# Lives Collide

## The Collide Series

### Book One

## Kristina Beck

ISBN-13:978-3-947985-00-5

Editing: Dori Harrell, Breakout Editing
Proofreading: Rachel Overton, Wordscapes
Book Cover Design: Sarah Hansen, Okay Creations LLC
Book Cover Image: David Koscheck
Book Formatting: Rik Hall, Wild Seas Formatting
Biography photograph: Fotografie Lehmann

To Christoph, Sarah, Anna, and Lucas

# Part One

# Chapter 1

## Lisa

I hear a loose shutter outside the window, fighting with the blustery wind. Every creak and bang tells me the wind is winning. I lift my head from my pillow and look out the frosty window. "That blows!" I forgot to pull the window shade down before I went to bed last night. The view outside would make anyone want to stay in her warm bed all day. Sleet with a mix of snow falls heavily from the gray sky. I hate New Jersey in February. The weather is mostly cold, wet, and windy. The sun peeks out sporadically, just to tease everyone.

I pull the heavy yellow down comforter over my head and lie there in a ball in my black-and-red flannel pajamas. Maybe I should pretend I'm sick so I can stay in bed. No matter how much I want to stay in bed though, today is grocery shopping Saturday. Mom will know I'm faking if I claim I'm sick. She's aware that I despise going. Every other week, I must go with her to buy two weeks' worth of food. Not the most thrilling Saturday morning activity for a fifteen-year-old high school freshman. I wish my older sister, Tina, would go once in a while. Lucky for her, she works every Saturday morning.

I hear quick footsteps coming toward my bedroom door. I hide under the comforter like a scared child. Someone knocks once and opens the door. I peek my head out and hear Mom sigh. She puts her hands on her hips. "Lisa, please get up and get dressed! Why must we go through this every time we need to go shopping? It's a hectic day for me. Tina needs to be at the pharmacy by nine. We should leave a little earlier than usual because the roads might be slippery. Then we have to go grocery shopping. After shopping, we need to get back home quickly because your dad and I have an appointment at a car dealer at eleven." She looks up and lifts her hands. "Finally, we found an advertisement for the type of car we want to buy. You have fifteen minutes to get ready."

"I'm up, Mom. Get off my back. I'll be ready soon," I mumble. My family knows I am not a morning person. She walks away but doesn't close the door.

I throw my comforter off and roll out of bed. I stomp over to the dresser and look at myself in the mirror. My shoulders drop as I groan. My long, wavy brown hair is a big rat's nest. Brushing it will be useless. I have no time to take a shower or wash my face. There is no way I'm leaving this house with my hair looking like this. Today is officially hat day.

Dirty and clean clothes are scattered all over the old, stained, yellow carpet. As I grab something hopefully clean to wear, my foot tangles with one of my school bag straps. I fall over and just miss hitting my head on the corner of the footboard. "It's going to be one of those freaking days," I say with clenched fists.

After standing up, I put on my favorite gray New York Mets sweatshirt and matching sweatpants. I look at my reflection in the full-length mirror. These sweatpants look stupid because they are too long. I look like a slob. However, January's *Teen* magazine said the sloppy look rocks now. Well, it better be fashionable enough for grocery shopping. With my luck, I'll see someone I know or a cute guy.

I leave my room and hurry down the stairs. Where the hell is everyone? I put on my pink ski jacket and ski hat. The weather calls for snow boots, but they will look dumb with this outfit. I slip on my grungy sneakers instead. I hear a car horn honk. I look out the front window and see they're already waiting in the car.

I run out the front door and almost fall on the slippery sidewalk. I continue slowly to the car, trying to dodge the sleet and snow. When I slide onto the backseat, I notice Tina is driving. She only has her permit. With this weather, I'm surprised Mom is letting her drive our ugly, old brown Chevy station wagon to work. It has to be at least twenty years old. I'm so embarrassed to be seen in it.

Dad has been a mechanic since he was eighteen years old. He refuses to buy a new car, but maybe he'll change his mind today. Whenever I ask him when we'll get a new *modern* car, he says, "Why do we need a new one when I can fix anything that goes wrong with this old one? It saves us money." I was surprised to hear Mom say they'll be shopping for a car today.

As we pull out of the driveway, I move to the middle of the backseat and put the seat belt on over my stomach. This Chevy doesn't even have over-the-shoulder straps. How is it legal to drive this car? I usually don't wear a seat belt, but this weather, mixed with Tina driving, makes me nervous.

"Tina, did you turn on the stupid heat yet? It's freezing in here." I rub my hands together and breathe into them to get warm. My sneakers are soaked just from walking from the house to the car. I regret the choice of shoes. At least I have my ski jacket and hat.

Tina looks at me in the rearview mirror. "Yes, I turned it on, but you know how long it takes for this shit car to warm up," she says as she rolls her eyes.

"Tina, can you please watch your language? I know this is how you talk around your friends, but I don't want to hear it when you're around me," Mom hisses. "Watch the road and make sure you're driving under the speed limit in this weather." Mom shakes her head in irritation.

I look out the foggy window. "Why did we take the Chevy today anyway? Doesn't Dad's car drive better in the snow?"

"Your dad had to take his car to the garage to fix something. Any more questions, comments, or complaints?"

I raise my eyebrows in surprise. I look at Tina in the rearview mirror again, noticing that her eyes are bugging out of her head at Mom's unusual annoyance.

We remain quiet for the rest of the drive. Big snowflakes stick to the windows. It's not a pretty, fluffy snow blowing around. It's a heavy, wet snow that creates puddles of mud Slurpees all over the

5

streets.

"Mom, the weather is getting worse. Can we please go home after we drop Tina off?"

"No, we can't. Stop making excuses not to go shopping with me. I need your help." She rubs her eyebrows.

What the hell is wrong with her today? She's usually the cheery one of the family.

"This bad weather makes me nervous. That's all I'm trying to say," I respond.

We arrive at the pharmacy, and Tina parks the car. The pharmacy windows are decorated with red hearts and cupids. I forgot today is Valentine's Day. Tina jumps out and leaves the door open for Mom. She doesn't even say good-bye to us. Snow blows into the car. Mom runs to the driver's side and gets in. She shakes her head to get the wet snow out of her hair. Normally, I would immediately jump into the front seat, but I'm too lazy and don't want to get wet again.

Mom cautiously pulls out of the parking lot, but the back tires spin.

"Be careful, Mom."

"I know, Lisa," she snaps. "Would you please stop worrying?" She turns left onto Main Street, which is a four-lane road that runs through Hillstown.

Knots form in my stomach because she's driving too fast. I don't want to say anything because I'll only annoy her more, but I need to. "Mom, aren't you driving too fast? I know you're in a rush, but the roads are slippery."

"The speed limit is fifty miles per hour on this road. I am driving fifty." As she says this, I notice a black pickup pulling out of a street on our right. The truck is not stopping for us.

"Slow down, Mom," I scream. I lean over and grip the top of the front seat hard, as if I can control the brakes.

Our car starts sliding, and the back fishtails. I hear Mom scream and then the sound of grinding metal. My body shoots forward. The seat belt catches me, then flings me back into the seat like a slingshot.

A sizzling pain burns in my stomach and back.

It takes me a few seconds to focus. The eerie sound of silence is worse than the grinding metal. I look around, and bile rises in my throat. We've hit a large oak tree head on. Blood is splattered over the dashboard and windshield. Mom is slouched over the steering wheel, not moving. Her head angles to the right, and blood covers her face. I fight the urge to throw up.

I cry out, "Mom! Mom, can you hear me? Please say something." No reaction. "I'll go for help!" Still no response. Her eyes are open— why isn't she responding?

My heart races as if it would jump out of my chest and run away. As instinct kicks in, I unbuckle my seat belt. When I open the door, I fall out and land in a pile of slush. My sweatpants and sneakers are soaked. I pull myself up by grabbing the car door. My legs are shaking and feel weighed down by bricks. Running is the only option, but it's almost impossible because I can hardly get my feet off the ground. The pain in my stomach grows worse. I push myself to move, and adrenaline suddenly pumps through my veins.

As I try to run, I hear a car. I look to the left and see a young guy driving up next to me. "Where are you going? You should stay near your car," he shouts through his open window.

"I need to get help," I cry.

He stops his car and quickly slides out. He takes off his brown leather jacket and puts it over my shoulders.

"I have so much pain. I can't run fast enough."

"Please sit in my car. You shouldn't be moving. I'll go get help." He leads me to his car and opens the passenger door. He talks to me, but I can't focus on his voice. He closes the door and runs off.

My body shakes profusely. I'm so petrified, wet, and freezing. I look out the window toward our car, which now looks like a damaged accordion. It's hard to see because the windows are fogging up. I need to help Mom, but my body won't move anymore. *How can I leave her there though?*

I see the guy running back to his car. He opens the door and looks in. "I asked someone to call for an ambulance. They'll be here as soon as possible," he says, out of breath.

"Please help my mom!" He nods and runs to my car. After a few minutes, he comes back with his head down. He opens the car door and lowers his head to look in. Before I have time to ask him about Mom, I look down and scream. My sweatpants are soaked with blood. I look up at him and see the sheer panic on his face. His big emerald-green eyes pierce through me like lasers. They are the last things I see before everything goes black.

# Chapter 2

## James

The ski slopes are covered in a fresh blanket of powdered snow, with clear blue skies above. The air is bitingly cold and tickles my lungs when I inhale. My breath leaves my lungs as a steamy cloud. There is nothing better than the smell of fresh snow. It reminds me of crisp, fresh sheets that have been drying outside in the sun all day. We couldn't ask for a better day for skiing.

It's January 2, and it's our last day of skiing. Every year since I was little, my family and I have vacationed in Killington, Vermont, for Christmas and New Year's. As usual, we are staying at the Snow Peak Lodge. We woke up early to hit the slopes today, anticipating a fresh blanket of snow.

I walk out of the lodge with my sister, Alexa. We head toward the ski lifts. I need to take advantage of this last day and enjoy it. My last semester at Johnson College starts in one week. My college is in New York State, but right on the border of New Jersey.

I start medical school in the fall. I was accepted to a few competitive medical schools, but I've chosen Clarion College of Physicians and Surgeons, also in New York, not too far from Johnson College. I like Clarion's reputation, because I hope to become a trauma surgeon. It's also close to my parents' home, in Clearwater, New Jersey—just a forty-five-minute drive south from where I'll live.

It might be my last time skiing for a while. Medical school will be difficult and time consuming.

I studied my ass off to get into med school. When I received the acceptance letter into Clarion, my hard work paid off. My dream of becoming a surgeon is closer to reality. Ever since I helped that young girl after that car accident when I was seventeen, I've wanted to study medicine. I remember it like it was yesterday. How helpless I felt when I couldn't help her or her mother. I was terrified I'd do something wrong. The paramedics were so quick and knew exactly what to do.

That day changed me forever. My future has been planned for the next eight years. Once I make a decision, I stick with it. Nothing will get in my way. I'm not flexible with time or planning my life. Flexibility is not part of my vocabulary.

I was completely overwhelmed with what I experienced that day. I still wonder what happened to her. She looked like she was fourteen or fifteen years old. I hope she and her mother survived. I looked in the newspaper for days to see if the car accident was reported. There was nothing. I wonder what she's like today. I guess she'd be around eighteen or nineteen. Does she still have my leather jacket? Would I recognize her if I saw her now?

The worst memory I have of her was her bleeding in my car. The passenger seat was a constant reminder. It took several months to stop replaying the accident in my head or dreaming about it. Slowly the amount of dreams decreased. But every once in a while, one still comes out of nowhere, and I see her big crystal-blue eyes staring at me.

My boss at the gas station fired me that day. I'd been late for work too many times in the previous weeks. He'd threatened to let me go if I was late one more time. He didn't care why I was late or even about the people hurt in the car crash. After what happened, I didn't care that I was fired. I did the right thing. Did he really expect me to drive away from an accident and just ignore the people who needed help? From that day on, I knew my future career would be in medicine. If I'm ever in a situation again when someone needs help, I'll know what to do.

Alexa and I are sitting on the ski lift, heading up to one of the new black-diamond slopes. She's wearing a bright-red ski suit with a matching hat that has a big pompom on top. She would be hard to miss, especially against the white snow. She likes to stand out in a crowd. I'm wearing mostly black with a red stripe on my jacket. I bought a new black ski helmet before I came on this trip. She laughed at me when I suggested she buy one as well. She would rather wear a hat with a huge pompom on it. Typical.

The brilliant sun reflects off the snow, blinding me. Even with goggles, the sun glare will be dangerous. This is a new slope; one I haven't traversed before. I'm a little tense. I'm not sure why, since I'm twenty-one years old and have been skiing since I was ten. I consider myself pretty experienced. However, I have too much to lose if I hurt myself. No matter what, I need to finish this last semester of college. I keep rubbing my hands together.

Alexa constantly makes fun of me. "Are you nervous, James? Don't be afraid, you fucking scaredy-cat. You have your new helmet. That will protect you," she says as she pulls the helmet forward.

"You have such a trash mouth. Do you kiss your million boyfriends with that mouth?" I joke while I fix my helmet.

"I'm from New Jersey. What do you expect? Like you never swear. Oh, wait—you don't." She laughs.

I swear, but only when I'm in stressful situations.

"You know why I'm like this. I need to graduate this year. It's too important to me."

"You need to lighten up. Stop worrying." She pokes me in the cheek.

"I'll go down first. Watch and learn." She's twenty years old and just as good at skiing as I am, if not better.

What adds to the danger today is that the slopes are overloaded with skiers. That's the one downfall with coming here during Christmas week. It's always too crowded. *Listen to me! I do sound like I'm scared! I'm tougher than this.*

My fear quickly turns into an adrenaline rush as we approach the top of the ski lift. The panoramic view of the snowcapped mountains is breathtaking. I secure my goggles properly. My ski boots are attached tightly. I look at Alexa to check she is okay. We hop off the lift and proceed to the top of the slope. She gives me a thumbs-up and takes off before me. I quickly follow, with an instant feeling of flying. I glide smoothly, side to side, snow shooting out from under me.

This slope is steeper than those I've skied before. I'm navigating properly, but I'm still cautious. Skiers crisscross from every direction. Little snow crystals hit my cheeks, filling the air from others' skis. A sharp right curve comes up, so I slow down and lean toward the right. A blinding glare reflects off the snow from the sun—I can't see anything.

Out of nowhere, something strikes me hard from the right like a freight train. I fly to my left. The wind is swiftly kicked out of my lungs. My body is airborne, and then gravity takes over and slams me back down. I land hard on my left side—head, left shoulder and arm impact as I plow through the snow. Agonizing pain shoots down my left shoulder all the way to my fingertips. My bones feel like they have been shattered like a glass pane. I'm having trouble breathing. My legs tangle with my skis.

In the distance, I hear skiers shoot past me. Finally, I stop sliding when someone pulls me gently to the side of the slope. It hurts to move, but the cold snow helps.

"What happened?" I cry in pain.

I hear a girl's angelic voice. "Someone was out of control and smashed into you at a very high speed. My sister went for help. You're lucky you were wearing a helmet. The other skier isn't wearing one and hit his head hard on the ground. He isn't moving.

"I'm going to take your skis off so you feel more comfortable. You need to lie still. We don't know what injuries you may have." She has a soothing voice, or maybe I hit my head too hard. The pain pulsates through me, so I know something, if not all of my bones, are broken.

"Does your neck hurt?"

"No. Just my shoulder down to my hand," I say through gritted teeth.

"Okay. I'm going to gently move your head onto my lap." She places my head onto something soft. Much better than snow. "I hope your head is comfortable now. You're shaking. You are most likely freezing or in shock." I hear her unzip her jacket. "I'm not sure how much it will keep you warm." She lays her ski jacket over me. It smells nice.

"Your voice is soothing. Like an angel's."

She giggles as she carefully takes off my goggles. I can't see her, because of the sun's glare. I shut my eyes tightly.

I hear someone yelling, "Lisa! Lisa, is he okay? The ski patrols are on their way."

"Did you hear that? Help is on the way. Please try to relax and not move. I know it's not easy to do when you're in so much pain." Her fingers tenderly stroke my cheek.

Suddenly, I hear Alexa screaming in the distance. "James! James, are you okay?" Fine snow shoots onto my face as she drops to my side.

My mouth is dry like the desert. It takes every ounce of energy to answer her. "I don't know, Alexa. Help is on the way. I can hear the sirens." She touches my arm. I recoil in response. "Fuck, don't touch me. Do you know how much fucking pain I'm in?"

"I'm so scared. I'm sorry I made fun of your helmet. It probably saved your life. I can't live without you. Please be okay," she pleads in hysterics. I hear people yelling and shuffling nearby. Seconds later, the ski patrols are at my side and bombard me with questions.

In the middle of the chaos, I only hear the girl's voice. "They will take care of you now. You're going to be okay."

I can't focus properly, because it feels like someone is hammering the left side of my body.

I hear her voice again. "They will prepare you for evacuation along with the other skier." She leans over me to take her jacket. "Good luck, James," she says as she rubs my cheek one more time.

With every ounce of energy I have, I grab her hand near my face. I press it against my cheek. I don't have the strength to open my eyes.

"Thank you," I reply as she pulls her hand away.

"Miss, please move. We need space in order to treat him properly." I try to move but freeze in place because of the throbbing pain. I don't hear her voice anymore. It's like she vanished. Was she real?

# Chapter 3

## James

I place the canvas bag on the old table assigned to me. It's overstuffed with an assortment of different pamphlets, pens, notepads or coupons for a free coffee at the campus cafeteria. It's the first day of the one-week orientation program for the new medical students at Clarion University of Physicians and Surgeons. I can hear the buzzing of faculty and students as their voices echo off the walls. The students wander around this big white modern auditorium, their eyes wide open. Absorbing their surroundings, not knowing where to start. Asking themselves, which clubs or organizations should I join? Are any of my teachers here? Is there free food? Some look terrified, holding their notebooks close to their chests like security blankets. Of course, there is always a handful of students who act as if they know everything and everyone. Walking with their heads held high, raising their hands up to say hello, like a politician. Meanwhile, I'm sure they are ready to wet their pants.

When I think back to my orientation, I acted just like these students. Excited, nervous, anticipatory, proud... It seems so long ago. I felt an overwhelming sense of relief. I'd finally made it to medical school and was moving forward with my dream.

I graduated from Clarion last June and started my residency program in July. I'm officially an MD. Medical school emotionally and physically drained me. I studied countless number of hours every week. Lived off little sleep and a high intake of caffeinated drinks. When I started med school, I cut out socializing and dating. I had done enough of that during undergraduate school. I missed out on a lot of fun while I locked myself in my room or the library here—but I met my goal.

My residency program is at the university hospital that's connected to Clarion. My former goal to become a surgeon was cut short because of the ski accident, when I dislocated my shoulder, broke my left arm in different places, bruised some ribs, and broke two of my left-hand fingers.

I'm left handed. I went through every kind of physical therapy to regain full function of my fingers as well as my arm and shoulder. I gained full function back in my arm and shoulder but not my fingers. My middle and index finger can't properly grip small objects such as medical instruments or tools used to perform surgery. Writing with my left hand is a catastrophe. Something so easy that I took for granted. My handwriting resembles a child's. I guess I fit in with the other doctors, who also have horrible handwriting.

I've opted instead to specialize in emergency medicine. I will need to complete three years of residency before I can apply for a medical license.

I'm attending Clarion's orientation today because I was asked to answer miscellaneous questions about this medical school and/or share my own personal experiences with the new students. It's 12:30, and only a couple of students have visited my table during the past hour. They asked questions I couldn't even answer. Of course, they took the coupons for free coffee.

Here comes a student now. "Hi. How can I help you?" I say with enthusiasm.

"Can you tell me where the bathroom is?"

My face drops.

*Are you kidding me?*

"Sure. See the sign about twenty feet away from us?"

"Oops. Sorry. Thanks." He walks away as I growl.

Another half hour passes. I love to organize, but how many times am I going to reorganize the buffet of pamphlets? The time is dragging, and I'm hungry. Do I really need to be here? I hope it gets busier, because I'm constantly yawning. I would rather be at the dentist having a tooth pulled.

Finally, more students visit my table. As I finish with one, I notice a young woman approaching. She is looking down, so I can't see her face. She stops and looks through some pamphlets.

"Hello. Can I help you?"

She lifts her head and looks at me. *I am not bored anymore.* I freeze and can't stop staring at her. She is breathtaking. She has beautiful hazel eyes with long, wavy auburn hair flowing over one shoulder. Freckles lightly dust her face. A pure Irish treat. I've never believed in love at first sight until this moment. I feel like I'm in a movie when everything is in slow motion and sappy music is playing in the background and birds are chirping.

Speechless is an understatement. I hear her laugh. *Is she laughing at me?* She asks me questions, but I'm not answering them. She has me in a trance.

Finally, my mouth is able to function. "Hi, I'm James Kramer." I hold out my hand to shake hers. She takes my hand in hers. *I am never going to let it go.* A soft tingle goes up my right arm straight to my chest. I'm shaking, and my mouth is dry, like cotton. I repeat myself. "Do you need help with something or have any questions about medical school?" *Great. My voice squeaked.*

"No, I don't need any help. I'm just walking around to see what each table represents. I'm a third-year resident in pediatrics at the hospital here. I was asked to help out today. I have a table over in the corner there," she says as she points in the distance. "After meeting you, I'm happy I agreed to come today." She grins.

*Is she flirting with me?*

"I'm Jessica Flynn, by the way."

"Wow, I'm impressed, Jessica. This hospital is known for its pediatric department. It's huge. Good for you."

She looks at her hand in mine, since I'm still holding it. I quickly let go, as if I'd touched fire. "It's okay. I didn't mind. Your hand was nice and warm."

"I'm a first-year resident for emergency medicine. You're way ahead of me. I'm jealous."

She leans against the table. *I wish she was leaning against me.* "The first years went pretty fast. Before you know it, you'll be done. It's not medical school anymore. You're working."

My body is drawn to hers. I want to keep talking to her, but I hear students saying, "Excuse me, sir. Can you help us, please? We have been waiting here for a few minutes now."

Of course, students line up now.

As I finally turn to face them, a female student tosses pamphlets back onto the table and storms away.

"Excuse me, miss. Can I help you?" I call. I guess not, because she ignores me. "Please give me a few seconds," I say to the students waiting in line. I hear some of them grunt.

I turn back to Jessica. She leans into me and whispers, "I see you are busy. I'll come back when it's slower. You're welcome to visit me, if you get bored. I can give you some information on the pediatric department, if you are interested. As I said, my table is just over there." She offers a jaw-dropping smile.

"I just might take you up on that. Hopefully, everyone will avoid this table. See you soon."

She grins as she turns around. I watch her slender hips sway.

A male student clearing his throat pulls me back to reality. "Yes, yes. How can I help you?"

It's 5:00, and orientation is finally over. Instead of being avoided, I was swamped all afternoon. But Jessica and I have been sneaking peeks at each other the entire time.

After most of the students leave, she approaches and stands in front of the table, facing me. "Hi, James," she says with a sparkle in her eye.

"Hey there," I say softly as I pack up the leftover pamphlets. "The past hours were a lot busier than I hoped they would be. I would've rather been talking to you." I glance at her hand as she traces a heart with her finger on the table.

"And now we're finished," she says as our eyes meet.

She steps away from the table and saunters around it. She stands a few inches away from me. Her closeness alone makes my pulse race. I unfasten the top button of my shirt. I'm suddenly very warm.

"James, would you like to go for a drink somewhere?" She bites her lower lip.

*What I wouldn't do to bite her lip right now. Whoa! What the hell is wrong with me?* "I'd love to, but I need to do a few things first, which could take a while. Can we meet at Kerry's Pub at seven? Do you know where it is?"

"Yes. That would be perfect. I'll wait for you at the bar. I look forward to it." She brushes my arm with her hand. "See you later, James."

I watch her walk away, counting the minutes until I will see her gorgeous face again.

I arrive a few minutes late because I couldn't find a parking space. Hopefully, she isn't annoyed. I walk through the doors and see Jessica sitting at the bar to the left. She hasn't noticed me yet, so I stand there and observe her. She changed her clothes. Damn, I didn't have time to change my clothes. Do I look okay? I push my hand through my hair nervously. I look down at my shirt to make sure there are no stains and then smooth out my khakis. Good enough.

She's older than me, and exudes maturity and elegance. Her hair is the same as earlier today. She's wearing a dark-green short-sleeve dress with sexy black high heels. Her legs are crossed, and one leg is revealed to midthigh. My head automatically goes to my pants. I shouldn't think like this. I need to behave and get a grip. It has been a long time since I've reacted to or thought about a woman like this. Actually, I've never felt this way before. I'm not sure I can control myself.

I don't know anything about her, but I'm lucky to be meeting her right now. I'm sure she has men constantly knocking on her door. Especially other residents. I wasn't expecting this today. I'm a planner by nature. My life has been planned for the past eight years while going through undergraduate and medical school. Structure is a necessity. When something doesn't adhere to my schedule, it throws me completely off balance.

I've dated occasionally, but there's never been anyone special. Perhaps in the back of my mind I was always searching for that girl from the ski accident. Alexa confirmed the rescuer was really there and wasn't a figment of my imagination. I waited for a long time, but I finally convinced myself to give up. I'll never forget the sound of her voice. The only thing I know about her is that her name is Lisa and she has black hair.

Jessica swivels on her stool and notices me. In this moment, I forget whom I was thinking about. She's the only person I see. Her smile grows as I walk toward her, and right then I'm hooked. The bar doesn't need any lights because her face glows enough. My heart is pounding, and my hands are sweating. *Don't shake her hand.* She stands up as I give her a gentle hug. She smells like fresh roses.

"You look incredible, Jessica."

"Thank you. You look quite sexy yourself."

It's going to be an interesting night. Will I be able to keep my hands off her? I never had a woman say something like that to me before.

I like it.

A lot.

"Would you like to sit here at the bar or move to a table?" I ask as I gesture toward the tables.

"Let's stay here. We can sit closer to one another."

She's killing me with these little comments. Some come out innocent and some come out downright hot. I'm not sure how to respond, so I just smile and motion for her to sit down. I claim the barstool next to hers.

"I see you already have a white wine. I hope you weren't waiting too long."

"Sorry. I was a bit nervous. I needed something to relax me. I hope you don't mind."

"Not at all. Let me order a beer and some food. I haven't eaten in a while." I wave the bartender over and order a Sam Adams as he hands me a menu. "Do you want to order something to eat? Maybe the nachos?"

"Please, I'm starving. I need to eat something, or this wine will go straight to my head."

I order the nachos and move my stool closer to hers. She shifts in her seat to get something from her handbag. Her hair moves in a way that blows a cloud of her rose perfume my way. I close my eyes as I inhale to savor the smell. I need to make small talk to keep from thinking about how good she smells, how pretty she looks, and how much I long to touch her.

"You don't seem like the nervous type. When I met you at orientation, you seemed quite confident. I mean that in a positive way."

"That's how people perceive me, but it's not always true. Men make me nervous because they only see me on the outside. Yes, I'm tall with a pretty face, from what people tell me, but I'm more than that. I want you to see past my appearance."

Now I feel bad. I have been thinking those very things. Tall, sexy, and beautiful.

"How old are you, James? I'm guessing around twenty-seven. Am I correct?"

"Twenty-six. Is that bad? Have you ever dated someone younger than you?" I question with slight apprehension.

She shakes her head. "No. Gosh no. I have no problem with your age. I'm only twenty-eight," she quickly responds.

"I'm only kidding. No worries," I tease.

She playfully taps me on the arm. "That's not fair. Be nice. You are supposed to make a good impression."

"Okay. Next question then. Where are you from? Are you from New York State?" I ask in a formal tone, still trying to tease her.

She smiles. "Yes, I am. I'm from a small town not too far from here. I'm the only child, so I wanted to stay close to my parents. Well, close enough that it would take less than an hour to drive to visit. Sometimes a little distance is better. Being an only child can be a bit tough. The focus is always on me. I need some space, which led me to choose this hospital for my residency."

"I'm assuming you didn't go to Clarion? I think I would have seen you at some point."

"No, I went to St. Clare's Medical School north of where I grew up. That medical school has a good reputation, but the residency program here is much better."

"Do you wish you had a sister or brother? My sister, Alexa, is one of my best friends. I can't imagine my life without her. She's one year younger than me and went to a college near mine. I went to Johnson College because it wasn't too far from where my parents live in New Jersey. She now lives here and works as a pharmaceutical sales representative."

"I do wish I had one or a bunch. It's lonely growing up with no siblings. When I get married and am ready to have children, I want at least two so they have each other."

"When I fall for the right woman, I would like to have two or four children. With three, one always feels left out. I don't want them right now though, since I'm just starting my residency." I gaze at her. She stares right at me with a sweet smile on her face. What is she thinking about? Hopefully, what I'm thinking. I look down and notice we are holding hands and are knee to knee. When did that happen? It feels so natural being here with her.

Finally, our food arrives. "Ladies first." I motion. She takes the first nacho and starts to slowly feed me. How is being fed nachos by a beautiful woman so erotic? If I saw someone doing this at another table, I would think it's completely absurd. I watch her put a nacho in her mouth, and I can't keep my eyes off her lips. She licks her lips to get the food off her mouth.

Because my mind is in the gutter, I drop my napkin on the floor. We both react at the same time and bend over to get it. We bang our heads.

"Ouch!" We say in unison and start to laugh.

"Are you okay, Jessica? I'm a doctor. Do you need me to check your head?" I ask playfully.

"Why yes, doctor. Can you please feel my head right here? Or maybe you should kiss it to make it feel better. I bet you have magical lips." She leans her face close to mine.

I lean in closer as I rub my hand up her thigh. Gently, I touch the red spot on her forehead with my lips, lingering there for a few seconds. The electricity between us is thicker than the humidity in New York during the summer. I slowly lean away and skim my fingers along her jaw. On impulse, I brush my lips against hers. I pull away but stay close while we stare into each other's eyes. Everything is in a haze.

"How does it feel now? Are you all right?" I ask in a sultry voice.

She nervously sips from her wineglass and sets it back down. "Perfect. I couldn't ask for better service from any doctor. Do you act this way with all your patients?"

"You are my only patient. I promise."

"I'm glad to hear that. I want to be the only one to look into those glowing green eyes of yours. They are quite breathtaking."

The loud noise of a chair scraping along the floor yanks us out of our bubble. We lean away from each other as if we've both suddenly remembered we are in a public place. I clear my throat to keep me sane.

"Do you have any hobbies? Do you ski or run?" A good neutral question.

"I'm sorry to say, I hate skiing. I tried it several times, but it's not for me. As for running, I find it boring."

No skiing or running. That's too bad. But then again, I haven't gone skiing since my accident. I don't even know if I could hold a ski pole.

"I would rather go to the gym or exercise at home by myself. Right now, I have minimal time to exercise, with my work schedule."

*It doesn't look like it to me. You are beautiful from head to toe. I can only imagine what is under that dress.* "I guess that means you won't run with me if I ask you. I run quite often," I say with my bottom lip sticking out. She laughs as her head falls back slightly. She has a natural beauty that's even more radiant when she laughs.

I am brought back to earth when she starts talking again. The time goes quickly as we talk about anything that comes to mind. Eating nachos and laughing without a care in the world.

She stifles a yawn. "I'm sorry. It's not easy to work the hours we residents do. I need to be up at four tomorrow morning. I haven't had much sleep this week."

"I agree with you there and I only started in July." I finish my beer and place it at the edge of the bar. "I'm lucky I have off tomorrow."

She looks at her watch. "On a normal night, I would force myself to be in bed by now. I'm surprised I'm awake. However, being here with you is the only place I want to be right now. It's worth every minute I lose of sleep." She squeezes my hand and looks directly into my eyes.

The noise and energy in the bar are blocked from my mind. There could have been a bar fight, and I wouldn't have noticed. I'd stay here all night with her if we could. But she needs to be at the hospital early in the morning.

"Let me pay so we can leave." I wave for the bartender.

While we wait for the check, she searches through her bag. She pulls out some mints. "Want one?" she asks as she pops one into her mouth.

"Please."

"Open up." My eyebrows shoot up.

I do as she says. She places one on my tongue as if it's normal to do that. I play with my shirt buttons again. I'm not sure I can restrain myself much longer.

I stand up from my stool and pull my wallet out of my pocket. "Where do you live? Should I call you a taxi? My car is parked too far away."

"I live in the Greenhouse Apartments. Do you know where they are?"

"Yes, I do. I pass them often when I go to the hospital. I would love to walk you home. I don't want you to walk alone at this time of night."

"That would be nice. Thank you." The bartender comes over with the check, and I pay it. Then I put my hand on her lower back and lead her out the door.

We walk part of the way to her apartment in silence. We talked nonstop but I forgot to ask her one particular question. I turn slightly toward her as we continue walking. "What made you want to become a pediatrician?"

She starts swinging her arms back and forth, with a smile on her face. "Let's see. The obvious one is I love children. I look forward to working with all the different age groups. I can have patients ranging from newborns to late teenage years. This field is stimulating as well as complicated, because I need to know different practices for the variety of age groups. There's a huge difference in developmental, psychological, and physical needs between these ages. I love to nurture and educate them and their families. I could possibly take care of a child from birth until they are in their teens. It would be amazing to see the developmental changes in one person during a long period of time. When I have a baby as a patient, it's a new life I'm taking a part of and caring for. However, there are times when I see a child suffering from a horrible disease or sickness. If I can help a child recover or make them smile, it's all worth it at the end of the day." She stops talking abruptly and covers her mouth. "I'm sorry. I got a little carried away. I hope I didn't lose you there."

I put my arm around her shoulders and pull her close. "Actually, you did the opposite. It's nice to hear how passionate you are about helping others and not just the paycheck you'll receive." She wraps her arm around my lower back and pulls me closer. If it's even possible to get closer to one another.

"Do you want to work in a hospital after your residency, or would you like to open up your own pediatric practice?"

"One day I would, but it'll be expensive. I have debt from school. My parents helped me with tuition, but I still have some small loans to pay off. I'd also like to gain more experience through the hospital before then."

"Isn't this your apartment complex?" I say as I tug her hand lightly to stop her.

"We're here already? That's too bad." She sighs. "My focus was on you, not where we were walking. I would have passed it if you didn't say something." She giggles.

"Which apartment is yours?"

"Number fifteen on the first floor to the left. A lot of medical students and residents live in this large apartment complex. They're nothing special, but the rent is cheap. To cut out more expenses, I decided to get a roommate since I have a spare bedroom. We don't see each other often because our schedules are different."

"Do you live nearby?"

I point in the direction where my apartment is. "I live about ten minutes in that direction from here by car. The apartment is small and not big enough to have a roommate. I enjoy my privacy. I'll show it to you some time, if you would like."

There's her beautiful smile again.

"I'd love to."

We arrive at her door, and it's time to say good night. I hear something behind us. I turn around to see where it's coming from. The lighting in the hallway is dull, but I think I see two people kissing like mad. They clearly have the same thoughts as I do. They hear us, so they stop immediately. Jessica and I both laugh and turn toward her door.

Should I kiss her or not? I really want to kiss her, especially after we spent the past hours together. The soft kiss I gave her at the bar made me desire her even more. Why am I questioning myself? I'm usually a confident man, but with her it's different. I have never tried to impress a woman before. This is how I know she is different from other women I've met.

"I had a great time tonight. It was the last thing I thought I would be doing when I woke up this morning. I would love to see you again," I say.

"I enjoyed myself too. I don't want the night to end, but my roommate is actually home tonight. Plus, I need to get up early. I'd love to see you again." She looks at her feet for a second and then up at me through her long eyelashes. "I have a confession. I deliberately went to your table at orientation because I saw you from my table. I'm usually not so brave, but I felt this pull toward you. I thought you were so handsome. I just had to introduce myself."

"I'm glad you did. This has been a day I will never forget. If you give me your phone number, can I call you tomorrow night? When is your shift done at the hospital?"

"Give me a call after five. I should be home by then." She pulls out a pen and writes her phone number on the palm of my hand. How can something like this send vibrations through my body? I need to leave before I push her against the wall and do things to her I shouldn't. Well, at least not on the first date.

She opens her bag and searches for her keys. As I start to walk away, she asks softly, "Aren't you going to kiss me good night?" She plays with her hair nervously as she waits for my reaction. I hear the keys jiggling in her hand.

"Would you like me to kiss you?" I ask. Wishing I could run to her rather than walk.

She nods without hesitation. I check to see if the other couple down the hall is gone. We are alone in the hallway. I stand in front of her. We are both breathing faster. I see the anticipation in her eyes. We are only inches away from each other now.

"I have been wanting to kiss you all night. Especially after the little kiss you gave me. You are such a tease," she says as she moves closer to me.

"I didn't notice because I was too busy staring at your lips. That brief kiss before was not enough. But if I kiss you now, I won't be able to stop."

"What if I don't want you to stop?" She looks at me with seductive eyes.

I cup her face with my hands and lean into her slowly. When our lips touch, we simply blend into one. Her lips are warm and soft. We know exactly how to kiss each other without thinking about it. It's better than I could have ever imagined. This night has been building up to this moment. My hands run through her silky auburn hair, then down her body, eventually resting on her backside. I pull her closer to me, not leaving any space between us. She lets out a slight moan. Then it hits me out of nowhere, like a billboard in Las Vegas. Soul mates.

We stand there kissing for seconds, minutes...I have no idea. I hear her purse and keys fall to the ground. I graze her neck. She tastes so sweet on my lips. I want to taste every part of her body every day. I feel like a teenager with buzzing hormones.

Eventually, we come up for air. Her lips are red and swollen. Her eyes are heavy, hopefully for desire for me and not because she's tired. I hate that her roommate is home. I want to kiss her for hours, among other things. For the second time, I need to leave. I must force myself to leave.

We slowly let go of each other. I already miss her touch. Our eyes lock, and I immediately see our future together. "Sweet dreams, Jessica," I say with a stupid grin on my face. *When did I become so soft?* As I walk away, I can truly say, I will marry her someday. Something tells me she feels it too.

# Chapter 4

## Lisa

The campus at Clarion University of Physicians and Surgeons is so beautiful in September. The last time I was here was in the dead of winter. It's not just the one-hundred-year-old historical buildings that are beautiful in the sunshine. The beauty also comes from the lively surroundings.

Large old oak and maple trees are scattered in every direction. They are still lush with dark-green foliage. Roots push up out of the ground, making the sidewalks uneven. Squirrels run around, collecting nuts or food of some kind. A pigeon pecks at a piece of bread on the ground near a garbage can. The weather still holds remnants of the summer heat, balanced by a slight breeze blowing through the trees. Students lie on the warm, bright-green grass, studying, napping, or socializing. Some play Frisbee or kick a soccer ball around. I'm enjoying myself so much I almost pass the sign for orientation.

I turn in the direction of the sign and hear music in the distance. There's a group of students in front of me, but I can't see where they are walking because I'm too short. I move to the side and smile instantly. There's a massive building ahead, which I assume is the auditorium. A huge rainbow made of balloons frames the entrance, and a big sign announces, *Welcome to Orientation*. My mother loved rainbows. When I see them, a sense of peace settles through me, as if she's watching over me. The rainbow arch pumps me with confidence as I approach the building. When I arrive at the entrance, to the right a band plays soft rock music. To the left, girls in red hand out welcome envelopes. I take one and walk through the doors.

I spin around in awe. Wow, this place is impressive. The undergraduate orientation at Johnson College was nothing compared to this. What a pleasant surprise. People are here already, but it's not too crowded. I should take advantage and walk around before lines form at the tables. The welcome envelope has a layout of the tables and what they represent: faculty, different curriculums, financial aid, campus health clinic, and hopefully some free food.

I find some tables particularly interesting. These have fourth-year and freshly graduated medical students talking about personal experiences during medical school. I have some questions and would love to hear what an actual medical student would say. I search for the nearest one on my map.

I try to act like I know what I'm doing as I approach the table. There's a line already, but I'm in no rush. A young man stands behind the table, with his back toward us. He's easily over six feet tall with wavy light-brown short hair. His backside seems quite attractive in his khakis.

*What? Where the hell did that thought come from?* I'm here for medical school, not for my hormones. He has such broad shoulders though. I wonder what it would feel like to touch them. *Stop it, Lisa!*

Unfortunately, I don't see his face, because he seems quite enraptured with a redhead behind the table. Isn't he supposed to help the new students? Can't he see the people waiting at his table? Probably not, since he only has eyes for her. He's acting like a puppy dog, hanging on her every word. He's probably drooling. Maybe I should offer him a tissue. She is quite beautiful though, with her long auburn hair and tall, slender body. Her hair is the type you would see on a shampoo commercial. It dazzles in the light and looks so smooth and bouncy. It must be nice to have such beauty.

The other students are impatient as well. I clear my throat to get his attention, but he doesn't even acknowledge me. After waiting again for what feels like an eternity, I slam some pamphlets back on the table and storm off. He must have heard me that time, because he calls out to me, but I walk away, never looking back. Why would they have someone like him here to represent the medical school? All he wants to do is pick up students, or whoever she is. Typical!

"Where should I go next?" I ask myself. I walk around and search to see what's interesting. After about a half hour, I see a table representing the faculty in the psychiatry department. As I approach, I feel something slam into my hip. I lose my balance and drop my things on the floor. "Shit." My bag slides off my shoulder and falls open on the ground. My phone flies out, along with empty candy wrappers, notebooks, and, of all things, a tampon. *Great! How mortifying!* A guy tries to help me pick up my stuff. I quickly rip my things out of his hands. My face burns and must glow like a fireball.

After I put my things back in my bag, I straighten, and as I walk away, I glance at him. I do a double take. *Well, hello there.* He's quite handsome. Blond disheveled hair, a bit of stubble, and chocolate-brown eyes. *Wow, does he have long eyelashes.* He's only a few inches taller than me. I don't need to look up too high. Out of embarrassment for staring at him, I turn away, but he grabs my arm lightly.

"Sorry about that. I wasn't paying attention to where I was going. Did I hurt you?"

"No, no, you didn't hurt me. I'm just a little embarrassed."

"Why are you embarrassed? I'm the one who ran into you. I should be the one who's embarrassed. What's your name, blue eyes?" he asks with a crooked smile.

"Lisa...Lisa Schmitt."

He takes my hand and kisses the inside of my palm. *Oh my gosh, that just vibrated through my entire body.* I imagine myself as a character in one of my steamy romance books. Who kisses your palm when you first meet him? Don't get me wrong. I'm not complaining. Am I blushing even more?

"Nice to meet you, blue eyes. I'm Bryant Callahan."

His name sounds fancy or like someone with money. Or one you would hear in movies.

KRISTINA BECK

"Since I knocked you over, can I please buy you a coffee? It's the least I can do."

I think about it a bit while watching him smile at me. His smile could make me do anything he wants. I believe he's flirting with me. However, I have no clue because I don't even remember the last time I was flirted with, let alone someone I wanted to flirt with. I didn't have many boyfriends in college.

"I would like to," I hesitantly say. "But, I just got here and orientation isn't over until five. How about we meet for a light dinner or drinks later in the evening? Maybe Kerry's Pub?" Since when do I initiate going to dinner or for drinks? And with someone I don't even know. It's a bit different from having coffee.

There's a pause on his part. Maybe he'll say no. I hope I'm not being too forward.

"Okay. Sounds like a plan, blue eyes."

I'm in over my head. When a guy smiles at me like that, it makes me weak in the knees. These feelings are so foreign. I have never had a guy so gorgeous flirt like this with me. I kind of like it though. It makes my body quiver in a good way.

"How about eight thirty?"

"Can't wait, blue eyes." He winks.

I watch him as he walks away. He looks good from every angle. His biceps flexed when he handed me my tampon. *A tampon!* At this point, I can only laugh at myself. I have a date even after that. Pure anticipation pulses through my veins. I have never been instantly attracted to a guy before.

Should I change my clothes? Do I have something nice to wear? Will I look like I'm trying too hard if I do? The last date I had was over six months ago, and it was a disaster. The dating scene was never my thing. I already have knots in my stomach.

I should ask my roommate, Emily, for some fashion advice. Emily and I don't live in a dormitory. We live off-campus. She rented the apartment first and advertised her spare room on the Internet. It's a little bit expensive, but when Mom died, she had a life insurance policy. Dad gave me and Tina money to help us with school. I answered Emily's ad, and we've been roommates for a few months now. We hit it off instantly. It's nice to have someone to hang out with and talk to. My few friends from college have moved on with their lives. We're still in contact, but randomly. I miss my sister, Tina. We are best friends, but she lives and works about an hour from here. I don't drive, so when Tina and I get together, she visits me.

Emily is starting medical school as well. I don't know why she isn't at orientation today. I didn't see her this morning. She probably went on another date last night and never came home. With her beautiful, long, shiny black hair and olive skin, she attracts men like a bee to a beehive. She has been on more dates in the past two months than I have had since I was sixteen. She will be shocked when I tell her I'm meeting someone for a drink. Maybe I can borrow some of her clothes.

After a thorough consultation with Emily, I chose a scoop-neck navy-blue jersey dress. Nothing too revealing but just enough to keep him guessing. It hugs my hourglass curves in all the right places. She suggests I wear her secret push-up bra to enhance my boobs. I can't believe it fits me. Now I know why her boobs always look so big.

She insists I wear a pair of her black high heels. I never wear them, so I choose the shortest heels possible, which are still two inches high. I practice walking in them for half an hour and am not confident it helped. Blisters are already forming.

"How do I look?" I say as I turn from side to side in front of the mirror.

"I'm not going to say it again. You look beautiful. If I had your body, I would show it off all the time."

"Okay, miss tall and exotic. We wear the same size in a lot of things. I wouldn't complain if I were you. Men obviously think you are beautiful because they line up at the door to go out with you."

She flips her hair over her shoulder and fixes her lipstick in the mirror.

"My makeup isn't too much?" Pushing her out of the way, I peer into the mirror at my eyeliner. She helped me with my makeup. She used black eyeliner to enhance my blue eyes, since he likes my eyes. I want him to recognize me, so I didn't change my hairstyle.

She sighs in frustration. "I'm getting pissed now. I'm not saying anything else."

"I'm sorry. I told you, I haven't been on a date in a long time. Especially with someone who's so attractive. I'm really nervous." I straighten the dress and put on her ridiculous heels. I am going to kill myself in these things. I rotate in front of the mirror. However, my legs do appear quite slender and longer. Running several times a week keeps my legs firm. Maybe I should wear heels more often. Every once in a while, it's nice to feel taller.

I glance at the clock. "Shit. It's time to go." I straighten the dress again and grab my handbag. This dress will be stretched down to the floor by the end of the night.

"Have a great time and stop worrying. Be yourself. If he doesn't like it, then you know he isn't worth it. You are both old enough not to play games." She opens the door and pats me on the butt as I walk out. "Go get him, killer."

Kerry's Pub is a five-minute walk from my apartment. I see the sign, a beacon telling me I'm almost there—and without killing myself in these heels. As I reach the pub, the door swings open and a few guys walk out. This pub is a popular watering hole for residents and doctors from the university hospital. Emily said if Bryant doesn't show up, I'll have a pool of other residents and doctors to pick from. I had to laugh, but what if he doesn't show up? What will I do then? I don't know how to pick up anyone.

"Radiate confidence when you walk in," I mutter to myself. I pull the dress down for the hundredth time, keep my back straight, shoulders back, and head up. My eyes roam the bar in search of

Bryant or an empty table. I notice a small group of people wearing scrubs. It isn't too busy tonight. After a few minutes of searching, I don't see him. I let out a sigh of relief.

There's an empty table in the corner, opposite the bar. I weave my way through the tables, praying I won't fall. As soon as I arrive at the table, I pull a chair away, blaring a horrible scraping noise. I sink into the chair to hide my embarrassment.

I lean my elbows on the table, with a napkin in my hand and wait for a few minutes. I look at the door again and then my watch. It's 8:40. Since he's late, I'm going to order a drink. I need to do something other than tear up this napkin or read the label on the ketchup bottle.

A waitress is nearby, so I wave to get her attention. She approaches with a friendly smile. "Hi there. My name is Gloria, and I'll be your waitress tonight. What can I get for you? Would you like to see a menu?"

"I'm waiting for someone to arrive. But I would like to order a Corona Light with lemon, please. I'll wait until my friend gets here to order some food. Can I please have a menu though?"

"No problem. I'll be back in a few minutes with your drink and a menu."

"Thanks," I say as my eyes wander to the door again. *There he is.*

My body stiffens. My heart rate picks up instantly as my stomach flutters. Shit, he is cuter than I remember, and it was only a couple of hours ago when I met him. Cuter isn't the correct word. Sexier is better. He changed his clothes, just like me. He's wearing blue jeans and a light-blue polo shirt. I'm annoyed he's late, but I'll disregard it because he looks so good. *I think I will eat him for dinner. What the hell is wrong with me?*

Do I get up and wave to him, or do I just wait until he sees me? Our eyes meet before I can answer. He approaches the table, never breaking eye contact. I stand up too quickly and lose my balance. At the same time, he reaches over to give me a hug. He hugs me tight and saves me from embarrassing myself. *These damn heels.* His scruff grazes my cheek as he lets me go. Goose bumps form all over my body.

"Hi, blue eyes. Sorry to keep you waiting. I had a private matter to attend to. I usually don't leave a beautiful woman waiting for me. Please forgive me."

"You're forgiven. This time anyway," I say as I bat my eyelashes. I try to flirt, but I'm not sure he notices.

"You look beautiful in that dress. It's too bad we're in public." He eyes me up and down. My blood instantly rushes to my face. The heat from his eyes burns me as they travel over my body. He sits down in the chair next to mine and motions for me to sit down.

I slide into the chair and immediately fire questions at him. "How was the rest of your day? Are you hungry? This place has the best nachos. Do you want to order some? I already ordered a beer. What are you going to drink?"

He smiles at me and proceeds to read the menu.

"Sorry, that was an overload of questions." I fold my hands in my lap. *Do not ramble, Lisa!*

"Nachos and a beer sound great. I plan on going to the gym tomorrow, so I don't mind."

*Red flag.* Should I worry about what I'm eating in front of him? I like to eat. I run every chance I get, so I don't count calories. I shouldn't care. If he doesn't like it, screw him, as Emily would say.

He waves over the waitress and orders a Yuengling and nachos. The waitress stares at him. She obviously likes what she sees. He sure has me melting at his feet. It's probably those damn eyelashes. He doesn't seem to notice how the waitress gawks at him. She finally walks away.

"Please tell me something about yourself, Bryant. How old are you? Are you a medical student or a resident?"

"I'm twenty-seven and a second-year resident in the pediatric department at the hospital here. I love being a pediatrician. To be able to make a baby, child, or teenager smile at the end of an appointment makes my day. The future pay scale is also very enticing," he says, wiggling his eyebrows.

*Red flag number two.*

"I guess if you are going to be surrounded by them every day, you should love to be around them," I remark with disappointment. More to myself than to him.

His face lights up when he talks. "I've always had an interest in medicine and becoming a doctor. When I started medical school, I had no idea which medical field to pursue. I took some classes revolved around children and cancer. It really hit me hard, because my cousin's son died of cancer at the age of seven. I found it fascinating and enlightening. I've always been surrounded by children and teenagers. My extended family is very big. Once I became more involved toward the end of medical school, I knew this was the medical field for me. No matter what, children always need doctors."

*He likes kids.* I should walk out of this bar right now. I'm setting myself up for heartbreak. He will split me into two. This is why I never get involved with guys. Once they find out the truth about me, they'll walk away.

"My parents are already pushing me or my sister to get married so they can have grandchildren." His hand flies up. "Can you believe it? I haven't even finished my residency, and I'm not even in a relationship or looking for one. The time will come for that, but not right now."

*Red flag number three.* But, why am I annoyed he doesn't want a relationship with anyone?

He looks toward the bar. "Hey, that's funny. Speaking of the pediatric department, the woman over there with red hair, sitting at the bar with that guy, is also a resident. Maybe she's on a date. I won't bother to say hello. I don't want to interrupt her," he says as he points to where she's sitting.

Interesting. She looks like the woman I saw today. "Do you know if she was at orientation today? I think I saw her at a table with that guy she's with." I only see the back of the guy's head again. He has the same color hair and broad shoulders as the other one. Maybe they are the two from orientation. "Funny coincidence if they're the same people."

"Yes, she was. She's a third-year resident in pediatrics. She helped out today. I've worked with her during several rotations. She's extremely smart. I've learned a lot from her," he says as he turns in his seat toward me.

Our nachos and his beer finally arrive. "Here's to bumping into a beautiful stranger and getting a date out of it," he says as we clink the bottom of our bottles together.

"Cheers to bumping." I blush again. *I can't believe I just said that*. We eat in comfortable silence as our knees rub together.

We stare at each other for a few seconds. Now his eyes are the color of light-brown sugar, with large specs of amber.

"You have beautiful eyes, Lisa. I've never seen eyes so big with the color of crystal-blue oceans. And you have a sexy body. You are perfect, especially in this dress," he says as he runs his hand up my arm.

*Oh my gosh*. I don't know what to say. I'm utterly clueless.

"Thank you. I'm not used to receiving so many compliments. Especially from someone like you."

"I don't believe it. Any guy would turn their head twice when you walk by. You are gorgeous, with a killer body and sexy legs in heels."

"Stop it now," I say. "You're getting me all hot and bothered." *Flirting is so difficult and exhausting.*

We talk for a while about casual things, but I find it weird he never asks me what I'm going to medical school for. *Red flag number four.*

Even though I find it strange, I can't help the attraction. Is it my hormones? I know I haven't been with anyone in a long time. To be honest, I'm still a virgin. I haven't been with someone I felt was worth it. It's also out of fear. Just being near Bryant makes me reconsider my virginity without even knowing him for more than a couple of hours. Is this what sexual attraction is?

Since he doesn't ask me about Clarion, I purposely withhold why I'm going to medical school to become a psychiatrist. Maybe it's a blessing he isn't asking me anything personal. I can't go down that path of explaining what happened years ago. It's not the time or place. That will only happen when I feel a relationship is serious enough to open up like that. Should I just walk away from this now, like I always do when it comes to getting close to a guy? This screams red flags. But...it's not like I am going to marry him.

"Hello to Lisa." He waves his hand in front of my face. "You seemed to have spaced out a bit. Everything okay?" He puts his hand on my thigh and keeps it there.

I nod. "Yes, I'm fine. I just remembered I need to do something tomorrow. Sorry. What were you saying?"

He laughs. "Where are you from, and how old are you?" His hand rubs my thigh.

"I'm twenty-three years old—well, almost twenty-four. My birthday is at the end of this month. I'm from New Jersey. I'm a genuine Jersey girl," I say proudly as I shake my body back and forth on the chair. "I'm starting medical school one year late because I took extra classes at Johnson College. I wanted to be more prepared for this."

No reaction. "Where are you from?"

"I'm from Vermont. I'm a genuine Vermont boy," he says mockingly.

My eyebrows shoot up.

*Red flag number whatever. Who doesn't appreciate a genuine Jersey girl?*

"Where in Vermont are you from?"

"I'm from a small town not too far from Killington. I'm assuming you know where Killington is."

"I used to ski there, since I was little. I haven't been in a while because of school and money. The last time I was there, I witnessed the most horrible ski accident. A skier in front of me was slammed into by another skier who was out of control. Both went flying through the air. I helped one of them until the ski patrol took him away. The skier who was out of control almost hit me. He shot right in front of me, missing me by a couple of inches. It was a terrifying experience."

"I'll bet. Injuries like that happen all the time on the mountains. I don't ski as much as I did in the past. I don't really miss it though."

Time passes quickly as he talks about his family and how they come from old money. He plays tennis and goes to the gym as much as possible. He doesn't visit his family often due to his schedule. We hardly spoke about me.

He looks at his watch and slaps his hands on the table. "I need to work tomorrow. Would you mind if we get the check?"

*So soon? Was I boring?* "Of course not. No problem."

He waves over the waitress and asks for the check. My gaze wanders toward the bar. The redhead is still there.

"Bryant, let me help pay for the check."

He puts his hand up. "No way. I knocked you over today, so I'd like to pay to say sorry. Where do you live? Shall I walk you home?"

Several red flags. Do I go with my gut or with my hormones?

"I would love that. Thank you." *Hormones win.* "I don't live far from here. Do you know the Greenhouse Apartments?"

"Yes. Let's go."

He opens the door to let me out first. As we proceed down the street, he grabs my hand. I'm confused, because after all the red flags, he doesn't seem to be the type to hold hands. He's hard to read.

I feel something almost electric. It prickles all over my body. My reaction to Bryant is bizarre. I'm either lovesick or just horny.

This has been one of the most interesting days I've had in eternity. For the first time, I need to just relax and enjoy going out with a guy without any expectations on either end. What can come of this anyway? He has his residency, and I start medical school next week. We wouldn't have time for dating. At least I try to convince myself of that.

We arrive at my apartment complex. "I live in apartment one." I point to my door. Do I just go inside, or encourage him to kiss me?

I've been fantasizing about kissing him and have never felt so attracted to someone. Maybe I drank too much.

I peer into his eyes, and I see something I have never seen before. Passion, lust...I can't tell. His hands tug my hips closer to his. My lips are so close to his that I feel soft puffs on my lips. The anticipation kills me, so I grip his shirt as he lowers his lips to mine. Our kiss starts off slow but then heats up.

He puts one hand around the back of my neck, and the other hand travels downward, brushing the side of my breast, then down to my backside. My body responds everywhere, especially between my legs. His lips are so soft but demanding. His tongue is so delicious, so arousing. Don't get me wrong—I have kissed my share of guys, but somehow kissing Bryant is a whole new ball game.

I don't want to stop, but I hear some people down the far end of the hallway. He quickly steps away. I giggle and am thankful the hallway is not very bright. I can barely see them, so I hope they can't see us.

"Can we go inside?" he whispers into my ear, sending my hormones into overdrive.

"I want to, but my roommate has friends over tonight." It's not the best night for this, no matter how much I want it. "I thought you needed to work tomorrow?" I smirk.

"I do, but that kiss is encouraging me to stay. I want to see you again. When or where can we pick this back up?" he says as his hands run up my legs, almost under my dress. "What I wouldn't give to have your body under mine right now." At this point, he has me pinned against my apartment door.

This is so unlike me to be like this. But no one has ever made my hormones erupt like this before. I want him to jump me right here in the hallway. I want to lick him like a lollipop. Is that wrong?

I peek down the hall, and the other couple is still there. I need to control myself. I push him away gently, so as not to make a scene. "I only have orientation this week. What's your schedule like at the hospital?" I ask as I lean my head against the door.

"I'm scheduled to work the next two days, but I'm free on Thursday night. Want to come to my place? I don't have a roommate." He smiles with a wink.

I hesitate so I don't seem too eager. "I think I can. Why don't you call me and let me know what time and where you live?"

In exchange for my phone number, he gives me one more demanding kiss that tempts me to pull him into the apartment. He turns around and walks away without saying another word. He didn't have to after a kiss like that. I think my dreams will be X-rated tonight. I can't wait to fall asleep and for Thursday night.

I walk into my apartment, close the door, and lean on the back of it. I'm overthinking every little thing. I need to enjoy this reaction to him. I'm curious where this will go.

Emily and her three friends are sitting on the couch, watching me. She walks over, her clan following. "I think someone had a successful date. I'm glad I lent you that dress. How did it go?" she asks. Her friends, whom I have only met once, have big grins on their faces.

I giggle. "It went really well. I never had a date like that. He was quite open about how attractive he thinks I am. I'm not sure about anything else. There were a lot of red flags. The conversation flowed just fine, but it was very casual. I guess that's to be expected on a first date." I shrug and hang my handbag over a kitchen chair.

"I can't ignore how attracted I am to him. We were all over each other in front of our apartment door. He is twenty-seven years old. I have never been with anyone so much older than me. It's a little intimidating. I'm sure he has more experience."

"We heard you outside. We all took turns peeking through the peephole and saw what was going on. He's definitely cute and a good kisser."

I slap her on the arm. "You did not?" My eyes question all of them. *How humiliating.*

I walk over to the cabinet to get a glass. I'm so thirsty after all those yummy kisses, or was it the nachos?

"When will you see him again?" Emily says.

"On Thursday night. He asked me to go to his place for dinner. It makes me a bit nervous." I retrieve the Brita from the refrigerator and fill a glass.

"Why does it make you nervous? Then again, everything makes you nervous. Just go and have some fun, and maybe you'll get lucky. You need it bad."

*Is it that obvious?*

"Don't overthink what happened tonight. We've been living together for a little while, but I see how you analyze everything and everyone. I'm sure you analyze lint on the couch pillows." She laughs. "Just go with the flow and see where the flow takes you."

Easy for her to say when she doesn't know my mental and physical issues. No one does, except for my dad, stepmother, sister and therapist.

After some silence, I say, "Okay. You're right. I'm just going to have fun and take it from here. We can enjoy each other's company for the time being, until real life starts again next week. A late-summer fling."

I drink a big gulp of water. "I need to go to bed. It's been a long day. Thanks for your help. Have a good night, everyone." I walk to my bedroom. I close the door and immediately kick off her horrible shoes. How do women wear these things all day long? I was lucky I could even stand with him in front of the door after we walked from the bar. My feet are covered in stinging blisters.

The bed calls to me. As I grab my pajamas, I notice the leather jacket on the back of my chair. I run my fingers over it. Is it time to put it away? It has been my security blanket since the car accident, years ago. I wear this jacket when I'm sad, stressed, or need to feel safe. It's the only thing I have from the guy who helped me and my mom. I'll never get rid of it, but maybe I'll put it away for a while.

I always thought the guy with the mysterious green eyes would pop into my life again. After tonight, it's time to wake up from that fantasy. The past is long gone. Maybe Bryant is the one I've been waiting for. I walk over to the small closet and hang the jacket far to the left, out of sight. I hope I won't need it anytime soon.

# Chapter 5

## Lisa

There is no damn coffee in any of the kitchen cabinets. I slam the last one shut. This is not a good way to start the day, especially when I have an important reproduction exam today. Definitely not my favorite subject. I slump over the counter. My brain is like oatmeal without my first cup of joe. I can't even remember what I was thinking about two minutes ago. I tap my fingers on the countertop. It had to do with the male anatomy. Oh, that's right. Bryant!

Bryant and I have been together for over a year—a record for me. Sadly, with his hospital schedule and my large amount of schoolwork, we don't see each other often. We want a relationship, but my studying and his residency come first. Sometimes it's only once a week for a couple of hours. It always seems like we fill our time together with incredible sex. Not that I'm complaining.

I want to believe I'm in love with him. I finally feel free from my past. Maybe it's because he doesn't ask too many questions. We don't talk about the future and don't see each other enough to have many serious conversations. I sense we don't want to make it too serious. But how much more serious can we get when we are having sex all the time and have been doing it for over a year now? I want to believe it's something more.

I shuffle through the refrigerator and find a can of Diet Coke. It's better than nothing. I usually don't drink soda for breakfast, but I'm too lazy to walk to Mocha Bean Café for a latte macchiato.

Even with all the stress, we balance each other. We understand each other's responsibilities and pressures. Our stress relief is each other. Whether it's on the kitchen floor, bedroom, or in the car, we always find time for sex. We can't get enough. However, we don't go on dates or visit family much. He met my sister once, but not my dad. I saw his parents and sister a couple of times. They didn't seem too impressed with me.

Does he want something long term? Is he someone I can see spending my future with? Neither of us has said "I love you." I still haven't told him about my past. I know I should approach the subject, but I don't want to ruin what we have. The longer I wait, the worse it will be. I'm terrified he'll walk away from me, either from the pressure of just talking about the future or because I can't give him what he wants.

I need to talk to him soon. If my heart is going to be broken, I want it done now, not later. This is the first time I will tell a guy about the car accident in detail or that I love him.

I tap a pen on my notebook. Come on, Tina. Pick up the phone.

"Tina Schmitt."

"Hey, Tina, it's Lisa."

"Hi, what's up? I haven't heard from you in over a week. School getting to you?"

"Yes, I'm studying like hell for exams as we speak. My schoolbooks and notes surround me on the sofa. But I don't want to talk about that right now. I need your advice."

"Sure. Hopefully, I can help you. If it's about men, can't help you there. I'm still going through a dry spell."

I take the heavy books off my lap and put them on the coffee table. "I'm going to talk to Bryant about our future. I want to tell him I love him."

I hear her sigh. "Do you really love him, Lisa? Are you in love with him or just love him? You hardly see each other and seem to only have sex when you are together. I know there's more to your relationship than sex, but still. I hope you don't think it's more than it appears."

I hug my knees. "I know. I understand what you're saying. You know me. I have never been with a guy like this or this long. I'm always running in the other direction. Maybe he's the one I don't have to run from."

"Well, if you're going to tell him you love him, then you need to tell him all of the details about the car accident and what happened to you. You haven't been completely honest with him."

"I know. You're right. He asked what happened when he saw the scar. I told him I had an accident. But, the conversation didn't go any further."

The first time we had sex, he was pretty surprised he was my first. When we both knew we were clean, I told him I went on the pill. A little white lie. I didn't think we would last as long as we have. I wasn't thinking about future consequences.

"I wish you wouldn't live like this. You don't fully open up to anyone. You're going to school to become a psychiatrist and have gone through so much therapy of your own. Haven't you learned people will love you no matter what? If they don't, then you don't need them."

I lean my head back against the sofa. "I'm broken. Who wants someone who's broken? If, and I say if, I think Bryant is the one to finally tell my secrets, I'll tell him everything."

"You act like you have a disease. I don't want to see you get hurt and then pull yourself away from the world again. Make sure you know what you are doing."

"I know. Neither do I."

"I have to get back to work. Let me know how it goes. Love you."

"Thanks for listening. I don't know what I would do without you. Talk to you soon." I turn off the phone and put it on my books.

I search through my handbag for my wallet. I pull out a folded picture of me and Mom at my middle school graduation. I miss her so much. Tina is my best friend and my only sister, but she isn't my mom, even though she acts like she is most of the time. No one could ever take Mom's place. I need her more than ever right now.

Bryant is coming over tonight for dinner. He has the night off. We can finally see each other for more than an hour. Emily is spending the night at her boyfriend's apartment. She's hardly ever here anymore. I have a feeling she will move in with him eventually.

He knocks on the door as he walks into the apartment. He knows I'm alone, so he doesn't care, and neither do I. I run to him and give him a big kiss. Which turns into us ripping each other's clothes off before we can even get to the bedroom.

I don't even know how long we have been in bed. We lie on our sides, facing each other. "I have something to confess," I say hesitantly.

His jawline stiffens.

"Remember how I told you my mom died in a car accident?"

He nods.

"I was in the car with her and obviously survived."

His eyes widen. "I'm sorry, Lisa. Nobody deserves to experience something like that," he says as he rubs my arm. "Why haven't you told me this?"

*Maybe it won't be so hard to tell him.*

I put my finger over his mouth to make him quiet. "I have more to tell you."

His eyebrows rise.

"I survived, but not without severe injuries. The scar on my abdomen is from the car accident. My seat belt dug into my lower abdomen when our car hit a tree. Due to the pressure of my seat belt, it severely damaged my left ovary. It had to be removed. Thankfully, the other ovary is fine." I need to take a breath because tears pool in my eyes. It's hard to talk about this. I don't look at him because I'm afraid of how he will react.

"Not just my ovary was damaged. My uterus ruptured on the same side, but the surgeon was able to repair it and stop the bleeding. Still, I was told it will never function properly due to the large amount of scar tissue. It wasn't necessary to remove my uterus, but I was told I'll never be able to have children.

"Because of the car accident, my mother's death, and that I can't have children, that's why I'd like to be a psychiatrist. I've been through a lot of therapy to deal with my issues. I would like to help others like I was helped."

He slides out of the bed. He remains quiet while he pulls up his jeans. He turns toward me. "Why haven't you told me this before? We've been together for a while now. You've basically lied to me all this time. You were never on the pill, were you?"

"No, I never was. I was afraid you wouldn't want to be with me if you knew I couldn't have children. It wasn't to hurt you."

"Did I ever say to you I want to have children or even to get married any time soon? I can't even think about that shit right now. My focus is on my residency. That's what comes first," he spits out.

*Ouch.*

"But you are a pediatrician, love being around children, and told me your parents are constantly saying they want grandchildren. I'm in love with you, Bryant, but I'll never be able to have your children. I'm broken." I barely realize tears are trickling down my face.

After a few minutes, he lies down next to me again. He pulls me in his arms and wipes my tears away.

"I'm mad you didn't tell me the truth, but I understand why. I love you, Lisa, but I'm not thinking about marriage or having children in the near future. I can't give you more than what we have right now. I thought it was enough for you. We're always busy, but we understand one another and have amazing sex," he says with a smile that is not necessary at the moment.

I sit up in bed with a sheet over me. "I told you I love you. I didn't ask for a marriage proposal!"

He flips onto his back and lets out a long breath. "I'm sorry. That didn't come out right. I'm happy you told me. It's just that I can't think further than tomorrow. We know what our priorities are. That's what I love about our relationship and why we have been together for so long. We don't let it get in the way of our goals."

All I can do is sit here and stare at him. Is this the reaction I was hoping to receive from him? Did I expect him to be more compassionate, angry, disgusted? I'm lost.

"Why do you feel broken? There are always other options, like adoption, surrogate mother..." He says it like it's so easy and no big deal. Almost as if I'm buying a watermelon at the grocery store. He's a man. How could he even comprehend this?

I stand up and put on my pajamas with force. "You make it sound like it's so easy. You are not a woman, so you can't possibly understand. Well, I wouldn't do any of those things. I feel this happened to me for a reason. I have no idea what that reason is, but I've been asking myself ever since I was fifteen. I'm not meant to have children."

He waves his hand in the air. "Whatever. Again, I can't think about these things right now. It's so far from my mind. Let's not put pressure on ourselves."

He says he loves me. But does he really? He doesn't think of his future with me? Ever? If he was in love with me, wouldn't that thought come into his head sometimes?

He gets out of the bed and reaches for me. "Let's just enjoy having time alone and the apartment to ourselves." He kisses my forehead. "Thanks for opening up to me. It had to have been hard. Let's make dinner. I'm starving."

And just like that, he acts like we never discussed my issue. I feel relieved I told him, but his response wasn't what I'd hoped. Are the red flags waving around again? Does he even want a future with me? Or should I ask myself, do I really want a future with him?

# Chapter 6

## James

My thirty-minute break starts now. I take a cafeteria tray and slide it over to the coffee machines. I pour a hot coffee and place an everything bagel with cream cheese on my tray. I pay and search for an empty table. I can't wait to sit for a little while. My feet and legs are tired. Jessica said she'll try to meet me here if it's slow in the pediatric ward.

Jessica and I have been inseparable for the past two years. I'm going into my third and final year of residency, and she has finished hers and received her medical license. She can finally make more money. Even though we've had a rough time with our residencies, we've been supporting each other. Any free time we have, we spend it together. We don't fight like other couples. Our friends and families think we are ridiculous because we are constantly touching and kissing.

Every time I see her, it feels like weeks since the last time, even when it's only been a couple of hours or days. I need her like I need water. She is my addiction. How did I handle life without her? I never want to know the answer to that question.

Our schedules don't match up often, but when they do, we spend time with our families. My parents have told me numerous times how much they love Jessica and think we're a perfect match. Both sets of our parents get along—they even get together once in a while without us. My parents stay over at Alexa's sometimes, to make it easier for us to all meet up. Jessica loves Alexa. They act like sisters.

I sip my coffee but almost spit it back into the cup. It's boiling hot. That just woke me up more than the actual coffee itself.

Now that Jessica has her New York State medical license, she can look elsewhere for a job. She still works at the university hospital, but she wants to keep her options open. We talk about getting married when my residency is over. But I don't think I can wait much longer. I know it's too soon since I'm not finished yet, but I want to at least ask her to marry me. I know in my heart it's time. When it's right, it's right.

I don't care if we don't get married right away. I just want her to be mine forever and ask her to move in with me. It seems to be the natural next step in our relationship. We spend most of our time at my apartment anyway. We have more privacy there. And it would let us save money for when it's time to get married.

I look at the time. I have only five minutes left of my break. I guess Jessica couldn't get away from the ward. I finish my bagel and leave the table.

This Saturday she's throwing a party to celebrate the end of her residency and obtaining her license. She's invited her parents, my family, our friends, and other residency doctors. I plan to ask her to marry me at her party, in front of everyone. I asked her parents for their blessing. They said they would be proud to have me as their son-in-law.

When I sought their blessing, Jessica's mother, Mrs. Flynn, showed me Jessica's grandmother's engagement ring. Her grandmother passed away a couple of years before I met her. Mrs. Flynn asked if I would like to give it to Jessica and ranted about how much her daughter loves this ring. I had planned to buy her a ring, but this seems more romantic and part of her heritage. Since she's the only child, it's the only chance to pass it down to the next generation. And we can pass it down to one of our kids someday.

I know I'm crazy, but I just can't wait. She doesn't suspect a thing. I'm confident she'll say yes. She told me she wants to be surprised when I propose. I think she will be floored. Only Jessica's parents know I plan to propose at the party. Not even my parents, Alexa, or my best friend, Matt, knows. It was so hard not to tell them.

I'm anxious and excited. I know exactly what I will say to her.

# Chapter 7

## Lisa

Don't I have Tylenol or Advil? I knock over a bottle of hand disinfectant into the bathroom sink. How can there be nothing in the bathroom cabinet? Maybe I have some in my handbag. I head toward the kitchen to search my bag. I wish Emily still lived here. She always had this apartment stocked with painkillers. She moved into her boyfriend's apartment about a month ago. I don't mind living alone at this point in my life. Especially when I'm sick.

Ha! I find a travel bottle of Advil in my handbag. I drag myself to the sink to fetch a glass of water.

I woke up with the chills and a headache this morning. Why do I have to be sick today? Ugh! I'm supposed to go to a party with Bryant tonight. His fellow resident, Jessica, is having a party because she finished her residency and received her license. She lives in an apartment far down the hallway from mine but I have never met her. Our paths have never physically crossed.

I've been looking forward all week to going to an actual party rather than staying home having sex. I like the sex, but there has to be more to a relationship. Right? Well, it's only morning. Maybe I will feel better later. Now that I've taken some medicine, I'll try to sleep it off.

Wishful thinking. I'm lying on the couch in complete misery. It is 7:00 p.m., and I still feel horrible. My fever and headache have returned. My stomach feels nauseated. Even if I take medicine again, I won't be well enough to go to the party. I hope he won't be angry. He should be here any minute. I'm pissed off because I really wanted and needed to have some fun tonight. Bryant as well. We've been working so hard these last weeks, which is probably why I'm sick. We need a break, even if it's only for a couple of hours.

I hear a knock at the door but don't move off the couch. Bryant walks in and notices right away I'm sick. His facial expression reflects sympathy but also disappointment. He walks toward me, but I put my hand out to stop him.

"Don't come near me. I don't want to get you sick."

He stops immediately.

"I'm sorry. I can't go to the party when I feel this sick. You know how excited I was about tonight. I shouldn't expose other people to what I have. Please understand. You need to go without me. I didn't call you because I hoped I'd feel better by now."

"Are you sure? I can stay here with you," he says, not too convincingly.

"No. Please don't worry about me. I'm just down the hall. Go for as long as you want. I have no desire to be around anyone. All I want is a cup of tea, a hot water bottle, and to lie in my warm bed. I've taken medicine, but this fever doesn't want to go away."

He moves forward again, but I don't have the strength to stop him this time. It's his fault if he gets sick. He puts the bottle of champagne on the coffee table he told me he bought Jessica yesterday.

He presses his hand against my forehead. "Yes, you definitely have a fever. Put a cool compress on your head. See if that helps. I'll go to the party for a couple of hours and then come back and check up on you later."

The chills are worse now. I sit up and pull a big blanket over my shoulders. "You can, but I have no idea if I'll be awake. It's probably better if you aren't around me, since you have to be at the hospital tomorrow. Granted, you are exposed to bacteria and viruses every day. Please have a good time and don't worry about me. Tell Jessica

I'm sorry for not attending her party." *Not like she'll care, since she doesn't even know me.*

I wrap the blanket tighter around me and walk him to the door. Before he can say anything, I practically push him across the threshold and close it.

I can hardly stand at this point. I need to make myself tea and a hot water bottle before I go to bed. He didn't sound too disappointed I'm sick. Maybe he didn't want me to go with him. He has been a little distant lately. Now I'm being paranoid.

Tina asks me why I stay with him. I ask myself the same question more than I should. If I truly loved him, I should have every reason to stay with him. But I don't.

# Chapter 8

## James

My palms are sticky, and my forehead has beads of sweat forming. I check for the hundredth time that the ring is in my pocket. My eyes search the crowded apartment for Jessica, and I finally see her. She stands in a circle of her resident friends, laughing about something. Every movement she makes releases all the tension from the last few years out of her body.

There is nothing to be nervous about. However, I never thought I would be proposing in front of so many guests.

She sees me and waves me over. Her smile relaxes me as I approach. She kisses me softly on my lips and slips her arm around mine. Her rose perfume encompasses me.

"Hi there, handsome. What took you so long to get here?" She puts her hand on my cheek. "Are you feeling okay? You're sweating. Did your old Honda break down again so you had to walk here?" She pokes me in the ribs.

"Maybe I'm getting a cold. I don't know. We're exposed to so many things at the hospital. Anything can happen." I jiggle the ring in my pocket.

She looks toward the apartment door. "Hey, another resident just arrived who I want to introduce you to." She waves him over.

He waves and walks up to us. "Hi Jessica. Congratulations on finally being free." He hands her a bottle. "Here's a bottle of champagne from me and my girlfriend, Lisa."

"Thank you so much. I will definitely enjoy this. It's such a relief to be done." She cradles the bottle in one arm.

"Where's your girlfriend? I have yet to meet her and we live in the same apartment complex. Granted I'm hardly ever here." She laughs.

"She sends her regards. She really wanted to come tonight but she's sick."

"I'm sorry to hear that."

He shrugs his shoulders. "It happens."

I extend my hand out to him. "Hi. I'm Jessica's boyfriend, James."

She giggles. "Sorry James. This is Bryant."

We shake hands. "Nice to meet you, James. You work in the ER. Right?"

"Yes, I do."

"Sorry guys." Jessica interrupts. "But I need to go help my parents. I see them trying to take something out of the oven." I take the champagne bottle from her.

"Bryant, go get something to drink and mingle. Enjoy the party," she says happily.

"Thanks. Talk to you both later." He wanders off into the group of guests.

Her hand flutters against my arm. "Want to come with me?"

I shrug. "Sure."

As I walk away, I space out after hearing the name Lisa. I haven't thought about my Lisa in a long time.

Jessica pulls me aside. "James, are you sure you're okay? You're acting funny."

"Everything is fine. I think I need a glass of water, or maybe a beer would be better." I'd like a shot, but I should stick to beer.

"I thought you said you were getting sick," she remarks in confusion.

*She got me there.*

"Maybe, but I need something cold right now. A cold beer sounds pretty good."

"Do me a favor. Please put the champagne in the refrigerator.

Then get yourself a beer." She kisses me on the cheek and walks away.

She has no idea. I love it!

I open a beer and walk into the living room.

Jessica's father approaches me. "Are you ready, James?" he whispers.

"I'm more than ready, Mr. Flynn," I say with a nervous smile.

"No more Mr. Flynn. After tonight, please call me Dad." He pats me on the back and walks away.

Interesting. For the last year, I have called him Mr. Flynn. I always thought it was too formal, but I wanted to be respectful. Now he wants me to call him Dad. That's a big jump.

More people arrive. I think the entire group of residents are here. This apartment is small, so it's packed. Maybe I should rethink this. I shouldn't care, because I'll only be looking at her when I propose.

I check my watch for the fifteenth time. I'm going to explode if I wait any longer.

It's showtime.

I stand in the middle of the living room. "Jessica, where are you?" I say it loud enough that her guests turn in my direction.

She comes around the corner. "I'm right here. What's going on?" She looks at me and then to her guests.

"Come stand by me, please," I say as I stretch out my arm for her to grab my hand.

I check to make sure our families are watching. I've gone over this moment in my head several times, but now I'm lost. I take her hands in mine and stare directly into her eyes. I calm down immediately.

"The moment you walked into my life at Clarion's orientation, you turned it upside down in the most wonderful ways. I knew my life would change for the better. All my friends and family know I've had my life planned out for the next ten to twenty years. Even though you were not a part of the plan, you easily fit in. Becoming a doctor was my number one priority since I was seventeen years old. After you entered my life, it became the second. You will always be my top priority."

Her grip on my hands increases, and her eyes glisten.

"The night we met at Kerry's Pub, when I arrived, you didn't see me right away. I stood there and observed you. I told myself how lucky I was to be there with you. I learned how passionate you are about being a doctor. We share the same passion. We want to truly help others.

"You are smart, beautiful, patient, and most of all, you are mine. I never knew my life was lacking something until you appeared. From the first time I saw your face, I knew it would lead me to this moment. The first time we kissed, my heart whispered you were my soul mate. I can't wait to build a future with you. I'll support you in every way I can, in all aspects of your life. When you fall, I promise I will pick you up. I hope one day you will be the mother of my children. I promise to show you how much I love you, every day for the rest of our lives. I know we agreed we would wait to get married. However, I can't wait any longer to ask you to be my wife."

I kneel on one knee and take out the ring box. "Jessica, I love you. Will you marry me?"

Tears form in my eyes. My hands shake as I take the ring out of the box. I take her trembling hand and slide the ring on her finger. I almost lose my balance when she screams, "Yes, yes, yes! I love you so much." I straighten, and she jumps into my arms and kisses me as if we are the only ones in the room. There's an uproar of congratulations and clapping.

"This is my grandmother's ring," she cries. We hold on to each other for a while, until we remember we are in the middle of all the guests. I'll always remember this moment. I'm truly the luckiest man in the world.

"Mr. Flynn—I mean, Dad—where's the champagne?" I yell cheerfully.

Alexa runs to me, squealing. "Congratulations, you sly dog. I can't believe you didn't tell me. Not even Mom and Dad. We are all happily surprised. I love that Jessica will be my sister-in-law. I love having a sister. No offense, James, but you are a guy. It's different."

"Thanks, Alexa. You can calm down now. I don't think we'll be getting married anytime soon. Go have some champagne and give Jessica a hug."

Dad clamps a hand on my shoulder. "We can't believe you didn't tell us," he says as Mom hugs me.

She wipes a tear from her eyes. "What a beautiful proposal! We're so happy for you both. I love that we were all surprised. We thought you were going to wait to get married."

"We'll wait to get married, but I really wanted to propose. This was the next best step to get us closer to that."

I watch while Jessica shows off her ring. I know she loves it was her grandmother's. That's why I love her so much. She doesn't need a huge diamond on her hand to prove I love her. She doesn't need money and fancy things to be happy. Unfortunately, her parents feel differently.

Her parents think money is essential. It puts pressure on me. She's the only child and has been doted on by her parents since she was born. I don't know how she's the type of person she is today. Money is not a driver in her life. However, once I start making money, I'll spoil her with anything she wants.

# Chapter 9

## Lisa

I'm dead asleep in my bed when I feel a hand on my arm, shaking me gently. I open my eyes and see Bryant came back anyway.

"How are you feeling?" he asks.

"I still feel like crap, but at least I was able to sleep for a couple of hours." *I'm not leaving this bed.* I'm annoyed he woke me up.

"I'm sorry I woke you up. I wanted to see if you need anything."
*Okay, maybe I'm being bitchy.*

I sit up, regretting it immediately. My head is pounding. I try to put a smile on my face. "So how was the party? Were there a lot of people there?" I say, faking interest.

"The party was actually a lot of fun. There were more people there than I expected. I knew a bunch of them from the hospital. I finally met her boyfriend. He seems like a nice guy."

"She must be ecstatic to be finished. Now she can practice anywhere she wants. I still have so much school ahead of me," I say as I fall onto the pillow a little too hard.

"Her boyfriend proposed to her in the middle of the party."

That got my attention.

"It seems everyone was quite shocked, including her. She jumped up and down and of course cried 'yes' like a total girl. He was on the verge of tears during his proposal, and then they were both crying. You could see how they truly love each other. They're like, the perfect couple. It was a true Hallmark moment." He ridicules.

"Why do you say it like that? Is it so hard to believe two people can be so in love?" I sound defensive, and I don't even know them.

Bryant only shrugs and stands up.

I guess I'm right then. *Red flag 5,000!*

"What's her fiancée's name?" I ask as I massage my temples.

"His name is James."

Instantly my stomach turns. It makes me think of James from the ski accident in Killington. I haven't thought of him or that experience in a while.

"Are you feeling worse, Lisa? You're making a weird face.

"I'm fine. The name James reminds me of the ski accident I told you about. His name was James. I've told you that story before, haven't I?

"It rings a bell." Bryant replies completely disinterested. Does he care about anything personal to me?

Now I'm just irritated. "Bryant, can you please leave? I'm not good company when I'm sick. I sleep better alone. Sorry you can't stay the night. Since it's not too late, why don't you go out with your friends?"

"Really?" He acts like a dog that was just asked if he wants a bone. He bolts to the kitchen to call his friends, with too much enthusiasm.

He ambles back into the bedroom. "I'm going to meet up with some of the guys at the Burning Tavern. Are you sure you don't mind?"

"As a matter of fact, I don't mind at all." *Please get out of my apartment!*

"Okay. Thanks! Feel better, and I'll talk to you tomorrow." He exits the bedroom like his pants are on fire.

When I hear the door close, I sigh in relief. I don't want him here tonight. The way he told the story about the proposal was like he was mocking them. As if it was so stupid to be that much in love with someone. What does it say about us? We definitely don't act like that, even though we supposedly love each other.

I can't think about Bryant anymore. It makes my head hurt worse. I need to focus on school and stop wondering how he feels about me. Our relationship works for the time being.

My thoughts wander to James. I wonder whatever happened to my James. Hopefully he wasn't seriously injured. I haven't gone skiing since I started medical school. That's probably why I haven't thought about him in so long. Would I recognize him if I saw him on the street? Probably not. I didn't see his face clearly. He had a helmet and goggles on most of the time. When the goggles were off, his eyes were closed. Even if I did meet him, he could be a total jerk. The one thing I do remember is when he held my hand and said thank you with such tenderness and sincerity.

I shake my head. Why am I even thinking about him? I need to lay off the medicine.

# Chapter 10

## Lisa

I exit the lecture hall and head toward my favorite café on campus. I'll be lucky if I passed that exam on clinical reasoning. My head is in another place.

I know something is wrong. Bryant and I are growing apart. I've seen it coming though—we've been fighting a lot. He doesn't come over as much, and he doesn't tell me he loves me anymore. I don't say it either. Well, not just because he doesn't say it. I'm not sure I love him either. Sex is nothing like it used to be. Maybe he's found someone else.

I take a latte macchiato to go and head home. Bryant finished his residency over a year ago. He received his license and accepted a job where he'd been employed as a resident, as he wanted to prolong his time there for a couple of years. He would like to open his own practice in the future. He also admitted he wanted to stay because of me. That was last year, but things have changed. His hours are not as bad as when he was a resident, but he hasn't increased his time spent with me either.

We used to talk about our future together, but that's also come to a stop. It's not like we talked about it much to begin with. Why did I ever think our relationship was normal? I can't open up to him. We had our good times, but they were never anything spectacular.

Let me see how he is when he comes over in a couple of hours. I'll make sure I'm irresistible when he arrives. Usually, he can't resist me when I'm wearing a dress and high heels.

I'm in the bathroom when I hear the doorbell ring. *Who could be at the door?* Bryant shouldn't be here until 8:00 p.m., and he usually just walks into the apartment. "I'm coming," I yell as I slip into my fluffy, pastel-green robe. I walk to the door and look through the peephole. Bryant.

I open the door. "Hi! Why did you ring the doorbell? You always walk right in."

He doesn't say anything as he steps inside.

"You're here early. What a nice surprise," I say as I give him a hug. A hug he doesn't reciprocate. *Now I am pissed.* "What is wrong with you, Bryant? And don't tell me there's nothing wrong. I'm tired of always making excuses for you. You've been acting suspicious for weeks, if not months." I stand with my hand on my hip as he avoids eye contact.

He strides toward the living room. "Come sit on the sofa with me."

I close the apartment door and walk over to him. I sit down as he takes my hand in his. I can feel what's coming.

"Lisa, we've had a great time together for three years now. We've had a lot of fun, and it has helped us get through some of the hardest times with your studying and my residency. You supported me in ways no one else did. You were so proud of me when I finally got my medical license. One of the reasons I stayed at the hospital to work was to be near you.

"However, I can't pretend I'm happy anymore. I haven't been happy for a while. We are now in two different places in our lives. You still need to finish medical school and then your residency. I'm finished with that. After I started working, I was okay for a while. Then I started to evaluate my life. I asked myself, 'Will I be happy if I stay here? Do I want to go to work for another hospital? Do I still want to open my own practice? Do I want to get married and have a family?'"

My heart pounds in my ears. I yank my hand from his and turn away.

"Please look at me, Lisa."

I force myself to look at him. He keeps rubbing his chin. "I met someone else. She's also a doctor at the hospital. She studied family medicine. I've never cheated on you, but we have been spending time together."

*Does he really expect me to believe he's never cheated on me?*

"I know what I want now. It's to open my own practice, but most of all, I want to get married. I see my future with her. We want to open a dual practice where she'll be the general family doctor and I'll be the pediatrician. We both hope to have a family one day."

*There it is. The punch in the stomach I was waiting for!*

I stand up abruptly and walk over to the living room window. "I knew I should have followed my gut the moment I met you. I told myself to walk away. But no, I convinced myself you were different and would accept me for who I am. I should have listened!"

I try hard not to shed any tears. Unfortunately, I cry when I'm angry. I turn to him with clenched fists. "Why were we together all this time? Why did I stay with you when my gut was always saying to break up with you?"

"I don't know. Why did you?" he asks accusingly.

"I guess I was good for the time being, but not for the long term." *I will never be enough for any man.* This is why I stayed away from relationships. He wants a family.

He rests his head in his hands. "No, that's not it at all. I thought we agreed we weren't thinking long term, or at least I wasn't. Marriage and children were so out of my spectrum the first years. I didn't think you were considering marriage with me either." He stands up from the sofa and holds out his hands. "We were coasting along. We hardly saw each other during the past years. Our schedules never matched up but we made it work. We didn't have time for anything or anyone else. We never spent more than a couple of hours with each other at a time."

He reaches for me, but I back away.

"Don't touch me."

"Don't be like this. You can't honestly tell me we were

head over heels for each other. As things started to settle, I thought about my life differently. I love you. But I'm not in love with you. If I was, I would stay with you no matter what. You deserve to be with someone you are completely in love with and who feels the same. You deserve that more than anyone. But I know I cannot give it to you. The time we've had together was special to me, but it's time for me to say good-bye. I'm sorry I'm hurting you."

I turn toward the window again, gripping the sill as I stare outside. My fingers are white from gripping so hard. I can't stand being anywhere near him. I want to scream out of frustration. I'm so angry and disappointed. Disappointed in him or myself? I don't even know.

I want to keep calm and show him I'm not hurt, but it's impossible. I turn around and start yelling. "I truly hope you're happy with your new girlfriend! Thanks for letting me be your fuck buddy for three years. Was that all I was good for? I should have followed my instincts, but I ignored them, hoping we would become more. Boy, was I stupid!"

As he opens the door, he stops, with his head hanging low, not even looking at me. "For what it's worth, I am truly sorry. I wish you all the best," he mumbles.

"Get out. Your apologies don't mean anything to me!"

I'm so stupid. I knew it would end like this. He found someone who can provide what he wants. They can have the white picket fence and all that goes with it. The past years were wasted on him. My heart knew he wasn't the one. Why did I ignore it? Was I scared to be alone again? Was I willing to settle? I can't answer such questions right now. I finally put myself out there, and this is what happens.

I officially close off my heart to all men.

I spin around in my apartment, searching for something to help me feel better. *Should I throw something across the room? Should I scream into a pillow?* I march into the bedroom and open the closet. I search to the far side and find what I'm looking for. I wipe the dust off the leather jacket and put it on. This is the one thing that has always been there for me and makes me feel better. I fall into bed and cry myself to sleep.

# Chapter 11

## James

I put on my scrubs and walk out of the bathroom. I toss my white jacket and raincoat over the arm of the sofa. Rain taps heavily on the windows. It's been pouring all day. Typical spring weather. Jessica will be home any minute. She wants to talk to me about something. Maybe she received an offer from another hospital. Applying for positions at other hospitals has been stressful for her. The university hospital has the best pediatric department in this area. She's doing well here, but she thinks she needs to move on. She hasn't been feeling well, on top of it. We both think she is rundown and needs a break. She has been exhausted lately and doesn't have much of an appetite.

I look at the clock on the DVD player. I need to leave for the hospital in twenty minutes. To keep myself occupied, I wander around our apartment, looking for things to straighten up. But this apartment is spotless and in order. That's mostly due to me. I'm very organized, and nothing is usually out of place. She's the messy one. I'm always running behind her, cleaning up. She gets annoyed because the first thing I do when I come home is straighten up. The only thing I hate to do is the dishes. The kitchen sink is full, so I guess I'll have to suck it up and do them.

I finish my residency in three months. The end of the tunnel is near. Once I have my medical license in hand, I can make more money to help pay off our loans.

Jessica's parents want to pay for the wedding. They want a big, fancy affair for their only child. Jessica says she doesn't need a fancy wedding, but deep down I have a feeling she does. I'll do whatever makes her happy. My parents insist on helping with the wedding also. I won't let them, since they helped me enough with medical school.

Finally, I hear a squeak from the apartment doorknob. I walk out of the kitchen as Jessica walks inside, a big smile on her face. I guess I was right about a job offer.

"Hey, babe." She shakes her damp hair and drops the wet umbrella by the shoe rack. I pick it up and open it so it will dry properly.

"What's going on? Did you get an offer from another hospital?"

She laughs. "No...that is definitely not it." She walks over to the sofa and tosses her handbag on the coffee table.

"So what's up? You're smiling for a reason. Spit it out. I'm dying here." I laugh.

"Maybe I should make you guess by asking different questions," she says as she taps her cheek with her finger.

"That isn't fair. It'll take too long. I need to leave in ten minutes. Tell me, woman!"

She plops down on the sofa. "Come sit next to me."

I fall onto it and try to guess what her good news is. "Did you win the lottery? You're acting strange."

"I'm pregnant," she blurts out. "I'm three months along already." She bounces up and down on the sofa.

"Wait. What? I'm going to be a father?"

She nods.

*How can she be pregnant? This wasn't in the plan.*

Her face changes because I have no reaction. I feel dizzy. I'm flabbergasted and excited at the same time. A smile finally appears on my face. I grab Jessica and start kissing her. I pull away quickly because I don't want to crush her.

"Wow, I can't believe it. I'm so happy, but how did this happen? You've been on the pill all this time."

"Remember when I was on antibiotics a while back? I forgot antibiotics can interfere with taking the pill. Being a doctor, I should remember these things." She chuckles. "It seems it decreased the efficacy of my pills."

I'm silent because I'm still trying to grasp the situation.

"When is the baby due?" I question in a daze.

"November eighteenth. Please tell me you're happy. Even though this is such a surprise and not within your timelines, I'm ecstatic. I know how you planned the years ahead for us already." She grabs my cheeks and squeezes them. "My little planner." She lowers her hands to her belly and starts to rub it. "We're going to become a family a little bit earlier than we expected. This is what we've always wanted. We're going to be parents." Excitement beams from her face.

"I'm more than happy. I've always wanted to have children with you. It's all so sudden. That's all. I need time to process this. We aren't even married yet. I'm thankful my residency will be over before the baby comes. I wanted to complete a fellowship to receive extended training. That will need to wait. I want to be home as much as possible when the baby is born."

"This is what we always wanted in our future. I'm already secure in my job. Maybe we can move our wedding up instead of waiting to have a fancy one. We can have something simple before the baby arrives and then have a big party after the baby is born. There are so many things to think about. We'll figure it all out." She rubs my thigh in assurance.

"We're very lucky because we hear about so many women in the hospital who cannot have children. We are truly blessed, no matter what. I love you so much."

She kisses me softly. "I love you too," she babbles.

She wiggles in her seat. "Now we know why I haven't been feeling good. I had a meeting with the chief of staff in the pediatric department today and mentioned I wasn't feeling well lately. Somehow during the conversation, she asked me if I was possibly pregnant. *No* was my first response, but then I started to think about my symptoms. When did I have my last period? It was a while. I thought it was because I was rundown and my cycle was off.

"When I had the chance, I went to my friend Jackie, a doctor in the gynecology department. You met her a couple of times. She gave me a pregnancy test immediately. The result was as clear as day. She took a scan, and there was our little peanut." She pulls the sonogram picture out of her purse.

She hands it to me and points to the little speck. At this moment, I don't care about anything else. This is our child in this picture. We have dreamed of this moment ever since we met. Tears well in my eyes, and I look at Jessica. Her eyes are watery as well. We embrace each other and sit in silence, gazing at the picture while I lay my hand on her stomach.

"I'm not sure what we'll do once the baby is born. We'll need to move into a bigger apartment and buy a new car. There are so many things to think about." My heart rate is already increasing.

Jessica takes my hand and kisses it. She's so relaxed. "James, whatever comes our way, we'll get through it as a family. We can't possibly expect every minute of our lives to go as planned. You need to learn to be flexible once in a while. Relax now. Everything will be fine."

I slouch my shoulders. "I know, but this is the way I am. I'll try to be more flexible, but it will take time."

She smacks her hands together. "I can't believe we're going to be parents. We have so much to be thankful for and to look forward to. The next chapter in our life is starting right now." She jumps off the sofa. "Let's call our parents to tell them the good news!"

# Part Two

# Chapter 12

## James

"What can I get for you, James? The usual?"

"Yes," I grunt without even looking at him. Jack knows me by name because I come here often. This will be another night when I'm going to get fucking drunk. I don't want to feel anything. *If I don't want to feel anything, then why do I come here?* How long am I going to torture myself? It's one year today. It's too damn hard. I'm lost in this black hole called my life.

"Here you go. Should I start a tab for you?"

I nod and snatch the whiskey and gulp it down. It burns as it glides down my throat. Just what I wanted. I smack my hand on the bar to let Jack know I want another one.

My parents and sister want me to seek help. They think I should talk to a total stranger about my feelings and experiences. I find pamphlets around the apartment about different support groups and therapists. No thanks! Talking to someone is not going to solve my problems. The only thing that will make my life worth living again is impossible. My anger and sadness are permanent, and no one or nothing will ever change that.

The barstool next to me scrapes along the floor. From the corner of my eye, I see a young woman with wavy light-brown hair sit next to me. Great. There are several empty barstools, yet she chooses to sit next to me. I aim my body away from her to avoid contact.

Jack asks what she would like. She orders a whiskey. She must be having a bad day as well. Whiskey is my alcohol of choice lately. It helps numb the pain fast. Jack puts her whiskey and mine in front of us on the bar. I raise the glass, but I don't even glance her way. She probably didn't even notice. I don't care either way. Actually, I don't care about anything anymore.

The whiskey is kicking in now, flowing through my veins like a drug, though it isn't taking my mental pain away. It's pulling me further down into the abyss. Getting drunk isn't working as well as it used to. I'm slowly dying inside every day because my life is total shit. Last year at this time, I had it all. I rest my chin on my clamped fists as tears form. I'm surprised I'm not dried up by now. Crying is my hobby.

Suddenly, someone taps my shoulder. I turn, and the young woman is staring at me. It's dark in here, so I can't see her face very well. Or is that the whiskey's effect?

"Are you okay?" she asks with concern.

"I'm fine. I cry when I brush my teeth with whiskey. Do you have a problem with that?" I snap as I turn away from her again.

She calls to Jack, "Two more whiskeys, please."

I sit there for a moment with my head down. Before I know it, I start talking or mumbling to myself or to her. I don't know at this point. Maybe to anyone who wants to listen.

"This is where our first date was. We sat here for hours on these two barstools. We could have talked all night, but we had to leave. I walked her home, and after our first real kiss, I knew we were meant to be together. My heart skipped a beat the first time I saw her face. It was so unexpected, but love is never planned. It was as if we were always together. Two missing links, pulled together instantly, and nothing could take us apart. Well, almost nothing. No matter how busy our lives were, we always made time for each other. We didn't have a lot of money and lived in a small apartment, but we didn't care. We were happy to be together, no matter what the circumstances." I rub my runny nose and wet cheeks with my sleeve. I see another whiskey in front of me. I take a big swig and slam the glass back down. Whiskey splashes onto my hand and the bar.

Jack walks up to me. "I will cut you off if you do that again. You almost broke the glass. I don't need customers breaking glasses and then cutting themselves. Be careful," he warns as he wipes off the bar.

I wipe my hand on my white button-down shirt. "I asked her to marry me earlier than I planned, because I couldn't wait any longer. When she was away from me, I felt like a part of me was missing. We were the lucky ones. These days, not many people experience the kind of love we had. So unconditional and pure. She was kind, smart, generous, beautiful...and most of all, mine. I always wondered why I was blessed to have someone like her at my side. She had her faults, and so did I. We accepted each other with all the good things and the bad. She was the best gift I have ever received. It was Christmas morning every morning when I woke up next to her. She was my best friend and my soul mate." I stop for a moment to catch my breath. I'm on the verge of another panic attack. I breathe in through my nose and out through my mouth. *Breathe in. Breathe out.*

My fists clench even tighter. "Overnight, my life changed. Every single thing was abruptly taken away from me. I live in a dark world now where nothing turns the light back on. My life was a brightly burning candle, and then someone blew it out. Now I'm here alone, feeling like I'm in fucking quicksand. Constantly being pulled down, but I have no will to pull myself back up."

The sound of a glass or bottle shattering on the ground brings me out of my stupor. *Did I do that?* I look over the bar and sigh in relief. Jack's at the end of the bar sweeping shards of glass into a pile. I turn to the young woman, surprised to see her still staring at me. "Did I just say all of that out loud?" I rub my face.

"Yes. Do you need a tissue, or would you rather use your sleeve again?" she asks as she searches through her big bag. She finds a pack of tissues and lays it on the bar.

I grab the pack off the bar. "Thank you." I take out a tissue and rudely blow my nose. "I'm sorry. It's hard to be in this place. Memories come back, and I replay them in my mind like a movie. As if it wasn't real. I can't stop torturing myself. You picked the wrong barstool to sit on tonight. I guess you're sorry you sat next to me."

"Not really. You're closer to the bartender, so I thought I could get some drinks faster." She lifts her hand. "Two waters without ice cubes, please."

Her joke makes me laugh...I think. *Did I laugh?* Smiling and laughing no longer exist in my world. I don't remember what they feel like.

"What's her name?" she asks softly. Her voice is smooth like silk. I don't know if it's the alcohol or if she truly sounds like that.

"Jessica." I turn my body a miniscule amount so I can see her better.

"Where did you meet her?" The words flow out of her mouth like a song. Almost hypnotic.

"I was beginning my first-year residency at the hospital here. It was orientation day for first-year medical students. I was given a table to answer random questions from the students. She walked up to me and smiled. We were together ever since." I stop for a moment and close my eyes, imagining I was there right now. Reliving that moment.

"She was so beautiful...long, wavy auburn hair and hazel eyes. She was a third-year resident. I remember I couldn't even speak right away when we first met. I was mesmerized by her beauty." I smile at the memory. *Wow, another smile.* "We told our story to everyone. We planned on telling our story until we were old and gray."

Jack brings the waters. She pushes one of the glasses in front of me. "Drink this. I think you need it after drinking your whiskeys so fast."

*I am pretty thirsty.* I drink the entire glass within seconds. Cold and crisp.

She turns her body toward mine and leans her head on her hand. "Did you go to medical school here?"

"Yes. I also finished my residency here last year, in emergency care." I stop talking because my whiskeys suddenly kick in. My head spins. I have no idea how many I have had. "I think I need to leave," I slur. I stand up too fast and lose my balance. She jumps from her stool and grabs on to my arm and shirt. She saves me from falling on my ass. Sadly, it wouldn't be the first time. One time I fell and almost broke my nose.

"Have you eaten anything in the last few hours?" she asks, sounding perturbed.

"No, because I'm not hungry." I push away from her.

She pays Jack while she speaks to him. They turn their heads toward me. She shakes her head and walks over to me.

"Ready?" She puts my arm over her shoulders, and her arm goes around my back.

*This is the closest I have been to a woman since Jessica.*

Wow, she's short. Her head comes only to my shoulders. She must be strong to be able to hold me up.

"What did Jack say to you?"

"He asked if I can handle you when you are drunk like this. Does it bother you?"

"I don't fucking care what people say about me." *I'm such a dick. I shouldn't be like this. She's only trying to help me.*

We walk outside, and the cool wind hits my face. It's refreshing and wakes me up. For a second anyway. I drag my feet over to the wall near the bar entrance and lean my body and head against it. Cars speed by, causing a vibrating ring in my ears.

"Is there someone I can call to come pick you up?" she says, out of breath.

Before I can answer, she interjects, "You are damn tall and heavy. That was tough holding you up."

"And your point would be?" I huff. "Sorry, shorty. You decided to help me. I didn't ask for your help." I feel like sticking my tongue out like a seven-year-old. She stares at me with a look that could kill.

"The answer to your other question. No. I don't want my family or friends to see me like this again. I can take a cab."

"Where would you go? Do you live alone?" She holds her hair out of her face as the cool wind kicks up.

"I live with my sister. Can you stop asking me so many questions? I can't even see straight." Spit shot out of my mouth when I snapped at her. She hands me another tissue. *I am such a disgusting loser.*

"Don't be stupid, nasty pants. You can come with me to my place. I live right down the street. You can eat something and sober up a little bit. Then you can choose what you want to do next. Okay? I think it's going to start raining any minute. Do you want to get stuck in a downpour? Well, then again, it might sober you up."

The door to the bar opens, and the stench of old smoke surrounds us. I crinkle my nose. Even though this bar is smoke-free now, you can still smell old smoke seeping out of the walls.

"Who uses the phrase 'nasty pants'? Are we in elementary school again?"

She pokes me in the chest. "I do when I'm dealing with a fucking child. Do you want to come with me, nasty pants, or should I leave you here in the pouring rain so you can throw up on the sidewalk?"

*Wow, she is brave to talk to me like this.*

I push her hand away and grunt in response. I have no choice but to go with her.

"Does one grunt mean yes?" She stands with her hand on her hip, waiting for an answer.

I grunt again, moving my head up and down, and shove away from the wall.

She lets out a long breath. "I guess that means yes. Put your arm over my shoulder." Once again, I lift my arm as she puts her arm around my waist.

"Are you sure I can lean against you? You are so damn small. How can you hold me up?" She ignores me and starts to walk forward. "Which foot goes first?"

"Be quiet and let's go. Don't put all your weight on me. I know you're drunk, but you need to focus and try to stand up straight so you can walk."

"Yes, ma'am!" I widen my eyes in order to focus. Everything around me is foggy, but I try my best to see straight.

"Now left foot forward, right foot forward. Can you do— Ouch, that was my foot, nasty pants!"

"Stop calling me that! Let's try this again. Left foot forward, right foot forward." It's working now, but my feet still scrape the sidewalk. We walk in sync, but slowly. Did I just feel a raindrop?

Her long hair blows everywhere as another strong gust of wind surrounds us. It tickles my face, and a strand sticks in my mouth.

"We need to pick up the pace. I have a feeling the sky is going to open any minute now. Do you think you can do that?" she says while walking faster.

I take a deep breath. "I'll try. But I have some of your hair in my mouth."

She flips her hair away from me.

"Much better. I can't promise I won't step on your foot again. What's your name, by the way?"

"Lisa Schmitt."

"Linda Shits is your name? I feel sorry for you." *Hiccup.* "I knew a Linda—or was it a Lisa?—once." *Hiccup.*

"Let me repeat myself slowly. Liiiissaa Scchhmmiiittt." She laughs.

"Are you laughing at me?"

"Yes. You are kind of a funny, sarcastic drunk."

"I'm only funny when I'm with someone who's so little." *Hiccup.*

"I'm not that short. I'm five foot three. People call me petite or short, not little. Great things come in small packages. Didn't you ever hear that before? I can't help it you are so damn tall." She digs her fingers into my side. "Anyway, what's your name? Do you remember who you are?"

"Look who the sarcastic one is now," I say as I dig my fingers into her shoulder.

"It hurts when you do that. Control your strength, big guy. I wouldn't be so wet if you weren't walking so slow. I'm surprised you can even speak rationally. The rain seems to help you."

People snicker as they walk past us. It must look funny when a short, skinny girl is holding up a big guy on the street when it's pouring. I hear someone on the street yell, "Drink another one, buddy."

"Again, what's your name?" She says it slower, as if I don't understand her.

Pulsing rain bounces off the sidewalk. "My name is James. James Kramer," I say as the rain streams down my face. I'm still leaning on her, but I swear her fingers dig into my side even more when she hears my name. "What the hell are you pinching me for?" I'm too tired and wet to focus or really care.

We walk longer than I thought we would. "Are we almost there yet? I'm soaking wet! I thought you live close by."

"Stop your complaining. We're almost there. We've been walking for maybe five minutes. Don't forget I'm also soaked. Get a pep in your step, and maybe we will get there faster."

She guides me to the left, and I see an apartment door with the number one on it. I hear her keys jingle when she opens it. She flips a switch, and a muted ceiling light blinks on. We enter directly into a cramped kitchen area. It has a table with two chairs, light-colored wooden cabinets, and a small countertop to the right. To the left is a narrow room with a washer and dryer. The smell of fabric softener wafts through the air.

"It's pretty dark in here, even with the light on."

"One of the lightbulbs in the ceiling lamp blew out. I haven't had the time to change it. I usually call the landlord to change it since I can't reach the ceiling. I don't have a ladder."

She puts her bag and keys on the counter. "I'm going to change my clothes. Stand there or sit at the table while I get you a towel," she orders. "Oh, can you please take your shoes off so you don't track dirt on the carpet?"

I grab one of the chairs and sit down. A sense of déjà vu hits me. This place seems strangely familiar. My eyes roam around the kitchen. While I try to focus, I can tell it's organized. No dirty dishes are on the counter, the appliances are all neatly placed and sparkling. Almost like no one uses the kitchen.

"Here's a towel to dry off." She hands it to me, and I immediately dry my face and hair. She's changed into sweatpants and a T-shirt. I kick off my shoes and leave them on the kitchen floor.

I stand up, holding on to the table. My balance is returning, but my vision is still foggy. "I need to shake the weasel."

She takes a step to the side and stifles a laugh. "Even though you're funny, I hope you don't talk like this when you're sober or talking to your patients."

*Little does she know...I'm not practicing anymore.*

She dries her hair with a towel. "You can use the bathroom if you want. Once you're done, go lie on the sofa." She points to the sofa with her thumb.

"I may be drunk, but I know what a sofa looks like," I snarl.

"I'll ignore your rudeness. I'll bring you a glass of water and something to eat."

She opens and closes the cabinets. I stumble into the living room, where I see three closed white doors. Two straight ahead and one to the left wall of the living room. I didn't see where she went to get the towels. I shuffle my feet along the light-green carpet to the one door straight ahead on the left. I peek my head in. Nope, not a bathroom. From what I can see from the light pouring through the window from the streetlights, this is a bedroom. I pull myself out of the room because I'm going to piss myself if I don't find a toilet.

I close the bedroom door and proceed to the one on the left. I walk with my head and shoulders hanging down. Forgetting the door is closed, I walk right into it. I bang my forehead hard and loud. My hand goes immediately to my head. *Fuck! Can I humiliate myself any more tonight?* I look over my shoulder to see if she saw me. It appears she didn't. Her back is facing me. I take a deep breath and open the door. Thank God! There's the toilet.

The bathroom is extremely narrow. I lay the towel on the sink. I could piss and wash my hands at the same time if I wanted to. As I relieve myself, I hold on to the counter with one hand so I don't lose my balance.

I flush the toilet and turn to the sink. I squint my eyes and look around. I feel like an old man without his glasses. This is definitely a girl's bathroom. It's tidy, with lots of girly things. Perfectly folded light-green and powder-blue towels hang on the towel rack. The walls are painted the same color green as the towels. A powder-blue candle sits on the back of the toilet, near the shower. Three bottles of perfume, makeup, and a jumbo bottle of hand sanitizer sit on the sink countertop. *I thought I was the only one who has that in the bathroom.* I pick up one of the perfumes and hold the bottle near my nose. I accidentally spray it on my chin. *Shit! Now I smell like fresh powder and vanilla. She will smell it on me when I leave the bathroom.*

I bend over the sink and rinse my face to lessen the smell and wake me up. When I finish drying my face, I see my reflection in the mirror. Only it's not me. The person I'm staring at has dirty, messy brown hair, dark circles under his dull, blood-shot green eyes, and a pale face. He hasn't shaved in days. He has a red bump on his forehead from running into the door. *This is what my life has become.*

This man is a stranger to me. I don't recognize myself anymore because I'm no longer complete. My sister describes me as an asshole living in an empty shell. What does she expect when my better half was ripped away from me? The old version of myself is gone and perhaps never coming back. I'm disgusted looking at my reflection. I take the towel and quickly exit the bathroom.

Ahh, there's the sofa. It looks so welcoming with those big green and blue pillows on it. *What is the obsession with these colors?* The sofa is inviting but maybe a little bit small for me. I don't care. I will lie on anything. I'll stay here for a minute and then leave. I don't even know this woman.

I've just fallen back onto the sofa, when I hear, "Wait! Your clothes are soaking wet. Please, dry off before you lay all over the sofa."

"Lay all over your sofa? I'm not a wet dog." I stand up and start to pull off my shirt.

"What are you doing?" she asks nervously, her eyes darting in every direction.

"I'm soaking wet. Unless you have a magic trick that will make me dry, I need to take my damn shirt off. I think we have seen worse things. Do you have a clothes dryer?" *Of course she does. I saw it when I came in.*

"Fine. Do what you want. Yes, I have a dryer." She turns away, as if she's searching for something.

*What's her problem?* I finally get the shirt off and proceed to dry my arms, shoulders, and chest.

"Am I dry enough now? I will not take my pants off, just so you know. Unless you have another pair of sweatpants. Yours seem pretty long on you, so maybe they'll be long enough for me."

"Is that another short—" She turns around and freezes. Her eyes grow wide, and just now I notice how blue they are. I watch her eyes move up and down my body.

"Why are you looking at me like that?" I look down to see if something is hanging out of my pants, like my junk or toilet paper.

"It's not an everyday occurrence for me to have a half-naked male stranger in my living room," she says as she tosses a towel on the couch for me to lie on. She moves closer and takes my hand, dropping two pills into it. Her hands are shaking. "Take these, please. I put a glass of water and a bowl of pretzels on the coffee table. Try to get some food in your stomach. I'll go put your shirt in the dryer." She turns away but stops. "Why does it smell like my perfume? Did you spray one of my perfumes in the bathroom?"

My eyes shoot wide open. I need to change the subject. "Wait. You didn't answer my question. Do you have another pair of sweatpants? My pants are soaked. Or would it be a problem for you if I wear only my boxers?" She stands there, rubbing her finger on her chin.

"Give me a second." She disappears into one of the rooms connected to the living room.

*That was a close one. I don't want her to think I'm a psycho.*

A few seconds later she comes out with another pair of sweats. "Here, try these on. They might be too short, but they're dry."

"They are fucking hot pink! You only have pink sweats to give me? That's just cruel."

She covers her mouth to hold back her laughter. "Sorry. The others are in the laundry. It's either these or your wet *khakis*? Beggars can't be choosers."

I rip them out of her hand and lay them on the sofa. "Turn around, please. I would like to take off my *khakis*. I don't have the energy to go to the bathroom. I'll keep my boxers on."

"Fine. I'll be in the kitchen. Yell when you're done stripping." She saunters away.

I empty my pockets and put my phone, keys, and wallet on the table. It takes me a few minutes to take my khakis off. I hold the sweatpants up in front of me. This is an all-time low for me. I try to put my leg in one side but lose my balance and fall face first into the sofa. *Get a grip.* This isn't going to work. I need to sit down. Finally, I can pull them up. The waistband is snug, and the legs are floods. They go up to my calves. This has got to be a joke.

"I'm finished," I yell. "That was exhausting."

She comes out from the kitchen and bursts out laughing.

"Hilarious. I guess I deserve it after all I'm putting you through tonight. Don't be taking pictures of me while I'm sleeping."

"Sorry. I'll stop. Thanks for making me laugh though." She grabs the wet pants. "I'll put these also in the dryer. Can they go in the dryer? Won't they shrink?"

"I don't care. Please dry them somehow." I wave my hand for her to go away. She mumbles something as she leaves.

Can I be any more obnoxious to her? It's not necessary. The dryer door slams in the distance, with the hum of the machine following right after. I'm still standing in the same spot when she returns.

She touches my arm lightly. "Please move for a second, pink pants."

I give her a nasty look as I step aside.

She spreads the towel over the cushions. "Now lie down." Before I can react, she pushes me onto the sofa.

"What the hell? Are you always this rough and demanding with men?"

"Wouldn't you like to know."

"Nope," I say under my breath.

She leans over me to pull a blanket off the back of the sofa. I can see up her shirt, but I look away before she notices. She peers down at me. I finally see her face more clearly. She's pretty. Her eyes seem even bigger and bluer. She stares back at me with concern. I'm unsettled by how familiar her eyes look. For a second, I'm back at the scene of the car accident when I was seventeen, looking into the eyes of the scared girl in my car.

I rise up on my elbows. She jumps back because our heads almost collide.

"Is it you?"

Her eyebrows press together. "Am I who?"

I shake my head. "Forget it. I don't know what I'm talking about anymore. I can't even think straight. For a second, I thought you looked like someone from my past."

She stares at me with her forehead wrinkled. I clear my throat, but I can't look away from her eyes.

"It must be the alcohol distorting my vision. I'm going to throw up now. I mean, I'm going to shut up now," I say as I burp like I just drank a can of soda. "Sorry!" I rub the back of my neck.

She presses her lips together and heads to the kitchen. One of the cabinets slam shut. She returns with a small bucket. "Just in case. I really don't want your vomit on the carpet. I only allow that when I know the person for more than twenty-four hours."

"You are either funny or very mean. I don't know if I should like you or hate you. Just remember—you insisted I stay here." She squints her eyes at me with a tight jaw. I shrug and down the glass of water and pills. I collapse onto my back and put my hands under my head. Shortly after, I watch the blanket float above me and slowly land on my body...

As sleep takes over, her voice switches to this angelic, soothing tone again. Like a symphony. "Go to sleep now. You have sobered up a bit, and the medicine will help. Maybe your hangover won't be too bad. I'll refill your water and place it on the table for you."

I crack my eyes open because her voice sounds so familiar. I could listen to it all day. Now she reminds me of the girl at my ski accident again. *I've gone mental.* I promise myself I will never get drunk again. She turns to walk away, but I grab her hand. I press it against my cheek as my eyes close again. "Thank you," I whisper as she slips her hand from mine.

# Chapter 13

## Lisa

I pull my hand from his and step backward. That was eerie. He placed my hand on his cheek and said thank you just like the James at the ski accident. Is it possible he's the same guy? *Don't be so stupid, Lisa!* The possibility of the James lying on this sofa and the skier being the same person is near nil. I shake my head and stroll to the kitchen.

As usual, I'd been contemplating my life tonight, which pushed me to Kerry's Pub. I went there to take away my depressing thoughts by getting drunk. Not to bring a drunk home with me to sleep on my sofa. If someone told me tonight would end up like this, I would have laughed in her face.

I'm not as sad as I was before I met James tonight. Helping him gave me some much-needed distraction.

I place James's dirty shoes next to the door and push the chair back toward the table. I wipe off the counter and the table, even though it's not needed. My brain is in overdrive.

I will never forget what he looked like when I saw him at the bar— like George Bailey in *It's a Wonderful Life*, when he cried at the bar after the money was lost from the bank. I know that movie by heart because it was one of my mom's favorite Christmas movies. We would always watch it together. I have watched it every year at Christmas since she died. Anyway, James seemed just as disturbed, if not worse.

He spoke about some woman he's in love with, or was in love with. He kept using the past tense, like she isn't around anymore. I could hear it in his words and how the tears fell down his face. I wonder what happened to her.

Tears form in my eyes.

I know what it's like to be so distraught. After my mom died, I wouldn't accept that she was dead. I was in denial. I didn't want to go to her funeral, but my dad and sister forced me.

I always asked, why did Mom die? Why didn't I die with her? If I died that day, I wouldn't have the feeling of dread every morning when I wake up. I wouldn't have a heavy weight on my chest from missing her so much. I wouldn't be so angry with everything and everyone. I wouldn't have this disgusting scar on my lower abdomen reminding me of a future I can never have, and I wouldn't be a burden to Dad and Tina.

I jump when I hear him cough in the living room. Please don't throw up. I run to him, but he's still out cold. One arm is stretched over his head, and the other is placed on his chest. I sit on the coffee table for a few minutes just to make sure he isn't going to get sick.

It was so beautiful to hear a man talk about a woman that way. I could almost feel it myself. She was lucky to have someone who loved her so much. There has never been a man in my life who spoke about me or to me like that. I don't think it's meant for me. I hoped I'd have something close to it, but I was wrong. It was all an illusion, and I was in denial for a long time. After Bryant...I've stopped searching for it. I was so naive and desperate for someone to accept me and love me. I'm ashamed I was willing to settle for what we had.

He startles me when he shifts his legs. The blanket falls to the floor. I lay it back on him and tuck him in like a little baby. He's probably gorgeous under all his facial hair, anger, and despair he projects. His green eyes alone would make any girl feel giddy. I can't imagine what color green they'll be in the daylight.

Seeing him without his shirt on was a pleasant surprise. A bonus for my good deed. His upper half is pure muscle. Never in my life have I seen someone so chiseled. He blows Bryant out of the park. The way his khakis were hanging off his hips made my hands shake and my mouth go dry. Tingles shot up my body all the way into my scalp. It was a weird but positive feeling.

I know I shouldn't think like this, but I can't help it. Thankfully, his sexy image disappeared when he put on those pink sweatpants.

My mind wanders back to him and Jessica. Is it possible they are the same James and Jessica who got engaged at the party Bryant went to a couple of years ago? Is she the Jessica who Bryant pointed out to me at the bar on our first date? James did say he met her at an orientation and their first date was at that bar. If yes, our pasts are so intertwined.

I rub my temples. What a crazy night. It's the most action I've had in a long time. My social and love lives are lacking. I see Emily often, but it's always for a short time. I haven't been on a date since Bryant and I broke up. I made medical school my focus until I graduated this past June. I don't see my family often because of lack of time and no car, but I talk to Tina several times a week.

I'm exhausted. I mosey to my room and grab my pajamas off the bed. As I walk to the bathroom, I hear him snoring. It sounds so cute. Similar to a cat purring.

I brush my teeth and think about his comment about brushing his teeth with whiskey. It sounds so disgusting, but I smile. Even though he was rude, he was also quite comical. I need to laugh more often.

I'm not sure I'll sleep well tonight. He might freak out when he wakes up, or maybe leave before I get up. He probably won't know where he is. I freeze in my tracks when I open the bathroom door. If she is the Jessica I'm thinking of, she lived in these apartments. I shrug my shoulders. I'll worry about his reaction when he wakes up.

# Chapter 14

## James

What is that noise? Something is vibrating or ringing. My head is pounding, and I really need to pee. I hear someone clear her throat. My eyes shoot open to see a young woman standing near me. She points to the coffee table and says softly, "Your phone is ringing."

*Who the hell is she, and why is she in her pajamas? Am I dreaming?* I jump up—*am I on a sofa?*—and instantly fall back down. I'm dizzy. My phone keeps ringing. I look at the screen. Alexa, probably checking up on me again. I ignore it.

I look at the woman. She observes me with big, beautiful blue eyes. Her hair is up in a messy bun on top of her head, with strands flowing down. Her eyes drop down to my chest. I glance down. I have no shirt on. *What the hell? And why am I wearing pink sweatpants that don't even fit me?* I cross my arms over my chest.

"Where the hell am I, and who are you?" I ask with a frigid tone. "We didn't do anything last night, did we?" *I hope I didn't have sex with her.* "Did someone put drugs in my drink?"

"You were pretty drunk and upset last night, so I brought you here to sober up. You were soaking wet from the rain, so I put your clothes in the dryer. I only had pink sweatpants for you to wear. Here are your clothes."

With hesitance, she stretches her arms out with my clothes, and I stand up and snatch them away. I put my shirt on as she says, "I couldn't let you leave the bar in the state you were in. You kept on talking about your girlfriend, Jessica."

I rub my eyebrows to relieve my headache.

"I encouraged you to come here so you could drink something other than whiskey and eat some food, but you fell asleep, or should I say passed out, on the sofa after you took some medicine."

I take in my surroundings. "I remember a little bit. I know I went to Kerry's Pub." I rack my brain long and hard as my head pounds. Memories pop into my brain in white flashes. My anger switches to embarrassment. "Oh...I cried to you, and then some," I say with regret. My shoulders slump, as I sit back on to the sofa. "You should have left me at the bar. You didn't need to take care of me. I don't even know you. Why would you even care?"

I need some water. "Do you have more medicine?"

She takes a bottle off the coffee table and hands me two pills. She points to the glass of water on the table. I gulp them down with water and wipe my mouth with the back of my hand.

"Thank you. Can you please tell me where I am?"

"You're at the Greenhouse Apartments."

My eyes bulge. "What the hell did you say?" My blood shoots straight to my head as I jump up. She leaps back in fright. "Is this some kind of sick, fucking joke?"

Her blue eyes shoot wide open as she shakes her head, the pill bottle rattling slightly in her trembling hand. "I live here. I'm sorry you're angry. I only wanted to help you," she says with disappointment.

"Did I tell you Jessica lived in these apartments?" My voice is full of disdain.

She shakes her head again and steps back.

*Am I scaring her?*

"I just wanted to help you. I'm sorry," she repeats, on the verge of tears.

I don't know what to say. Thankfully, my phone rings again. I turn away and answer the call. "Hey, Alexa," I whisper.

She starts yelling, "Where the hell are you? Why didn't you come home last night?"

I pull the phone away from my ear. Of course she's pissed off because she couldn't get hold of me. I've been at my worst this week.

"I stayed at a friend's place last night," I respond, my voice low.

"Which friend? You haven't spoken to any of your friends in months."

"I'm at my friend Lisa's apartment." I glance over at Lisa, hoping that's her name. "I ran into her last night and ended up crashing at her place."

"Who the hell is Lisa? You've never mentioned a friend named Lisa, ever! You better not have slept with her—"

"I'm not even going to respond to that comment." I clamp my teeth together. *I will never sleep with another woman.* "Listen, I'll call you later." I hang up and turn around.

"Your name is Lisa, correct?" I ask her softly.

She nods.

"I'm sorry for yelling at you. I've been going through an extremely hard time for the past year. Jessica, whom I have been speaking about, lived here for a while. When we started dating, she lived in apartment fifteen. Did you know her?"

"I knew of her, but I never met her. My ex-boyfriend knew her through the residency he was doing in the pediatrics division at the hospital."

Curiosity takes over. "Really? What's his name?"

"Bryant Callahan. I think you met him once at a party Jessica held."

"His name sounds familiar, but I don't remember when I met him."

"I was supposed to go to a party with him at Jessica's, but I was sick that night. Maybe we would've met then, but it just wasn't meant to be, I guess." She swings her arms back and forth.

Now I know who he is. I met him at Jessica's party when I proposed. Now I'm uncomfortable. There is silence for a few seconds. "Listen. Again, I'm sorry about last night and for yelling at you. I usually don't dump all my shit on strangers. I usually don't tell anybody anything. The alcohol was talking. Not me."

I look at the khakis in my hands and then at her.

"I'll leave you alone so you can get dressed. If you need anything, I'll be in the kitchen," she says.

"Thanks." I put them on in record time but notice they are snug. I walk into the kitchen.

She's sitting at the table, her hands around a cup of coffee.

"Did you happen to put my khakis in the dryer?"

She looks me up and down and grins. "Yes, I did. They look a little tight now. Your shirt looks a little snug as well. I asked you last night if they could go into the dryer. You said it was okay. Don't worry. You look fine."

*Serves me right.*

My socks and shoes are near the apartment door. She follows me as I fetch them. "I'm sorry I disturbed you. I'm sure you had better things to do than babysit me. For all it's worth, thank you for saving me last night. I don't want to know what the outcome could have been if you weren't there."

I reach for the doorknob, but she stops me.

"I'm a first-year resident at the hospital here. I'm scheduled to work today, but I don't need to be there until one p.m."

*Why did she tell me that?* "Okay, but I'll leave now anyway. Again, I'm sorry and very embarrassed and confused about this whole thing." *Stop repeating yourself.*

She slightly hops on her feet toward me and says, "Why don't you stay for breakfast? I think you need some food in your stomach. It won't be anything fancy, but I can make a mean batch of pancakes. You're welcome to shower while I make them. But only if you want to. No pressure."

I linger by the door, my hand on the doorknob. For some unknown reason, I say, "Okay. I am pretty hungry, even with this hangover." *What am I doing?* Well, I love pancakes. She also puts me at ease. "A shower sounds great right now. Are you sure it's all right with you? I have already overstayed my welcome. I promise I'll make it quick."

"It's more than all right. If I'm not scared or angry with you already, I think breakfast will run smoothly." She smiles, and I can't help but smile back.

*I have no right to take a shower here.* I should have recognized the design of the apartment. It has the same layout as Jessica's. *Where I proposed to her.* The decorations and colors are different. Lisa has light-green and sky-blue colors. Jessica was more into neutrals. The kitchen is the same though.

Lisa seems easygoing. She could have reacted completely different to my outburst, but instead she offered to make me pancakes. Who would do that? She seems familiar because of her soft voice and her name.

According to Alexa, the girl Lisa, from my ski accident, had black hair though, so it couldn't have been her. Her eyes also look like the girl I helped in the car accident. I will not even attempt to ask her if she is either one of those girls. I'm just imagining things. I laugh at myself. *Yes, James, she is both girls wrapped up in one little package.* I'm a lunatic.

I finish showering and brush my teeth with the spare toothbrush she'd told me was in the medicine chest. The mirror reflects someone who looks human now, even with this ugly beard I have. As I open the bathroom door, I smell something delicious. I take in a deep breath. My stomach growls, as if it can smell pancakes. *When was the last time I ate pancakes...or any decent food?*

Steaming pancakes are already on the table. My mouth waters in anticipation of the warm, sweet taste of maple syrup.

With caution, I approach the small table adorned with orange juice, coffee, syrup, and butter. "Hi. The shower was just what I needed. Sorry I took so long. It's not pleasant to put clothes back on that smell like sweat and alcohol. It should teach me a lesson."

She sits at the table and watches me. She's still in her pajamas...without a bra. It must be cold in here. *I need to look somewhere else. Stare directly into her eyes. Nowhere else.* She puts her arms in front of her. I guess she noticed. *Shit.*

"You clean up nicely. Please sit down. Eat as much as you want, before they get cold."

I place my phone and wallet on the table. I slip into the chair across from her and motion with my hand. "You made the pancakes so please take the first ones."

She puts a good-sized stack on her plate. Nice to meet a girl who likes to eat. We are sitting close to one another. My knees touch hers sometimes. We can't avoid it, since the table is small...almost intimate.

I stab a stack of pancakes and plop them onto a plate. "How many people were you cooking for? There are a lot of pancakes." I put a huge chunk of butter on the top and pour a large portion of maple syrup. I cut them up and put some in my mouth. My eyes close as a moan comes out of my throat. "These are spectacular." I open my eyes and notice her staring at me with a grin.

"I'm happy to see you're feeling better after last night. That was quite the outburst when you woke up. Maybe you need to eat more the next time you want to drown yourself in whiskey, or, as you said, brush your teeth with whiskey." She chuckles.

I drop my fork on the plate. "Brush my teeth? What do you mean?"

"Last night you said you were brushing your teeth with your whiskey. Quite original."

My jaw drops. "How did I come up with that one? I must have been very entertaining last night." I rub my forehead. "I need to lay off the alcohol."

"Sure, sure. That's what they all say." She grabs the coffeepot and asks, "Do you want some coffee? It's fresh and hot." She sets the pot near my plate.

"Wow, what treatment. I should be making you pancakes and coffee. I'm the one who crashed on your sofa last night." I pour some coffee into my cup.

She offers the milk and sugar, bobbing them up and down.

"I take it black. It's quicker to make. I was always in a rush during medical school and my residency. I lived off coffee or anything with caffeine."

I drink some coffee. The hot liquid coats my stomach. There's nothing like the first sip of coffee.

"Next time I'm drunk and need a place to stay or something to eat," she says, "I'll call you. Then we can call it even."

I raise my coffee cup. "Sure. I can agree to that." *Like hell. I will never see you again after today.*

"I know your name is Lisa, but what's your last name?"

She swallows her mouthful of pancakes. "At least you remember some things. Last night you thought I said my name was Linda Shits. Even though you were drunk and nasty, you made me laugh several times. My last name is Schmitt."

"Just to remind you, my name is James—"

"Kramer." She smirks. "I wasn't drunk, so I remember everything."

I change the subject to focus on something other than last night. "I come from a small town in New Jersey called Cleartown."

Her eyes grow large as she begins to cough. She grabs a napkin, wipes her mouth, and takes a sip of her coffee. "Sorry. That's so weird. I'm from Hillstown."

I lift my left eyebrow. "Seriously? That's only two towns north of Cleartown. I used to work at a gas station on Main Street in Hillstown when I was a senior in high school."

"Yeah, I know where it is. Next to the small convenience store. My sister, Tina, worked at the pharmacy next to it."

I shake my head in disbelief. "I'm having breakfast with a true Jersey girl. It's been a long time since I've met a Jersey girl around here, and a pretty one, no less."

Her cheeks turn red, and she won't look at me.

*Why did I just say that?*

"You probably wouldn't think I was pretty when I was sixteen years old. I had big, frizzy Jersey hair and superlong fingernails. That phase didn't last very long."

"You must hate pumping your own gas."

"I don't drive," she responds dryly.

"Really?"

She clears her throat. "Anyway, so where did you go to college? If you don't mind me asking." She licks syrup off her thumb. "I don't want to invade your privacy, if you don't want me to."

I wipe my sticky hands with a napkin. "I don't mind. I went to Johnson College, not too far from here. After college, I attended Clarion and finished my residency at the university hospital. I received my medical license in emergency medicine about a year ago. Did I mention that last night? If I did, I'm sorry for repeating myself. I don't remember much of what I said last night."

I stare off into space. I don't want to talk about my residency or practicing medicine. It only reminds me of how shitty my life is right now.

She pulls me from my thoughts. "Wait a second. You went to Johnson College? I also attended there. I just graduated from Clarion in June. I started my residency in July." She shivers. "How is this possible? I'm kind of freaked out. Is this *Candid Camera*?" she says, looking around with a hesitant smile.

"No, it's not *Candid Camera*. I agree—it's quite strange. All those years growing up in towns not too far from each other, going to the same schools, and we still never met. At least not until now. Interesting. It makes you wonder why. Maybe it's our age difference or...did fate play a hand in this, Lisa?" I wink at her. *Since when do I wink at people? I can't even remember if I ever winked at Jessica.*

"How old are you, anyway?" I ask.

"I'm twenty-seven," she answers. "And you?"

"Thirty."

"You're not that much older than me. Even with the age difference, I'll need to think about all these coincidences. Analyzing things or people is what I do best. I'm a psychiatrist." She smiles and takes a drink of her orange juice.

"Seeing me at my worst last night probably reminded you of some of the patients you have seen or read about during your medical school years."

Her face becomes serious as she puts her fork down. "I guess you can say that, but it isn't just that. I truly like to listen to people so I can help them get through whatever problems they are dealing with," she says. "I would rather listen than talk. Sometimes it's easier for individuals to talk to a stranger or, let's say, a doctor. The doctor won't judge you like your family or friends will. It can help people let things out without someone trying to interrupt or put pressure on you. They listen and make suggestions on how to solve your problems. Which is why I wanted to become a psychiatrist. I want people to open up to me. My main focus is to work with patients who are suffering with issues similar to post-traumatic stress disorder." She clamps her mouth shut. "I thought I said I would rather listen than talk."

"So am I your guinea pig now?" I cock my head to the side.

Her head pops up. "Only if you want to be. You need to want help, or it will never work. You need to want it for yourself. Not for your family, not for your friends." She looks directly into my eyes, as if she is reading my mind. It's unnerving.

I break eye contact. Do I want help? Do I want to keep living this way? I don't really need to think about it. I know the answer. Yes, I want help. After last night, I'm disturbed by what I'm doing to myself. If I continue down this road, I'll destroy myself and cause suffering for my family and friends.

I finish my coffee and wipe my mouth and hands. "It's time for me to get out of your hair. You need to get to work soon. I'll call my sister to pick me up. Again, I'm sorry about last night, for unloading my shit on you, passing out on your sofa, and taking a shower. Oh, and eating breakfast here. You are too kind to strangers. I know I'm repeating myself and babbling. I can't say sorry and thank you enough." I take my dishes to the sink.

I grab my things off the table and head to the door. She places a piece of paper on the wall and scribbles something. She comes over and hands it to me.

"James, here's my phone number. If you ever want to talk, I'm a good listener. I'm not trying to treat you like a patient. Let's think of it as a new friend trying to help a new friend. I know what it feels like to experience something tragic. I've had my own traumatic experiences. I don't know what you are battling with, but it might help to talk to someone who has suffered from a similar type of pain. My schedule is awful with the hospital, but we can work something out."

"Thank you, new friend. I might just take you up on that." I step into the hallway but turn around before she closes the door. She looks at me with her electric-blue puppy-dog eyes and a hint of a smile. *She is so damn cute with those pajamas on.* "Good luck with the first year of your residency. It won't be easy." I smile and wave good-bye.

After she closes her door, I lean against the wall. Man, the last twenty-four hours have been so out of control. Maybe it's my wake-up call. I take a deep breath and escape the one place that holds so many of my memories with Jessica. *Forget where you are...forget where you are,* I repeat to myself until I'm outside on the street. I need a swift kick in the ass for letting myself get so drunk last night. I can't handle another mental breakdown.

I speed-walk down the street, wishing I had running gear with me. Running or the gym would be the best thing right now. I could blow off some steam and the alcohol.

I should call Alexa and ask if she can pick me up. She answers after one ring.

"James?" she yells. Of course she's still annoyed with me—I hung up on her. I can't blame her. I haven't been easy to deal with this year.

"Sorry, Alexa. I told you what I did last night. Someone helped me, and that was it." Silence. "Alexa, are you still there?" I sigh. "Can you not give me the silent treatment? This is the first time in a long time I don't feel like total shit for at least thirty minutes. Believe me—

I still feel like I'm going to lose it since I was at Jessica's old apartment complex. But it's not as bad as usual."

"Are you fucking kidding me? You stayed in the same apartment complex where Jessica used to live? What were you thinking?" she shouts.

"I didn't know until I woke up this morning. Believe me. I was pretty pissed off."

"Why are you doing this to yourself?" she asks desperately. "Why do you keep torturing yourself?"

There are days when I feel like I can't breathe or gravity is pulling me even closer to the ground. When I wake up in the morning, for a split second I think my life is normal and Jessica is lying next to me. Then I reach over to the other side of the bed and feel nothing but cold and emptiness. I look around, and realize I'm in Alexa's apartment. Then the memories come flooding back. I miss Jessica so much—and my son, who I never had the chance to know. A constant, terrible constricting ache has settled in my chest.

"I'm in front of the Mocha Bean Café. Can you please come and pick me up? Can you get out of work?"

"You called at a good time. I just finished a sales appointment. I'm heading to my car now."

"I'll be waiting at the curb. There's a reason I was there last night. I'll tell you when you pick me up. Okay?"

"Yes. I'm sorry, James. I didn't mean to upset you. I'm always worried about you. It's never going to stop. When you didn't come home last night and then you tell me you stayed in the same apartments where Jessica lived and where you proposed to her, I have a right to be concerned."

I hear the chirp of her car door unlocking.

"I'll be there in twenty minutes."

# Chapter 15

## Lisa

Once I shut the door, I release my breath. His fiancée, Jessica, lived on the other side of this long hallway. He's the James who proposed to her at the party I was supposed to go to with Bryant. I need to ponder this realization.

I roam to the messy kitchen table and begin to clear it off.

His first date with Jessica was at the same bar as my first date with Bryant. I remember seeing Jessica at the bar that night. Bryant pointed her out. I get chills thinking about this. We were each there last night because we were upset about those two people. Well, I wasn't there entirely because of my relationship with Bryant. It was a part of it though.

I bang my hip into the corner of the table and almost drop the coffeepot. *Focus!* I clear the rest of the table quickly before I do break something.

The odd thing is, he took away some of my pain as I listened to him talk about Jessica. The connection he feels to her was once in a lifetime. I think Bryant and I loved each other, but we were never in love. I think we loved the sex more than anything. If we truly loved each other, our relationship would have lasted. At the end, I was the one hurt. He proved me correct. One of the reasons he left me was because he wanted children. It wasn't the only reason, I know. But it's the one I focus on the most.

Is it right for me to expect him—or any man I meet—to give up having children? But if he loved me, he would have. Wouldn't he? I'm so annoyed. I know I didn't love Bryant.

I fill the sink with water and add dish soap, swirling the dishcloth to create suds. I drop the sticky silverware into the water.

I hate this confusion, the constant back-and-forth in my mind. Ever since we broke up, I've been living behind a wall. All I do is work, go for a run, and come home. It's a lonely life, but it protects me. Dating is a no-go. I won't let my heart be torn apart again. Tina is concerned about me. She worried about this happening way before Bryant and I broke up. She tried to convince me it wasn't love and to cut him loose, but I refused to see it.

With my training, I'm aware my lifestyle isn't mentally healthy. I became a psychiatrist to help others. I should be ashamed of myself, since I'm the one who still needs help. Maybe it's a good time to start over and change my nonexistent social life.

Last night, James didn't confess what happened to Jessica. He always spoke of her in the past tense. Did she leave him for someone else? The way he spoke about her makes me think she died. How horrible to lose the love of your life. Especially at such a young age. They had their whole lives ahead of them. After he freaked out when he woke up, I could understand why he reacted the way he did. That must have been a nightmare.

I can't believe some of the things we have in common. How is it possible we grew up just two towns away from each other, went to the same college and medical school, and have never met before? Was this some kind of fluke? Or was it because of our age difference? My gut tells me no. There has to be a reason why we have finally met now. Maybe it's to help us move on with our lives.

I've been washing this frying pan for several minutes now. A splash of water lands on my pajama top. I look down. *Ugh!* I can't believe I didn't wear a bra while he was here.

Last night put my problems into perspective. It was nice to focus on him. Offering breakfast seemed like the right thing to do. When he came into the kitchen after his shower, I was blown away by how cute he is, even with his crazy beard and hair. His brown wavy hair was still wet from the shower, but it looked good that way. Gorgeous green eyes. Tall with wide shoulders. The beautiful upper half of his body matches his face perfectly. He's a yummy package I will never forget.

While analyzing, I pick up the towels scattered around the apartment and put them in the washer. I fold the blanket and fluff up the pillows on the sofa.

I enjoyed the easy, relaxed banter between us. I think I even made him smile once or twice. It was quick, but it was there. It's amazing how a smile can change someone's face. He was even more handsome. His green eyes lit up for a split second. They may have even twinkled. I smack my forehead. *Oh, who am I fooling? This is not a Disney movie.*

I shouldn't think about him like this. Yet, his eyes were mesmerizing. I still notice attractive men even though I avoid them. It's simply not appropriate to think anything remotely sexual or romantic. He's dealing with his own turmoil.

Arghhh!

But it's been a long time since Bryant. The tingling sensation I felt when I was near James was an unexpected but delightful surprise.

Giving him my phone number was a last-minute decision. If he calls, maybe he'll tell me what happened. It would be a great experience for my medical training, though it's not only the training I would appreciate. I enjoyed talking to someone new. He knows nothing deep or personal about me other than where I grew up and went to school.

Our encounter can't be over.

# *Chapter 16*

## *James*

Here comes Alexa in her shiny new red Volkswagen Beetle. It must be nice to have a good-paying, successful career. A year ago, I dreamed it would be me.

I open the car door and get in. Before I can even close the door, she speeds off.

"What the hell, Alexa? Are you trying to kill me?"

I struggle to put the seat belt on.

"No, you are doing a good job by yourself."

I ignore her comment.

"Thanks for picking me up. I didn't want to take a cab home." I feel her eyes drilling holes in my head. "Can you please pay attention to the road? You're freaking me out."

She turns her head forward, clearly waiting for an explanation.

I break down and tell her what happened. I think she's speechless, because she's quiet. She is never quiet. "Say something!" I yell as she pulls into a parking spot by our apartment.

She bursts out laughing. "You really woke up shirtless and wearing pink sweatpants that were way too small? That's hysterical!"

I stare at her with my mouth open. "That's what you have to say? Nice way to support your brother." As we get out of the car, she finally stops laughing.

"Sorry. I'll be serious now." She pushes on her cheeks to keep from laughing again. "I'm intrigued. Her name is Lisa Schmitt. We don't know anyone with her name, although we grew up only a couple of towns away from hers. You both end up going to the same college, medical school, and residency. She lives in the same apartments as Jessica did. You both end up at the same bar last night. It's as if you've been living parallel lives with near chances to meet but something always interfered. Until now."

We walk into our apartment complex and toward the elevator. "You watch too many romance movies, little sister."

She pushes the button for the elevator. "You have been so closed off and ballistic since everything happened. You are different this morning. A little lighter, if I can describe it that way. Or maybe, happier?" she says with caution. "You actually thanked me for picking you up."

"Me? Happy? You're stretching it."

"James, you're mentally more stable right now than you have been for the past year. You wake up every morning pissed off at the world. Anger and sadness seep out of you like a bad smell. Everyone's afraid to talk to you or approach you about anything. You've stopped caring about life in general. The only thing I'm happy you still do is exercise. You do it obsessively, but it's better than nothing."

The elevator door opens, and we walk in. When the door closes, she takes hold of my shoulders. "I observe you now, and it's as if a miniscule part of your shell has been chipped away. Your body movements and the way you talk aren't as abrasive as usual. You also haven't used the word 'fuck' since I picked you up. That's a miracle in itself." She leans against the elevator wall. "Don't get me wrong—you are nowhere near back to normal, but you are better than yesterday. I'll take anything I can get."

I scratch my beard. "Last night was an eye-opener. I hit rock bottom. It was one year yesterday since it happened."

Her face droops. "I'm sorry. I forgot it was yesterday." She hugs me tight.

"I need to change something. I can't live like this anymore." I cringe, thinking about Lisa helping me. *I am such a dick.*

She lets me go and turns around as the elevator chimes. "I'm happy you finally realize this. That's a great sign. Hopefully, this revelation sticks with you.

"I can only take it one day at a time. I can't say what will happen tomorrow." I'm scared about tomorrow. Will I turn right back into an angry monster?

"We don't expect you to change in one day. Hearing you say you *need* to change is a huge step forward." She unlocks the apartment door and steps inside. "Did you tell her what happened to Jessica and the baby?"

I freeze. Hearing "Jessica and the baby" shoots pain through my heart.

Alexa stands by the open door. "Are you coming in or staying out in the hallway?" She's clueless to my reaction.

I walk in and go straight to the kitchen. I grab a bottle of water out of the refrigerator and drink most of it. "No, I never told her she died or that she was pregnant. I couldn't say it out loud again. It hurts too much when I do. I only talked about Jessica. I know you, Dad, and Mom always try to help me. You ask me to open up, but I can't. Always pushing me to seek professional help. Well, she's a professional, all right."

"Maybe Lisa is your guardian angel, sent to you when you needed her the most."

She sounded like an angel, but I hadn't seen a halo. I drink the rest of the bottle and pull a chair away from the kitchen table. I turn it around and sit on it backward.

"She was a stranger, not an angel. Alcohol makes people do stupid things. I know I sound totally crazy. *I know I'm crazy.* Sleeping, showering, and eating breakfast at her place was so inappropriate. Who the hell does that? I guess people who are as desperate as me. But it wasn't complicated, and she didn't dig for details. She didn't have to do anything for me, but she did. Maybe she was using her psychiatrist skills."

I stand up to take the piece of paper out of my pocket. I hand it to Alexa. "She gave me her phone number, just in case I want to talk." I step back and refill the water bottle at the sink.

She leans against the kitchen counter, staring at the paper. "I think you should keep her info. She helped you last night and this morning. Maybe she could help you even more, since she's a doctor. But don't think of it as going to a doctor. Think of her as a new friend." She gives me the paper back.

I raise my eyebrows. "Funny you say it like that. Lisa suggested the same thing. She also insinuated she has been through something tragic."

"She wouldn't have given you her number if she didn't want to hear from you or see you again. Please keep the paper for now. Put it in your wallet for another bad day. Her number might come in handy." She puts her hands together to beg me. "Please, James, do it for your little sister." She bats her eyelashes, as if it will work.

I wag my finger at her. "Don't play that game with me. You can't have your way all the time. This isn't a game. This is my life we're talking about. I'm not one of your boy toys."

She punches me in the arm and starts laughing.

"I'm going for a run. I need to burn off the rest of the alcohol in my body." To make her happy, I put the paper in my wallet. "Thanks again for picking me up and for listening."

She plays with one of the rings on her hand. "Is she pretty?" She asks it like she's asking if the sky is blue.

I whip my head in her direction. "What? What do you mean?"

"It isn't a difficult question. Is she pretty? Cute? Ugly as sin?"

My blood is hot as lava under my skin. I point my finger at her. "I haven't looked at or noticed another woman since I met Jessica. It'll never be the same with someone else. My heart belongs to her and only her. I don't want to be with anyone else." *Who am I trying to convince? Her or me?*

She raises her hands. "Hold on. You don't need to get so defensive. I only asked if she is pretty. I didn't ask if you wanted to date her. Even if you did find her attractive, there's nothing wrong with that. You can find anyone attractive. It doesn't mean you want to jump her bones. Chill out!"

My thoughts are all over the place. I start pacing the kitchen. Lisa is quite pretty, even when she just wakes up. I wonder what she would look like any other time. I don't remember how she looked last night. I was drunk, and it was dark, with pouring rain. She has long, brown wavy hair and big, beautiful blue eyes. She was pretty cute with her pajamas on and her hair up. My hormones kicked in when I noticed she wasn't wearing a bra. She has nice curves, which I know I shouldn't have noticed.

I stop pacing. "Fine! Yes, she's pretty but completely different from Jessica. She has brown hair and blue eyes. Happy now?"

"Actually, I am happy. It shows blood still pumps through your veins." She rubs my arm. "I'm sorry I made you angry. I didn't know you would react that way."

I nod in understanding. "I'll keep her number, but I won't promise I'll call her."

She claps, with a smile so bright it almost blinds me.

"Thanks again, and I'm sorry for being such an asshole all of the time."

"It's understandable." She points at my pants. "Please throw those stupid khakis out, since they're too small now. You need a makeover!"

I throw the empty water bottle at her. She waves and disappears into her bedroom.

*I will never call Lisa.*

# Chapter 17

## Lisa

I stand at the entrance of the Cool Mount Park with my eyes wide, amazed by the beautiful surroundings. I'm so annoyed I have never come here before. It's perfect for running, with paths outlining the bright-green border. Colorful flower patches of golden dahlias, pure white roses, and light-purple chrysanthemums are well maintained and in pretty designs. It is a bee's fantasy. I take a deep breath. The smell of freshly cut grass swirls through the air. The leaves have slight hints of red, orange, and yellow. Fall is my favorite time of year. I can't wait until the leaves are at their peak.

I need to thank my running sneakers. They beckoned to me for a good run this morning. I have a ten-hour shift, starting late this afternoon. This run better give me a temporary jolt equal to ten cups of coffee.

I spot a park map hanging on the iron gate entrance. This park is too big to run in one day. I can explore one corner and come back to enjoy the others. I walk to the side to stretch my legs. There are two paths going in different directions. My gut tells me to go right.

There are several runners and walkers cutting themselves off from the world. I notice an old couple holding hands as they walk along the flower beds. A pregnant woman walks her dog and pushes a stroller as her cute daughter picks flowers. An old man sits on a bench, talking to himself with a bottle in a paper bag. They all have their own stories.

After the car accident, I went to a psychiatrist and therapist separately. My therapist encouraged me to find a sport or hobby to help me refocus and to distract myself from negative thoughts. It was either try her suggestions or take medication. I took up running and skiing. The adrenal rush that pumped through my veins from both was addictive. It gave me a high no drug could ever give. Within minutes, my mood lightened. My anxieties dripped out of my body in the form of sweat.

I wish Emily was with me today. It would have been nice to have her company. The last time I spoke to her, she asked me if I wanted to go out for my birthday, which is on Friday, September 25. I agreed with slight regret afterward, but I need to make positive changes. Celebrating my birthday will push me in the right direction. I vow this year will be a new beginning for me. I pray I have the guts to change things for the better.

I pick up the pace, but my foot slips on the dirt path. My right hamstring freezes up, and I almost lose my balance. I cautiously limp over to a large patch of grass ahead. As I sit not so gracefully, I scare a couple of sparrows away. I stick my right leg out and bend over to release the ache. I rub and shake it to loosen it up.

"Lisa? Is that you?"

I look up and see James about ten feet away from me. Am I dreaming?

"James? What...what are you doing here? Did you see me almost fall right now?" *Now I feel like an ass.*

"Yes, but I didn't realize it was you until I stopped to help."

"You look different. I almost didn't recognize you with a baseball hat on—and you shaved your beard." He still has a good amount of scruff but I can see he has chiseled cheekbones, a broad jawline, and full lips. It's a pity to hide something so beautiful behind a bushy beard.

He rubs his chin. "Did you hurt yourself?"

"It's just my hamstring. It froze up on me. It's been a while since I ran last. My muscles need to warm up a little bit more."

"It's strange to see you here today. Don't get me wrong—it is nice to see you again, but...you know what I mean. I run here several days a week and have never seen you before. Granted, I only met you once before. I'm usually in a zone when I run. I was running behind you and saw something happened."

Is he nervous? He's babbling, which is kind of cute. "I agree it's odd to run into you here. I wondered if I would ever see you again." I press my hamstring with my fingers. "This is my first time here. The weather is perfect, so I thought I'd try a new place to run. I was just wishing my friend, Emily, was here to run with me. Do you always run alone?"

As I ask this, he takes off his Mets baseball cap, squirts some water over his head, and runs his hand through his hair. *Wow!* That was by far the sexiest thing I have ever seen. I could see his arm muscles flex. His sport shirt is wet, which reminds me of how he looked shirtless in my apartment. *Tingle alert. I need to start running again, or I will just sit here and drool all over his body or myself.* His eyes are mint green. It's amazing how much brighter they appear today.

He walks over and sits next to me. "I usually run alone. No one likes to run with me because I run like I'm on a mission." He brushes his hand over the grass.

"And now I'm interrupting you. Please keep going if you want. I don't want to keep you from your mission." I lean into him and tap his elbow with mine.

"It's okay. I've been at it for a while now. I can take a break. Do you want me to help you with your hamstring?"

Before I can answer, he faces me and starts to massage my entire thigh. I don't know what to do or say, because I'm enjoying it too much. He is sweaty, but he smells good. I never thought I'd say I like the smell of sweat. He has such strong fingers. His hands move under my leg to my hamstring and massage it directly. I twitch because it hurts, but in a good way. He'd better not massage any higher, because my hormones will go into overdrive. His hands are magical. *I wonder what his magical hands would feel like on other parts of my body...*

"I'm sorry. Did I hurt you?" His eyes make contact with mine. My breath catches. Is that a dimple I see? He's even more beautiful than I thought. *Damn.*

"No, you didn't hurt me. It felt really good. My hamstring feels better. I think I can run again. Thank you. I should get massages more often. Do you want a running partner today? I can't say I can match your pace with this leg of mine."

He looks around, as if the answer is hidden in the bushes somewhere. "That would be nice for a change. How long were you planning to run?"

"I just got here, maybe thirty minutes. What's your plan?" I watch two chipmunks zoom by like they're on a mission too.

"Thirty minutes sounds good to me. After that, it takes me about five minutes to run back home. I don't live too far from here. That's why I run here a lot."

*I bet the women love watching you run here. Do not start with these thoughts again!*

I push off the grass with one hand. He reaches down for the other to help me up. I grab his hand, and a jolt shoots straight to my stomach, creating butterflies. I pull my hand away and almost fall back on my ass. "Did you feel that?"

His forehead wrinkles. "Feel what?"

I wave my hand. "Nothing. I thought I felt a tremor of some sort or something like static. My stomach feels kind of weird. I must be hungry. Or there will be an earthquake. Never mind."

*I'm making a fool of myself.*

"Should we continue in the same direction? I think I'll follow you, since you know your way around here. You can give me a quick tour of at least some parts of the park." I stretch one more time before we start.

"Sounds good to me."

We run off in total silence. I'm afraid to ask him questions. Maybe he's so out of breath he can't speak. Maybe he forgot I'm running with him. He said he cuts himself off from everyone. Maybe he doesn't want to talk at all. *That's a lot of maybes. Stop overthinking again. It's just a run with an attractive guy. Chill out.*

"I guess you're a Mets fan."

He turns his head toward me. I point at his navy-blue baseball hat.

"Yes, I am." He smiles.

*Dimple alert. I got him to smile again. Brownie points for me.*

"You're a genuine Jersey girl. You must be a Mets fan too—or are you crazy and love the Yankees? Don't even say you don't watch baseball, because I'll stop running with you right now." He pretends to run away from me.

"Get back over here, nasty pants."

He whips his head toward me. Ha! I got his attention. "Of course I'm a Mets fan."

He smirks and lets his head fall back a little.

"The Yankees are good too," I say, "but I favor the Mets. I used to go to games, but that was a while ago. I feel like life stopped once I entered medical school."

"The cap I'm wearing now is at least ten years old. I bought it when I was at a game when I was sixteen or seventeen. I wear it when I run. I'm surprised I'm not bald from wearing it after so many years. There are some things you can never throw out."

"My dad's a big Mets fan. You should see his basement. It's full of Mets paraphernalia. We went to a lot of games when I was younger. Well, when he could afford it. A mechanic doesn't make much money. The last game I was at was when I was fourteen. My dad bought me a great sweatshirt and sweatpants set. I was in an accident and never saw it again. It was hard to give up that outfit."

"What kind of accident, if you don't mind me asking?"

*Oh no.* I set myself up for that one. I'll pretend I didn't hear his question. "James, have you always been a runner?"

"Let's see. I started running in medical school. It helped me get my head on straight. It was the one part of the day I didn't have to think. My feet were in charge, not me. It helped relieve stress. I didn't run as much once I started my residency. About a year ago, I picked it up again more regularly. It helps me deal with my issues right now. It's either this, go to the gym, or get drunk. As you've already seen, sometimes alcohol wins."

*The gym is working well for you.*

"I don't like going to the gym. When I'm stressed or anxious about something, I run or ski. Since skiing is a seasonal thing, running is what I do most. I haven't had much time in the past several years to go skiing. Maybe one day I'll go again."

My hamstring freezes up again, and I grab his arm before I fall. "Damn, my hamstring again."

He puts his arm around my waist and hauls me to the side of the path. It feels nice to have his arm there. I fit perfectly against him. *Snap out of it, Lisa.*

Our eyes lock for a moment, lost in our own world. People run past us, children play on the playground, and dogs bark. We don't seem to notice.

"You have the most beautiful green eyes, James. Right now, they are a lime color in the sunlight. But when you were angry the other day, they were a deep, dark, evergreen."

He looks away from me.

"I'm sorry. I didn't mean to make you feel uncomfortable. I'm sure you have heard this your entire life."

"Actually, you're the first in a very long time. Well, you're the first girl I've had a decent conversation with, other than my sister, in the last several months. Thank you for the compliment though. I'm sure you have heard it about your eyes, too. They are the color of ripe blueberries in an electrical storm."

"Well, that's original. I'm not sure if it's a compliment or a joke." I shove him with my hand. He pretends to fall backward.

"It's a compliment. You have beautiful electric-blue eyes with a tinge of purple in them. Quite unique, actually."

A smile peeks out. "Thanks. I never heard someone describe them like that." I massage the back of my neck.

He looks at the path and then at me. "Seriously now. Are you feeling better?"

I massage the back of my leg. "Not really. My hamstring is screaming right now. I don't think I should run anymore. Maybe it's a sign I'm getting too old. Friday is my twenty-eighth birthday. Next time, I'll run with a cane, like the elderly." I laugh at myself.

"Happy early birthday. Have anything special planned? Hopefully you don't have to work."

"No, I don't, which is a nice surprise. My friend Emily wants me to celebrate with our friends that night. My sister, Tina, might come. We're going to a bar called Cloud Nine. It's a martini bar that has a menu with near fifty different types of martinis. It's a great place. Emily says I need to let go and have some fun. I was excited when she first asked, but now I'm not sure."

He crinkles his eyes. "Why not?"

I groan. "She tries to fix me up with different guys all the time. I have a feeling she'll try again that night. She knows I'm not interested in dating right now. The night I was at the bar with you...I went there because I was sad about my relationship with Bryant and life in general."

I stop speaking for a moment because he dropped his head as soon as I mentioned the bar. I continue anyway. "Strangely, that was where our first date was too, and on the day of my orientation at Clarion. I find everything so ironic. It's been a long time since Bryant and I have been together. I really missed him at first, and I was a bit lonely the night you and I met."

I take a drink of water from my bottle. "When you spoke about Jessica, you gave me a whole new perspective of what love could feel like. I've never had a man talk or feel about me the way you do about her. It really made me think about my relationship with him differently." I hope I'm not pushing this subject too far. *But if I never see him again, I will never be able to say this to him.*

"The way he broke up with me was as if I wasn't enough for him. I hate that I wasted years of my life on him. But after meeting you, I feel better somehow. I've come to the conclusion I'm better off without him. I'm really glad I saw you today, because it's my turn to thank you. You really helped me that night."

His facial expression changes into one I can't read. Did I say something wrong? Oh! If I think about what I just said, it means his state of misery helped me feel better.

"I'm sorry, James. That didn't come out right. I don't want you to think your grief helped me. I just wanted you to know that your love for Jessica was an eye-opener."

He remains quiet and stares at the ground. *Awkward.* I take a step back. "So. Okay. Well, I guess I'll head on home. It was nice to run into you. No pun intended," I joke. "If you still have my phone number, give me a call. Maybe we can meet up for a run again. I promise I'll stretch an hour beforehand." Still no reaction. *I guess I'm not all that funny.*

I turn away, but he mumbles something. "I'll go with you if you want."

"To my apartment? Now?"

"No, to Cloud Nine."

"Really? You want to go?" That came out of left field. A tick of excitement runs through me. I twirl my ponytail.

"It's just a couple of blocks away from where I live. It's right next to City Theater. A lot of people who attend a show go to Cloud Nine for a drink first. Neither one of us want to be involved with anyone. Your friend will hopefully back off because I'll be there with you. Not that I'll be there as your date. But you know what I mean. Right?"

I shrug my shoulders. "Sure...I guess." *Why do I feel a tad disappointed he won't be there as my date?*

"I promise I won't get drunk this time. It'll give me a chance to say thank you again for saving me the other night. My sister and parents will be thrilled I actually want to go out for once."

"It would be great if you stopped by. Besides, I like hanging out with you, so it's easy for me to say yes. I'll make sure you have a good time without the need to drink." I can't stop grinning.

He puts his baseball hat on backward. *He needs to stop making himself look so damn yummilicious!*

"Great, well, how would you like to do this? Do you want me to meet you there?" He tosses his water bottle from one hand to the other.

"I already agreed with Emily we should all meet there at eight p.m. You can meet me there any time after that. If you change your mind, I'll only be a little offended. At least come to wish me a happy birthday. Even if you only stay for five minutes."

"It sounds like a plan. Can I bring my sister, Alexa?"

"Yeah. Sure. You can bring your sister, your friends. Whomever you want. The more, the merrier!"

I bend over to stretch again. "I need to leave now. It'll take me a little while to walk back home with this leg of mine."

"Wait. Let me go get my car. I can drive you home if your leg is really bad. I told you already—I'm only a five-minute run from here. Do you mind waiting? Do you have time?"

"Thank you for the offer, but you don't need to." *Because I hate being in cars. But I really want to go with him anyway.*

"I wouldn't offer if I didn't want to."

"You win... Um, are you going to be all right driving me back to my apartment? I don't want you to feel uncomfortable." I cringe as I wait for his response.

"I'll be fine. I need to deal with these things. If I wanted to avoid everything that reminded me of Jessica, I shouldn't live in this city." He takes my hand and puts it through his arm. "Here, let me help keep some weight off your leg."

Goose bumps prickle on my skin like bubbles in champagne, and I shiver.

"Are you cold? Should I bring you a sweatshirt even though it's eighty degrees out?" He laughs.

"I just got a chill from the light wind. No sweatshirt needed. I'll survive."

We walk—well, I limp—toward a bench about a hundred yards away, near the street. "Are you always such a gentleman with girls you hardly know?" *I shouldn't say things like this. He doesn't want to be with anyone. It's also clear he hasn't been with another woman since Jessica.*

He frowns. "No, I'm not. Alexa says I've become a real asshole. *Gentleman* is the last word she'd use to describe me. I told you it's been a long time since I've been around another woman. You seemed to have changed that."

"Why?"

He cocks his head to the side with a slight smirk. "I have absolutely no idea."

"I usually analyze everything by nature. Maybe this time we shouldn't. Let's just go with the flow and enjoy each other's company. No pressure. No romance. No expectations. No analyzing. Nothing."

He gives me a thumbs-up. "Sounds good to me." He motions to the bench. "Sit here while I run to get my car. It should only take about ten minutes, depending on how fast I run."

I sit down and rest my sore leg on the bench. I wave my hand. "No problem. You don't need to hurry. I have time. I can enjoy the warm sun."

"Good. I'll be back soon." He salutes me and runs off.

*Even his backside looks good.*

This screams trouble.

I raise my face to the warm, morning sun. Cars zip by in the distance, but the noise doesn't distract me. I could get used to this. What does distract me is something wet tickling my ankle. I shake my leg, thinking it's a bug. There it is again. I crack one eye open and see two wet noses from blond Labrador puppies sniffing my ankle. *I'm in complete heaven.* Carefully, I stand up so I won't scare them. I scan the park, looking for their owner. No one is in sight. How can someone let two puppies run around by themselves? They could wander into the street.

They follow me as I sit on the grass. "Come here, cuties." One puppy paws at me. I reach out and scratch behind his ears. His tail wags as fast as hummingbird wings. "Aren't you the happiest puppy?" I guess the other one is jealous because he jumps on me, which makes me fall backward. They climb all over me, smelling and licking my face profusely. Their fur is soft like pussy willows. I learned in medical school that playing with baby animals lifts your spirits. As a psychiatrist, I completely agree. Forget being a doctor. I want to play with puppies all day.

"Having fun?"

James's voice distracts me.

"Is this what happens when I leave you alone for ten minutes?"

"This is the best. Come and play with us." I encourage him.

He kneels next to me. One licks his hand. He laughs as he picks up the puppy. It proceeds to lick his cheek.

"There you are," says a woman, marching toward us. "You both run too fast for Mama." A woman in her fifties joins us, a smile on her face. "Sorry about that. I should have them on their leashes. I hope they didn't bother you."

I stand up and wipe the dirt off my shorts. "Not at all. They made my day. They're beautiful."

"They definitely keep me on my toes. Thanks for taking care of them. Have a nice day, both of you." She puts leashes on them and walks away. I hear a puppy bark in the distance. I giggle and spin toward James.

I press my fingers on my arms, noticing how sticky they feel. "That was awesome. I think I will be smiling for the rest of the day. I have a lot of puppy slobber on me, but it was totally worth it. I'm sticky and stinky." I crinkle my nose when I smell myself.

My eyes wander back to James, and he smirks.

"Do I want to know why you are smiling like that?" I chuckle.

"It was fun to watch you play with them. You were in your own little happy puppy bubble. They loved you. You must taste good with the number of licks you received." His laser-green eyes burn through me.

"I don't know about that," I respond, not knowing how to take the comment. "One big salt stick, maybe from sweating so much. I definitely need a shower when I get home."

He turns in the direction of his car. "Shall we go, petite one?" He peeks over his shoulder and flashes his dimple.

I limp toward him. "Hey. So you do remember some things from the other night. No short jokes today," I command with sweetness.

He turns around and runs up to me. "I'm sorry, little one. I should be helping you. Not a gentleman anymore, am I?" He puts his arm around my waist again.

So much for not visualizing him touching other parts of my body. I need to get home fast and take a cold shower.

"I'm only playing with you about being short. You shouldn't worry about your height. You are a cute little package."

I'm too busy replaying how his hands feel on me when I realize we are walking to an old silver Honda Civic. I freeze in my tracks.

He stops in response. "What's the matter?" he asks.

"I hate riding in cars. I wanted you to drive me home since I'm having trouble walking. Now that I see your car, it makes me think differently." *Just get in the damn car!* "Please don't drive fast. I'm known to panic."

He unlocks his car. "Why?"

"I was in a car accident once, and it scarred me for life, mentally and physically."

He nods but doesn't press me for more details.

He opens the passenger side. I slide in and buckle my seat belt with shaking hands. He starts the car and pulls out slowly at first but then presses the gas.

My blood pressure escalates as my heart starts pounding. "What the hell are you doing?" I screech as I put a death grip on his arm.

He starts laughing but stops as soon as he sees my panic-stricken face.

"I was serious about being afraid in cars."

He slows to the normal speed limit. "I'm really sorry. I thought you were joking." He peels my hand off his arm and squeezes it. I pull it away even though I like it there, and stare out the window.

"It's fine." I rub my hands on my thighs. I look at his arm and see I've left nail marks.

"Sorry about your arm."

"I think I'll survive. Do you want to talk about it?"

I shake my head. "Nope."

"Ooookay. That was a big fat *none of your business* if I ever heard one." He bursts out laughing, of all things.

I belly laugh for no reason as well.

"We are mental cases. A match made in heaven."

"Hey, we agreed. No pressure or romance, petite one."

We joke around and laugh until we arrive at my apartment. *I like his laugh. I like a lot of things about him.*

He parks in front of the complex. I need to make this quick so he doesn't freak out. Before I take hold of the door handle, he's already opening it for me.

"I can take it from here. No worries. I know you don't like being here."

"It's not a problem. I wouldn't do it if I didn't think I could handle it. To be honest, I have no idea why I'm able to."

My arm is hooked around his as we walk to my apartment. I let go to search for my keys in the jogging sack around my waist. I unlock the door. "Thanks a lot for driving me home. It was great seeing you again. It made my day. Well, the puppies did too." I chuckle. "I look forward to seeing you on Friday if you can make it. See you soon." *I'm talking too much.*

I enter my apartment and turn around to close the door. James is frozen in place, looking at me with his eyebrows squeezed together.

I walk back to him and push my finger between his eyebrows. "James, what are you thinking about? I'm the one who thinks too much. Are you like that too?"

"I haven't smiled or laughed during the past year until I met you two weeks ago. It feels both good and bad. I want good to win. Thank you for lifting my spirits. I'm glad we saw each other today."

My heart does somersaults. "You're welcome. Don't feel bad about being happy or showing signs of it. There's nothing wrong with being social." I place my hands on his cheeks. *Should I be touching him like this?* "I don't know what happened to you or what you have experienced that brings you so much pain and sadness. I can only say, you are allowed to have fun, no matter what's happened in your past." *Maybe I should follow my own advice.* "If you want to get out of your apartment and smile a little more, come to the bar on Friday. Take baby steps. I think we both deserve some fun. I'm sure my friends will entertain you." I pull my hands away from his conflicted face.

He nods. "Put some heat on your hamstring. It will help loosen it up." He waves good-bye and turns on his heels.

I'm such a hypocrite. I don't even follow my own advice. It's time to change that. Maybe James and I can do it together. This is going to be an interesting birthday.

# Chapter 18

## James

I glance down the long hallway toward Jessica's old apartment. I encourage myself to walk to it. Once there, I stand to the side with my hands in my pockets. I close my eyes and block out my surroundings. Memories of this apartment resurface. Our first kiss...our first Thanksgiving, when she burnt the turkey. I can still remember the pungent odor that lingered there for weeks. My heart squeezes tight when I replay our engagement, but the nightmare that came after brings its own pain.

Should I feel guilty to be here with someone else? It isn't like we're dating. But I don't feel guilty, and that makes me feel guilty. No matter what, I feel guilty. Something is going on with me, and I don't know what. Maybe I'm finally waking up; it feels as if I were in a deep sleep for a year.

When I met Lisa at the bar, it changed me for the better. She saved me. I never thought it would be possible to meet another woman who could make me feel alive.

I rub my hands up and down my face and take a deep breath. I turn around, and with a heavy chest, I leisurely stroll to the car.

I pull out of the parking spot, exhausted from thinking too much. I'm surprised I agreed to meet Lisa on Friday night. I have only seen her twice. It's just a favor, right? There are no memories of Jessica at Cloud Nine. That makes it safe.

Lisa helps me forget. Is that wrong? It's strange I saw her at the park. I was running behind her—well, a young woman I didn't know was her—and checking her out in ways that made my hormones come out of hiding. I noticed her thin waist, perfect backside, and toned legs. It has been a long time since I've been aroused by another woman. My hormones are tired of my dry spell. When I saw the woman almost fall, never in a million years would I have thought it was Lisa. We never met one another with our parallel lives, but now we've met twice within two weeks.

When I squeezed her hand to help her stand up, I played it off like I didn't feel anything, but I did. It felt like a bolt of lightning zapped my arm, sending heat through my neck toward my face. My face flushed, but it wasn't from exertion.

Running with Lisa seemed natural. It distracted me from my constant depressing thoughts. She didn't ask what happened to Jessica. When or if the time is right, I'll tell her. She didn't want me to talk about her car accident either.

I drive on autopilot through the streets.

When I saw Lisa playing with those puppies, the armor around my heart cracked. The happiness that beamed off her opened my eyes. For a split second, I remembered what complete bliss felt like. The surge of heightened pleasure and happiness that connected Jessica and me. Will I ever experience something like that again?

I park my car and walk into my apartment building. Should I tell Alexa? Well, I need to because I'm going to ask if she wants to go to Cloud Nine with me. I open the door and see she's on the phone. She says good-bye and then looks up.

"Hi, James," she says as she hops off the couch. "How was your run this morning?"

*How was my run?* "Entertaining."

She snorts. "How can running every day be entertaining? Don't you get bored?"

"I ran into that girl, Lisa."

"Get out!" She slaps my arm. "And? What happened? Was she happy to see you?"

I divulge the encounter in detail. "Out of the blue, I offered to meet her at Cloud Nine if she wanted. She complained her friends always try to introduce her to different guys. She doesn't want to date anyone right now. I don't either. I thought maybe it would help if I'm there with her. Her friends won't bother her, and other women won't bother me."

"You actually agreed to go out with a girl? This is huge!" She smacks her hands together while jumping up and down.

I roll my eyes. "We're only friends, Alexa. There's nothing else to it. I've only seen her two times. I hardly know her."

"You hardly know her, yet you slept at her apartment and now agreed to meet her on her birthday. I just think it's great you are getting out there and socializing. You're acting more like a human and less like an ass."

"Do you want to come with me?"

"Hell yeah! I love Cloud Nine. Maybe I'll attract some fresh meat." She wiggles her eyebrows.

"Be careful, Alexa. Of course, any guy would be better than the dick you dated a couple of months ago. He was more of a dick than I was then."

She tilts her head to the side. "Now that's the brother I've missed. Please keep talking to her. She brings out the old you." She squeezes my cheek and prances to the bathroom.

Do I even want to be the old me again? I was too regimented and inflexible. I was so driven by becoming a doctor. I didn't focus on anything else. Well, until Jessica came along. I allowed my focus to include her. Creature of routine and never willing to change.

"Shouldn't you be at work?" I yell to her.

She yells back. "You know my job. I get to make my own schedule. I only need to check in with my boss and sales team a couple times a month. I don't have any appointments today."

She walks back out, spraying perfume on her neck and wrists.

"I'm so excited for Friday. I can't wait to meet Lisa." She puts her arm through mine. I cough on her perfume cloud. "Let's go get something to eat. How about our favorite pizza place? Maybe we can even go shopping for some new clothes for you. All your stuff is so old and nerdy. You need a major makeover. You need to show off your muscles."

My stomach growls when I hear *pizza*. "I'm starving, so why not? Don't push it with shopping though."

She sniffs me and waves her hand. "Eek. Go take a shower. You stink!"

"Do I really?" I panic. My arm was around Lisa when she was limping. I lift my arm up to smell myself. I give Alexa a dirty look. "I'm going to get you for that one."

"Just kidding. I thought you didn't care and Lisa's just a friend." She elbows me.

I punch her lightly on the arm. "Enough. I can't win with you. Think what you want. I do need to shower first. I'll be ready in twenty minutes." I walk away, shaking my head. *What have I gotten myself into?*

# Chapter 19

*Lisa*

I stare into the closet, wondering what to wear for my birthday gathering tonight. My closet lacks pretty clothes. I search through it, pushing my options to the opposite side, listening to the wire hangers scratch against the metal bar. I choose three possible outfits and display them on the bed. One is a pair of light-blue skinny jeans and a frilly, sleeveless black top. The second is a flowing white skirt and red short-sleeve V-neck shirt. The third is a basic black halter dress. I guess I do have some nice clothes. I forgot I bought them, since my wardrobe lately consists of ugly green scrubs. It shows I don't go out often.

This is hard to admit and probably wrong, but I want to impress James. He's only seen me in pajamas or sweaty running clothes—with puppy slobber. I need to convince myself he sees me as a friend. Nothing else.

I pull on the skinny jeans that fit in all the right places. The black shirt looks great with it, but I know I'll sweat my ass off in these jeans. *Option one, denied.*

I look at the white skirt and push it to the side. What was I thinking? I can't wear white when everyone will be drinking colorful martinis. This skirt will look like a rainbow by the end of the night. *Option two, denied.*

I slide the black dress on and stare at the mirror. I turn left and right. The dress fits my curves and perks up my boobs. My slender back is shown off with the low V of this dress.

*Option three, perfect.*

I can wear the only pair of black heels I have. They will give me some height and make my legs look long and thin. The dress makes me feel comfortable but sexy. James won't be able to make any short jokes tonight. *If he shows up.*

Now on to my hair. I lift some hair up with my hands and turn sideways in front of the mirror. With a halter top, I think pinned up with little strands falling loose will be prettier. If it's hot in the bar, having it up will be more refreshing. I ruffle my hair while staring at the mound of clothes on the bed.

*What's happening to me?* Most of the time, I don't want to socialize. Since I met James, I've actually felt happy. Other residents at the hospital have commented about how cheerful I have been. Asking me if I'm in love or won the lottery.

I sift through a box of hair accessories that just fits in the cabinet under the bathroom sink. I find a handful of hair clips and lay them out for later.

I'll put all this effort into making myself look beautiful and he won't even show up. I'll be disappointed if he doesn't, but my birthday will be fun either way. *I have become my own cheerleader.*

# Chapter 20

## James

I walk into the kitchen and see Lisa and Jessica talking by the sink. What the hell are they doing, and how is it possible they are in the kitchen together? Both turn to me and smile as they walk toward me with their arms open wide. Who do I go to first? My heart races as sweat pools on my forehead. I try to breathe, but my lungs aren't functioning.

"Hercules!" I jerk back to reality. The owner of the gym, Tyler, approaches me by the barbells. "It's time for you to stop. You have been pushing yourself hard since you got here two hours ago."

I finish the last rep of bicep curls and drop the barbell to the ground. I wipe my face, neck, and arms off with an already soaked towel.

"I know you have shit going on in your life, but you've pushed yourself way too far this time. I don't need clients passing out in the middle of the gym." He tosses me an electrolyte sport drink. "Your face is bright red, veins are popping out of your neck, and you are completely drenched."

I glimpse at myself in the mirror. I don't care.

"Cool down and stretch, then I want you to go home."

I nod and grab a mat.

It's true. I've been killing myself for the past few hours. I keep replaying the dream I had last night. I woke up covered in sweat and anxious. I needed to burn it off.

I don't remember all of my dreams, though I often wake up feeling like I'm having a heart attack. This time I remembered it vividly. I woke up before I chose Jessica or Lisa. Why is Lisa an option in my dream? I plan to keep any relationship with her platonic—no expectations and no romance. Why do I feel like I need to choose, if I only see her as a friend? *Because you are attracted to her.*

I finish my drink, then lie on the mat to stretch my muscles. Lethargy kicks in.

Every day is new and different. I have no idea how I'm going to feel. Yesterday was a good day because I was excited to see Lisa today. Then the guilt kicked in again. I shouldn't be thinking about another woman. Jessica is the only one for me.

Guilt is a destructive emotion. It eats away at me like a caterpillar on a leaf. One little piece at a time. I know I need to accept Jessica and the baby are gone. But when I try to move an inch forward, the guilt kicks me back again. This inner conflict sucks the life out of me.

I flip over onto my stomach to stretch my quads. Tomorrow I'm going to regret these two hours. My quads are screaming.

I fell asleep last night holding my favorite picture of Jessica, taken when she was six months pregnant. She has her hand on top of her pregnant belly. Her glowing smile reflects how healthy, happy, and excited she was for our baby to be born.

Every time I look at it, I beg myself to get better. I dig deep to find a speck of motivation, a positive outlook, or even the slightest bit of hope of ever being happy again. But the pain of losing them is so fucking crippling.

Spending time with Lisa has been like a breath of fresh air, as if I were stuck in a house with all the windows closed on a hot day without air conditioning and someone finally opened the windows after a thunderstorm. She helps me find pieces of myself I have lost. I've smiled and laughed more with her during those two encounters than I have over the past year.

After stretching, I disinfect the mat and put it away.

Do I meet Lisa at the bar tonight, or do I stay home like every other night? I feel I owe it to Alexa because she's ecstatic I said yes. She would be disappointed if I backed out. A part of me really wants to go, but I don't know what this urge is to see Lisa. Is it because she doesn't remind me of the past, like everything else does?

To be honest, she does remind me of the past, but a very distant one. The girl in the car accident had similar eyes as Lisa. The girl's name from the ski accident was Lisa, and she also had a soothing voice. My emotions and thoughts twist like Chinese noodles.

I haven't mentioned these things to Alexa. I'm sure she would send me straight to a loony bin. It would sound so outrageous to say it out loud. Maybe I'm just obsessed with big blue eyes and soothing voices. At least Lisa's eyes do not remind me of Jessica. Actually, nothing about Lisa, as a person, reminds me of Jessica.

# Chapter 21

## Lisa

Cloud Nine is packed. There is a show next door at 8:30 p.m. I hope several people will be leaving. I have only been here once before, but I love the atmosphere. The lighting is dim, offering a romantic touch. Over the bar tables are small, round, crystal lamps that hang from the ceiling. The shimmering light from the crystals glimmers on the dark-red walls. A big square bar of shiny new mahogany dominates the middle of the room, with matching barstools lining each side. Martini glass after martini glass lines the shelves on the mirrored walls behind the bar.

At first, I don't see Emily or Tina. I make my way through the crowd, surrounded by the buzz of conversations. I circle the bar one more time and see Emily there, with Tina behind her. I sneak up to them from behind and tap their shoulders. Both turn with big smiles on their faces and grab me in a three-way hug.

"Happy birthday, Lisa," Tina shouts. "Wow, you look awesome tonight. Are you hoping to get lucky?" She leans over and whispers into my ear, "With James maybe?"

I scan the bar to make sure James isn't nearby. I pull Tina aside. "Be quiet. He might be here. Also, Emily and the others don't know about him. I never told them what happened."

"What are you two whispering about?" Emily says as she sips her bright-turquoise martini.

I crinkle my nose and I elbow Tina. "That color reminds me of the antifreeze Dad always stored in the garage."

"Ha! That's too funny. I don't know why he stored so many

containers of that stuff in the garage. I guess it's a mechanic thing."

"It's a Curacao martini. Blue Curacao makes it this color. Add a little orange bitter, clementine juice, vodka, and gin, and violà." Emily gestures with her hand. "It's yummy!"

"We need to get you a drink to kick off your birthday celebration," Tina says.

Emily holds up her hand. "I'll order it. This drink is on me. What's your poison for the evening?"

"I'll start off with something basic. A cosmopolitan for now. I'll experiment later," I say as I tap my fingers together.

"Suit yourself. It's your birthday, so you make the rules. We found some tables over in the corner—go say hello to everyone." She points to a spot not too far from the main entrance. That's good. I can watch out for James.

Emily taps my arm. "I brought a friend from work to party with us. He's really nice, and I told him all about you." She gives me a devilish smile.

I roll my eyes. "Please don't start with me tonight. Let me enjoy my birthday without you trying to fix me up with some random guy again."

She winks at me and walks away. I have to give her points for trying. James better show up now!

Tina puts her arm around my shoulder. "I'm so glad I'm here. A last-minute meeting was scheduled, but I refused and walked out the door. I'll probably get in trouble on Monday, but I don't care. I hate where I work." She squeezes my shoulder to the point it hurts. "I have missed you so much!"

"It means a lot to me that you came. My schedule is so random it's hard to plan anything lately. I'm glad it worked out for all of us tonight."

I search the unfamiliar faces in the crowd. This bar attracts an older clientele, not the college-age crowd—the drinks are too expensive.

"Maybe there will be some cute guys for you to flirt with." I tap her hip with mine. "You look hot tonight. Black sequined shirt, red skirt, and sexy black sandals. Mile-long legs. Gorgeous!" We giggle like little girls.

She blows a lone strand of hair off her face. "Whatever. On top of hating where I work, my love life sucks. I never meet anyone nice, let alone worth talking to for more than five seconds. They're always so boring. But that labels my life perfectly right now...boring."

"What do you expect when you're a brilliant software developer and website designer? Everyone just stares at the computer and ignores each other."

She nods in agreement. "Let's talk about you. Are you sure you didn't dress up for James? You're looking pretty exceptional tonight yourself. You haven't looked this good or smiled so much in years. I'm so thrilled to see you this happy. I know it has something to do with him."

Her comments make me smile even more. "No, I didn't dress up for him. Well, not really. Okay. Maybe just a little bit. The other part of me is sick of wearing scrubs that smell like disinfectant and stale urine. And I still have four more years of this."

She plugs her ears. "I don't want to hear about what you experience or smell in the hospital on a daily basis. No more talk about our jobs." She tugs me toward our table. "You need to say hi to your friends. Let's have fun."

We arrive at the table, and I scan for James as I check my watch one more time. It's after eight. My heart sinks. I have to admit, seeing him is a big reason why I'm fired up tonight. But if he doesn't show, I can't let it bother me. No man will bring me down again. This is the start of a new year for me, where I change things for the better. No matter what happens, I will enjoy this evening with my friends. If he comes, he needs to look for me. *Good motivational speech. It better work.*

My friends scream "Happy birthday, Lisa!" and then start to sing. All eyes are on me. Once they finish singing, the crowd starts clapping. I want to crawl under a table. I'm never in the spotlight.

Emily hands me a cosmopolitan. She lifts her glass. "Happy birthday, Lisa. We all wish you a great night and year ahead. May all your wishes come true."

We lift our drinks.

"Cheers to that," I yell and take a sip of the cold martini. *One of my secret wishes is for James to show up.*

"Lisa, let me introduce you to my friend from work."

I plaster a smile on my face and follow her. He looks pretty cute. Black hair and blue eyes, wearing glasses like Superman. I can talk to him for a few minutes.

"Lisa, this is Bert."

*Bert? Where's Ernie?*

"Hi, Bert. Nice to meet you." I sigh to myself. Hopefully, Tina will pull me away from him within a few minutes. Sisterly intuition.

# Chapter 22

## James

"Alexa, it's 8:15. We need to go! What the hell is taking you so long?" I yell as I pace back and forth in the living room. "How much hairspray could you possibly need?"

"My hair is done. I'm changing my outfit," she responds nonchalantly from her bedroom.

I rub my temples. "Again? You looked fine with the other two outfits. Come on now!" I growl.

She walks out of her bedroom. "I'm just kidding. I'm trying to get a rise out of you. I see it's working. Relax. I don't know why you're so nervous. The martinis aren't going to run out," she remarks as she cleans the lipstick off her teeth.

"This is my first time going out in over a year. I want to go, but I also want to stay here. You can't possibly understand." I let out a big breath as I turn away.

Alexa walks up behind me and puts her arms around me. "I'm sorry, big brother. If you think I don't understand, you are correct. I hope I never do. My wish is for you to relax and enjoy yourself tonight. You deserve it more than anyone I know. Maybe you will actually have a good time." She squeezes me extra tight. "Keep an open mind. Forget everything that has happened, and relax. If it becomes too much for you and you want to leave, just say the word, and we're out of there."

She plays with her hair one more time. "Let's get going. Lisa awaits."

We are out of the door by 8:25. The bar is two blocks over, so we arrive within a few minutes. There is a big crowd in front of the theater, so we have to squeeze our way through to find the entrance of Cloud Nine. I feel so out of place. Going to a bar to socialize is not what I do. During the past year, I've only gone to bars to get drunk and be antisocial.

I had my hair cut a couple of days ago. *Why do I care? I'm not trying to impress anyone.* As part of the makeover Alexa gave me, she suggested solid color T-shirts that are a little snug to show off my shoulders and arms. Even though this is not my typical attire, I followed her advice and wore basic blue jeans and a plain gray T-shirt. I pat down my shirt before I walk through the door.

"What are you waiting for? Go inside." Alexa pushes me forward.

"I'm going. Impatient much?"

She pushes me to the side and goes through the entrance first. I follow. I hate to walk into a place where I don't know anyone. Alexa runs off, leaving me alone. I try to act casual and walk around the bar.

I freeze and do a double take. There she is, standing by a table in the corner. There's a lamp over the table reflecting specks of light on her skin. She shines like a diamond. The last two times I was with her, I thought she was pretty. Her black dress hugs her at all the right places. Her hair is up with little curls coming down, which exposes her neck and back. Her shoes show off her slender legs. The first word that comes to my mind is *stunning*. My body goes on immediate high alert.

She laughs at something with one of her friends. Her heart-shaped face lights up the room when she smiles. Her friend looks in my direction. She whispers something in Lisa's ear, and Lisa glances my way. Our eyes lock, as if by some magnetic pull. A lump forms in my throat when I see her glistening blue eyes and giant smile. The man who ends up stealing her heart and waking up to her smile every morning will be a very lucky man. Her ex-boyfriend Bryant was a jackass. Maybe he didn't make her smile. *Is she smiling like that because of me?*

I pull my lead feet off the hardwood floor to walk over to her. She meets me half way. "Happy birthday, Lisa." I lean in and give her a kiss on the cheek. My lips linger longer than they should. They tingled when they touched her feather-soft, warm cheek.

"Thanks, James. I'm so glad you came."

My eyes trace her face. "You look beautiful."

She fiddles with her earring. "Well, isn't that a nice thing to say. Thank you. I almost didn't recognize you. Short hair and cleanly shaven. We have never seen each other in normal clothes." Her eyes scan my body. With a slight grin, she says, "You look really good in jeans. But I also liked the stubble on your face. You look sexy either way." She giggles as she traces her fingers along my jawline and then drops her hand to her side. "I'm sorry. I shouldn't have done that." Her face turns an instant shade of crimson as she looks down.

I will pretend her comment or her touch didn't surprise me. "I'm sorry I'm late. I blame my sister. It took her forever to get ready. We're here now, so that's all that counts." I wink. "I'm sorry I didn't get you a present."

She rubs my arm gently. "No worries. You joining us tonight is all I wanted for my birthday." I can see, by the way her eyes shine and how she nervously touches her neck, she is being honest.

"Where's your sister?" She looks over my shoulder.

"She's around here somewhere. She'll make her appearance in due time, I'm sure. She left me as soon as we walked into the bar.

"Speaking of sisters, did your sister come?"

"Yes, she did. She's the one I was talking to when I saw you. Let me get her over here so I can introduce you. She knows about you." Lisa looks behind her. "Tina, come over here." She yells and waves her over to us.

Her sister picks up two martinis and walks over to us. She hands Lisa one.

"James, this is my sister, Tina."

She shakes my hand, looking me over with wide-open eyes. "Lisa, you said he's good-looking, but he's a lot more than that. Look at your eyes, James. Wow!"

Lisa nudges her and whispers something in her ear. Tina grins.

"I saw you when I was talking to Lisa, and right away I knew it was you. I saw those eyes of yours."

Lisa nudges her again.

"It was nice to meet you, James. I need some water. We can get to know each other later." She downs her martini and walks away.

"Sorry about Tina. She already had two martinis, which is more than she usually drinks. She's usually the mother hen."

*Did she really tell her sister I am good-looking?* I lift my head up high and push my shoulders back.

"It's no problem. I have a sister too. I'm used to it. Your sister looks nothing like you. Brunette with brown eyes, and tall. She looks similar to the actress Anne Hathaway. What a contrast. I would have thought she was your friend, not your sister."

"That's not the first time someone says she looks like her. Everyone says I'm a replica of my mother. She had the big blue eyes and petite figure. I was blessed with them."

*She used the word "had." Did her mother die? I remember she said she's been through some tragic experiences herself.*

"Tina looks just like my dad. He's tall, dark, and handsome."

I look over her shoulder at her friends. Their eyes are darting back and forth from me to Lisa. *What's their problem?* Something tells me she didn't tell them I was coming tonight. Interesting.

I grab Lisa's hand and stroll up to them, with her behind me. "Hi, everyone. I'm James. Lisa invited me here tonight to celebrate her birthday with you all. I hope that's okay, since it looks like it's an all girls' party," I say, a little too sugarcoated as I let go of Lisa's hand. I'm not sure why I started to hold it in the first place.

Everyone gawks at us, not saying a word. I put my hand on her open back and lean in and whisper, "I'm going to get a drink. Do you want something? I can see your friends want to interrogate you." I get a view of her neck and smell a trace of vanilla. *I wish I could give her a birthday kiss right underneath her collarbone.* I gently trace my fingers along her skin.

She shivers in response. As she takes a sip of her martini, I notice her hands are shaking. I smile to myself.

She leans her head toward me and looks up. "Don't worry. I'll only say nice things about you. Well, in reality, I don't know a lot about you, so I can't say much. I'm kind of enjoying the reaction you're getting. They are completely surprised, wondering who this gorgeous guy is and where I have been hiding him." She looks in the direction of her friends. "Why don't you get yourself a drink? Can you please get me a glass of water? I want to pace myself tonight. I still have this one I need to finish."

I nod and walk away, knowing I'm the one who's shaking now.

What is this effect she has on me? She's more attractive every time I see her. I was so close to her when I was whispering in her ear. Her neck and back are completely exposed. It's so sexy and enticing. I had to touch her skin to see how soft it was. Smooth like satin.

This is unfamiliar territory. We agreed to keep this platonic. My heart belongs to someone else, but my hormones tell me something different.

I order a dirty martini and her water. I hear Alexa behind me. Finally, she makes her appearance.

"So where is Lisa? I want to meet her," she asks while sipping a bright-red martini. Not surprising, since she's obsessed with the color red.

"Please don't embarrass me. I'm warning you. This isn't a date. I agreed to come here for her birthday. That's all."

She pouts. "Don't be such a party pooper."

I take our drinks and lead her over to Lisa. She's talking to a guy at the table. My body stiffens. Who is he? Of course, she will attract other guys. She certainly has my eye. Do I feel jealous or protective? She can talk to whomever she wants. *It's your hormones, jackass.*

She said she didn't want to meet anyone, so let me have some fun. I proceed to where they stand. Her lovely back is facing me. I wrap my arm around her waist and hand her the water she asked for. "Here's your water, babe."

She doesn't miss a beat. Her hand goes around my waist in response. "Thanks, honey." The guy's face is priceless. His eyebrows press together as he takes a step back.

He takes his drink off the table and mumbles, "Sorry. I didn't know you were here with someone. See you around, Lisa. Have a good birthday." He walks over to Emily and whispers something in her ear. She looks back at us and mouths to Lisa, *I'm going to kill you.*

We try to hide our amusement by facing the other direction. "That was perfect timing. Thanks for the save. As you can see, Emily brought him here for me. He's nice, but he's not for me. I don't know who is, as a matter of fact."

*I'm the one for you.*

She peeks over my shoulder with a curious look.

"What's up?"

"I think your sister's heading our way. I can tell by her eyes."

Before I even see Alexa, I move to the side. "Lisa, this is my sister, Alexa."

Lisa smiles and extends her hand. "It's so nice to meet you. Thanks for coming out tonight. I see you both inherited the same beautiful eyes."

"Unfortunately, his eyes are even prettier than mine. It's nice to finally meet you. Thanks for inviting us. Happy birthday."

She points to Lisa's drink. "Are you drinking water? This is supposed to be your birthday party. Can I buy you a birthday martini?"

"Sure. So much for pacing myself. I'll take you up on your offer. Let's go scan the menu for something fun. I should try something new tonight." She turns toward me. "Want to come with us?" Her hand touches my lower back.

"No. You go ahead. I have a martini. I'll stay here at the table until you both come back." I have this urge to kiss her cheek before she walks away. I refrain.

I watch them walk to the bar, my eyes focusing on Lisa's backside. I force myself to turn around and almost bang into a girl.

"Hi, I'm Emily," she says while twirling a strand of her hair. "I'm Lisa's old roommate-slash-best friend. We're all a bit surprised about you. Lisa never mentioned you. I could see how happy she was when you arrived. No one seems to make her smile like that."

She leans into me with inquisitive eyes. "I saw how you both had your arms around each other. You scared my colleague Bert away. I was trying to fix her up with him."

"She told me you do that often."

Her eyebrows perk up, and then a smile forms. "This makes me even more curious. Is there something I should know about?"

She's invading my space entirely too much. I take a step back. I'm not surprised to be interrogated. She's excited to see Lisa happy. Little does she know nothing is going on between us. *I think.*

"We met a couple of weekends ago and again the other day under strange circumstances. She mentioned she was celebrating her birthday here, so I asked if I could come along. I live not too far from here." I act casual.

I keep my mouth shut after that, just to keep her guessing. It's none of her business. Lisa didn't tell her for a reason. It's for her to explain to her friends, not me. I think I will enjoy this night, just watching her friends. Thankfully, Lisa and Alexa approach us with their drinks. Emily walks away when Lisa arrives with a purple martini.

"What type of martini are you drinking? It looks sweet as hell. Just looking at it makes my teeth hurt."

"It's a Purple Lamborghini. It isn't too sweet. It has cranberry juice and grenadine in it. Try it." She hands it to me. There is something very intimate about drinking from her martini glass.

I squeeze my eyes shut. "Wow, that's a mix of sweet and sour. It could be deadly because you can't taste the alcohol. I think I'll stick to dirty martinis tonight. Yours is too girly for me." I sip my martini, trying not to laugh. "Don't drink too many, because then I'll need to take care of you tonight. Maybe it would be fun."

Alexa's eyes bore through me. Her mouth transitions into a

knowing smirk. I break eye contact, not wanting to know what thoughts spin a web in her head.

Lisa takes the martini back and brings the glass up to her lips. I see the tip of her tongue touch the rim. Why do I wish I were her martini glass? I wonder how her full pink lips and tongue would feel on mine. *Have I gone completely mad?* My face feels warm. I need some ice cubes to cool off. I didn't imagine Lisa would make me feel like this. Then again, she always makes me feel something, something positive and sexual.

Lisa and Alexa have moved away from me. They seem to be hitting it off. Alexa is animated in their conversation, with her arms flying around. Who knows what the hell she is talking about. Hopefully, nothing about me.

I walk over and stand at Lisa's side. Alexa walks away. "I hope she isn't telling you embarrassing stories about me." *Or my secrets.*

Lisa responds, "No. She's pretty funny though. I like her outgoing personality. She's so classy with her blond bob and stylish red clothes. Your parents created beautiful children."

Tina sneaks up behind us and chimes in, "I'm personally very happy to be here tonight to see Lisa happier than she's been in a very, very long time." She stares at me a little longer than I feel comfortable with and then hurries off.

"Again, please ignore Tina. She's trying to annoy me. We haven't seen each other in a while, so I think she needs to make up for lost time."

"I was just interrogated by Emily. Why didn't you tell her I was coming? She told me about that guy you were talking to. You weren't exaggerating about her trying to fix you up tonight. I'm glad I'm here for you."

"Well, I was afraid you would change your mind. I didn't want to mention you and then if you didn't show up, I knew how they would react. I would've been embarrassed. It was a lot more fun this way. You're the mystery man."

"Let them talk. This is the most entertainment I've had in a long time. Better than any reality TV show. I'm glad I came." I lower my voice and run a finger down her arm. "You have this charming way about you... You'd better be careful. I might need to have you around all the time."

She bats her eyelashes. "Sorry. I'm basically married to the hospital for the next four years. I can give you my schedule so you can get your daily dose when I'm available."

"Sounds good to me, beautiful."

# Chapter 23

## Lisa

This is the best birthday ever! When I saw James for the first time when he arrived, my heart skipped a beat, and my stomach jumped. I couldn't help it. He stands out in the crowd. His green eyes are the first thing anyone notices. They almost glow. He's dressed casually tonight, but he looks stylish. His T-shirt fits his chest, biceps and shoulders perfectly. Not too tight but just enough to give a peek of what's underneath. *I've seen what's underneath.* His jeans attract my attention to all the best places. *I wish I could see those places.* I'm done with drinking. I don't want to make an ass out of myself by jumping on him. He's only here because it's my birthday.

Tina nudges me and nods toward the restrooms. "Come with me to the bathroom." Does she want to talk to me, or is she not feeling well?

"Sure."

She hooks her arm with mine and starts to drag me with her.

I peek back at James and say, "I'll be right back. Stay where you are."

He nods while he eats the olives from his martini.

We enter the bathroom, and Tina looks around to see if it's empty.

"What's up with you? Did you meet a cute guy?" I say, full of curiosity and excitement for her.

"Don't try to deter the subject."

I play dumb. "What are you talking about? I thought that's why you're so peppy."

She cocks her hip and points out the door. "There's so much electricity sparking between you and James I'm surprised the lights aren't flickering. How can you stand there and say there's nothing going on between you two?"

"I won't deny it, because I truly feel what you see. However, nothing will come of it. He has some dark secrets, and he wants nothing to do with relationships, just like me. I need to ignore the chemistry and just be friends. Simple as that."

"Something tells me it won't be so easy. I'm not going to push you. If you can't or won't do anything about it, at least enjoy it tonight."

I check my hair in the mirror and say to Tina's reflection, "Go pee. I want to go back outside. I'll meet you out there." I wash my hands and pop a mint into my mouth.

"Okay. Go back to your yummy man out there. I wish he had a twin brother." She chuckles as she locks the stall door.

"You're definitely tipsy, if not drunk. Lay off the martinis for a little while. I've never seen you drink this much. Oh, and wash your hands! You don't want to know what kind of germs are lying around in here." I rub hand sanitizer on my hands.

"Yes, Dr. Lisa," she yells as I walk out the door.

As I walk out of the bathroom, I hear the song "Fix You" by Coldplay. I haven't heard this song in so long. It's one of my favorites from this group. I think of James instantly. Maybe I can fix him.

I look through the crowd and see James hasn't moved from where we were standing. However, a tall, slender blonde chats with him. As I creep closer, I zone in on her hand, which is on his arm. She leans closer to him.

Why doesn't she press his face into her cleavage? *Is it my turn to interrupt, or does he want to talk to her?* He jerks his arm away from her.

There's my cue.

James notices me behind the blonde. He lifts his chin and flashes me a smirk. I can't help but feel warm and fuzzy. He's so damn cute.

This is so much fun. Once I'm near the table, he scoops me into his side.

"There you are, beautiful." He leans down close to my cheek. I turn my head toward his, and our lips brush and linger for a couple of seconds. We slowly put space between us, never losing eye contact. My breathing is heavy. My pulse blasts through my body. Our kiss was only for a mere few seconds, but it was the best kiss I have ever had.

"What's the matter?" Tina interrupts.

We are jerked from our zone, and I act like nothing happened. The blonde is nowhere to be seen.

I clear my throat. "Nothing's the matter. Why do you ask?" It's not like the kiss meant anything.

"You both looked really intense. Like something happened."

"Oh. There was a blonde chick flirting with James, and I saved him from her. No big deal."

James remains silent. Did he like the kiss as much as I did?

"Here comes Alexa," I say.

"There you guys are! I couldn't find you. Are you having fun? Why don't we order you another martini?" Alexa suggests.

I take a deep breath. "Before I have another, I think I need some fresh air. The martinis are hitting me." I rub James on the back. "Do you want to come with me?"

"Sure. Let me finish this first." He drinks it in one gulp and sets the glass on the table. He places his hand on my bare back, pushing me gently forward. "Let's go."

"We'll come with you. If that's all right? I could use a dose of fresh air." Tina's words slur.

"Sure." *But I want him to myself for a few minutes.*

We walk through the doors and are hit with a blast of cool air. It's so refreshing, like an ocean breeze. I was sweating in there, and not only because of the crowd. His lips were so soft and inviting. *How am I going to stay away from him now?*

The show at the theater must have just finished. A large group of people are filtering out of the theater doors and dispersing in different directions. We walk closer to the street to find some space.

"I hope you're having fun tonight. Thanks for coming to celebrate with us."

I'm standing next to James and Alexa, but neither look at me or even respond. They're focused on something or someone in the crowd. James is frozen. I stare at him, wondering what he's looking at.

"What's wrong?"

He keeps rubbing the back of his neck with one of his hands, as if he's in a total panic. Alexa looks uncomfortable as well.

"What's the matter? You're both catatonic."

I finally get his attention. He whispers, "Those people approaching us are Jessica's parents." My stomach lurches to my throat. My heart starts racing so hard I feel it in my ears. I don't know what to do, so I just stand there. *Why am I nervous? I don't even know what the story is with Jessica.*

They approach us with caution.

"James, I'll give you some privacy."

I try to walk away, but he grabs my hand. "Please stay. I need you next to me." He squeezes it too hard. I don't complain.

I squeeze his hand back. "All right. I'm not going anywhere."

"Hi, James, Alexa," Jessica's parents say in restrained unison.

"Hello, Da—Mr. and Mrs. Flynn. It's been a long time. How are you both doing?" James asks with a sullen voice.

"It has been really hard, but I'm sure harder for you. Every day is a battle, but it's slowly getting better. We wish you would return our phone calls. We are worried about you. We haven't seen you in at least six months. We spoke to your parents a couple of times. Did they tell you?"

"No. No, they didn't. I think they know it would upset me."

There's obvious sadness in their eyes, especially when they look at me.

"Did you see a play just now?" James says.

"Yes, we've had tickets for a while now. Your parents gave us a gift certificate a long time ago, so we finally decided to use it," Mrs. Flynn responds.

James nods in acknowledgment.

This is very awkward. I cut in to break the tension. "Hi, I'm Lisa, and this is my sister, Tina." I let go of James's hand, which I didn't realize he was still holding. Tina and I shake hands with the Flynns. I feel out of place. They saw us holding hands.

"I'm a friend of Alexa and James." I say Alexa first, hoping it might sound better. *But we have nothing to hide, because we aren't dating.*

"Nice to meet you, Lisa and Tina. We're Jessica's parents, if you haven't already guessed," says Mr. Flynn. "Well, we'll let you enjoy your evening. We're staying at the Belvedere Hotel tonight. James, maybe we can meet for lunch or even coffee tomorrow. Alexa, send our regards to your parents." They both force a smile.

James gives Jessica's mom a quick kiss on the cheek and shakes her father's hand.

We stand there in silence until they are out of sight. I look at Tina for some guidance, but she just shrugs her shoulders.

James starts to walk away but stops and spins around. "Come on, Lisa. Are you going to dissect this situation by using your fucking psychiatric tools?"

"James, that was extremely rude and uncalled for. Lisa didn't deserve that at all. You should apologize," Alexa snaps in return. She points her finger at him with anger radiating off the tip, like a wand.

"What did I do to deserve such an asinine comment? I'm standing here wondering what the hell just happened. That was obviously very hard for you, but don't take it out on me," I hiss.

Alexa comes up to me and whispers, "I know it's your birthday, and I'm asking a lot, but can you please stay with him? I'll stay behind with Tina. We'll tell Emily you left with James. Is that okay with you?"

I nod.

Tina kisses me on the cheek and whispers, "Are you all right with this? You don't need to be his babysitter."

"I know, but this is what I went to med school for, and I care about him. He might do something rash. I also want to know what the hell happened to Jessica."

"It's not fair. It's your birthday. It's your choice, but be careful." Tina gives my hand a gentle squeeze, then hurries off with Alexa.

I turn to James. "Do you want to be alone? You don't need to stay here."

"Alone is the last thing I want to be. All I wanted tonight was to have fun for the first time in a year. Ironically, I run into Jessica's parents." He shakes his head and groans. "I need a drink. Do you want to come with me to my apartment? I told you it's not too far from here."

I'm reluctant. His eyes are squinted, reflecting a disturbing murky-green color. His jaw is clenched. He spins on his heels and strides ahead of me.

"James, can you please slow down? I don't have long legs like you do, and I'm wearing heels."

He eases up but doesn't look at me. We don't speak a word. His hand shakes as he reaches for his keys when we arrive at his apartment building. He's nervous, or maybe it's his adrenaline. I follow him to the elevator. *Silence.* He's hurting, and I want to be here with him and for him. He needs someone, and that someone is me right now.

He presses the elevator button.

As we get into the elevator, I can't stop thinking about holding his hand and our minor kiss before. It felt so natural, as if our hands were made to fit each other's perfectly. Like two puzzle pieces lost somewhere in a child's bedroom and then somehow found again.

I snap out of it when I hear the bell and the clatter of the elevator door sliding open. James bolts out. I follow him with long strides. I don't want him to be alone, but does he really want me here? He sure doesn't act like it. I need to stop him from doing something stupid, like getting completely drunk again. Thankfully, he only had one martini. Not that I was counting.

He enters his apartment but doesn't check if I'm behind him. He does leave the door open. I guess that's a good sign. I step in and quietly close the door. The first thing I see is a spacious living room with highlights of red. Definitely Alexa's apartment. Even though it's modern, it's decorated in a way that makes it cozy and cheerful. It matches Alexa's personality perfectly. The black sectional couch is facing a large picture window. Several multisized, colorful pillows are neatly scattered on it, enticing me to dive into them.

To the right is an open kitchen that connects to the living room. The cabinets are modern, glossy apple red, with a black countertop. Between the kitchen and the living room is a black dining table with a glass top that seats six people. Red seat cushions adorn the matching chairs.

From what I've seen so far, Alexa has good taste and makes a good living in pharmaceutical sales or whatever the hell she does. Good for her.

I stay where I am in front of the door. James walks into the kitchen and takes a tumbler out of a cabinet. He strides over to what looks like a liquor cabinet. He opens it and pulls out a large bottle of vodka. At least he sticks to the same alcohol as his martini. He pours a lot more than he should.

"Do you want a drink?" he asks with anger dripping from his words.

"James, do you really need to drink alcohol? Let's talk about what happened a few minutes ago instead. I know this is your way of dealing with things. Maybe we can try something else to help you."

"Am I one of your patients, Lisa?" His says my name with thick disgust.

*What the fuck?*

He walks away and stands by the couch. "Where's my chart so you can jot some notes down," he asks loudly, dripping with sarcasm. "Do you even know who or what you are dealing with? You don't have a clue what I've been through, what I'm still going through!"

He runs his hand through his hair repeatedly. I think he might rip it out. I'm worried and angered by his nasty attitude. But I can handle it. I need to handle it. I would rather he take his rage out on me than drown it in alcohol. Rage seeps out of his skin, creating a dark cloud around him.

I have the urge to get in his face. "You're right, James! I don't know what the hell is going on. I know you love or loved a woman named Jessica. You talk about her in the past tense. Tell me what happened so I can understand."

He throws the glass of vodka against the red wall. I jump back as air whooshes out of my lungs. Vodka drips down the paint, like lava. Glass shards blanket the carpet.

"You want to know what happened to her? She died along with our unborn child! Are you happy now? Is that what you wanted to hear?" he yells.

I put my hand over my mouth.

"That's right. You didn't know she was almost seven months pregnant. I had to bury both of them." His voice cracks.

*Oh my gosh, she was pregnant. This is much worse than I thought.*

"We had our entire fucking life together in front of us...and it was taken away"—he snaps his fingers—"just like that...from one minute to the next. How do you think you would handle it, Lisa? I didn't lose just one person—I lost two. I'm so pissed off all the time. There's a storm brewing within me. I want to jump out of my own skin."

His face is mottled, and his fists are clenched. Is he going to punch something?

"I finally decided to go out tonight. The first time since they died. I was in a good mood and actually excited. It was a safe place to meet you because I have no memories of Jessica there. And then Jessica's parents suddenly appear. My little chance of happiness was sucked right out of me in those couple of minutes they spent talking to me. It's as if I'm not allowed to move on or try something to get me out of this shit hole of a life."

I tiptoe over to the couch but stay behind it. I'm a bit scared to approach him because he is breathing so hard. "What happened to her and the baby?" I ask with caution.

His eyes dart to mine. They reflect grief. He paces from one wall to the other, not aware he is stepping on the broken glass. I inch my way around the couch and stand by the coffee table, separating us still.

"Tell me what happened. Let it all out. I'm here for you."

He turns away and stares out the window, with his arms crossed. He speaks low while wiping the tears from his face.

"She was due in November. She was still working in the hospital. The baby was healthy and developing perfectly. She was so happy during her pregnancy. She never complained even when the summer was so hot. We didn't want to know the gender. We wanted it to be a surprise. I was working several hours a week, since I had just obtained my medical license.

"One morning I woke up like I always did. She was still in bed because she had the week off from work and could sleep in. She had complained about a sore throat and being exhausted the few days prior, but we just assumed she was getting a cold from being around sick children all the time. It was strange, because even if she was just a little bit sick, she would still get up with me. I went to check on her, but she was still in a deep sleep. She was a bit sweaty but I attributed it to the hot and humid weather. Our window air conditioner was broken. I decided to let her sleep. At that time of the pregnancy, it's common to be exhausted. I thought nothing of it. I rubbed her back and kissed her lightly on the cheek. She moaned a little bit, but I just took it as she wanted to sleep. I left and started my day.

"I should have recognized the signs." He bends over, shaking and sobbing. My heart breaks for him. I approach him and put my hand on his shoulder, fully expecting him to shrug it off, but he doesn't.

"What happened next?"

He rubs the tears from his eyes and walks to the couch. He grabs a tissue from the box on the coffee table. He rubs his nose and throws it on the carpet. He plunges onto the couch.

"As the morning went on, I didn't hear from her. Not a day would go by she wouldn't send me a text message or call. I sent her text messages, but she never responded. She always had her cell phone with her. For a little while I just thought she was still asleep. It was nearing lunchtime, and still no response. I had a sick feeling in my stomach. I finally called her. No answer. I called several more times, and still no answer. I paged my boss and told him I had an emergency with Jessica and needed to leave. I took another doctor with me just in case."

He leans back against the cushion, pinches the bridge of his nose, and closes his eyes. I take the opportunity and settle down next to him.

"Thankfully, we lived very close to the hospital. I drove as fast as I could. I knocked on the door while trying to unlock it. Praying she would open the door and be okay. But nothing was okay. I opened the door, and it was silent in the house. I yelled for Jessica as I ran from room to room. I found her on the floor in our bedroom. I have no idea how long she'd been laying there. She felt cold and wasn't breathing. The other doctor immediately called for an ambulance as I performed CPR. My biggest and worst nightmare. It was completely horrifying.

"We both tried everything to resuscitate her, but nothing worked. We tried to find the baby's heartbeat or any kind of movement. Nothing. I knew in my heart they were both gone. I didn't feel them anymore. I always knew when Jessica was nearby."

He shudders and shifts forward to rest his head in his hands. I rub his back lightly.

"I held her in my arms until the paramedics arrived. Two of them had to pull me away from her when I started shouting and crying. I wouldn't let go of her. I thought I was dreaming. My fiancée and unborn child were lying on a stretcher in front of me.

"I'm an ER doctor, and I couldn't save them. I should have seen the signs. Her sleeping longer than normal, her sweating and complaints of a sore throat—they should have given me a clue. When I proposed to her, I promised if she ever fell, I would pick her up. I couldn't keep my promise."

His breath hitches. "I promised her, and I failed."

I want to shower him with comforting words, but I know it won't help. I'm also afraid if I interrupt, he won't tell me everything.

"I rode in the ambulance with them. My head lying on her as I cried. They confirmed both of them were dead before we arrived at the hospital. The other doctor tried to convince me it wasn't my fault, but I know it was." He stabs his chest with his thumb.

"Several doctors and nurses were waiting for us when we arrived at the emergency entrance, since it was called in. They were shocked it was Jessica. They knew her well from the hospital. They took her away but made me wait because my emotional outbursts were hard to control. I felt like I waited forever. Finally, the doctor led me to an empty office. He didn't need to say anything. I broke down, knowing it was final.

"It appeared like she died from septic shock. He asked me if she was sick that day or recently. I told him how she wasn't feeling well the days before.

"When the mother suffers from severe sepsis and then shock, the baby has no chance of survival in such a quick onset. If she had been able to get to the hospital quicker, there would have been a slightly better chance." He pauses for a moment, as if deep in thought.

"Let me get you some water." I move to push off the couch, but he puts his hand on my thigh before I can.

"Please don't leave. I want to tell you everything. I need to tell you everything."

I put my hand on his. "I'm not leaving. I'll do anything you want."

He rubs his eyes several times.

"They needed to take the baby from her by caesarian section. They asked if I wanted to be in the room and whether I wanted to see the baby. I wanted both. I needed to be there. I needed to see our baby one time. I sat next to her as if she were alive and having a C-section.

"It was a boy. They wrapped him up in a blanket like they would do for a newborn. They handed him to me and quickly took care of

Jessica. They left me alone with them. I just sobbed uncontrollably until I had no tears left. I didn't care who heard me. He looked like he was sleeping. I sat holding him in one arm and stroking Jessica's face. Telling her how beautiful he was. That it was all a dream. A sick, twisted dream, and we'd wake up from it. But we didn't. I only woke up to complete hell.

"I didn't want to give him back to the nurses, but I had to. I held him close and kissed him good-bye, which was one of the hardest things I ever had to do. The worst was saying good-bye to Jessica. I wanted to hug her and kiss her to make it all better, but I couldn't. I'm a fucking doctor, but I couldn't save them. I should have recognized the signs. All the training I had, and it didn't help at all." His fists clench again.

Now I need a tissue because I'm the one crying. My heart hurts because I know what it's like. It's different to lose a parent versus losing your fiancée and unborn child, I'm sure. But all his emotions are completely warranted.

He reaches for my hand and starts talking again.

"I finally had to leave the room. When I did, I saw my family and Jessica's parents waiting for me. They all started hugging me while we all cried. We didn't know what to do or say. I tried to explain to them, with bursts of crying in between, what happened and maybe it could have been prevented, but it didn't matter. In the end, they were both gone.

"My life changed exponentially. I stopped working at the hospital, not knowing if I would ever go back. My parents drove me back to a quiet apartment filled with Jessica's things and all the new baby clothes, toys, and furniture. Even though I wanted to be alone, the quiet was unbearable. I went straight to bed and held on to Jessica's pillow so I could smell her rosy scent. She always smelled like roses. I associated roses with her. Now I can't stand the sight or smell of them. Next to the bed was the crib we'd bought. A crib that would never be slept in. I cried until my head was going to explode."

He lets go of my hand and leans on his elbows. His head hangs toward the floor.

"During the days leading up to the funeral, I found out Jessica died from septic shock due to a common streptococcal infection. Since she worked in the pediatric ward, she was probably exposed while working. It's extremely rare, but there have been similar cases reported. Since she was dead for a couple of hours before we found her, the baby couldn't survive.

"I had to plan the funeral with Jessica's parents. The worst part was picking out a coffin. I wanted my son to be buried with his mom. I couldn't imagine it any other way. Our son was growing in her until the last day of their lives. He needed to stay with his mom. He was positioned on her chest like he was sleeping. They looked so beautiful and so peaceful. I wanted to be laying in there with them. Who was I without them?"

He faces me. I watch a single tear fall down his cheek. My shaking hand raises and catches it as it drips from his chin.

"I named him Jacob. We had a list of names, and Jacob was one of the three boy's names we'd chosen. Her favorite name was Jacob. If the baby was a girl, I would have named her Rose. I looked at the list today, wondering how different my life would be if they were still alive."

*He thought about this today?* I feel a ping of disappointment or maybe jealousy. I'm so selfish to even think this way, with the torture he has been through.

"Days after the funeral, I shut down. I didn't want to see anyone. Getting drunk was my only way to numb the pain. Getting rid of their things was unthinkable. I wanted the apartment to stay the same. I didn't go back to work; I took a leave of absence. How could I be a doctor if I couldn't even save their lives?

"A couple of months went by, seeing my family, Jessica's parents, and friends randomly. They would come over sometimes to give me some food, clean the apartment, or do some laundry. Slowly, my friends and Jessica's parents stopped calling because I refused to answer their phone calls or to see them. I haven't spoken to my best friend in months now. Alexa and my parents are the only ones who stayed to help me. I hardly showered or shaved. I was depressed and sickly looking.

"Alexa came over one day and told me—not asked me, told me—I was moving in with her until I got back on my feet. I needed to be watched because I was having random suicidal thoughts. Thankfully, not all the time. But those moments snuck up on me when least expected. At that point, I knew she was right, and I had to get myself out of the apartment. The one place that had promised to fill our lives with our future was suddenly filled with death and tragedy.

"One month later, I moved into this apartment. Thankfully, Alexa has a second bedroom. It's more luxurious than mine was. It was a change I needed, but it didn't solve my problems so quickly. I had to pack up the apartment. Give all their stuff away. I gave a lot of Jessica's things to her parents. Alexa took control of giving away Jacob's things. I couldn't do it myself. If I could have, I would've brought all of it with me. I only kept the special things I could never part from. Pictures of us together, little notes and cards we wrote each other, sonograms of Jacob as he was growing. Those little things meant more to me than their clothes and furniture."

He clears his throat and swallows.

I get off the couch. "Let me get you some water." I scurry to the kitchen and retrieve the water within seconds.

He takes the glass and takes one gulp. He lowers the glass and lets it dangle from his fingertips. Before he has a chance to drop it, I gently remove it from his hand. I rest it on the coffee table. I lightly rub his arm to encourage him to continue.

"Moving in was a good direction to go, but it was still very difficult for me. I dwelled in my own misery. Alexa and my parents tried for months to pull me out of my rut. I would sit in the dark for hours, talking to Jessica as if she were still there.

"They asked me numerous times to go to a therapist or self-help group for people who are grieving. I refused to go. I thought no one could cure me. I didn't deserve happiness again. I vowed I'll never love anyone again or have another child. My heart belonged to Jessica and Jacob. I would feel guilty if I was with anyone else. I couldn't take the chance to possibly go through something like that again. I wouldn't survive. No one could ever replace Jessica.

"I refused to see Jessica's parents. They were too much of a reminder of her. I couldn't do it anymore. I know they were and still are grieving, but so am I. No one could possibly understand what I was going through. Yes, they lost their daughter and future grandson. But I lost the love of my life and my son."

He hunches over and lets out a deep sigh, as if all energy has been sucked from his body.

"The night you saw me at the bar was when I was rock bottom. Ready to give up, torturing myself. Then you appeared next to me when I needed it the most. You were there because of your sadness, but you chose to help me instead. My thoughts and mood changed after you helped me that night. Alexa noticed it the instant she picked me up the next morning. I still have my relapses with drinking though. When I saw you again at the park, it lit me up. The weight I always carry on my chest slowly goes away when we're together. I don't understand this effect you have on me, but I like it."

He stops talking, but I wait to see if he'll begin again. I want to do something I know I shouldn't do. He needs it though. I wrap my arms around him. He's facing forward, and my arms are around him from the side. My cheek rests against his shoulder. I settle there to see his reaction. He angles his body toward mine and hugs me back. At first the hug is a little tight, but he releases a minimal amount. I can breathe better now.

We start rocking back and forth ever so slightly. Who started it first, I don't know. It's soothing, as if in a rocking chair or being held in my mom's arms when I was little. We slowly loosen our grip but continue hugging as we fall back against the couch. Somehow his head is lying on my chest, but I'm okay with it. My heartbeat should be comforting to him. I wonder how long it has been since he allowed someone to actually hold him.

After several minutes, I whisper, "James, are you all right?" No response. *Is he sleeping?* He's breathing heavily. His weight is mostly on me, so it's not the most comfortable position anymore. Very carefully, I release my arms. I push him off me slightly in order to get out from under him. Finally, I'm off the couch but still trying to hold him up with every piece of strength I have. I gently lower him onto his back.

I elevate his legs so he's lying in a straight line. I place a pillow under his head and pluck the burgundy cashmere blanket off a corner of the sofa. Before I drape the blanket on him, I stand there and stare. I'm shaken by how stunningly handsome he is when sleeping. Even with spiked, unruly hair. I keep telling myself I shouldn't be having these thoughts and feelings, but it's too hard to ignore them. I kneel next to him and gently rub his cheek. I whisper, "Sweet dreams, James."

Ten minutes pass as I watch over him. Should I stay and wait for Alexa, or leave and go back to the bar? Before I go, I need to clean up the glass and try to wipe down the wall. It smells like vodka in here. I find cleaning products and a garbage can in the kitchen. After a few minutes, the mess is cleaned up. The smells of vodka and cleaning liquid circulate the room. I hope Alexa isn't too pissed when she sees this.

It's hard to process his loss and depression. I've had a lot more time to come to terms with my mom's death. No one gets over the death of a loved one. You learn how to cope and accept it. You can heal, but you will never be the same as you were before.

It still feels like yesterday when it all happened though. People say I'm so strong for being able to deal with the outcome of the accident, but deep down I still feel weak. I know I've hidden behind medical school and residency.

There are five stages of grieving the death of a loved one. Denial, anger, bargaining, depression, and then acceptance. James seems to be stuck in between depression and acceptance. He hit rock bottom the night we met. He hit a wall tonight, but maybe now that he let it all out, he can start to move on. It doesn't help to keep everything in. It builds up until you burst.

I rotate in place with my arms swinging back and forth. I'm really lost as to what to do next with him. Would it be better if I'm here when he wakes up? Or should I wait until—

"Stop thinking so much, Lisa."

I freeze when I hear him whisper. I kneel by his side.

He turns his head toward me and speaks in a soft tone, as if he has no energy left. "I know you are racking your brain, trying to figure out what to do with me." He gives me a little smile.

I rub his cheek. "How did you know that? I don't want to leave you. I should wait until Alexa comes back. I cleaned up the broken glass and vodka on the wall and carpet. I'm not sure how Alexa will react when she finds out."

"For some reason, I feel as if I've known you forever. You don't need to leave unless you want to. I'm sorry I ruined your birthday and for being such a dick when I'm upset."

He takes my hand from his face and holds it on his chest. "Now you know my story and why I'm so screwed up. I have no idea what to do next. I'm so lost. I don't know who I am anymore. I'll never be the same as I was before."

When I look at him and he says these things, I want to pull him into my arms again and make it all go away. But I can't. "James, I think the first thing you need to do is sleep now. We can talk about this another time," I say as I run my other hand through his hair.

He looks into my eyes. "How do you do that?"

"Do what?"

"You change your tone of voice. It's almost celestial. It wraps around me like a blanket. Is this your doctor's voice? Your patients must love it when you speak to them."

"I never really noticed. A long time ago someone said that to me, but I just laughed it off. Since then, you're the only one who has mentioned it. Maybe you are the only one who hears it this way."

"Will you help me, please?"

He catches me off guard. How can I say no? "Yes, I'll help you as long as you promise to stop throwing glasses of alcohol at the wall." I poke his chest. Another smile appears briefly, then fades away. "I like it when I make you smile." I want to help him, but I don't know if I can.

He closes his eyes and whispers, "You are the only one who makes me smile."

After a few minutes of me stroking his hair, he falls back to sleep. I carefully remove my hand from his and push up from the couch. I turn around in a circle. I've been here for a good hour, but I didn't really look at the apartment itself. I was too focused on him. We could have been in a dark alley, and I wouldn't have even known or cared.

A long table against a wall in the living room holds several picture frames. I wander over to them and look at each one. One picture is of James, Alexa, and I'm assuming their parents. His family is so attractive. He's smiling along with the others. Out of curiosity, I peek at the other pictures to see if Jessica is in any of them.

I look at James to make sure he is still asleep. I sift through the living room to search for other pictures. There are no others. I snoop in the kitchen, and again nothing. Do I look for pictures in his bedroom? I shouldn't snoop like this. But I can't help it.

My hands shake as I approach one door. I hesitate to open it as I look over to the living room again. One would think I was breaking into a house. I turn the knob, careful not to make any noise. The door slowly opens, but it's dark. I move to the side to let some light shine in. With the low light, I can see light-colored walls with a plain blue comforter on the messy bed. It looks too plain to be Alexa's room. Hers would be decorated in bright, happy colors.

My ears are on high alert for any noise. The last thing I need is for Alexa to come home and find me in here. I look quickly back at the couch to see if there's any movement. I step into his room and turn on the light. My eyes dart quickly to all corners. I see a couple of items on the nightstand next to his bed. Sweat beads on my forehead.

Walking quickly toward the nightstand, I see it's the list of names and the photo of Jessica he mentioned. Picking up the picture is not an option. My stomach turns when I see how beautiful she is, or was. She's the complete opposite of me. Pregnant, tall, long auburn hair, light skin. I'm not sure about her eye color. I'm short and curvy, with light-brown wavy hair, creamy skin, big blue eyes...and I'm not pregnant and never will be. I have feelings for James I don't understand, but when I see this picture, those feelings are completely irrelevant. With that, I turn around and exit the room. Sadness tugs on my heartstrings.

Just as I'm glancing at James one more time, the door opens slowly, and Alexa and Tina mosey into the apartment. I put my finger up to my lips and point to him on the couch.

I tiptoe over to them and whisper, "We should go. He needs to sleep. Alexa, will you be here all night to watch him?"

"Yes. I'll be here. How's he doing? He looked like he was going to destroy something when he walked away from Cloud Nine. I'm so sorry I asked you to go with him when he was in that state of mind. Especially since it's your birthday. It was extremely selfish of me." She hesitates. "You seem to have a special touch when it comes to dealing with him."

I shrug. "He's sleeping like a baby. I hope he is anyway. He threw a glass of vodka at your wall." I point to the wall that was hit. "I tried to clean up the mess. You can still smell it though. The red paint on your wall seems to have survived."

She looks toward the wall and then the couch. "That's the least of my worries." She turns back to me. "I guess he told you what happened? I'm sorry you found out the way you did."

She looks at Tina. "I told Tina what happened to him because she was concerned about you and wondered why he was so upset."

Tina gives me a sympathetic look as she puts her arm around my shoulder for a brief squeeze.

"I'm so pissed off," Alexa continues. "He was in such a good mood tonight. He was actually enjoying himself. I could tell by his facial expressions. Then Jessica's parents were there, standing in front of us." Her face turns a shade of red as she massages her eyebrows. "I can't stand that he's constantly running into walls. He can't seem to find a way out of his maze of misery."

I rub her arm. "He was frantic when we arrived, but he finally broke down and told me everything. It's good he let it all out. He told me he doesn't talk openly about it to anyone. He scared me when he threw the glass at the wall, but I stayed anyway. My own experiences helped me understand him more. Maybe more than other people could."

She looks directly at me with her moss-green eyes. "The only time I have seen him happy lately is when he has been with you. You are changing him somehow. I know it isn't easy for him to be around another woman. Yet you bring out some of the old James we've missed so much." She stops to take a deep breath while tears well up in her eyes. "I try to be the strong one for him, but it's difficult to see him hurt so much. Sometimes I need to cry myself."

She grabs my hands. "Please don't let tonight scare you. Please don't walk away. I know he's not your responsibility and he has a lot of baggage, but maybe you can help him more than any of us can. I don't want you to treat him like a patient. More like a friend. I think he likes it that you are new in his life. You help him see outside his world of pain."

A weird silence settles between us.

I sigh. "I'll do what I can. I'm not a miracle worker. Tonight has been very unusual. I need to think about everything and work on top of it. It'll be hard for me to be in contact with him. I don't want him to think I'm blowing him off. Tell him to call me. He has my number."

I look down at my watch. "I'm sorry, but I really need to get some sleep. I need to work in six hours." I look around the apartment frantically. "Please tell me one of you brought my handbag. I completely forgot about it."

Tina shakes her hand with it hanging off her finger.

"Thank you! My keys are in there."

Alexa hugs me. She feels like a sister to me. I can see how much she loves him.

"Thank you from the bottom of my heart. I know this is a lot to digest and to take on. No matter what happens, I hope we'll see each other again," she says.

I smile at Alexa, and then Tina and I walk to the elevator. How, I wonder, did I get into this situation with James?

The time at work will give me some distance and clarity. Maybe I can convince myself my feelings for James are only sympathy. Nothing else.

# Chapter 24

## Lisa

I drag my feet into the grocery store and see it's closing in fifteen minutes. There's nothing like buying dinner at 9:45 p.m. As I reach over to grab a grapefruit, I hear a familiar voice. My body stiffens. I slowly turn in the direction it's coming from. *It can't be.*

It's Bryant, and he's talking to someone. I crouch behind the grapefruit stand with only my eyes peeking over the top.

I stay there for a few heart-banging seconds. As if watching something in slow motion, a woman appears. He walks up to her, kisses her forehead, and rubs her big belly. Her pregnant belly. The grapefruit slips from my fingers to the ground, rolling toward his feet. He turns in my direction, and our eyes briefly meet. His eyebrows rise.

I start to tremble as my heart leaps out of my chest. He can't see me like this. I leave the basket on the floor, searching for the quickest exit. I take my time as I walk to the cashiers to avoid making a scene. Once I'm near an empty one, I dash through the line.

I run out of the store and feel like I am going to puke on the sidewalk. Why can't I handle this? I'm such a fool. He finally got what he wanted. Another slap in the face, reminding me of what I already know. Is there a hole around here I can crawl into? I run toward my apartment, keys already in my hand for a quick entrance.

After dropping the keys twice, I'm finally in my apartment. I slam the door and throw my handbag across the room. I lean my back against the door as I gradually sink to the floor.

I thought I could handle running into him. It's been so long since

I've seen him. Didn't I come to the conclusion I'm better off without him? But why does it hurt so badly? Here I am trying to help James and other people with their problems, when I can't even deal with my own.

I drag myself to the bathroom, strip off these disgusting scrubs, and get under scalding water. I sit down in the bathtub while the shower streams burn my skin. I have no energy left to stand. I rock myself back and forth, just as I did with James. It's soothing, but I wish Mom were here instead. She would take me for a secret hot fudge sundae.

After a while my skin is almost raw. I'm clean, but I don't feel any better when I get out. I stagger into the bedroom to find my pajamas and see the leather jacket hanging over the desk chair. I put on the pajamas and then the jacket. This jacket will get me through the night.

I wander to the kitchen with a desperate need for a glass of wine. I search and realize there's not one damn drop in this apartment. Funny, I don't want James to drink his sorrows away, but it's the first thing I want to do. Food would be better for me now, but my appetite left the moment I saw the woman's pregnant stomach.

It takes me a few seconds to acknowledge the ringing phone in my handbag. I run to get it. It's probably Tina. She has this weird psychic ability. She always knows when something is wrong.

"Hello." I try to mask my misery.

"Hi, Lisa. It's James."

I want to start crying when I hear his voice.

"Hi, James. How are you?" I ask with a flat tone.

"I'm good. Are you okay? You don't sound good. I hope I didn't wake you."

"No, you didn't wake me." Before I know it, I break down over the phone. I tell him how I saw Bryant with a pregnant woman.

"Lisa, I'm coming over."

*He wants to come over?*

"You don't need to come over. I'll be fine when I wake up in the morning. I'm tired from working so many hours." *I'm completely embarrassed.*

"I'll be there in ten minutes." He hangs up.

I can't help but smile through the tears.

He was serious. The doorbell rings in less than fifteen minutes. I open the door, not caring what I look like. He's already seen me in pajamas. I step aside so he can come in. He saunters into the kitchen and puts a bottle of white wine on the table. He turns around and watches me for a while. *Why does he look so damn good all the time? I want to punch him in the face or maybe rip his clothes off.*

I close the door and walk straight to the wine bottle. I can feel his eyes trailing my every move. Is he waiting for me to break down like he did? I will after I wolf a glass of wine.

I sift loudly through the kitchen drawers, trying to find the corkscrew. When I find it, I slam the drawer shut. James takes the corkscrew from me and proceeds to open the bottle. I grab two wineglasses from the cabinet.

As he unscrews the cork, he says, "Lisa, tell me what's going on in your head. I thought you were over Bryant. That you're better off without him. Why are you so upset he is married or with someone and they're having a baby?"

Just hearing him say it out loud makes me boil. I hear the cork release and wait until he pours me a glass. Within seconds, I swig half the wine down and bang the glass back on the table. I take a deep breath and look up at him. "Now it's my turn to yell."

He nods, "I'm listening. Let it out. You have the stage." He stands there with his legs spread slightly apart, his arms crossed like Superman. I'm sure going to need to be rescued when I'm finished.

"Let's see! Where should I start?" I stomp away from the table. I spin around and give him the evil eye. "When I was fifteen, my mom died in a car accident. Well, I was in the car with her. She died and I survived. I only survived because I decided to wear a damn seat belt that day. What teenager wears a seat belt? For some reason, I wore mine. Why did she die and I survive?" I hit my chest with my fist.

"I got to see it in slow motion—our car slid off the road and crashed into a big tree. Right on Main Street in my town. She died instantly. I tried to get help as fast as I could. Some guy helped me. I sat in his car while he called for an ambulance. I had blood all over my sweatpants. I only remember his eyes—green, like yours. I woke up in the hospital, and they told me my mom died." I squeeze my eyes shut, as I replay every horrible detail of the accident.

I take a deep breath. "I wore my seat belt, the kind that only had a lap belt. Due to the pressure of hitting the tree, I was severely injured by the seat belt. That's why I had blood all over my sweatpants.

"The doctor told me one of my ovaries was severely damaged and had to be removed. Then he proceeded to tell me my uterus was severely injured as well. It was not removed, and I had surgery to repair it. Due to the injury, the doctor, and many more after that, told me I will never be able to have children. So my mom died, and I found out I couldn't have kids all in one fucking day."

I walk back to the table and drink the rest of the wine. I go to refill it, but my hands are shaking. James gently removes the wine bottle from my hands and stuffs the cork back it. He puts it in the refrigerator. *He's the one who loves his alcohol, and now he's taking it from me. Real nice.*

"They told us if that guy wasn't there to call for an ambulance as quickly as he did, I could have died along with her. That was a lot to handle for a teenager. Why did I wear my seat belt? Why didn't she wear hers? Why did I survive?" I spew questions out like they taste disgusting on my tongue. I growl in frustration as I pull on the collar of my leather jacket.

"At that young age, I didn't fully understand. But as I got older, I had to come to terms with it. It was much harder to accept once I understood. Ever since then, I've felt like I'm never going to be good enough. No man will ever love me, because I'm broken.

"I've been to countless psychiatrists, psychologists, and

therapists to help me get through this. They helped me in many ways, but there wasn't much more they could do for me. Well, other than putting me on medication. I refused to go on meds. I'll never fully accept the outcome, but I've learned to deal with it." I walk over to the sofa and start fluffing the pillows roughly because I can't stand still. James follows me into the living room but doesn't interrupt.

"I never want someone to feel like I do. I want to help people who have gone through a horrible experience. That's why I vowed to become a psychiatrist.

"Bryant was the first guy who made me feel something physical. We had a good connection, so I let go of my fears. I saw the flags the first months we dated. He loves kids. Of course he does—he's a pediatrician. I tried to ignore it. After we were dating for a while and I thought we were serious about one another, I broke down and told him. He was mad I didn't say anything, but he promised he didn't care as long as we were together. I thought he understood and meant he loved me." I throw the last pillow across the room, just missing a lamp. *It's probably more exhilarating to throw a glass of vodka at a wall.*

"Long story short, we drifted apart. I decided to confront him, but before I could, he dumped me. He admitted he'd met someone else. He thought he could accept that I couldn't have children, but he was wrong. He wanted a family of his own."

I walk across the room and pick up the pillow and toss it back on the couch. "So you see, I'll never be enough for any man. I'm not saying there aren't men out there that don't want kids. But it sure does feel like it. My married friends all have kids now. One big fucking happy family. I can't provide that to anyone."

I rub my forehead to relieve the pounding in my head. "It kills me, knowing I'll never have kids. I'm broken—I always will be. I never let myself fall for anyone until Bryant came along. We had instant chemistry and just clicked from the second we met. But it was all an illusion. It was probably just sexual attraction. But what did I know then? Or now? I have nothing else to compare it to. I don't know what love feels like.

"Only when I met you did I realize Bryant and I were never in love." My eyes drift over to James as I play with the zipper of my jacket. He looks terrified.

# Chapter 25

## James

My feet are stuck to the ground. Did I hear her correctly? Can this even be possible? Was she the one I helped at that car accident years ago? I've wondered this several times but just ignored my instincts. It doesn't matter, because I need to listen to what else she's saying. She's crying and talking, so it's hard to understand her sometimes.

She's throwing pillows and roaming around the living room and kitchen. I finally comprehend what she's focusing on. She can never have children. I understand now. It's not just the death of her mom she suffers from. This explains a lot.

It's so quiet right now I could hear a pin drop. As seconds go by, she begins to play with her jacket zipper. Zipping it up and down. Then I notice it. She's wearing my old leather jacket! After all this time, she still has it. I'm completely blown away. I didn't notice it when I arrived.

She looks up at me, and I see it now. Her eyes are just as radiant blue and sad as they were years ago. I knew it was her, but I didn't believe myself.

How do I approach this without sounding like a lunatic? I've always wondered what happened to the girl I helped that day. Now she's standing in front of me. This would explain the strange bond between us. We have met before.

As I stare at her, I know she doesn't want me to show pity. What I'm going to say right now will be far from it.

"James, why does it look like you have seen a ghost? Did I say something wrong?"

I close my eyes to calm myself. "The day of your accident, was it on Valentine's Day?"

"Yes. How could you possibly know that?" she asks with fear in her tone.

"Was it bad weather? On a Saturday morning?"

"Yes. James, how the hell do you know these things? You can't possibly know! Who are you?"

I don't respond.

"Fucking answer me!" she demands, shaking her head, moving a few steps away from me. Her eyes pierce mine as she waits for an explanation.

I lift my hands up in peace. "Please don't be angry or frightened. Just listen and let me explain myself. Okay?"

She nods and crosses her arms over her chest.

"I was on my way to work that Saturday morning. I told you I worked at the gas station on Main Street. Remember when I mentioned it to you? It's not too far from where the accident occurred."

She lifts her chin. I guess that means yes.

"I was in a rush because I thought I was going to get fired if I arrived late again. It was snowing heavily and cold as hell. It was quiet on the roads. I was driving down Main Street when a black truck pulled onto the road without stopping. Your car lost control and hit a tree head on. I drove around your car and saw you trying to run away. By impulse, I drove up next to you to help you. The leather jacket you're wearing now is the one I gave you."

She looks down at it and wraps it tighter around her.

I focus on a speck on the wall as I recall everything. "I put you in my car to help keep you warm. I ran to the nearest house to call for an ambulance. When I got back, you were shaking and crying about your mom. I went to check on her, but fear took over when I saw her. I had no idea how to help her or you. I just prayed the ambulance would get there in time.

"When I got back to the car and opened the door, you were

screaming about blood. There was blood all over your sweatpants." My eyes connect with hers. "You looked at me the way you are now. I remember your eyes. They have been engraved in my memory ever since. I've thought about your accident several times since we met a couple of weeks ago. I believed I was going crazy, thinking you were her." A chill runs up my spine.

"I've always wondered what happened to you and your mother. I've always questioned my actions. Did I get help in time? Was it okay to have you sit in my car? Should I have pulled your mother out of the car? Were your injuries worse because of me? I read the newspaper for days to see if your accident was reported."

She interrupts me. "I tried to find out who you were. I searched this jacket to see if your name was in it. I went to the police station and asked around. Your name wasn't in the police reports, which I found very strange, since you were a witness."

The need to touch her is becoming too strong. I continue to distract myself. "After that experience, I vowed to become a doctor. I never wanted to be in that type of situation again. I felt so helpless. I'm sorry your mother died and you had to experience something so terrifying. And your injuries...I wish I could have done more for the both of you." Every muscle in my back and shoulders is tight.

She drifts toward me. Her watery eyes look up to find mine. "I can't believe it's you. I waited for you for so long. Never, ever apologize for helping us. There was nothing that would have saved her. However, you saved my life. I could have bled to death if you weren't there to help me. Tina called you my guardian angel. I believed that then, and now more than ever."

She leans up to me and pulls me into her arms.

*She feels so good in my arms. She is so petite but fits perfectly against me.* I instantly relax.

"I remembered your eyes. They were so big and green. I didn't remember your hair color, how tall you were, nothing. Your eyes were what stood out the most. There were times when I thought I saw your eyes. But I always figured I was imagining things. It flashed through my head when I met you. But I put it behind me like you did. I believed it would be impossible."

She leans away and props one hip and shoulder against the wall. "Now I can finally say thank you after all these years. The only thing I had from you was your jacket."

"I can't believe you still have it. I'm surprised it wasn't thrown away."

"This jacket has been my sanctuary. When I'm sad, angry, lonely, or in need of comfort, I put it on. It makes me feel safe. Maybe it sounds stupid, but I needed something to hold on to at that time. So much changed. The smell of your jacket was so soothing. A mixture of leather and pine. It doesn't smell like that anymore, but I think I would still recognize it if I smelled it again. After all these years, I couldn't part with it. Call it my security blanket." She smiles warmly.

"I tried to forget about the jacket when I was with Bryant. I had to learn to lean on something else. It worked for a while. But as soon as we broke up, I immediately pulled it out of the closet. I've been wearing it again ever since. Please don't make me give it back," she pleads, gripping the jacket tightly.

Knowing what this jacket means to her, I would never take it back.

She leans against the wall. She lowers her head and puts her face in her hands, laughing like she's crazy. "Why is this happening? I don't understand."

I move carefully toward her. "Don't be afraid. I'm just as confused as you are." I pull her hands away from her face and pick her chin up with my finger. Her tear-filled eyes look into mine, and I feel it. There's a connection between us I can't ignore anymore. *We* can't ignore.

I close the gap between us as her eyes close. My thumbs caress her cheeks as I lower my lips to hers. She's resistant for a split second, then starts to reciprocate the kiss. Her hands move up my arms. She dips her tongue into my mouth as my tongue desperately searches for hers. Our mouths are dancing to a tune I have never heard. We kiss in unison without hesitation, drenched in the heightened emotions swirling around us.

She wakes up my body with her taste, her lips, her touch. I don't want to stop. I lift her so her legs are around my waist. I push my body against hers as we lean against the wall. She responds by rubbing against mine. I kiss a path down her neck, hearing her breath catch.

Then the moment is over. She breaks our kiss, so I lower her down. She presses her fingertips to her lips and looks away from me. "I'm sorry, James. I can't do this. I'm not in the right mind, and neither are you. We're both overwhelmed by what we have discovered. I don't want to ruin anything between us by getting involved this way. You are still grieving, and I'm upset over seeing Bryant."

She looks back at me. "I have thought about kissing you so many times. When our lips briefly touched at Cloud Nine, I knew I was in trouble. It was so hard to push you away just now. If we want to do this, it has to be for the right reasons—because we care for each other, we are attracted to each other. Not because we are sad, lonely, and horny."

I exhale deeply. "We also need to digest all this. It makes me happy it was you all those years ago. I can't comprehend how odd this all is. What are the chances we would ever meet again? And why now?"

She puts her arms around me and squeezes. Her touch is comforting. I breathe in the fresh scent of her hair as I hug her back.

"Things happen for a reason. If you didn't get in that car accident, maybe I wouldn't have become a doctor. I wouldn't have met Jessica. I wouldn't be suffering so much, and I wouldn't have met you, and I wouldn't be standing here with you right now. If you didn't get into the accident, you would have a mother, you would be able to have children, you might not have become a doctor, you wouldn't have met Bryant, and you wouldn't be standing here with me. No matter what the scenario, would our paths have crossed anyway?" My head is fucked up thinking about all of this. I need a glass of the wine I brought.

"James, I think we need some time to come to terms with it. Thank you so much for coming over here to rescue me. I feel so much better." She traces her fingers up and down my back, which causes my entire body to quake.

"You would think with all the therapy I've had, and medical school too, I'd be able to handle all of this more calmly. Getting lost in hospital work was my coping mechanism. Seeing Bryant with that woman made me snap. You called just when I needed you. Maybe our paths are crossing now because it's the time we need each other the most."

Her arms release me. "Even though I want you here, I need you to leave now. I'm exhausted." She rubs her eyes.

"Okay. Anything you want, I'll do it."

"When you held my hand at the park and your lips brushed mine at Cloud Nine, I felt our connection then. Even though the kiss was an accident, it was the best one I ever had...well, until our kiss now. I felt it all over me. I don't think I can trust myself if you stay here any longer."

I nod and stuff my hands in my pockets. I know she's right, but my body is protesting.

I'm pretty exhausted after all of this too. I lean down and wrap my arms around her again. *I can't resist hugging her. I want to hold her all night.* I kiss her forehead and move away first.

"I always thought your eyes were beautiful, Lisa. I think it even more, knowing who you are now. Don't worry. We'll figure this out together. Get a good night sleep. You deserve it. I'll call you soon." I ease myself toward the open door.

"Thanks. You really helped me tonight...and all those years ago. You are such a good man. I'll be thinking of our kiss when I fall asleep tonight. Sleep well." She blows me a kiss as she leans against the side of the open doorway.

I walk away and can't let myself turn around. If I do, I will run back to her and wrap her in my arms again. Kissing against the wall wouldn't be the only thing we would do. She needs space. But I don't know how long I can wait. She woke up something inside me I didn't think existed anymore.

I open the door to find Alexa on the couch watching TV. She turns her head and sees my face. She sits up. "What happened? You look like shit."

I walk over to the couch and drop onto it. "You will never believe it. I don't even know where to start."

She sits on the coffee table, facing me. I explain everything. She sits there with a look of shock and disbelief.

"This is just fucking weird...but very exciting. Like you were meant to be in each other's lives and have influenced each other's paths in life."

"How have I influenced her life?"

"You possibly saved her life. She could have bled to death if you weren't there to help. And because of that situation, you wanted to become a doctor."

I think about it for a moment.

"After we discovered everything, I kissed her."

Her eyes open wide. She smacks me on the arm. "What the hell did you say? You kissed her? Holy shit! That's awesome! How was it?" she squeals.

"It was like our mouths were made for each other. It was a jolt to my heart I never felt before. I haven't desired another woman since I met Jessica. Now that I've kissed Lisa, I'm not sure I can walk away. It scares the shit out of me. It would have gone further, but she stopped us. She thinks we aren't in the right mind-set. I was disappointed, but she's right. She thinks I'm still dealing with Jessica's death, and then figuring out I was the one at the accident...it's too much for one night."

Alexa taps her chin. "She's a smart girl. I think one kiss is good for now. You definitely have chemistry. Take it slow. She's opening you up again. We're all so relieved someone is finally getting through to you."

"I need a drink. Come into the kitchen with me."

She follows me and sits at the table. I stand in front of the open refrigerator. I debate whether I should have a beer or just water.

I want alcohol but I take a bottle of water instead and lean against the counter. "What if I just want her because I haven't had sex in a long time?"

"Do you really think this is only your hormones acting up? There's so much physical and emotional chemistry between you two, I can practically smell it." She pinches her nose.

"If something else happens between us, she wants it to happen when we both want it for the right reasons. I respect her for that. I don't know what I want. I love being around her. She makes me happy and helps me look forward to the future."

"I wish I had the answers for you, but I don't. This is something you need to figure out yourself. I don't want either one of you to get hurt in the end."

"I still miss Jessica and Jacob. That will never change. I've felt guilty even thinking about Lisa. Am I letting them go?" I push off the counter in frustration. "I thought I would feel guilty after kissing her, but I didn't. If anything, I wanted to kiss her more. After what we discovered, I felt it was right. We're more than a mere coincidence."

I walk over to the window above the kitchen sink. I gaze outside at the stars. What do the stars have planned for me? "Could I start a relationship with her? I vowed I would never love someone again, nor have another child. I couldn't take the chance of it happening again. I would never survive, Alexa. I can't do it again."

"Maybe it would work with Lisa. She can't have children," she says.

I shoot her a dirty look. "That's not a reason to have a relationship with her. I can't be with her just because it's safe. She deserves so much more. I don't want to give her false hope. She already feels like she isn't enough for anyone to begin with."

She rises from her chair. "Why don't you see what happens next. Mom and Dad are coming over for dinner Friday night. Why don't you ask her to join us? Do you know what her schedule is?"

"No. You know how hard I worked as a resident. She works like a dog. Isn't it weird to ask her to have dinner with Mom and Dad? Doesn't it sound like, *I want you to meet my parents*?"

"We aren't in college anymore. Screw that stuff. Now that you know she was the one from the accident, I feel we already know her. She also lived so close to us when we were kids. It's okay. Take the chance. What do you have to lose? The old James never took chances. Maybe it's time to change that."

I crush the water bottle and throw it in the recycling bin. "I'll wait until tomorrow morning. I'll send her a text message and then leave it up to her. I don't know how to do this anymore. All I know is it feels right and I don't want to walk away."

# Chapter 26

## Lisa

I sit on the sofa, staring at the same magazine article regarding a new depression medication for fifteen minutes. I slept like hell last night. My head was swirling like a typhoon over the connections in our past. And our kiss. It was so sensual, so steamy. He really knows how to kiss, or we have great chemistry, or both. There was nothing awkward about it. Usually, the first real kiss, not accidental, can be a little strange. But with James, it was as if we have kissed before. We knew each other's movements beforehand. It was so smooth, and he tasted luscious. I was close to giving in, but I knew it was a bad idea. What if he was thinking about Jessica when he was kissing me? What if he did it because we were both overwhelmed?

I can't think about this anymore. I drag myself into the kitchen. While I wait for the coffee machine to finish, I list the things I need to do today on a piece of paper. My energy level is at an all-time low.

I need to check my phone. Maybe Tina responded to the text I sent her. I wrote I needed to talk to her as soon as possible. I place my coffee cup on the table and plunk onto the sofa. I pick up my phone and see two new text messages, one from Tina and one from James. I can't help myself. I read the one from him first.

*Hi Lisa, I hope you are better today. I don't know your schedule but wanted to ask if you would like to come over on Friday night. My parents are coming for dinner. Alexa is going to cook for us. No pressure at all. I'll leave it up to you. If you have time and you want to come, dinner is at seven p.m. I hope you can make it. Thinking of you, James.*

I drop the phone onto the sofa like it burnt my hand. Isn't it kind of weird to meet his parents? I need to talk to my sister. I don't even read her text message. I dial her work number. I shouldn't call her at work—

"Lisa? What's up? Is everything okay?"

"Well, I sent you a text message saying I needed to talk to you. I didn't read your response though. Do you have a few minutes to talk?"

"Yeah, sure. Let me go somewhere quiet. I'll go hide in a conference room. Give me a few seconds." I bite my thumb while waiting. "Okay, what's up?"

"It's about James. I'll tell you the short version because I know you have to work."

"This sounds juicy already. Do tell."

I wrap my favorite seafoam-green fleece blanket over my legs. The next minutes are consumed with me telling her what happened with Bryant and how James came to my rescue. And then I divulge the most important detail. That James was the one from the accident.

"Holy shit! I love this. I can't believe he's the mysterious guy from the accident." She giggles like a little girl. "It's fate. You are meant to be together in some way. Whether as a couple or just good friends, it doesn't matter. The question is, do you have feelings for James, other than a friend?"

"Well—" I hesitate as I pick the lint off the throw pillows and blanket.

"Don't *well* me. I want honesty now. No, you know what? I already know the answer. I just want to hear you say it."

"Fine." I pull my knees to my chest. "When I first met him, he was too drunk and rude. The morning after the bar incident kind of changed my feelings toward him. I didn't know exactly what those feelings were. Maybe sympathy, empathy, attraction. Or all of the above. After we ran into each other at the park, I noticed him more. I just thought it was because I haven't had any contact with a man in a long time. He's hard to miss when he's sober. As we get to know each other more and more, I adore him as a person. He's a good man. What happened to him was tragic."

"I feel like I'm listening to a romance audiobook. The anticipation is killing me."

"Behind his sadness, I can see another part of him. He makes me laugh. He's devoted and very kind. When he came to my apartment right away last night, it showed me he really cares about me. It was nice to be taken care of for once. When he kissed me, that cinched the deal. It's evident we both have feelings for each other. More than I would like to admit. I stopped us before it went further."

She interrupts me by screaming, "What did you say?"

I swear I felt my hair blow away from the phone.

"He kissed you and you stopped him? Are you out of your mind? You could've had some awesome sex, or at least foreplay."

I toss the large lint ball on the table and throw the blanket off my legs. "Tina, this is not about sex. I'm scared about how I feel and the weird connection we have. I don't know if I should be freaked out or take it as a blessing. He's also still in mourning. Let's not forget about that."

"I don't care. This is freaking fantastic. I have a good feeling about this. It's natural. Please, for once in your life, take a chance and see where it goes. You can't ignore the connection. You both need each other right now."

"Hey, I took a big chance on Bryant, and look where that got me."

"I know, but James is completely different from Bryant. Thank God! Bryant was an asshole. James helped you get over him and see it as it truly was. This situation is different and worth the chance. I always knew Bryant wasn't good for you, but you had to learn that by yourself."

"I know. Thanks for reminding me." It's a hot poker in my stomach every time she says that. "Anyway, James asked me to go to dinner at his apartment on Friday night. Alexa will be cooking, and his parents will also be there. Is it weird for him to ask me to come over when his parents are there?" I bite my lower lip.

"No. Not really. You know him even more now. Who cares if his parents will be there. Be confident and go. Do you have that day off?"

I sit on the edge of the sofa and stare at my calendar. "I'm scheduled to work during the day. I have the late shift on Saturday. Maybe I'll wait until Friday to make a decision."

"I'm already excited to hear the next chapter of this book," she says.

"I'm glad we are so entertaining for you." I laugh. She has always been a good influence as well as my cheerleader.

"Sorry, I need to go. I have a stupid meeting in a few minutes. I'm not supposed to be on the phone anyway, but it was totally worth the chance of getting caught."

"No problem. Talk to you soon."

"Follow your gut, Lisa. It never lies."

My gut says, *Go for it!*

# Chapter 27

## James

It's 6:30 p.m. on Friday, and I haven't heard from Lisa. I guess she isn't coming. I'm sure she has been working nonstop. That's why she hasn't responded. Right? I was hoping she would call and surprise me last minute. I want to give her space if she needs it, even though I want to see her more and more each day. Something changed within me that night. I wake up in the morning without so much dread. My sadness is decreasing. Because of her.

"Alexa, can I help you with something? You're doing everything. I need to keep busy."

She stops chopping the peppers with annoyance. "I said no, like the million other times you asked me. Stop being so anxious. I have a feeling she'll show up."

"What if it freaked her out when I mentioned Mom and Dad will be here? Or what if she never got the text message?"

"Now you sound like a girl. Would you please relax." She waves a knife toward me.

"Sorry. I can't stop thinking about her. This yearning to see her or hear her voice has me unhinged." I groan as I crack my knuckles. "Is it wrong of me to feel this way?"

"First of all, stop cracking your knuckles. It's disgusting. Second, no, it's not wrong. You deserve another chance in life. You haven't been living. You are finally coming back to us. Have some faith." She wipes her hands on her red apron. "Mom and Dad should be here soon. You know they are always early." She pulls plates out of the cabinet and hands them to me. "Set the table please. That'll keep you busy for five minutes."

When the doorbell rings, I almost drop a plate. My heart rate jumps up a notch as I walk to the door. *Please let it be Lisa.*

"Hi, Mom and Dad. How are you?" I flash a fake smile to mask my disappointment.

"We are good, sweetie! How are you after all this craziness in your life?" She shakes my shoulders in excitement. "You look really good. Like your old self with new clothes. It's good to see you in a pair of jeans for once." Mom wraps me into a big hug.

Dad pats me on the back.

"Thanks, Mom...I guess. Did I dress that bad back then?"

"It's not that. You seemed a bit stiff in your pressed khakis and starched shirts. You looked so formal all the time. Jeans make you look more relaxed and casual. It's always fun to mix things up a little bit."

"Sure, Mom. Whatever you say." I close the door. "Dinner is almost ready. Alexa has outdone herself again, even though I have no idea what she's making. She can tell you herself."

They walk toward the kitchen to greet Alexa. "Oh, by the way Mom and Dad, if by small chance Lisa comes, please don't bring up the accident and our connection unless she does. Let's make this night casual. I want us to have fun."

Mom pretends to zip her lips.

We're all in the kitchen, laughing, when the doorbell rings. I try to act calm and cool, but inside my stomach flips over. I open the door, and she stands there, wearing the leather jacket and holding a bottle of white wine. Seeing her with that jacket on makes my stomach calm down. It gives me hope she feels the same way. I flash her a huge smile.

"You're here. I assumed you weren't coming, since I didn't hear from you."

"Sorry. I had decided not to come, but as the day went on, I changed my mind. I needed to see you...I wanted to see you," she whispers.

I can't help but be sucked in by her beauty, not paying attention she's still standing in the hallway.

"Can I come in?" She giggles.

"Of course, but not before I give you this." I pull her into a hug and kiss her cheek. I whisper in her ear, "I'm so glad you came." I grin and step to the side. "Nice jacket, by the way."

"Thanks. I got it from someone very special a long time ago." She winks as she walks in the door.

We finally acknowledge everyone and notice they have been watching us. "Lisa, you already know Alexa." I motion to Alexa. "Mom and Dad, this is Lisa."

Mom doesn't hesitate to give her a hug. "Well, aren't you the prettiest little thing."

Dad shakes her hand. "Nice to meet you, Lisa. Glad you could make it. We've heard so much about you."

"Thank you, Mr. and Mrs. Kramer. It's nice to meet you both as well."

"Please call us Kathleen and John. Mr. and Mrs. Kramer is too formal for us," Mom says with an animated smile.

"Alexa, sorry I'm late." Lisa gives Alexa a hug and kiss.

"You aren't late. You are just on time. I knew you would come."

Lisa stands in front of her with one hand propped on her hip. "You look like a chef on the Food Network channel, with your red apron and gourmet kitchen. Do you always look cute and fashionable? You need to give me some fashion and cooking tips."

"Thanks. I try...you never know who you will meet." Alexa giggles and turns back toward the stove."

"Oh, here's a bottle of white wine. I hope you like white wine."

"I like any wine, darling. Thanks. Can you please put it in the fridge for later?"

"Let me do that for you." I take the bottle from Lisa's hand and place it next to a bottle of champagne in the fridge.

Lisa leans over the stove. "Everything smells so delicious. I'm starving. Hospital food is nothing to write home about. Actually, it's pretty disgusting. This meal will be a real treat. What are you making?"

"Tuna carpaccio for the appetizer, Thai vegetables with chicken and rice for the main dish, and for dessert, homemade lemon sorbet."

"Wow. I wasn't expecting a meal like this. I'll come here more often."

*I hope so.*

"We have a bottle of champagne," I say. "Why don't we open it?" I take it as a yes when Mom pulls out the champagne flutes from the cabinet.

Lisa's smile stretches from ear-to-ear. "I love champagne. I can't even remember the last time I had some."

I carefully open the bottle, praying it doesn't shoot out. I fill the flutes to the rims.

Alexa grabs her flute. "Let's make a toast."

"What are we toasting to?" Mom questions brightly.

"Did you buy a new pair of shoes?" I joke.

We laugh.

"Just for that comment, I should throw my champagne in your face. Be nice to me, James." Alexa clears her throat. "Can I please finish?" She raises her flute. "To James and Lisa officially meeting each other after all these years." She looks at Lisa and me. "Cheers to you both. You are lucky to have found one another. Since you have met, little by little the old James is peeking through. We couldn't be happier or more thankful."

Lisa and I clink our glasses together with our eyes locked. The intimate moment is interrupted when everyone else tries to clink our flutes.

I put my arm around Lisa and kiss her forehead. "Are you all right?" I whisper.

"Yes, I'm better than all right. Your family is very warm and friendly. I feel comfortable here."

"I hope so. They seem to be fascinated with you," I say as my parents walk to the dinner table.

To prove my words, Mom says with enthusiasm, "Lisa, come sit at the dinner table and talk to us." Her bracelets tap on the table as she seats herself. "I hear you are a psychiatrist. That has to be an interesting medical field. I hope it's not too depressing."

Lisa walks over and sits across from Mom. I proceed to sit at the end of the table between them.

"It can be a bit draining at times. But there are days when I see the medical team has made positive progress with a patient. It makes it all worthwhile. I doubt I'll work in a hospital once my residency is over. I would love to open my own practice one day." She pulls her chair closer to the table. "My goal is to specialize in helping people work through traumatic experiences or losses or something related. This can be done one on one or in a group setting. Have you ever heard of post-traumatic stress disorder, PTSD?"

"Yes, just a little bit. Soldiers suffer from something like that when they come back from serving in a war or battlefields. Correct?" Mom says.

"Yes, that's correct. However, it's not just an experience like that. It could range from losing someone close to you, having some kind of serious accident that you were directly involved with or witnessed, domestic violence, or being a rape victim. There are many reasons why someone can suffer from that."

She sips her champagne. "I'm sure James has told you about our connection with the car accident."

She smiles at me and looks back at Mom. "Because of the accident, I've dealt with similar problems common to PTSD. It took me years of therapy to come to terms with issues caused by the accident and to deal with the death of my mom. I still hate driving in a car. I had one specific therapist who really helped me, and I couldn't be more thankful I found her. I still have bad days after all these years, but I know how to cope with them. Since then, I decided to attempt a career in medicine. I want to help people in need, as my therapist helped me."

I sip some champagne as I watch them talk to each other with ease. I realize Lisa still has her jacket on.

I rub her knee. "Should I hang your jacket? Sorry I didn't ask you when you arrived."

She shakes her head. "No thanks. I'd like to keep it on if you don't mind." She smiles.

Mom grabs Lisa's hand. "We are sorry you lost your mother. We were speechless—weren't we, John?—when James told us what you both figured out. What are the chances? We remember the moment he came back home after the accident. He was pretty upset and a little bit in shock. It's amazing you still have his leather jacket." She reaches over and brushes her thumb across the jacket sleeve. "He always wondered what happened to you both. We tried to help him find information regarding the accident, but nothing was in the papers."

After Mom stops talking, Lisa looks at me. I can't read her face. Maybe she's having a moment of clarity. Talking about it openly with other people confirms it was really us. It gives *me* clarity.

"Mom, can you help me bring the food to the table?" Alexa yells from the kitchen.

"I can do it, Kathleen. You stay right here." Lisa gets up from the table and walks into the kitchen.

"Thanks, dear."

My eyes follow her as she walks away, and Mom notices.

She nudges me with her elbow. "She's really nice and quite beautiful. I can see by the way you look at her that there's chemistry between you two. Enjoy it." I don't say anything, but I know she is right.

I stand up to help Lisa place the dishes on the table. I whisper into her ear, "I guess Alexa has good timing. I hope it didn't upset you we were talking about your accident. Your face was hard to read."

"Actually, it did the opposite. It's really nice to be open about it. I feel like I can be myself in front of your family. It's such a breath of fresh air to talk freely about it."

# Chapter 28

## Lisa

"Let's eat, everyone! I'm starving." Alexa prances over to the table while taking off her red apron.

Minutes pass by as we eat. The only sound in the room is from the silverware scraping the dishes.

"Alexa, this is absolutely delicious. You've outdone yourself this time," Kathleen proudly says.

"Thanks, Mom. You taught me how to cook." Alexa reaches over and gives her a hug. I can see how they really love each other. It makes me miss my family.

Kathleen then puts her hand on James's arm. "James, we have a surprise. We are staying at the Snow Peak Lodge in Killington for Christmas and New Year's. We haven't gone there since your accident. You never had time when you were going to medical school. Would you be interested in going with us this year? Would it scare you to try to ski again? I wonder if you would be able to hold a ski pole securely with your left hand."

I chime in with a smile. "I used to go to Killington all the time. I think the last time I was there was when I was a freshman in college. I love skiing. I skied as much as I could back then." I pause to wipe my mouth with a napkin. "James, what kind of accident did you have? Was it bad?"

He angles in my direction. "Yes, it was bad. I was going into my last semester at Johnson College. The college we both went to." He squeezes my hand. "Mom and Dad, did I tell you that? We both went to the same college and medical school."

"Seriously? How spooky," she says as she shivers. Alexa seems to have her mother's personality.

"Anyway, we always stayed at the Snow Peak Lodge. Alexa and I went out to the slopes early that morning."

I'm listening attentively and choke on my champagne when I hear he was hit by another skier and a girl named Lisa, with black hair, helped him before the ski patrol came. I had black hair at the time.

Alexa interrupts and explains how she was at his side, crying. I remember Alexa. I thought she was his girlfriend.

He describes the severity of his injuries and why he couldn't become a surgeon. He keeps talking, but I can't hear him anymore because my ears are buzzing. I stare into space as my heart races and my stomach turns.

"Lisa, what's wrong? Are you feeling sick?" James asks as he touches my shoulder.

"Yes, I'm feeling nauseated. I think I need to go home. Can you please call me a cab?" I try to stand up, but my legs are like rubber.

"No, I'll drive you home myself. Let me get your handbag. I'll grab a bag in case you need to throw up." He rushes into the kitchen.

"I'm so sorry, Alexa. Maybe I'm allergic to something. I'm so embarrassed." I stand up and steady myself. It's taking everything in me not to lose it right now.

"I hope it wasn't something I cooked," Alexa says. "Please feel better. James will take care of you. Come back soon." She rubs my back.

"Nice to meet you, John and Kathleen. I probably picked up a bug or something from the hospital."

"Do you have everything, Lisa?"

I look around and see he has my handbag, and I'm still wearing my jacket.

"Yes. Are you sure I can't just take a cab? I don't want to ruin your evening with your family." I extend my arm to take my handbag, but my hands shake profusely. His eyebrows squeeze together in confusion. He yanks it away.

"You are not taking a cab," he says with a sharp tone.

"Fine, then please take me home as fast as possible."

James drives very carefully. He probably thinks I'm going to throw up. That would be the least of our problems. I don't want him to know the real reason for my actions. We aren't talking, which makes the silence unbearable.

"Do you think it was the food?" he asks.

I nod.

"Do you feel like you are going to throw up?"

I shrug.

"Close your eyes for a little while. We'll be at your apartment in a few minutes."

As he parks his car, I jump out and sprint to my apartment. He's right behind me. As he gets closer, I try to close the door so he can't get in. He's too fast and pushes the door open.

"Lisa, what the hell is going on? I have a feeling it has nothing to do with the food you ate tonight. Talk to me, or please let me help you," he shouts with his hands on his hips.

"James, please go home. I can't be around you right now."

"What the hell is that supposed to mean? Is there something you aren't telling me?" He enters the apartment a few feet and slams the door. "I'm not going anywhere until you tell me what's going on. You know you can tell me anything."

He's in the kitchen while I'm standing in the living room, leaning against the back of the sofa. I drop my head because I can't look at him. Why am I so scared?

"I was there," I whisper.

"Lisa, I can't hear you. Please look at me."

My stinging eyes roam up his body to his face. "I was there, James."

"You were where?" He grimaces.

I stab my chest with my finger. "*I* was the girl who helped you when you had your ski accident. Your head was in *my* lap. *My* fingers were caressing *your* face. It was *my* voice that was soothing to hear," I exclaim.

"I had black hair at the time. Back then I changed my hair color regularly. You are lucky you didn't see it when it matched my pink ski jacket." I cackle nervously.

"I remember Alexa. I thought she was your girlfriend. She wore a bright-red ski suit. She screamed your name over and over again. Every time I heard the name James after that day, I thought about you. Tina was with me. She helped get the ski patrol.

"I'm looking at your eyes right now. When we met those couple of times in the beginning, I would always think of the car accident, then the ski accident. Your eyes and your name. It was all so confusing and seemed completely impossible you could be the same person. I ignored my instincts. Your eyes are so beautifully unique, and now you are standing in front of me. How can you be the same fucking person from both accidents?" I slam my hands on the back of the sofa.

My voice rises. "How did we not recognize each other right away? It's all so frustrating, so frightening. I couldn't believe what I was hearing. Why are our lives so intertwined like this? Why have we only reconnected now? I thought things like this only happened in books and movies."

# Chapter 29

## James

"No! This can't be true," I blurt out, but everything she said *is* true. I shake my head in disbelief.

I take a moment to reflect on that day. "It *was* your voice I remembered. How it soothed me and kept me calm while we waited for the ski patrol. When I slept at your apartment the first time, I remember you talking to me right before I passed out. Your voice was the same. That's why I put your hand on my cheek to say thank you."

I inch toward the living room, careful not to get too close to her.

"These last weeks have been surreal. Everything we've experienced and discovered has yanked me out of my anger and depression. I can't say I'm healed, but I think I'm on my way. Lisa, you're the best thing that has happened to me in a long time." I keep my distance, even though my body aches to touch her.

She looks at me, her eyes wide. "When I brought you home when you were drunk, you looked at me and asked, 'Is it you?' You recognized me but just dismissed it. I'm blown away it's you, but every time I go through it in my head, I'm more mental than I already was." She tugs on her hair. "It's so much to process in such a short amount of time."

My body and mind encourage me to go to her, but I'm not sure she wants me near her. "Don't worry. We're in this together. I agree this seems impossible, but almost comical as well. I believe we're meant to meet properly at this time in our lives. We have helped each other in our past, which helped shape our future. We each have had our ups and downs, but it's our time to be together. Must we analyze it? Or can we just follow our hearts and see what happens?"

"I don't understand how you can be so calm, while I'm freaking out inside." Her arms are wrapped around her stomach, as if trying to give herself comfort.

I want to be the one to keep her safe and warm. Our eyes lock as I step closer. I put my hands on the back of the sofa, caging her in. A single tear drops down her cheek.

I inch forward and whisper, "I have no idea why I'm so calm. What I do know for sure is I want to kiss you." Her chest moves rapidly up and down. My lips skim over her cheek and stop where our lips are bound to touch. "Are you going to stop me again?"

She shakes her head.

In an instant, my lips collide with hers. I run my hands down the sides of her body. She wraps her arms around my back and pulls me against her. I taste the salt from her tears. Where should I touch her first? I have wanted to touch and taste every part of her body for so long now.

We stop to take a breath. I step back to see if she will stop me. Thankfully, the opposite happens. She walks away from the sofa, stops, and turns around. She brings her hands up to her red sweater. I watch her slowly pull it up over her head, revealing a lacy red bra. She drops the sweater to the floor, then reaches forward and opens the bra's front clasp. It slides down her arms and falls to the floor. I memorize every beautiful curve of her body.

"You are beyond perfect."

I follow her lead and pull off my T-shirt, tossing it to where her sweater lies. Her eyes sweep over my bare chest. We both move a few steps closer to one another. She's close enough I can touch her. I reach out and graze her skin with my fingers. She throws her head back and takes a deep breath. I see her neck, and I want to bite it. I grab her and turn her around so her back is against my chest and her head is to the side. I push her hair away and start to kiss and suck on her neck. *I don't care if I leave a mark.*

"I wanted to do this to you on your birthday. I love this part of your body. Your neck and back were completely exposed with the black dress you wore. I could have licked you right there in the bar. It was so hard to keep my hands off you. I fought it, but I can't anymore."

She raises her arm and puts her hand in my hair, pulling me gently, encouraging me to explore her body more.

I reach in front of her and cup her breast with one hand as the other one travels lower. Her body was meant for me. She arches her back while rubbing up against me. I'm going to explode if I don't slow down. I turn her around and kiss her long and slow, this time enjoying every movement we make.

She puts her hands on my shoulders and softly pushes me away. She takes my hands and guides me toward her bedroom. She turns on a small lamp next to her bed. It gives off a soft glow that lets me see all of her.

She proceeds to remove her pants, revealing a matching red thong. My thoughts are jumbled. The only words I can say are "come here" as I sit on the edge of the bed. She smirks and teases me by taking her time as she comes closer. She stands in front of me now, almost naked, and it's all for me. I pull her closer and eagerly kiss her waist. Her hands glide through my hair, pulling me closer.

# Chapter 30

## Lisa

James's mouth is so warm, and his tongue tantalizes my skin in ways that make me tremble. I straddle his legs as his kisses burn a trail up to my mouth—kisses that will emotionally scar me for life. I want to feel that burn everywhere. My bare skin against his.

He stops kissing me so he can watch me unbuckle his belt and then his jeans. "This is all I have been thinking about since the night we kissed. I can't resist you anymore. I tried so hard not to think of you in this way. But every time I see you, you take my breath away. I need to see all of you. Touch all of you." I trace my fingers down his chest and then to his stomach. His ab muscles contract. His body is beyond my every fantasy.

His eyes close, and he whispers, "I want you to touch me. All of me. My body is yours. Look how I respond to your touch. Let your walls fall down."

My body shakes in anticipation as I push his black boxers down. My throat goes dry, and my breathing becomes even more irregular. "You make my body react in ways I didn't think were possible. It's euphoric. You see the real me. I'm not like this with anyone. I have never been like this with anyone."

He traces his fingers up my waist, continuing to my breasts. He teases me by massaging them ever so lightly but then continues up and over my shoulders down to my lower back. Goose bumps chase his fingers as I hope he will explore other parts of my body. He hooks his finger around my thong to pull it down. His eyes look me up and down, making me feel beautiful, not shy or embarrassed.

We can't stop exploring each other with our eyes. Desire explodes in the air as our bodies collide. Our lips meld together, never separating as he lays me on my back. He climbs over me, giving me even more of a glimpse of his delectable body. I like to watch him explore my every curve with his hands and his eyes. His jaw clenches in passion.

He traces my skin with his lips. "You are so much more than I could have ever wished for. I want to devour you, but I also want to slowly enjoy every part of you."

He starts moving down as he kisses one breast at a time and then meanders to my stomach. It's bright enough that he can see my scar. It's not as noticeable as it used to be, but he sees it. When he stops there, my instinct is to cover it. I try to put my hand there, but he stops me. He takes my hand in his and brushes his lips against the scar. It's so touching that tears form in my eyes and something tugs at my heart.

"Don't ever be embarrassed. It's a part of you. You have endured so much. It's a reminder of how strong you are. Don't hide it from me...especially me." His lips linger there, then proceed to move even farther down. *Oh my gosh, I am going to lose my mind.*

"Yes, James. Your lips are pure magic. Don't stop."

He does as I wish, but he takes his time, like I'm his favorite candy. Touching, licking, and sucking until I feel electricity pulse through every inch of my body all the way to my fingers and toes. I see stars shooting before my eyes. I have never felt a sensation so intense.

As I slowly catch my breath, his warm skin brushes against mine as he moves up my body. "James, that was—"

He puts his finger against my lips. "We're not done yet," he whispers.

He hovers over me as he brushes my hair away from my face. We stare deep into each other's eyes, as if reading each other's minds. I feel him against me. Without talking, we know what we both want. Our kisses become more passionate and urgent as we become one.

What is this feeling? I can't put it into words because it's indescribable. Our bodies fit perfectly together. We move slowly at first, but it quickly becomes more urgent. Our eyes stay locked the entire time. Our connection is now so much deeper. It's spiritual. We are heading toward a new level I don't think we can ever turn away from. Well, I know I won't be able to.

This is the second moment in my life when I'm changed forever.

I can only respond to him with my body. He fills me so deliciously. I'm rendered speechless. We both go over the edge explosively. All our inhibitions and worries melt away. I see a prism of color behind my eyelids as tears well. My fantasies were nothing compared to what we just experienced. I finally understand what it means when people say they see fireworks.

# Chapter 31

*James*

My body trembles, and my heart tries to jump out of my chest. That was completely insane, but in the best way imaginable. I have never experienced something so explosive physically or emotionally. She tasted so good and felt perfect around me. This connection between us is from another dimension. Every moment since she found me at the bar has led us to this. My attraction to her goes far beyond the physical.

Her breathing has finally slowed, as has mine. I slide to her side and put my arm around her. "Lisa, I can't find the words to describe how I feel. This month has been life altering for both of us. Somehow our lives have collided and brought us to this point. This is where we are supposed to be. I was afraid of my attraction to you. I tried to resist it. But now I've let all my fears and guilt melt away. This is where I want and am meant to be."

She responds by holding me tighter.

"Are you feeling okay? I hope you don't regret this."

She flips over, facing me with tear-filled eyes.

"Don't cry." I rub my thumb under her eye.

"My tears aren't from sadness or regret. I don't think I could regret this even if I tried." She half laughs. "If you walk out that door right now and say you never want to see me again, I would still never regret this. What we just shared was the most beautiful and amazing experience I have ever had. You are the best thing that has ever happened to me. You see all of me and know all my secrets and insecurities."

She runs her fingers along my jawline. "You have changed my life for the better. You make me look forward to the future. I was living my life like a robot. I want to see where this goes. If you are ready and willing, James... I know it's soon to say all these things to each other. But I feel like we have known each other for so long."

"Let's take it day by day. We need to get to know one another better. I want to learn every little detail about you." I pull her closer, hiding my face in her hair. "My life's a mess, and I need to find my way again. Are you willing to be patient with me? I have issues I need to work through."

"I'm not going anywhere. If you want my help, I'm here."

I pull away and lie on my back. "My career is at a standstill. I have no idea if I can ever be a doctor again...but I don't know anything else. It was my life and passion. I can't live off Alexa and my parents forever. You have your residency and very little time for anything else. We'll figure out something."

She leans her head on my chest. "I know. Now that I have you, I'm never going to let you go. No matter what happens," she says while kissing my chest.

We lie wrapped around each other as if we can't get close enough. The one thing I'm sure of is she is a shining light in my life. I never thought it would be possible for another woman to capture my heart. Well, Lisa has become that woman. She gives me hope. An emotion I thought I would never feel again.

My body sampled her just now, but I want more. A lot more. We won't be getting a lot of sleep tonight, but I don't think we'll be complaining in the morning. She nips at my lips, telling me exactly what she wants and what I crave.

# Chapter 32

## Lisa

I flutter my heavy eyes open. The sun shines happily through the edges of the window shades. Was it all a dream last night? Did we really have sex, and more than once? Something heavy is around my waist. I look down, and relax. It wasn't a dream, because he's sleeping like a baby next to me. His arm hugs my waist tightly while he purrs like a cat again. I will never get sick of that sound.

I carefully sidle out of bed so he doesn't wake up. I grab my thin powder-blue robe from the back of the desk chair. Our clothes pool on the floor by the bed. My stomach flips in delight, remembering his body against mine. It's hard for me to move away from the bed because I can't believe he's here with me.

I leave the bedroom unwillingly and go into the bathroom. I look in the mirror and am surprised. James did not lie. He really does like my neck, because there are a couple of faint marks on one side. Well, this is a first for me. I can't stop myself from giggling. Can I smile any bigger?

I wash my face, brush my teeth, and put my hair up into a messy bun. Maybe James will find this robe sexy. It reaches midthigh and reveals my legs. I leave nothing on underneath. Before I make coffee, I check to see if he is still asleep. He is, so I close the door. There is not much food for breakfast. Maybe I have enough ingredients to make pancakes again.

More clothes are scattered in the living room. I shake my head in delight as I tiptoe into the kitchen. Good, all the ingredients are here. If all goes well, I can make the pancakes and serve them to him in bed.

The pancakes are finished and still no sign of him. I'm thrilled he's sleeping so well. When he awakens, will he act the same as he did last night? After we made love, he was so affectionate, holding me and showering me with kisses. I said I will never regret being with him. I still don't regret it this morning.

I stroll into the bedroom to find him lying awake, holding my pillow. His eyes light up as his smile spreads from ear-to-ear. I could look at his eyes all day.

"Is that smile for me or because I made you pancakes?"

"Both, I promise you." He grins as he sits up.

"How did you sleep? I have no idea how long we slept. It's now nine twenty-five."

"I haven't slept this well in months. I almost feel drunk. You wore me out last night."

I lay the tray full of breakfast in the middle of the bed, just like a picnic. "Since we seemed to have enjoyed our first breakfast full of pancakes, I thought I'd make them again. Well, to be honest, I didn't have anything else."

"I don't care. Pancakes are my favorite, and I'm starving."

"They are the best, aren't they? Diner pancakes are better though. You're easy to please. When is your birthday?" I ask as I shove a huge forkful of syrup-soaked pancakes into my mouth.

"June twenty-first. I already know your birthday."

I can't respond right away because my mouth is still full. I take a sip of orange juice. "How about we ask questions to get to know the little things about each other? Like playing twenty questions."

He bobs his head in several directions as he attempts to answer the question. His first forkful of pancakes was larger than mine.

"Does that mean yes or no?" I laugh at him. "You have so much food in your mouth I can't understand you."

After he swallows, he says, "I get to go first since you already asked me when my birthday is. Do you mind if I get serious?"

"Sure. When the topic is off limits, I'll tell you."

"What happened the day of the car accident?"

I place my dish and coffee on the nightstand. "It's not something I usually talk about. With you, I feel I can tell you anything." He listens without interrupting as I go through the events of that morning. "Normally, I would have moved to the front seat, but I was too lazy. If I moved, I probably wouldn't have put my seat belt back on and I wouldn't be sitting here right now." I cringe and get up to get tissues. "Are you finished with your pancakes?"

"Yes. I'm more interested in what you have to say."

I take the tray of food and set it on the dresser. I sit back on the bed as I face him, pulling a blanket over my lap. "I still remember the pain I felt. I'll never forget my mom's face when I called to her. She didn't respond, but her eyes were still open."

He nods. "I remember."

I rub my stomach and swipe away a tear. "I'm sorry you had to experience something like that."

He takes my hand in his. "Should we talk about something else?"

"I'm fine. It's healthy for me to talk about it. I haven't in a long time." I kiss the top of his hand. My body shivers as I unload every detail and how the doctors told me I could never have children.

"Your seat belt must have been at a very specific angle to cause so much bodily damage."

"That's what everyone said to me. The doctors had never seen or heard of a seat belt causing that severe of an injury. The story about my injuries was written up in a couple of medical journals. I became famous in the medical arena at that time. Lucky me."

He massages my hand. "Would you ever consider adoption? Or—"

"Surrogate mother?" I finish his sentence as I try to pull my hand away. But he won't let it go.

"I'm sorry. Did I say something wrong?" His forehead crinkles from concern.

I sigh. "No, it's not a bad question. You aren't the first person to ask me that. The answer to adoption and surrogate is no. My injuries happened for a reason. I'm convinced I'm not destined to be a mother." I look away from him.

He pulls me to him so my head is lying on his smooth chest. He plays with my hair, which relaxes me.

I look up and smirk. "Wasn't that two questions? I thought you were only allowed one."

"I couldn't help it. I always wanted to know what happened."

"Aren't you sweet. Well, now you know, Curious George." I tap his nose. "My turn to ask you a question. We always talk about me."

"Fine. Fine. Be gentle. There are some things I'm not ready to talk about."

*That's not fair.* We talk about me all the time, but he still doesn't want to discuss personal things about Jessica or Jacob. I will ignore it for the time being.

I dive right in. "Do you talk to any of your friends? You never mention anyone other than Alexa."

His face contorts. I prop up on my elbow with my head resting on my hand.

"I did in the beginning, after they died. My best friend from high school, Matt, was there for me continuously, even if I didn't want him near me. As I said, I was a real asshole. Alcohol was my new best friend. He tried to distract me so I wouldn't drink. I became bitter toward him because he was hovering over me, together with Alexa and my parents. Finally, out of annoyance I told him to leave me alone and I didn't want to see him again. I didn't say it so nicely. He was completely offended and disappointed. He wanted to help me, but all I wanted to do was be left alone. I haven't seen or heard from him in over six months." He takes a deep breath and doesn't say anything else.

"Do you miss him?"

"Sure, I miss him. I'm embarrassed by my behavior. He didn't deserve how I treated him. I'm afraid to approach him. He knows the little things about me, like your accident and mine. I think he would be happy to hear our story."

With my hand, I brush soft strokes over his chest. "Don't you think he would like to hear from you? It has been a long time since you spoke to him. You were best friends for years. It's not easy to sever a friendship like that. You should think about it."

"I'll think about it. But he's probably in Europe somewhere. He's an awesome pastry chef. He always wanted to go to a top cooking school in France or Italy. He applied to several schools but I have no idea if he ever got in. His dream is to own an upscale bakery in New York City someday. Serving unique pastries, cakes, and even chocolate."

"It makes my mouth water just thinking about it. Tina would love him. She's a junkie for anything that resembles dessert. But then again, she eats everything. She has no fear when it comes to food."

"He's been on my mind lately. I hope he's doing well and is happy. I wouldn't be surprised if he talks to my parents or Alexa. Just like they didn't tell me Jessica's parents called, I'm sure they did the same with Matt."

He pats me on the butt. "Why don't we stop here with the questions, even though I'm sure you have more? I need to go to the bathroom."

I wiggle away from him and prop myself up on my knees. "I need to go to the bathroom too, but you can go first. I'll bring the dishes to the kitchen."

He kisses me tenderly. "Thanks for breakfast and for last night."

He rises from the bed, and my mouth drops. "You are so damn yummy without clothes on! Go to the bathroom fast before I pour maple syrup all over you and lick it off."

He gives me a devilish smile and proceeds to the bathroom as slow as possible, giving me a nice show of his backside. I throw a pillow at him. He is so hot. I can't believe I slept with someone like him. It makes my hormones bubble. I'm not sure I'll be able to keep my hands off him once he gets out of the bathroom.

I gather our plates and leftover food and take them into the kitchen. The dirty dishes can sit in the sink while I put everything else away. I hear him walk back to the bedroom. My turn in the bathroom.

When I enter the bedroom again, he sits against the headboard with the blanket over the bottom half of his body. I know what he wants, because I want it too. He's already making love to me with his radiant eyes. Electricity runs up and down my body, traveling across the room directly toward him. I climb onto the bed and straddle him. I lean my forehead against his. We sit there in silence.

He lifts his head from mine as he starts to gently touch my hair. "I love your hair up like this. You wore it like this the morning I woke up in your apartment. You looked so innocent standing in front of me with your hair up and wearing those cute pajamas. And no bra." He wiggles his eyebrows. "Your big blue eyes were staring right through me even though I was a mean asshole. I'm sorry. I'll say it a million times," he says with a pained stare.

"At first, you did surprise me with your outburst. But I wouldn't have offered you my delicious pancakes if you didn't redeem yourself." I brush my hands through his hair.

His eyes wander all over my face as his hand reaches for the back of my neck, pulling me closer. "You have some syrup on the corner of your mouth."

"Really? I didn't see it when I was in the bathroom. How embarrassing." I wipe my mouth, but he grabs my hands. He proceeds to seductively lick off the syrup.

"If you continue like this, we'll never leave this bedroom."

"That's my intention." He slides my robe slowly down my arms until it pools around us.

In full daylight, I'm completely exposed to him from the waist up. I'm usually bashful, but with him I'm the direct opposite. "Do you see the little marks you left on me last night?" I angle my head. He drags his fingers over every spot. My body tingles everywhere. He drives me insane with just the touch of his finger. "If you want to do that again, please leave marks somewhere my patients can't see them."

"That'll be no problem. I like seeing my marks on you. I intend to explore every part of your beautiful body over and over again. I think I can find several secret places."

He takes my face in his hands and kisses me deeply. We taste sweet like syrup with a hint of mint. He's pleased to see I have no underwear on. He tosses my robe away from us. I lean up on my knees so he can remove the barrier between us.

James gazes at me with such intensity. "Lisa, I never thought I could or would open my heart to someone after what happened. It scares me to death, but at the same time it feels so good and completely right. Most of all, you give me the strength to move forward." As if my heart is whispering to his, I grab his face and kiss him with all I have.

Within seconds we become even more intense than we were last night. He lifts me up to connect us one more time. We move in sync as he trails kisses down my neck and chest. I let my head fall back so he has better access. He gently loosens my hair from its bun so it drapes down my back.

His hands roam over the most sensitive parts of my body, leaving me breathless. He pulls me closer in a way that pushes us over the edge. We remain in this position, waiting for our bodies to calm down.

We lie in bed for a while, dozing off and on. This is the best thing I have ever had. I don't know how I will ever go back to the person I was yesterday. Not even one day with him like this, and I'm already in too deep. Didn't I promise myself I would never give my heart to someone else? That promise has been shattered to pieces.

# *Chapter 33*

## *James*

We lie in bed, twisted in her sheets like a cocoon. "What time do you have to work today?"

"I start at two p.m. I wish I had the day off. I would rather spend the day together...naked. I'd like to ask you more questions," she says as she showers me with little kisses.

"I don't want to leave you, but it's almost one. Which means you need to get ready soon. What's your schedule like the next few weeks?"

"The rest of October is pretty bad. After then, I'll work Monday to Friday every week and then one weekend during the month. I like it that way much better. The holidays are coming up quickly. Hopefully, I'll have at least Thanksgiving or Christmas off. My mom always made those two days special for us. Tina and I have tried to keep up the tradition, even with our stepmother, Beth." She waves her hand in the air. "Whatever. Christmas is far away. I can't think so far ahead."

"I know work will fill most of your hours, but I hope we can find time to spend together. I'm not sure how long I can wait until I see you again." I squeeze her against me.

"I know. Even before last night, I always wanted to see you. Now I'll miss you as soon as you walk out that door," she says with glowing cheeks.

She puts her robe on and tugs me out of bed. "Come take a shower with me. A real shower. I don't have time to be frisky anymore. So behave yourself. If you don't think you can behave, then you stay right there in bed."

"Then I'm staying here. You have woken up my body, so it's your fault I can't keep my hands off you."

She rolls her eyes. "Okay, sex machine."

"I didn't hear you complain a few minutes ago."

She looks over her shoulder. "You're one to talk." She drops her robe and throws it at me.

"You are such a tease, woman!" *My woman.*

"Control your hormones. I'll be out in a few minutes. You can stay here until I need to go to the hospital. You can walk me there if you'd like. If you think you can handle it." She closes the bathroom door.

My hormones are controlled now. I fall back onto the bed. I haven't been near the hospital since Jessica and Jacob died. I'm not sure I can face it yet. My old boss calls me now and then to see how I'm moving along. He assures me I have a job if I want to go back. I just don't know if I can, even though I miss working in the hospital. It's been over a year. How long will my boss be willing to wait? I'm sure not much longer. I need to stop hiding.

She comes out of the steamy bathroom with wet hair and no makeup.

I stand up from the bed and watch her. "You are so beautiful. You don't need any makeup. Your eyes light up your face."

"That's the sweetest thing anyone has ever said to me." She pecks me on the lips and quickly jumps away as I try to grab her. "Go take a cold shower, or I'll be late for work." She taps me on the butt and points to the bathroom.

"Okay. You win. It won't be so easy next time. By the way, I'll walk you to the hospital. I'm not sure how I'll react when I get there, but it's worth a try. It'll be the first time since they died."

"Let's do it together. I know it's a big step for you. Always come to me when you need me."

She closes her apartment door and locks it. "Let's go."

I concentrate on this moment, not on my past here. Even though I still want to leave as fast as possible. When I'm in her apartment, I don't think about where I am. Outside her apartment is a different story. As if she gets it, she grabs my hand and pulls me away from the building. She's so patient and understanding without even saying anything. She knows what it's like to lose someone she loves.

We hold hands as we walk down the busy street. It feels natural and comforting. Everything appears familiar but different because I'm different. I can breathe again. That evil dread is missing this morning. Lisa is the reason. Well, amazing sex can do it too. I smile to myself.

"Why are you smiling like that? I hope it's because of me."

It comes out as a joke but with a touch of insecurity. I can't read her mind, but with her twitchy voice, maybe she wonders if I'm thinking of Jessica and not her.

"I was replaying our incredible night and morning in my mind. Wishing we could do it again." I stop and pull her to me. I kiss her senseless so she understands how amazing it was to me.

"Kisses like that make me weak in the knees. Will I be getting more of those?"

"I will give you more than kisses. I hope your schedule will allow for that soon." I rub my nose against hers.

"I told you it's horrible for the rest of the month. Maybe we can start running together. Even though I'll be tired, I'll need it. We can see who can run the fastest or longest."

"Sounds like a plan. If I'm the fastest, do I get something special?"

"You sure will. I'll make you smile for days." She hauls me to her by the shirt and grabs my butt.

"Now I really look forward to it."

Without noticing, we're now in front of the hospital, not too far from the emergency room entrance. I freeze and just stare. My heart pounds in my ears, and I start to sweat.

"James, breathe through it." She encourages me. "Your reaction is completely normal. I still have problems when I'm driven near the site of my accident. You need to face it to move on. I know I sound like the psychiatrist side of me, but it's what I've learned. I understand from both sides of the spectrum. It will take time."

"I know. If you were anyone else, they wouldn't understand like you do." I hug her and say, "You need to get to work. Don't worry about me. I promise I'll consider your advice. Call me soon. You know where to find me."

Our hands drift apart. "Thanks for last night. It's going in my book of favorite experiences. Maybe even the top favorite," she says as she steps away from me.

She waves one last time before she enters the hospital. I've been blessed with her, but I hope I don't ruin her or what we have. I turn around without looking back. Maybe next time I'm near the hospital, I can walk inside. *Wishful thinking, James.*

# Chapter 34

## Lisa

It's the end of October, deep in the middle of autumn. The leaves are bright and colorful. I'm almost done with my horrible work schedule. Time with James has been limited, but we take advantage of my free time and make the best of it. He has plenty of free time still. We have been very strict with running together. I like the challenge of keeping up with him. I'm on my way to meet him at the park again.

We haven't spoken about how he is doing. Our time together is more enjoyable when we think in the present. I don't press him for information. Maybe I can approach it during our run today.

I walk through the gates of the park and scan for some sign of him. I jump when someone puts his arms around my waist. I know it's James, because he always kisses my neck. He can't resist it when my hair is up. I turn around and am blown away by how sexy he looks. *Again.* He is wearing his old Mets cap backward, with a little scruff. His eyes glow bright green.

"I'll never get tired of looking at you. How can you look so damn sexy all of the time?" I hug him tightly, wishing I could stay there forever. "The first time we met at this park, you poured water over your head because you were sweating. I found it so incredibly hot. Maybe you can reenact that for me." I put my hand up. "No. Forget I said that. I might have to jump your bones, and we don't have much time."

"I'd rather you jump my bones, but we're in a public place. I'll behave." He pats me on the butt.

We run at a good pace for a while. I want to ask him some

questions, but I'm afraid he will get defensive. We're always honest with each other, so I shouldn't worry.

"James, can I ask you a question?" I ask through rapid breaths.

"Sure, if you don't mind me breathing heavily while I answer it."

"Have you thought about what you want to do? Do you consider going back to the hospital? You can't keep going on like this."

He stops abruptly, and people swerve around us. "Going on like what?" His eyes are dark-green slits, warning me.

"You're in limbo. You told me you hope to figure out what you want to do. Have you come up with any ideas or answers?" I try to catch my breath. "Let's move out of the way so people can pass us."

He wipes his forehead with his arm. "There is one option. I had a discussion with my dad. He owns a big real estate agency in New Jersey, which focuses on luxury houses and apartments. I can train for a license to become a real estate agent." He looks toward the ground.

"Is that what you really want? You worked so hard to become a doctor. I would hate to see you walk away from it forever. You can always go and work for a pharmaceutical company, like Alexa, where you can still utilize your medical background." His head is still down. "Can you please look at me?"

He finally raises his head. His face is like stone. "Please don't push me. I think about my future every damn day, wondering what the hell I'm going to do. I have no fucking clue. That's why I spoke to my dad. He understands and encourages me to do it if that's what I want. Is it what I really want? Probably not. But I need to get out of Alexa's apartment and get back on my own two feet. I need a job and money." His eyes are full of pain.

"I'm not trying to upset you. We always talk about me and my issues, but we hardly ever talk about you. We should both be open and honest with each other. That's what girlfriends and boyfriends do."

He smiles. "Boyfriend, huh? I like the way that sounds. Do you want me to be your boyfriend? Or do you mean sex toy?"

I stifle a laugh. Discussion over, I guess. At least for now.

"I consider you both of those things. Is that okay? We never discuss what we are to each other. As far as I'm concerned, I want you to myself. I become insanely jealous when another woman looks at you." I'm admitting too much. I feel my cheeks heat up, and I can't look at him.

He tips my chin up with his finger. "My thoughts completely. You are my girlfriend. I never thought I would say those words again. I'm proud to say it. Should I say it out loud so everyone can hear it?"

I shake my head. "Don't you dare, James!" I pull on his arms. "Don't embarrass me."

He steps back, points at me, and shouts, "Hello, everyone. This is Lisa, my beautiful Jersey girl, and I couldn't be happier. She's saved me in so many ways she will never know." Some people walk by clapping their hands, while others look at him like he's losing his mind.

I put my hands over my face and laugh. "You're crazy! Let's go."

"That I am...crazy about you." Now his eyes are bright green again. I am falling so deep. I am terrified.

# Chapter 35

## James

I drop my head on a book about New Jersey real estate law. I hoped sitting in a café would perk me up. This is a painful read.

I've begun training to receive a real estate license for New Jersey and New York. All I can say about this training is...*boring!* I don't know how my dad has done this for so many years. He is successful and enjoys it. Good for him. I'm going through the process with little interest. Lisa supports me, but I have the feeling she disagrees with my choice. She doesn't pressure me, and I love that about her.

Sometimes I think I can go back to the hospital, but then I have a bad dream, and that feeling goes away. My dreams replay the moment I find Jessica on the floor. One night I had the same dream, but instead of Jessica lying there, it was Lisa.

I still miss Jessica and will always love her. In my dreams, she comes to me and talks to me like she would if she were alive. She wears the same summer pastel-purple dress she was buried in, and holds Jacob against her chest. When I reach for them, they dissolve into a misty cloud.

At least I don't wake up in a panic anymore. Well, I don't when Lisa is lying next to me.

Little by little, Lisa is taking Jessica's place. What if something happens to Lisa too? I couldn't live through it again. It makes my stomach turn just thinking about it.

I flip through the next pages, hoping for something to catch my attention. The only interesting thing in this café is the smell of coffee beans and the sound of frothing milk. I slam the book shut and gather my things. I need a breather.

How could something happen to Lisa? Why would we finally meet if we'll only end up apart? We're connected in ways most people will never be with another person.

I dispose of my coffee cup and walk out into the cold wind and rain. I open my umbrella.

Do we both want a future together? We don't talk about it. We live in the current day, never tomorrow. Since she's so busy with her schedule, and I'm obtaining my license, it helps us have our space. During the time we're apart, I can think about what I want for my future. In the end, I know what I want. I want Lisa. She makes me whole again. I'm a better person when I'm with her.

I proceed down the sidewalk toward my apartment. The store windows are loaded with Thanksgiving decorations. I find myself in front of a jewelry store with a huge display of engagement rings. Do I want to marry Lisa? I had the chance to marry Jessica, but I insisted we wait until after Jacob was born. I regret I never married her. I regret not being more flexible. I regret a lot of things.

I lost Jacob before he was even born. Lisa can't have children. I don't care, but is it because I accept her for who she is or because I'm a coward? I've always wanted a family, but maybe God has another plan for me.

Lisa feels broken, and so do I. I'm broken because I'm afraid to lose her. I'll always have the fear of loss and death on my shoulder. Sometimes I become distant because these thoughts circulate through my mind when I'm with her. I see how much she already means to me and how devastated I would be if she was taken away from me. Armor still surrounds my heart. Little pieces are missing, but it's still protecting me. Will I ever be able to open it so my heart can beat freely again?

Thanksgiving is tomorrow. We are spending Thanksgiving Day and that night at her dad's house. It's the first holiday we'll spend together, and I'll meet her dad and stepmother. On Friday, we plan to visit my parents and then head back home on Friday night. It's convenient our families live near each other.

I'm nervous to meet her family, but I don't know why. Lisa gives me no reason to be nervous. She keeps saying how excited she is for the next couple of days. She talks about her family more as we spend more time together. She's close to Tina, but she doesn't talk about her dad much. The first time I met Lisa, I would describe her as mellow and shy. Now she's more outgoing and animated. She's patient, soft-spoken, and caring. When she describes the way she was before she met me, it's hard to believe she is the same person. I remember Tina saying something similar on Lisa's birthday.

I see my apartment building in the distance as I pass Cloud Nine on the left.

My parents visit us frequently at Alexa's apartment. I still don't feel comfortable saying it's my apartment. We have a great time with them. Lisa and Alexa get along well. I get the feeling if they met at another time, without me in the picture, they still would have become good friends.

The one thing I'm worried about is taking Lisa to my parents' house on Friday. I have memories with Jessica there. I don't want to get nervous or sad. Especially not in front of Lisa. Months ago, I asked Mom to remove all items in the house that would remind me of Jessica or Jacob. I hope she listened.

# Chapter 36

## Lisa

"Wake up, sleepyhead," I whisper in his ear as I shake his arm lightly. "Happy Thanksgiving!"

He rolls over toward me and opens his sleepy eyes. I give him a sweet kiss as he maneuvers me on top of him. "I'm cold," I say as I shimmy the comforter over us. He holds me tightly as I melt against him with my head resting on his warm chest. His heartbeat is slow and rhythmic.

"I like waking up next to you." He kisses my head. "You give me a sense of peace that stays with me. How are you always so cheerful when you wake up in the morning?"

"I was never a morning person. Coffee was about the only thing I interacted with during the first hour after I woke up. I've only been like this the past couple of months."

"What made you change?"

"You." I kiss his chest. "Waking up next to you is better than any legal stimulant available. I'm a lucky girl to have such a sexy man in my bed." We cuddle, not paying attention to the time. We're in no rush to leave for my dad's. It's a nice change of pace for me to hang out in my pajamas.

He clears his throat. "Are you nervous to introduce me to your family?"

"What?" I ask with a high-pitched voice. "Of course not. Why would you ask me that? I've told you several times how excited I am for you to meet them. Especially since you are the mystery man from our accidents. Tina has been looking forward to seeing you again.

Even more so, since she also witnessed your ski accident. She didn't have much time to talk to you on my birthday."

"Oh really. I hope you only told them good things about me. I want to make a good impression today."

I don't think he's joking. I lay my chin on his chest in order to see his face. "I think you are the one who's nervous. Am I right?"

"A little bit. I know I shouldn't be."

"What is there not to love? You have turned my world upside down. I couldn't be more alive, and that's all they want to see. This is the first holiday I've looked forward to in years. I want to show you off."

"You already met my parents, and they loved you even after your weird behavior after dinner at Alexa's." He snorts.

I jerk my head up. He's goading me. "That isn't funny. They know why I acted that way. Must you rub it in?"

I push up to get off him, but he attacks me and tosses me onto my back. He tickles me under my arms and then the backs of my knees. I hope he doesn't go to my feet. He knows I will either kick him where it hurts or pee in my pants. We play like this until we are naked and breathless.

"Lisa, you drive me insane. I want you all the time. This is the best Thanksgiving ever. Will I get this kind of treatment every holiday?"

*Will there be more holidays?*

"You are like a kid in a candy store. You can't get enough of sweet things. Just remember—from now on, I'm your favorite sweet thing."

His demeanor changes within a second. He holds on to me tightly. "You are. Thank you for this morning. It's nice to live carefree for a change. Playing around like little teenagers in our pajamas. I haven't looked forward to a holiday in a long time either. You've changed that for me."

I kiss the tip of his nose. "I'll do my best to always make you smile and think happy thoughts." I break away from his steel hold and slide out of bed.

He sits up and says, "It's supposed to be sunny today but pretty cold. Make sure you wear and pack warm clothes. The sun won't be spending Friday with us though."

"Well, aren't you the cutest weather forecaster."

I blow him a kiss and go to take a shower. One more piece of my heart belongs to him. Soon my heart will be completely his.

Knowing I am almost at my dad's house, I relax into the seat. James drove carefully and held my hand the entire way, talking about mundane things. It's ridiculously embarrassing I'm still like this after so many years. Will it ever change?

"So this is the street I grew up on." I point to the leafless trees. "I love how big the oak trees are now. They line the street on both sides and produce a green canopy overhead during the summer. You should see it during autumn. The canopy turns scarlet red. It gives this section of town some charm compared to the newer parts."

"Which one is your house?"

"It's a couple of houses down on the right. See the Dutch colonial with the light-gray stone front with black shutters and front door? We can park in the driveway."

He shifts the car into park. "This is a nice house, a nice piece of property. All the houses on this street are well kept. I love Dutch colonial–style houses. How old is this house?"

I unbuckle my seat belt and open the door. "My parents bought this house when I was born. They didn't build it. It's around forty to fifty years old." Before I close the door, I lean back in the car. "Are you going to get out? You can see the house better from out here."

He laughs. "Sorry. I'm curious. I learned about different types of houses and how they are built while studying for my license. The Dutch colonial was one of them. It's common in the tristate area."

I look away from him so he can't see my face. I want to gag myself. How can he go from being an ER doctor to a real estate agent? There's nothing wrong with being in real estate. But it's not him. He's a doctor and always will be! I want to scream at him.

The sound of old leaves winding in circles on the ground flutters through the air. I breathe through my nose to enjoy the scent. The cold seeps through my black wool coat. "Damn, it's cold. Let's get our bags and go inside."

He pops the trunk open and bends over to grab our bags.

"I'll take mine. Can you please grab the flowers I bought Beth? They're in the backseat on your side."

"Sure." He takes his bag out. "Just make sure you close the trunk."

"No problem." When I grab the handle of my bag, I notice a red first responder emergency medical kit stuffed to the side of his trunk. It's not a black leather bag like people imagine all doctors carry. I know what's inside. I wonder if he remembers it's in here or if he pretends he doesn't see it. It's a fairly large bright-red bag, so I highly doubt he doesn't see it. I close the trunk and keep quiet.

I stop and look at my house. James comes around the car and hands me Beth's flowers.

"What's the matter? Why aren't you going to the door?"

"Nothing's wrong. I'm surprised how good the house looks. It looks better than the last time I was here. Dad must have had it painted." *Or I see it differently because I am different.*

We start up the sidewalk, and Tina swings the black door open and runs toward us. She pulls me to her.

"Careful. You almost crushed the flowers I bought for Beth."

"Oops." She cringes. "Sorry. I heard your car in the driveway. We're so thrilled you are both here." She looks at James, bright eyed and smiling. "Hi, James. It's great to see you again. Hopefully, we'll find the time to chat a little bit more this time." She hugs him.

"Hi, Tina. It's good to see you also. Sorry about last time. I didn't mean to steal your sister away. I promise I won't do it again today. We'll be here until tomorrow morning, so we'll have plenty of time to get to know each other better."

We stand there for a few seconds while Tina rocks back and forth on her heels.

I clear my throat. "Can we please go inside now? It's cold out here."

"Yes, sorry." She giggles as she hops to the side to let us in. "Dad made a fire. It's nice and cozy inside."

I nudge him with my elbow. I whisper, "This is new for me. Bringing a man home was not a frequent thing. In fact, you are the first."

He raises his eyebrows. "What? Bryant was never here?"

I shrug my shoulders. "No. I had no desire to bring him here, and he never pushed it. That should have been another flag to add to the list of a million. Lesson learned. I'm glad to be here with you." I lead him into the house. The smell of turkey roasting mixed with a hint of apple-cinnamon crumble wafts through the air. We place our bags on the staircase in front of us.

"Lisa, happy Thanksgiving! We're so glad you are both here." Dad pulls me into a tight hug as he lifts me in the air. Beth is at his side with a wide grin on her face.

I'm happy we're here. I've missed being home.

"Happy Thanksgiving to you as well. It's so good to see you both and to be back home. Beth, these flowers are for you. Maybe they will look nice on the table when we eat. I love the mini orange gerberas and the red daisies."

"They're gorgeous. I know exactly where I'll display them," she responds as she places her hand on her chest. Appreciation gushes from her.

I pull James close to me. "Dad and Beth, this is James." My smile stretches from ear-to-ear. I'm so proud to have him with me. It makes this Thanksgiving so special.

"Nice to meet you, James. Please call me Mike. Welcome to our home."

James shakes both of their hands. "Thank you, both. I'm happy to be here. Beth, I'm already hungry after Lisa told me about the delicious apple crumble you are known for. She told me you're an excellent cook."

"Lisa said that? What a compliment. I can't keep the smile off my face." She puts her hand to her cheek as she blushes the shade of a tomato.

"Don't act bashful. You know you are. Just smell this house. I can't wait to see what you have made."

She waves her hand in the air. "Stop it now. I don't know how to handle all these compliments."

She hands Dad our shoes and coats. "Mike, will you please put their coats and shoes in the foyer closet while they get settled upstairs?"

"You betcha."

"Lisa, your old bedroom is set up for you both. Take your things up and come down for a glass of wine. We will eat within the next couple of hours. Little appetizers are already sitting out."

We nod and haul our bags upstairs. I stop short when my feet touch the carpet in my old bedroom. The rich cream-color carpet is so plush, as if I'm stepping on fluffy white clouds. I wiggle my toes. I can see the tracks left behind from the vacuum.

"Wow! Beth redecorated this room. I love it." Three walls are painted powder white, and the fourth wall, where the headboard leans, is a light slate gray with a tinge of blue. The queen-size dark-wood sleigh bed has a duvet and sheets with a mix of delicate white and pastel-pink textures. Matching luxurious pillows are arranged perfectly on the bed. The sun beams through sheer white curtains, casting warm light into the room. How romantic, as if we are at a cozy bed and breakfast.

I twirl in a circle. "I'm stunned. My room has never looked this beautiful. Last time I was here, it still had the ancient yellow carpet and ugly sun bleached lemon colored curtains."

I do a Nestea plunge onto the bed. "Oh, I love Beth. This is a feather bed. It's pure luxury compared to the one at the apartment. My bed feels like I'm sleeping on a camel's back compared to this." I pat the bed. "Come lay next to me. You need to try it. I can't wait to sleep in it."

"Behave, little one. We have to go downstairs," he says as he lowers himself onto the bed. "You're right," he moans. "This is awesome. When can we go to bed, and I don't mean for sleeping?"

"I said sleep. You always have your head in the gutter. I'm not having sex in my dad's house."

"Well, I guess I'll go stay at my parents' house if I'm not going to get any action." He crosses his arms and pouts like a little boy.

"Oh really? I'll show you action." I whip a pillow at his head.

"That's it! You're in for it." He straddles me and pins my wrists above my head. "I'm bigger than you are, so don't even try to fight. You won't win." We play around until we hear a tap on the door.

Tina stands in the doorway. "Sorry to disturb you lovebirds, but we're waiting for you both downstairs. You have plenty of time to do whatever you are doing...later." Tina walks away, clicking her tongue.

Before he can move away from me, I tug his shirt. "I kind of liked the way you were holding me down. Maybe we can try it again some time."

His Adam's apple bobs as he swallows.

I flash him an innocent smile and pull him out of the room. "Let's go, tough guy."

We're greeted in the kitchen with crystal glasses of white wine. "I would like to make a toast," states Tina with a grin as bright as the sun.

*I've been celebrating a lot these past months.*

"Happy Thanksgiving, everyone. I couldn't be happier to have the whole family together on this holiday. It's been a long time since Lisa has been home. I'm also thankful she brought James with her. She has never been happier. The story of how you both met is a true fairy tale." She lifts her glass, and we follow. "Here's to always being thankful for what we have. Cheers!"

"Cheers," we all say in unison as we clink our glasses.

I gaze at James intently. He's grinning with a certain glow in his eyes—eyes that aren't vacant anymore. My heart warms, knowing I've helped return the sparkle to his eyes.

He squeezes my hand. "What are you thinking about this time?"

"I'm watching your expression and how sweet you look."

He leans down and kisses me on the cheek.

"Beth, you have outdone yourself with these appetizers. You said they are little ones. There are five big dishes full. We won't have enough room for turkey after munching on all of this." I stand at the counter, perusing the choices as my mouth waters.

"We still have a while before the big meal. It's been a long time since we've all been together, let alone on a holiday. It's also special to have James with us." She grabs a dish from the table. "Try this spinach and artichoke dip. It's heavenly. Here are some homemade bread cubes to go with it."

Beth continues to explain the appetizers as she points to each one. "This is the typical veggie platter with fresh hummus. These are mini meatballs with a spicy chili sauce on the side. Extra-large stuffed mushrooms, which won't fit into your mouth in one piece. I know what I'm talking about because I tried it myself. It wasn't a pretty sight." She laughs. "Last but not least, an assortment of different cheeses. Stilton, brie with a grape and walnut compote, and goat cheese wrapped in dill."

Dad interrupts. "Hey, James, do you watch football?"

"Of course I do. I think the Giants are playing right now."

"Yes they are. It's a nice change to have another man in the house." He rubs his hands in excitement. "Well, let's load up some plates and watch the game in my man cave in the basement while the girls gossip in the kitchen."

"Hey," I say as I stand there with my hands on my hips.

Dad laughs as he and James take hearty helpings of food. James follows him out of the kitchen.

I yell behind them. "Real nice, Dad. Don't show him pictures of me when I had braces or big Jersey hair and ridiculous makeup in high school."

I turn around to two sets of eyes staring at me.

"Lisa, he's so damn sexy. He looks even better today than on your birthday. His eyes alone would drive me nuts," Tina gushes.

I slap her arm. "He's mine, sister."

"Play nicely children," Beth teases as she peels some sweet potatoes.

Tina lays her chin in her hand. "I'm so jealous. I wish I would meet a nice guy. No offense, maybe one with a little less baggage though."

"Hey, I have baggage too, but we still want to be together. Everyone has baggage. If you love someone, you love the good and the bad."

Tina coughs on a bread cube. She wipes her mouth and says, "Did you say love?" Her eyes are wide open in disbelief.

I nibble on a carrot. "I didn't say I love him." *Do I love him?* "We like each other very much," I casually say as I sit in a chair next to Tina.

"Why are you afraid to say you love him?"

It must be an interesting question, because Beth stops peeling the sweet potatoes to give me her full attention. I look around to double-check James didn't come back.

"I'm afraid he could never love me like he loved Jessica. I know we care about each other a lot and have this unique bond. Is that enough for him to finally put Jessica behind him? I don't expect him to forget about her, but I wonder how he's dealing with it. I don't ask him questions because he gets defensive sometimes. And I'm afraid to hear the answers." I'm getting antsy, so I take the wine bottle out of the ice bucket to refill my glass. I motion to ask Tina if she wants a refill. She nods.

"I'm also scared because I promised myself I would never open my heart for a man again. Somehow, he has managed to do exactly that. If he walked away from me, it would crush me a hundred times more than when Bryant left. I wouldn't regret a minute of it, but it would ruin me." I sigh as I take a gulp of wine. Do I really want to get into this kind of conversation? Let me put food in my mouth so I can't talk anymore.

Beth walks over to the table and sits down next to me. "I had the same worries when I met your dad. He was an empty shell, almost lifeless, when I met him that day at the bank. I dropped something on the floor, and he picked it up for me. I saw the sadness on his face and in his eyes. His eyes were like a puppy's. That was it for me. I fell in love with him instantly. I asked him if he wanted to go for a coffee, and we've been together ever since.

"He told me his wife died, but he didn't tell me what happened with you and your mom right away. She was the love of his life. High school sweethearts and all that. How could I compete with her? After we started dating, he admitted he felt something when our eyes locked for the first time." She smiles as she munches on some cheese.

"Felicia will always be a part of his heart and soul. He fought his true feelings for me for a while because of guilt—from the accident and being with another woman. Finally, he let go of his past, and the guilt slowly decreased. He was also afraid of losing me just like he lost your mom." Her face looks sad as she stares off blindly at the appetizers. "He worries about me. He can be overprotective at times."

She turns in her chair and takes my hand. "I want you to know I understand completely what you are battling. You're both scared. It's a very complicated situation. However, you can't ignore it for long. You need to talk about it and be honest with one another. Communication is so important. The sooner, the better. I waited a long time for your dad, but it came to a point I couldn't compete with your mom anymore. He either had to deal with his issues and move on, or lose me. He needed to make a choice. Since I'm sitting here, he obviously made his choice. He will always love your mom, but he loves me just as much. I can feel it in my heart."

I mull over what she said. It's frightening how similar Dad and Beth's relationship is to ours. It never even occurred to me. How could I have been so blind? "I'm sorry, Beth. I never even thought about you going through this same situation. Thank you for your advice."

"Stop. You are going to make me cry. Crying isn't allowed on holidays." She dabs the corner of her right eye and laughs it off. "I can only say this—he was definitely worth the wait. Please consider what I have said. You make your own decisions, but I'm here for you if you ever need to talk."

I lean over and give her a big hug. "Thank you. This means so much to me. I'm sorry I don't visit so often. Ever since I met James, I feel reborn. I look at my life so differently, as if I can finally see in color. Everything was black and white and completely boring before him. Now everything is vibrant and exciting. I look forward to my future and what is beyond my residency. I have taken too many things for granted. For starters, spending time with my family. I promise I'll make a better effort in the future. You and Dad should visit me as well."

She holds me tight and then stands up and walks back to the counter.

"I need to finish some side dishes. You girls go somewhere and talk. I'm fine finishing up here."

Tina looks at me and motions for me to follow her. "We'll be right back. Call us when you need our help."

"Take your time. Everything is under control here. Take some of the appetizers with you. The refrigerator is already too full."

Tina and I look at each other and shrug our shoulders. "Sounds good to us," we say in unison. We fill our plates and head on up to Tina's old room.

# Chapter 37

*James*

I scan the basement layout. It's the size of the entire first floor. The walls are muted white, with a light-tan carpet. There are two windows at the other end; rays of sun pour natural light into the dim space. There are two wooden vertical support beams in the middle of the room. The adjacent wall near the TV has a bookshelf with large model cars displayed.

"So this is what a man cave looks like? It's huge." I look around, impressed. "I think I will need one of these for myself one day. It's a bunch of rooms mixed in one."

We place our food on the table in front of the huge TV hanging on the wall. "When Beth wants to watch her lady shows, I'll come down here to watch my shows. That's why I have a large flat-screen TV and nice brown leather recliner in this section of the basement. Every man needs a good recliner." He slaps the top of it with his hand. "I bought that small sofa to go with it for visitors. This part of the room is under the living room."

We move along the floor to the middle of the long rectangular room. "We don't have the space in the living room for a liquor cabinet, so we keep all the alcohol down here. Here's a small refrigerator to keep wine and beer cold."

Pictures and paraphernalia of the Mets and NY Giants hang on the wall. I notice a picture of Lisa and Mike with Mets caps on. Both have big foam fingers on their hands, with huge smiles on their faces. She looks so happy.

I point to the picture. "When was this picture of you and Lisa taken?"

"I believe Lisa was thirteen. Every once in a while we would go alone to a game. She enjoyed the games more than Tina. After Felicia died, we never went to a game together again."

He claps his hands together. "How about a beer?"

"Sounds great."

He walks back to the refrigerator. "I have Budweiser and Heineken. What'll it be?"

"I'll have a Heineken, please."

"Good choice. Me too." He pours our drinks into cold beer mugs and leads us back to the TV area.

Her father is relaxed and down to earth. He's wearing light-blue jeans with a casual long-sleeved gray shirt. He seems to be in good shape for his age. I don't feel the need to impress him because I'm dating his daughter. I hate to compare him to Jessica's dad, but I never felt quite this relaxed with him. Her dad always dressed in crisp black pants and stiff white button-down shirts. Never jeans or more casual attire. Then again, I wore the same kind of clothes at that time. It dawns on me I was just like Jessica's father. I'm not that person anymore. Is it wrong to be happy about that?

We lift our beers and take a swig. "There's nothing like an ice-cold beer."

"I second that." I take another long swig.

"I'm glad you were able to spend time with us. We don't see Lisa very often. Maybe it will be different after she finishes her residency. Granted, that's still years away. Was the drive down okay? Is she still nervous when she's in a car?"

"Yes, but I was able to distract her for a while. It's amazing how afraid she still is after all these years. It's a good thing the drive down here isn't too long."

He motions for me to take a seat on the sofa, while he sits down in his recliner. I notice he hasn't turned on the football game. Maybe we aren't really going to watch the game.

"Thank you for helping Lisa during the car accident. It feels like yesterday when it all happened. She was a mess for a long time. We all were." He replays what happened and says things I already heard from Lisa. I let him talk because maybe he needs to.

He becomes animated. "Now you are in our house. The chances of something like this happening are almost zero." He takes another sip. A little bigger this time.

"Mike, can I ask you a question? I know we don't know each other, but we both have something in common."

He holds up his hand. "I know what you are going to ask. You don't have to. But before we go in that direction, I want to say how sorry I am about your fiancée and son. No one deserves such heartache. It's one of the worst, if not the worst." He rubs his mouth and puts his beer on a Mets coaster on the table.

"I know what you are going through. As you know, it happened to me. I lost Felicia that day and almost lost Lisa. It was a horrific nightmare. I blamed myself because I made her take that bloody old Chevy out in horrible weather. I'm a mechanic. Why the hell did I even keep that hunk of shit? It was so old there were no airbags, and the seat belts in the back had no over-the-shoulder straps. What was I thinking? It should've been scrapped long before the accident. I've asked myself *why* for years!" he exclaims as his voice gets higher.

"She was pissed at me she needed to drive that car in such bad weather. The last time I saw her, she was angry with me." His hands squeeze into fists. "If I'd just told her to stay home and forget about grocery shopping, she would have been safe at home. That very day we had an appointment to go look at a new car for her. I should have taken Tina to work. But I didn't. It made me crazy thinking about it constantly. Why did I do this? Why not that?" He scratches his chin in frustration.

*I feel your pain.* "We can talk about this another time, if you would like. Believe me. I would completely understand."

He shakes his head. "I need to." He sits on the edge of the recliner with his elbows on his knees and says, "I know the gut-wrenching pain. It does get easier after time. It never fully goes away, but I promise it'll get better. Felicia was my high school sweetheart. She was the love of my life and soul mate. I'll always cherish the time I had with her. Every moment, every memory is a gift. Every time I look at Lisa, I think of her. Lisa has her eyes and is petite like she was."

"I've never seen a picture of Felicia, but Lisa said they look alike. It's funny how Tina looks just like you. The dark hair, eyes, and height."

He smiles in response, then continues. "However, I needed to move on with my life. There came a time when I knew I had to let go and move forward. It hit me that I had two daughters who needed me more than ever. I wasn't there for them for a long time. A lot fell on Tina's shoulders. She took care of us."

He turns his face in my direction. It looks like stone. "You need to move on, James. You are the one living; you're not dead. Don't waste your time being miserable, like I did. It will never change the past. Do you think she would want you to live like this? I'm sorry— what was your fiancée's name?"

It's hard to say it. "Jessica."

"Do *you* still want to live like this? Or let me reverse it. If you were the one who died, would you want her to live the way you do? If she found a great man to love her and who she loved as well, wouldn't you want that for her instead of being miserable?"

*Did he just say love?*

"You appear to be very happy with Lisa. But to be truly happy, you need to relieve yourself of the guilt of what happened and the guilt you feel being with Lisa." He shakes his head. "I'm sorry for being so direct. I don't want to see you waste your life like that. You need to be strong."

"It's okay. I need to hear these things, even if I don't want to. It's good to speak to someone who's had the same experience."

"I felt so guilty and unfaithful when I was with Beth those first months. I never thought I would look at another woman, let alone touch one. As time went on, I saw how Beth was pulling me out of my darkness. The hole I had in my heart was mending because of her. I felt happiness for the first time in a long time. She was very patient with me, but a woman will only wait so long. She didn't want to be second best and knew the turmoil going on in my head. She is different from my first wife...in a good way. I would never want a replica of Felicia. She was one of a kind."

I start to fidget and stand up. "Mike, can I interject for a second?" I sound like a lawyer.

"Please. I need a break from talking anyway." He relaxes in his recliner.

"Besides guilt, aren't you afraid of losing her like you lost Felicia? After everything happened with Jessica, I vowed to never love another woman. With Lisa, I'm second-guessing that vow. It scares the shit out of me. I couldn't survive losing her too."

"Like you, guilt wasn't the only problem I was dealing with. I'm terrified to lose Beth like I lost Felicia. To go through that again makes my stomach turn to even think about it. Beth says I'm a little overbearing sometimes. I'm Mr. Safety now. Always making sure she's okay." He stands up and bends over the table to look at the food we brought down. I haven't even noticed how hungry I am.

We eat in comfortable silence. Once he's finished, he stands up and walks over to a wall with several framed pictures hanging from it.

"Do you have any pictures of Felicia hanging in the house?" I ask as I follow him. I look at other pictures on the wall. One of them is a picture of Lisa and Tina skiing. They are maybe ten years old. Another is of Lisa graduating high school, with her big Jersey hair and a Mets T-shirt on under her graduation robe. I laugh to myself.

"There are no pictures hanging, but I still have them. I put them in boxes or gave them to Lisa and Tina. You should ask Lisa to show you some pictures. You'll see how much they look alike."

"I'll do that. Lisa doesn't have any pictures displayed in her apartment." I pause for a moment. "I don't have any pictures out anymore either. I have one picture I look at sometimes. It brings me so much heartache to see photos. I won't get rid of them because they are a part of me, but I don't want to look at them either."

"Beth understood why I couldn't get rid of them. Actually, she never asked me to get rid of them. She's such a blessing to me. I've realized there is more than one soul mate for everyone. Life is strange and complicated. We can't plan our future down to the minute. We don't know what will happen tomorrow. We can only live one day at a time."

"It's funny. I was always organized and a planner. To be honest, I started planning right after the car accident. My goal was to become a doctor. I was never flexible. Once I had a goal, I stuck to it. When I met Jessica, I rearranged my plans but never deterred from them. I should have enjoyed my life more during those years with her."

He walks over to the refrigerator to fetch another beer. "Want another Heineken?"

I shrug. "Why not? I'm not driving."

"No, you are not. Just relax and enjoy yourself."

"What is hard for me now is I don't have a plan anymore. I'm not that driven, organized planner I used to be. That part of me is long gone. I'm not sure I even want to be that person again. Is that wrong? It makes me exhausted when I think about what I used to be like."

"In a way, that's good. Your life is a blank piece of paper. You decide what to do next—no one else. All I can suggest is, follow your heart and learn from your past. It'll tell you what to do, if you don't already know. Face your fears." He sits back down on the recliner.

"Beth and I were shocked to hear you were the one in the ski accident. It's a great story to tell people how you both met years later again. Your lives collided at this moment in time for a reason. Why now? Who knows. Maybe you can both heal each other. When I look at Lisa today, she has changed for the positive. She's happier and more confident. I think that has a lot to do with you."

A warm sensation fills my chest.

"How about we take a break from this serious conversation and watch the game. We still have time to watch the second half."

"I couldn't agree more. Thanks for the talk. Now let's see what the score is. I bet the Giants are winning," I say with a sense of relief that my anxieties are justified.

# Chapter 38

## Lisa

"Did you see how awesome Beth redecorated my old room?" I ask as I trip up the stairs, almost dropping my food.

"You are cut off from the alcohol, young lady." Tina giggles as she stops short before she bumps into me.

"Whatever. I'm not drunk. The last time I was even close to getting a buzz on was at Cloud Nine." I stop in front of Tina's bedroom. "Now, two months later, I'm introducing James to Dad and Beth."

Tina opens her door and I stand in the doorway with my eyes wide open. "Is Beth taking interior design classes? Your old room looks just as pretty as mine. It's so lovely and feminine. Did she redecorate the office downstairs as well?" This room has white crown molding with light creamy-beige walls. The carpet is the same color and just as plush as the one in my room. The oak wood bed is decorated with a solid dark-beige luxuriant comforter. Draped over the end of the bed is a white filigree blanket with powder-blue flowers. Powder-blue accent pillows are spread across the comforter.

As I'm feeling the fabric of the matching curtains, Tina says in her sisterly tone, "I'm not really in the mood to discuss how Beth decorates the house."

I turn away from the window and look at her.

"How are you really doing? Are things going well between you two?"

I point to my smiling face. "Isn't it evident when you look at me? I told you downstairs how I feel. I wouldn't lie."

Before Tina sits on the bed, I air dive onto it, shooting pillows all over the floor.

"Yes, you do radiate something. Maybe a lot of good sex." She laughs and sits next to me with her dish of food.

My chin drops.

"Ha! Just kidding." She bites on a cucumber stick loaded with dip.

"Be careful. We don't want to ruin this nice bedding."

"Fine. Let's sit on the floor then." Tina slides off the bed and sets her plate next to her. I do the same and stuff two meatballs into my mouth.

"Why don't you put three in your mouth?" Tina jokes.

I finish chewing and remark, "Hey, I didn't eat breakfast this morning. I'm starving."

She rolls her eyes with a smirk. "Sex for breakfast." She puts her hand up. "Sorry, let's get serious now."

"Not until you get the spinach out of your teeth."

"I have spinach in my teeth?" She immediately covers her mouth. She speed-crawls over to the full-length mirror to check her teeth. I burst out laughing as she turns around and gives me the evil eye.

"I had to do it. Your reaction was priceless. Now, come sit back over here if you want to get serious."

She lets out a belly laugh and crawls back over.

"What do you want to know?"

"Are you happy with him? Be honest. I haven't had a good conversation with you since you found out about his ski accident. You've been slammed with a lot of information in the last couple of months. Especially since the last time I saw you. That has to make your head spin."

"Head spin is the simple way to say it. He came into my life more like a tornado. It has been turned upside down, but I couldn't be happier. It's bizarre to think about our connections in the past. I told you how freaked out I was at first. He was the calm one." I rub my eyebrows. "It still feels strange to me, but in a good way now."

"You never really opened up to me about that night. When we left Alexa's apartment, you were quiet and didn't want to talk about it. We haven't had much time to talk since then."

"I wanted to tell you, but that night was intense. The first half of the night was full of fun and happiness, and then it turned into a night of sadness and rage."

"He looks happy today. When I first met him on your birthday, he was more reserved, as if trying to hide something. I noticed how he looked at you. The mood of the evening changed so quickly when Jessica's parents showed up. His face changed completely to stone, like he was possessed. Do you think it could happen again?"

"That was his first time out on a social level since Jessica died. Give him some slack. He told me how he battled with the decision before he came. His outburst at his apartment helped him get all the pent-up energy out. He told me it was a relief to get it out. Why did he need to do it with me and not his parents or Alexa? I don't know. What I'm trying to say is he has changed in so many positive ways since his outburst. So, I don't know if it will happen again."

I take the hairband off my wrist and put my hair into a ponytail. "I keep asking myself, why did we experience such sorrow and tragedy to meet each other now? But I think we could ask why until we're blue in the face. I don't think we will ever find out the reason."

"Why do you even care? You are together now, and that's all that matters."

"It breaks my heart he had to lose Jessica and his unborn son for us to be together. One side of me is happy he's mine, but the other side knows if she was still alive, he wouldn't even give me a second glance."

"Again, it doesn't matter. The past can't be changed. You are together now. People experience the death of loved ones every day, but it doesn't mean they aren't allowed to love again. Look at Dad and Beth. Didn't you learn how to deal with issues like this in your psychology classes? You're a psychiatrist, for crying out loud."

I rest my head on the side of the bed. "You're right, but with this situation, I'm not sure how to handle it. It's me being nervous Nelly again. I'm afraid the bubble will burst. He makes me happier than I ever thought possible. He brings out the best in me and helps me be more open about my inner battles. He doesn't judge me or seem to care that I can't have children. It's so refreshing to relax and not worry about what he'll think. I'm not embarrassed anymore. I wake up happy and go to bed smiling."

"Please focus on the positive things then. You have such a connected history. It's so romantic in its own way." She squeezes her hands together while fluttering her eyelashes. "It would be a pity if you didn't stay together. I hope what Beth shared with us will help you if things get rough."

"I need to hear those three words from him. He needs to show me he's able to move on and love again. We're having such a good time right now. I don't want to rock the boat." I stop talking as I pick food from my teeth.

"Real attractive." She squishes her face in disgust as she laughs. "Do you pick your teeth in front of James?"

"No, I pick his teeth." I stick my tongue out at her.

"I love you, Lisa. If anyone deserves true love, it's you."

My heart squeezes, hearing her say that. "Thank you. That means a lot to me. Maybe your knight in shining armor will show up, unexpectedly, when you need him the most." I rub her knee. "I miss our talks. Time is so limited. I look forward to when I have more time on my hands."

"Yeah, in three or four years when your residency is over. One way or the other, we'll find the time," Tina adds.

"Hello up there. Come on, girls," Beth yells from the bottom of the stairs. "The turkey is ready to be carved, so I need help putting the side dishes on the table."

We both stand up. "We didn't realize we've been up here for so long. Sorry! We'll be right down."

Tina turns to me with a devilish smile on her face. "The last one to the kitchen has to do the dishes." We both bolt out of the room and bang into the doorframe. I'm able to get ahead and run into the kitchen, yelling, "I'm first. I won."

"Shit!" Beth shrieks as something clatters on the kitchen floor tiles. I spin in her direction to see her bending over in pain as she wraps her hand in a towel. It's turning bright red.

"Shit, I cut myself with the carving knife. You scared me when you ran into the kitchen. It fell out of my hands. I went to catch it. I think I need to go to the hospital!"

# Chapter 39

## James

"That's how you do it! Another touchdown for the Giants," Mike shouts as we high-five.

My back stiffens. "What was that?" I say as I look up at the ceiling. "Was that a scream?"

The basement door blasts open, and Lisa shouts, "James, Beth needs you. She's cut herself badly. Come quick!"

I jump from the sofa without even thinking. "Hurry, I'm right behind you." Mike motions for me to go before him. I take the stairs two at a time.

I dash straight to Beth. She bends over the sink, running water over her hand.

"What happened?"

"Beth cut her hand with the carving knife on the counter," Lisa says with a shaky voice.

I gently take her hand to examine it. "Let me see. This will hurt, but I need to check how deep the cut is."

She flinches from my touch.

"It looks like you cut in between your thumb and pointer finger." I gently wrap a clean towel around her hand and put light pressure on it. "It's pretty deep. Please put your hand where mine is. Put pressure on it so I can take my hand away and elevate it." I face Mike and Lisa. "Do you have any rubbing alcohol and bandages in the house?"

Beth chimes in before anyone else. "No. We're bad at keeping stuff like that in the house. We may have a couple of Band-Aids somewhere."

Lisa jumps from her spot in nervous excitement. "Wait. James, you have your first responder medical kit in the trunk of your car. I saw it when we took our bags out when we arrived."

The light bulb goes on in my head. I snap my fingers. "That's right. I forgot it was there. Let me run outside to get it. Keep your hand elevated and keep pressure on it." I dart toward the door, but Lisa stops me.

"Wait with her. Give me your keys so I can get it."

I pat down my jeans pockets hoping they are there. They are. I pull them out and throw them to her. I can't believe I still have that medical kit in my trunk. Or was I aware of it but just pretended it wasn't there? I bought it when I finished my residency, and I immediately put it in the trunk. It would be irresponsible for an ER doctor to not have one in his car and/or house. I'm shaken from my thoughts as Lisa runs through the door.

She hands me the bag, and I snatch the items I need without even thinking. My body and mind are on autopilot. It's been over a year since I've worked in the ER, but everything I've learned and experienced is still imprinted in my brain. With supplies in hand, I line them up in the order of when I will need them.

"Beth, I need you to sit in a comfortable chair at the table. The light is brightest there. Can I please have a few old, clean rags you don't mind getting blood on?"

"We have some in the laundry room. I'll go get a few," Tina replies.

"I have what I need to give you stitches. Unfortunately, I don't have anything to numb the area around the cut. You need to breathe in and out to help alleviate the pain. Bite on your hand or on a towel. Or better yet, Mike, come over here so she can squeeze your hand."

He moves over to her side and holds his hand out so she can take hold of it.

"Squeeze my hand as hard as you want," Mike says as he rubs her back.

"Lisa, I'll need you to hand me particular supplies when I ask for them. Please put on some rubber gloves."

She nods and proceeds to do so.

Tina comes back and freezes. "Here are some rags." She tosses them to me. "I can't watch this—I'm already queasy." She cringes and turns her back on us. "I'll stand over here." A nervous chuckle slips from her lips. "This is why I'm not a doctor."

"Thanks, Tina. Lisa can help me from here. It won't take long."

I pull on a pair of rubber gloves. "I'm going to start now. Again, make as much noise as you want and squeeze his hand until it's blue. He's a big guy. I'm sure he can handle it." I wink at Beth. "But you need to stay as still as possible."

She cracks a smile, a few tears trickling down her face.

From then on, I'm in a zone. There's complete silence other than occasional whimpers from Beth or me asking Lisa for something. My hands have their own language and grace while mending her. I'm back in my element, with adrenaline coursing through my veins. This type of rush is unforgettable, even though it's only from stitches. I've missed it.

"I'm almost done. You're doing better than I thought. Four stitches were all you needed. It was deep but not wide, and didn't hit the nerve." I look at the rest of the supplies on the counter.

"Lisa, can you please hand me the bandages so I can wrap her hand securely?" I remove them from her hand and look up at her. "Thanks."

Her cheeks are red, and her eyes shimmer. She glances to Beth and then back to me.

"Finished. The bandage is secure for now. You will need to change it once or twice a day. I'll leave some extra bandages for you. It's not good if it gets wet or is on for a long time. In a week, you will need to go to your general practitioner to have the stitches removed. Put some ice on it now and keep your hand elevated for a little while longer. That also means no more cooking for you."

I face Mike and say, "Mr. Safety, you need to go to the pharmacy or grocery store tomorrow to load up on some things. I'll create a list of basic items you should have in your medicine cabinet at all times."

He gives me a salute. "I will, Dr. Kramer. Thank you for your time and expertise. One more thing to be thankful for this Thanksgiving." He pats me on the back with a smirk. "Good job, son."

Beth sits in her chair, with her hand elevated above her head. "My hand stings and pounds like my heartbeat. I've never had stitches before."

"You should take some ibuprofen for the pain. Do you have any?"

"Yes. That's something we do have. Mike, can you please go get me two pills? The bottle is in the cabinet in our bathroom."

He smiles and walks out of the kitchen.

She touches my arm while I pack everything back into the medical bag. "Thank you so much. You are a true natural, performing that with such ease. You can be my doctor anytime. It would've ruined our Thanksgiving if I'd gone to the hospital. From now on I'll make sure our house is stocked with the things on your list. It's ironic. Mike is overly protective, but we don't have something as simple as bandages here."

"It was my pleasure to help you. Now go sit in the living room. Doctor's orders." How can I joke around about this? I haven't been a doctor for over a year, but it still feels natural.

Mike returns with her medicine.

"Mike, you need to cut the turkey now and place it on the platter," Beth says, waving her good hand. "I hope it isn't dried out and cold. Lisa and Tina, you need to put the rest of the side dishes on the table. I don't want anything to get cold. Or maybe while he cuts the turkey, heat up the oven and put some of the dishes in there to keep warm. The table is set and ready to go. Call me when it's time to eat."

Beth walks into the living room. Lisa wraps her arms around my waist. She kisses my neck and whispers, "They are right. You are a natural. You were amazing."

I'm walking on cloud nine, but I won't admit it. Not even to myself.

# Chapter 40

## Lisa

I lie awake in the luxurious new bed in my old room. It's been a long time since I have been here. My life has changed so much since then. I know it's only November, but it feels like James and I have been together for much longer. He made a good impression with me yesterday, as well as my family.

I've never seen him in doctor mode before. He took charge and mended Beth's hand with such confidence and compassion. Right then and there, I knew my entire heart belonged to his. Toward the end of the procedure, our eyes locked for an instant. If my eyes could have screamed *I love you*, I think the windows would have shattered.

After he finished with Beth, he cleaned up and acted like it never happened. But it did, and we can't pretend it didn't. When we gave him an abundance of praise, he shrugged it off and said, "It was only stitches." It might have only been stitches, but medicine is his domain, his calling. Did this open his eyes to reality? I should have asked him last night, but I didn't want to ruin his good mood.

I turn on my side and watch him sleep peacefully. He was antsy during the night. I was too exhausted to ask him what was wrong. Sleep finally took him under. I wish I knew what he thinks about. He stares off into space once in a while. Does he have other internal battles I'm not aware of? If so, why doesn't he confide in me? I hope being with me isn't his excuse to avoid facing his problems. I love it that I comfort him, but is that all I am? My gut says no, but I know there's still a little wall between us.

His eyes flutter open. Two glossy peridots pierce mine. "How long have you been watching me?" he grumbles. He rolls over onto his back and drapes his arm over his face.

"Forever. I like watching you sleep. I could stare at you all day. Especially when you sleep without a shirt."

He turns his head toward me and yawns. "Are you only with me for my looks? I'm offended." He tries to act serious but a smile cracks through.

"Do you know you purr like a cat when you sleep? It's so sweet. The first time I heard it was when you slept on my sofa."

"I have never heard that before. Do I do anything else while I'm asleep?" he asks as he pulls his pillow over his head.

"No worries. You look cute no matter what."

He grunts in response. Someone is cranky this morning.

"I smell breakfast cooking downstairs, and it makes my stomach growl. Not that I want to eat after the food we ingested yesterday. I won't fit into my scrubs when I go to work tomorrow. What time did you say we need to be at your parents' today?" I sit up and stretch my arms over my head.

"We can take our time. Mom told us to arrive between twelve and one p.m. Why don't you give me a tour of your town? I want to know where you played with your friends, where your schools are, and all the little things you can remember. I'm only familiar with the area by the gas station where I worked."

"Sounds like a plan. I'll think about where to go while I take a shower. Go back to sleep if you want, Dr. Kramer. You had a busy day yesterday. You were quite enticing to watch when you turned into a doctor." I kiss his bare shoulder and jump up from the bed. I turn around and see his face is contorted and his jaw clenched. "Is something wrong?"

"I'm fine. Just tired. I didn't sleep well last night," he mumbles as he rolls onto his stomach and hugs his pillow.

Maybe I shouldn't have called him Dr. Kramer. I don't care at this point. It's not fair I walk on pins and needles when it comes to his battles. We have a fun day ahead. To keep the air cheery, I chirp, "I can't wait to see your parents and Alexa." I walk out of the bedroom with a pep in my step.

"Sorry we have to go. We had a great time yesterday. It was nice to be home. I promise to be back soon." I squeeze Dad tightly. I walk over to Beth and hug her as well. I buzz softly into her ear, "Thank you for our long talk. It was really helpful. I'll keep you posted."

"What's with the whispering?" Dad interrupts playfully.

"I thanked her, among other things. Girlie things, to be exact. Nothing you need to know."

"If it's girlie talk, then you are correct." He takes a step back with his arms up.

"Beth, thank you so much for all of the delicious food. I hope your hand feels better soon. Call me if you have any questions or problems." James kisses her on the cheek. Her face turns a quick shade of red.

He walks to Dad and shakes his hand and pretends to whisper. "Thank you for our talk yesterday. It was very helpful." He looks over his shoulder with a devilish smile. "Sorry. Guy talk."

Dad looks at him and says, "Anytime. Please come back soon. I enjoyed having another man to watch the football game with."

"I'll be sure to do that. Enjoy your man cave this weekend."

"It would have been nice to say good-bye to Tina. Why did she leave so early today? Oh. It's Black Friday. How could I forget? She loves battling those crowds." I shake my head. "She's nuts. I wouldn't be caught dead near a shopping mall today." Beth and I laugh.

"Anyway, I'm not sure when I can visit next. I'm scheduled to work both Christmas and New Year's. I'll let you know, or maybe you can come visit us. Thanks again, and I'll call you soon."

"We'll think about it. Have fun and tell your parents happy Thanksgiving, James."

We walk to his car holding hands as the wind kicks up behind us. "No sun today. Hopefully, it won't rain," I add.

He puts our stuff in the trunk.

"Now I'll show you some places in my town. Drive slowly though. Especially if it starts to rain," I warn as I point my finger at him.

He grabs my finger and pretends to bite it.

"Don't bite my finger," I squeal.

"No more pointing your finger at me. I know I need to drive carefully. You have nothing to worry about. Sit back and enjoy."

For the next thirty minutes, I show him my high school, where I used to run, where my high school friends used to live, a tree I climbed and fell out of, where we went sled riding, and my favorite pizza parlor. Anything I could remember that was worth showing.

We're now at one of my favorite places when I was a child. I relax into my seat. "This is my elementary school. Behind the school building was a small field full of giant blackberry bushes. Maybe the bushes are still there." I look in the distance, as if I'll see Tina and me as little girls. "It looks like the field is gone. That's a shame." I sigh. "Anyway, during late summer, Mom would ask us to pick a few bowls of blackberries so we could make jam. She made us wear long-sleeved shirts and long pants even when it was ninety degrees."

"Why would you wear such warm clothing?" James asks.

"The first time we went to pick some berries, we had scratches all over our arms and legs when we returned home. Some scratches were deep enough they bled."

"What was out there that scratched you?"

"Blackberries have thorns on the branches. Hence the long clothes." I can almost feel the sting from the scratches. I rub my arms. "By the time we'd return home, our clothes would be covered with hitchhikers. Do you know what hitchhikers are?"

"Someone who tries to get a ride from a stranger." He gives a goofy grin.

"You're a real comedian. I'm feeling nostalgic, so pretend to enjoy my story." I smack his thigh. He grabs my hand and kisses my fingertips.

"Sorry. I was just playing with you. I like to hear your stories. Go on."

I'm putty in his hands. He makes me melt when he says things like that to me. "Hundreds of these little brown parts or seeds of a plant would stick to our clothes like Velcro. We had to pick every single one off." I sigh and bring James's hand to my heart. My body tingles with warmth as I think of those summers when Mom was alive.

He puts the car signal on. I notice it's to turn right. "James, you need to turn left instead of right to drive to your parents'."

"I know. I'm taking us on a detour."

"Where are we going?" I say under my breath, a bad feeling in my gut.

"You'll see. Somewhere I think we both need to go and see."

*Oh no.*

"James, I don't think I can do this." I rub my hands up and down my legs.

He grabs my left hand. "We'll do it together. It's where we first met. I've never been back there. Have you?"

"I tried to leave flowers by the tree once, but Tina had to do it for me. I wouldn't get out of the car. It's something I can't handle, no matter what I do."

"There's the gas station I worked at. Well, it was a gas station at the time." He points his finger at the now-deserted building. It's such an eyesore.

"There's the pharmacy Tina worked at. Surprisingly, it's still in business even with all the pharmacy chains around here." I point out.

Now we're driving toward the site of the accident. I chew the inside of my mouth. James holds my left hand and I rub my sweaty right hand up and down my right leg. I can see the large tree ahead. James parks the car on the side of the road near the tree.

"Do you want to get out, Lisa? I'll go with you."

I don't answer right away. The devil on one shoulder whispers I'm weak and can't handle being here. The angel on the other side encourages me to get out of the car. I bang my arm against the car door and pull my hand from him. "I hate that I'm so terrified to do this. Why am I still like this after so many years?" I scream. "I thought I was better after so much therapy, but it's obviously not true. How can I possibly help others if I can't even help myself?"

"Have you ever been able to say good-bye to your mom? Maybe this is what you need. I didn't bring you here to upset you. We connected here. That day changed both our lives, which led us to this very point in time. I think it will be good for the both of us." His hands take hold of my shoulders and turn me to him. "Let's do this together."

I squeeze my eyes shut while I breathe in and out several times. My heart rate begins to slow. I open my eyes when a flash of energy accelerates through my body.

"You're right. I need to face this. Something good came out of that day. You were with me." I take one last deep breath and open the door. I take slow steps toward the tree, with James next to me. Visions of the accident fly through my head. I start to quiver. I can still feel the wind and the snow blowing in my face.

James pulls me to him and tucks me inside his jacket against his chest. "You're shaking. Let me warm you up."

Still shaking, I walk away from him. I push my way through some bushes growing in front of the tree. I'm surprised the tree is still alive; a large section of the trunk is stripped of its bark and damaged. Scarred. Just like me. I brush my fingers over the rough edges of the bark. Rain begins to sprinkle my face.

My voice cracks. "I miss her. I remember so many things about her."

"Tell me what you miss about her. What do you remember the most?" He rubs my back.

"She made the best grilled cheese sandwiches. She used a special cheese that would ooze out the side like honey from a honeycomb. She French braided my long hair perfectly and stuck little flowers in it. She had a funny sense of humor. She loved being goofy, especially when I had a bad day. It's not easy to cheer up a hormonal teenager, but she could do it."

I put my scarf to my nose, smelling my past. "She used the best fabric softener when she washed my clothes. I use the same one still. Even if she hadn't died in the accident, I would have been injured the same. She would have been there for me. I know she would have been my rock." I grieve.

Things would be so different if she was still around. But would I have met James anyway?

"She would bring me a glass of warm milk with honey and sing to me when I couldn't fall asleep at night. We would secretly go for hot fudge sundaes any time of the year alone, no matter how cold it was. It was our little secret." My mouth waters remembering how sweet and warm the fudge was on my tongue.

"She was very beautiful. When I was little, I would stare at her. I told her every day she was beautiful and looked like an angel. Sadly, as I got older, I told her less and less." I laugh to myself because I'm sure she thought I was joking.

"She smiled even when things were stressful. She had this infectious personality. What makes me sad is she wasn't smiling a lot the day she died. She seemed so annoyed or angry. I remember it so clearly." I sniff.

"Here's a tissue, sweetie."

*That sounds nice. I've never heard him call me sweetie before.*

"What angers me the most is she missed out on a lot of things. Mothers should be able to enjoy their children's proms, graduations, weddings—all that stuff. No one understands what it's like to lose a parent, especially at such a young age."

I look up at James and see the sadness in his eyes as rain collects on his nose. "What's wrong?"

"It pisses me off how much pain we've endured. We shouldn't have to suffer anymore. I brought you here to encourage you to find a sense of peace. I hope it brought you comfort knowing I was there with you then and now."

I wrap my arms around his waist. Again, my heart wants to sing

*I love you* to him, but my mind zips my heart shut. It isn't the right time. I need to hear him say it first. We're always confronting my issues or talking about them. I need to find a way for him to do the same. Not today though. I've had enough.

"Thank you for bringing me here. I should have done it years ago. I'm glad you're here with me. Now give me a kiss that will make my toes curl."

His left eyebrow rises. "I love it when you are so demanding."

He leans into me, and boy, does he kiss me. Good enough that I forget we are on the side of the road getting wet. Some cars pass us, honking their horns. We burst out of our love bubble as the sunshine breaks through the clouds. We look up to find a rainbow streaming proudly across the sky. Right then I know I've faced one of my biggest demons. Mom is here with us. Does this mean I can move on and not be so afraid anymore?

"Let's get back to the car before it starts raining again. I'm wet enough," he says.

We run back to the car. Just what I needed to get out of this frame of mind.

"Thank you so much, James. I know I said it already back there, but I have to say it again. It feels good that I came here and that you're with me. One more weight is off my chest now."

"You're welcome. God knows I have my own demons to face. I'm glad I was able to help you with yours."

*At least he admits it.*

He adds, "Let's go to my parents' now. Can you believe I'm hungry?" Once again, discussion is over before it can hardly begin.

"You're always hungry. You need to feed your sexy muscles," I tease.

He flexes his bicep. "We need to use our muscles later, if you know what I mean." His fingers trace up my thigh.

I squiggle in my seat. "You're lucky I have the same idea. I'm glad we're going home tonight."

# Chapter 41

## James

"Here's my parents' house," I announce as I maneuver through the driveway's iron gates.

Lisa hits me on the arm. "You never told me your parents are rich. This house is huge."

When I park the car in front of the garage, Lisa jumps out without closing her door. "It's beautiful, James."

"Dad's company is very successful," I say as I shut the car doors. "He bought this house when it was half the size and value it is today. It was originally a thirty-year-old, four-bedroom Cape Cod that needed a lot of work. When he started to make a good living, he renovated it and eventually built an addition on the right side, which leads into the back." I point to the right side of the house.

"Mom's dream was to have a white house with black shutters. And a garnet-red front door. Dad gave her exactly what she wanted. I remember her always working in the garden to make it look like it does today. You can't see it now, since everything is cut back and the leaves are off the trees. You should see it in the spring when everything is in bloom. We have a lot of flowering trees that brighten up the garden after a long winter. Don't ask me which kind. I have no idea when it comes to gardening. The rose section alone should be presented in a garden magazine." *Roses. Jessica.*

"The flowerpots under the windows are full of colorful flowers flowing over the tops. She knows how to make it look nice. They are quite proud of this house and how far they have come, especially since they didn't have any money to begin with."

She tugs on my arm. "By looking at this large garden in the front, why do I have a feeling you have a pool in the backyard and maybe a water fountain?" Lisa says, barely containing her excitement.

"You are clever. Yes, we have both. The pool was put in when I was around ten. We had a lot of great pool parties. Especially when I graduated high school. People who weren't even invited showed up because they heard the noise from the street. Mom was pretty shocked because she didn't know half of them. I thought someone was going to call the cops by the end of the night. It was one of the best parties I've ever had."

Lisa's teeth chatter. "My high school graduation was celebrated pretty low key. I went out to dinner with Tina and Dad. He'd just started dating Beth. Things were still hard for us. It wasn't the same without Mom. But let's not talk about it now."

I rub her arms. "You're cold. Let's get you inside." We follow the long path leading to the front door.

"Dad loves his job. I think it's why he's so successful. I'm going for my license so I can follow in his footsteps and maybe even take over the business when he retires." *Who am I trying to convince I'm happy about this? Myself, Lisa, my family, or everyone?*

Stitching up Beth's hand yesterday gave me that simmering rush through my blood. I miss the rush as if it were a drug. I played it cool in front of everyone, but...it was a very big deal, especially to hear them call me Dr. Kramer. Even with the rush, I'm still petrified.

*I couldn't even save Jessica and Jacob.*

"Happy Thanksgiving, James and Lisa," Dad greets us midway up the path.

"Happy Thanksgiving, Dad. Where's Mom and Alexa?"

"They went to buy a couple of groceries. They should be back any minute."

He steps over to Lisa. "Hi, Lisa. It's great to see you again. We're glad you could make it. It's convenient your family lives close by."

I hear the gates open. Alexa drives up and honks the horn.

"Here they come." Lisa beams.

We stroll over to the car as Alexa jumps out. She runs to Lisa and hugs her.

"Hey, James. Can you please get the grocery bags out of the trunk for me?" Alexa says.

I can't even answer before they both walk past me. "Happy Thanksgiving to you, too. What am I? Chopped liver?" I complain.

They gobble like turkeys and continue toward the house.

"Hey, Mom. Happy Thanksgiving. How was your day yesterday?" I ask as I haul the full bags from the trunk. I thought Dad said they were getting a few groceries.

"It was nice but quiet with only Alexa here."

We proceed to the kitchen. I put the bags on the counter.

Mom comes up to me and takes my hands in hers. "Let's change the subject. How was yesterday?" she asks with concern.

"It was great. Her father, stepmother, and sister are really nice. Her sister, Tina, is a little bit like Alexa. Outgoing and bubbly. I felt very comfortable with them."

Mom sighs in relief. "I'm so glad to hear that, honey. I was a bit nervous."

"No need to be nervous. There's no reason why I shouldn't meet her parents when we spend every free second together. It's a natural step." I purposely leave out Beth cutting her hand.

"You know what I mean, James. I know it's not easy in general. I'll leave it at that."

I look away from her. "I'm curious where Lisa and Alexa are? I'm going to go search for them."

"Go ahead. I need to start cooking anyway. We'll chat later."

*Should I be more nervous?* I just met Lisa's family. It felt natural. To be honest, I felt more relaxed with her family than I had with Jessica's parents. Jessica's parents gave me the impression she was their princess and she deserved everything. She was the only child, so all their focus was on her. Jessica didn't act like that necessarily. She was independent, but she was always taken care of. Always given the best of everything. Her parents ran the show when it came to their daughter. I'd loved Jessica and wanted to give her everything, no doubt.

With Lisa—she doesn't need to be taken care of. She's been on her own for a long time and doesn't care about money and fancy things. She just wants to be loved and accepted for who she is. I hate comparing the two. I know it would hurt Lisa if she knew what I think about occasionally. It's also disrespectful to talk about Jessica this way. My internal battles suck the life out of me sometimes.

I leave the kitchen to see where Lisa is. Alexa is probably showing her around the house. I walk around the corner into the great room and stop short. Lisa is staring at a picture frame. Her face in distress. She doesn't seem to notice me. I take a silent step back so I'm out of sight. What picture is she looking at? I hope it's not a picture of me and Jessica.

Alexa calls her from another room, so I take advantage and peek around the corner. I see Lisa fumble with the picture and set it back into place.

I move back because I hear Alexa coming. I sneak into the bathroom so they don't see me. "Let me show you upstairs," Alexa says. Their voices trailing behind them up the stairs.

I want to see what picture she was looking at. I creep out of the bathroom and walk quickly to the picture frame. My stomach clenches. It's of me and Jessica, minutes after I proposed. It was one of my favorites. Oddly, it feels like a lifetime ago. It's also Mom's favorite picture of us, but I'm pissed she has this out.

"James. Where are you?"

I jump when Alexa yells. I thought they were upstairs. "I'm over here in the great room." She comes around the corner. "What's—"

I put the picture behind my back. "Where's Lisa?" I whisper.

"She's upstairs in the bathroom. Why?" Her voice low.

I hand her the picture. "I saw Lisa looking at it. Why does Mom still have this picture on display? I asked her not to."

She shrugs. "It's from our past, not just yours. She was a big part of our lives. Or maybe she forgot to put this one away."

"I couldn't read Lisa's face. It made me feel bad because I'm sure she had a million thoughts twirling in her head."

"James, do you ever talk to Lisa about Jessica? Are you open with her when she asks you questions?"

"She doesn't really ask me questions about her. She asks more questions regarding my career in medicine, not real estate." I put the picture in a cabinet next to the TV. "If I were in her shoes, I'm not sure I would want to know if she always thinks about her deceased husband and child. Could I even compete with him knowing how much she loved him, even though he's dead? I would be afraid to hear the answer." I pull on my hair and groan.

"I never looked at it from her perspective. How can she be so patient with me? I don't deserve her." I turn away from Alexa.

She pulls on my shirt. "Look at me, James." I turn to face her. "If you want a future with her, you need to be honest, no matter how hard it is for you or her. She deserves all you can give. She has been open with you from the beginning. She deserves the same from you."

"I know, Alexa. I know. It's just not that simple." *Life is never simple. Suck it up.*

I want to tell her how Beth cut herself, but she'll only push me till I'm annoyed. I don't need pressure during this holiday weekend. I know what she would say. It's what they would all say.

*Get back on the horse.*

# Chapter 42

## Lisa

Water splashes all over the sink and my shirt as I take out nervous energy on my hands. I should have prepared myself for something like this. It was heart wrenching to see a picture of James with Jessica. I didn't expect there to be pictures of them around the house. But why not? I'm sure she was here a million times. She was considered part of the family.

Of course, they looked deliriously happy in the picture. I'm so pathetic—I'm jealous of a dead woman. Why did she have to die for us to be together? Why did he go through something so horrific? Should I feel guilty because he's mine now?

When we make love, we're in another world. I hope to God he thinks about me and not Jessica. Even though I'm paranoid he compares me to her, I don't like it that I compare myself to her either. It was good to talk with Beth. She helped me understand the situation differently. How patient will I be in the next months? Will we move forward or just ignore the elephant in the room?

I dry my hands and wipe down the sink.

December will be a busy month. I need to work a lot and don't have any more holidays free. I think James will be going to Vermont with his family. I'll be on my own. Maybe it'll be good for us, even though we don't see each other as often as I'd like.

Enough rehashing the day. I've been hiding in the bathroom long enough. They're going to think I'm sick again or have drowned. I flinch when I hear a knock.

"Lisa, are you in there?" Alexa asks.

"Yes. I'm coming out now."

"Are you okay?" Concern thick in her voice.

"Yes, just pondering some things. Typical me." I open the door and find Alexa waiting for me to say more.

"What are you pondering about?" She wiggles her fingers like quotes when she repeats the word *pondering*.

"Nothing and everything." I shrug my shoulders and walk past her.

I look around to see if James is nearby. "Is James still downstairs?"

"Yes. Why?" She takes a step closer to me.

"Did he tell you my stepmother cut her hand yesterday? He gave her stitches right there in the kitchen. He was so impressive and in his element. He's making a huge mistake training for his real estate license. That isn't what he wants. I know it. He's so stubborn and apprehensive. I hoped it would give him a little boost. If it did, he's a good actor, playing cool." I'm pissed just talking about it.

"That's interesting. He didn't mention it to me yet. Let's see if he brings it up when we're all together. We're disappointed about the career change, but we need to be supportive. He's trying to find himself again, but it's taking a long time. I want to say be patient with him for a little while longer. But we understand when enough is enough. Worry about yourself and your residency. That's your priority."

"I saw a picture of James and Jessica in the living room. It was hard to look at. It hurt a lot. Yesterday was such a great day, but today seems off. I'm on Jessica's territory now. She spent a lot of time here. It has to be weird for him to be here with me."

"I don't know what to say to make you feel better." There's that face of sympathy I can't stand. I have seen it too many times in my life.

"I don't expect you to. But it's difficult. I'm in love with him, Alexa. I know deep down inside I am. It's hard for me to admit this to you. I haven't even told him yet because I know he isn't ready to hear it. I keep questioning whether it's too early to say it. I'm waiting for him. Maybe I'll need to walk away so he can work it out himself."

"I know you're in love with him. We see how you act toward him. I truly believe you are meant to be together. After everything you both have gone through, I can't imagine you will drift apart. After meeting you, he has changed from night to day. It's amazing how one person can bring you so far down you feel you can never survive, but then another person can lift you as high as the stars. You have done that for him. Be patient."

I want so badly to believe her.

"You'd better be right, or you'll owe me a new pair of expensive shoes. Not red though. I'm not sure I can pull off wearing red shoes."

"That's a deal." We shake hands and walk down the hallway toward the stairs.

"Thanks for letting me vent. My chest feels lighter now."

"No problem. That's what I'm here for. This is why I don't have serious relationships. It's too exhausting." She pushes her hair behind her ears.

"I need to go downstairs and find James. I feel like we have gotten lost in this big house." I laugh but wonder if we're avoiding each other.

I find James in the living room, not the great room, looking out of the large bay window facing the covered swimming pool. At what, I have no idea. I sneak up behind him and wrap my arms around his solid waist. He moans softly and puts his hands over mine.

"We seemed to have lost each other in this big house. It's a beautiful home. Sometimes big houses have a cold feeling to them. Not this house. It's so welcoming and warm. It has a country feel to it. Isn't it too big for your parents to live here by themselves?"

"Dad had not a cent in his pocket when he started his business. He's proud to have come this far financially. We were a little nervous with the house crisis years back. His business was hit, but it slowly picked back up. They love this house and don't want to sell it. Would you want a house like this when you're finished with your residency and finally start making more money?"

"I don't need a house this big, because I won't have a family to fill it," I say, more bluntly than I intended. It hurts to say the truth out loud. "I would love to have a house big enough to run a practice out of it. Maybe a house with two or three bedrooms, like my dad's. In all honesty, I don't think so far ahead. I still have a long road ahead of me."

He turns around and puts his arms around me, laying his chin on my head.

"Did you and Jessica want a big house like this?" I say it and then recoil.

His arms squeeze me tightly. "We talked about it but knew it would take a while to make good money for a house this big. I don't need a big house. She wanted it more than I did, especially if we had more children. I would be happy living in a smaller house. Status and money were never a goal in my life. I just wanted to do what I loved. As you and I have experienced, we don't always get what we want."

We stand there in silence. I can't let his comment about having more children bother me. That was before she died. Yet, now, he says he doesn't think he could ever have another child.

This visit is depressing us. He has memories here. He doesn't at my dad's house or most of the places we visit. This was bound to happen. I just wish it wasn't this weekend.

With that in mind, I pull away and say brightly, "Where's your family? I feel like we're alone here. Aren't we being a little rude?"

"Since it stopped raining, Dad set up the fire pit on the open terrace. Everyone is outside sitting under blankets on the Adirondack chairs. Enjoying the warmth from the fire and, I'm sure, some cocktails."

"It sounds like fun. Let's get our coats and join them."

He squeezes his arm around me and tugs me with him. It makes me feel a little bit of relief, but why do I feel a storm is brewing?

# Chapter 43

## James

The months are flying by. I've had my real estate license for a month now. I travel back and forth to Dad's office to learn on the job. It keeps me busy, and I'm finally making money. I stay at my parents' when I work. The time with Lisa is limited. I miss her. Being away from her has made me realize how attached I have become to her and how much she truly means to me.

It's Valentine's Day, and I have decided to surprise her with a candlelight dinner. She hates this day because it's the anniversary of the car accident. But it's also the anniversary of the first time we met. It's time to change the way she feels about this day.

I'm waiting in front of her apartment door, shivering, with a bouquet of different-colored tulips. She knows I will never give her roses. I want to ask her to come with me to Alexa's place. We'd have the apartment to ourselves tonight because Alexa is away until tomorrow. We always stay here, so I thought it would be nice to have a change. She had a stomach virus a couple of days ago. I hope she's feeling better and can eat.

She should be home any minute. I feel like an idiot standing here with a bouquet of flowers in my hand. Guys stare at me when they walk past me. Of course, the girls smile because I look romantic. I turn toward the sidewalk when I hear footsteps. When she sees me, her face lights up with the smile I miss. I can't help but smile right back.

"James, what are you doing here? What a special surprise! I thought you were at your parents'." Her cheeks are red from the cold.

I smile and hand her the tulips. "Happy Valentine's Day. I thought I would surprise you. I've missed you."

She takes the bouquet and leans in for a kiss. "No one has ever given me flowers. They are absolutely beautiful." She squeezes them tight to her chest. "Thank you. This is a real first. You make me feel so special."

"The flowers are not all. I would like you to come back to Alexa's for the night. She won't be back until tomorrow. I'd like to make you dinner, if it's okay."

"It's more than okay. I would love to. Let me pack some things. I'll take a shower there. I'm so excited." She walks happily into her apartment. I follow her in, and she goes directly to the kitchen to grab a sea-green vase. She makes a nice bouquet and runs into her room. Within ten minutes we're out the door.

She goes directly into the shower when we arrive. That gives me time to set up the table and get the food prepared. I hope she likes what I'm making. I'm not a good cook, but she mentioned a food she likes. It was a staple when I was in college and medical school.

As soon as I hear the shower turn off, I light candles in the living room and kitchen. Champagne cools on the table, and the lights are dim. I have never done something like this before. Not even for Jessica. I know how much Lisa will appreciate this. I want to see her surprised and happy.

She opens the door while towel drying her hair. She freezes. Her jaw drops. The towel falls to the floor. Her hands go to her face. "James, I don't know what to say. I have never been more surprised." Her eyes are big pools of sapphires.

"I wanted to do something nice for you. You've been working so hard and are so supportive of me. You deserve to be treated like a queen. You dread this date every year, so I want to try to change that for you."

I pull out a chair facing the living room. "Please take a seat. You can't look into the kitchen. As you have experienced, I don't cook very well. But there's one thing I'm good at making. It's something I think you'll laugh at when you see it. Let me open the champagne so you can relax with a glass while I make dinner. It won't take too long."

I pour her a glass. She puts her hand up to gesture it's enough. "I can't drink too much tonight because I need to be at work by twelve tomorrow instead of three p.m. So annoying."

"That's too bad. I was hoping to get you drunk and take advantage of you."

"You can take terrible advantage of me with or without the alcohol. I won't mind."

"Happy Valentine's Day, my little Jersey girl. Sorry, *petite* Jersey girl." We clink our glasses together. I drink some, then put my glass down, lean over, and press my lips against hers. "Hmmm. You taste good." I lick her lips. Before she can react, I walk away toward the kitchen.

"You are such a tease!"

I laugh. "How are you feeling? I'm sorry I wasn't there to help you when you were sick. Do you feel better now?"

"My appetite is back, but once in a while I get this weird pain in my abdomen. Maybe it's from standing all day. I only feel the pain when I move a certain way. It's probably a pulled muscle. My period is also weird. I spot once in a while, and that's it. It happened yesterday, and nothing today. It's normal for me to an extent. Since the accident, I've never had a normal period. No big deal. Maybe we're having too much sex." She smirks over her shoulder.

"No peeking! There's no such thing as too much sex. I can't help it I can't keep my hands off you. If you could only read my mind about what I fantasize about when you are near me."

"Don't make me attack you before you even feed me. I'm starving." She playfully threatens me.

"Be patient. I'll let you do that to me later." She drives me nuts. I would do anything to press her against the wall and make her love Valentine's Day.

She probably knows what I'm cooking. The smell of butter and bread frying in a pan fills the apartment. "Dinner is ready. Close your eyes. I want it to be a surprise. But you probably already know what it is just by the smell."

She wiggles in her chair like a little girl.

"I have an idea, but I'm not going to say. If it's what I think it is, you really do listen to the little details."

I place the dish in front of her. "You can open your eyes."

She opens them and starts laughing. "Oh my gosh. I knew you made me a grilled cheese sandwich. You remembered what I told you about my mom." She grabs my hand and looks at me with so much emotion in her eyes. "You are so thoughtful. I can't believe you did this for me."

She stands up and hugs me. "This is the best surprise after the long week I've had. I can't say thank you enough. It's so special to me. It's better than any five-star restaurant. I swear I could cry. I'm a bit emotional these days. Let me try this sandwich to see how it compares to my mom's. I can still remember the taste of hers." She sits back down.

"I feel so much pressure. I hope it's close." I watch as she takes a bite.

She stops midchew, closes her eyes and moans in delight.

"It's that good, huh?" I smile with pride.

"Absolutely perfect. It's not the same as my mom's, but I don't expect it to be. It's cooked by you, so that makes it my favorite now. It's truly excellent. The cheese oozes out of the sides, and the bread is perfectly crisp and buttery. Yummy! Do you have any ketchup?"

"You eat yours with ketchup?" I crinkle my nose. "I never tried it with ketchup."

"I don't really like ketchup, but I eat it with grilled cheese sandwiches and hotdogs for some reason. But the ketchup needs to be mixed with spicy, hot mustard when I eat hotdogs."

"Good to know for when barbeque season starts. Now let me get some ketchup for you and grab my sandwich. I'll be right back." I hear her moan again as she munches. I need to pat myself on the back.

I put mine on a plate. I turn on the CD player and start a song I know she'll like. It's a classic. I sit at the table with her. "Lisa, I know you hate this specific day. I know what it represents. But it's also the anniversary of the first time we met. February fourteenth holds bad memories, but the one positive is us. Maybe we can think of this day differently. It can be sad but also happy."

Her head perks up when she hears the song. She steps away from the table and comes and straddles me. She puts her arms around my neck. "You are the sweetest and best man I know. I can't fully describe how much this night means to me. You make me so happy. This song is one of my favorites since I was little. Bruce Springsteen's 'Jersey Girl.'"

"This song reminds me of you. You are my true Jersey girl. In the summer, we should go down the shore. I haven't been there since high school. We can walk along the beach, go to the boardwalk, and eat cotton candy. It'll be hard to resist you when you're wearing a bathing suit though. What do you say?"

"It sounds perfect. Everything is perfect." She brushes her lips against mine.

"Do you want another grilled cheese?" I ask as my hands wander down her back, pulling her against me."

"It depends. What's for dessert?" She trails kisses along my jaw.

"Dessert will be served anywhere in this apartment. I don't think we'll be thinking about grilled cheese for long when you see what I have planned."

"I say no to another grilled cheese. Dessert sounds more enticing. Is chocolate involved?"

"As a matter of fact, it is. In the liquid form." She sits there watching me. Her eyes look like blue crystals as they glisten in the candlelight.

I push my hand through her hair. "You are so beautiful in every way. I don't know how to tell you in words how I feel about you. I'm so lucky I found you."

"Well, I can help you show me." She opens the top two buttons of her shirt. She pulls the fabric away, revealing a sexy black bra.

I swallow deeply.

"I'm starving for dessert," she says seductively as she traces her finger down my chest and toward my jeans.

As if on cue, she pulls my shirt off in one movement. I stand up with her legs wrapped around my waist. We kiss in desperation, as if it's the last time we will see each other. She pulls her shirt off as I push her up against the wall. I pull her bra to the side. My mouth starts teasing and biting until she's squirming in delight.

"This is one of my fantasies tonight. I could have taken you against the wall while I was cooking, but I knew the anticipation would be better if we waited."

"We have too many clothes on! They need to be off, now!" she demands in passion.

I slide her down the wall so I can obey her sexy order. I yank down her pants and mine and have her up against the wall in five seconds flat.

I kiss and lick all over her chest and neck. She digs her nails into my shoulders while gliding on me.

"I'm so needy. I have missed you so much, James. It's been too long." She doesn't have to say it twice.

I'm more rough with her this time, but she seems even more turned on by it.

"It feels so good, James. Don't stop. My body has a mind of its own. It wants to consume you. I can't get enough of you."

I grab her mouth with mine, hoping she feels how my body belongs to her. That my hammering heart beats for her. That I am 100 percent hers and only hers.

# Chapter 44

## Lisa

We have never been this aggressive. It's the hottest thing ever. I love that he is strong enough to hold me up against the wall. He makes me feel like a feather. He makes me feel a lot of things. With every move we make, our hearts speak to each other. Things we are afraid to say out loud.

The way he kisses me, holds on to me tightly, treats my body like paradise, shows me his love for me.

Breathing heavily, I say, "James, I need the bed."

He holds me in place as he walks us to his bedroom. We are connected as one, just how I want us to always be. He slowly lowers himself onto the bed and lays back while I'm still on top of him.

"Should I get the chocolate syrup?" he says with a husky voice.

"No! I never want to separate from you, ever. I love feeling you in this way."

His hips lift to entice me. "Does this feel good?" he asks through gritted teeth with forced restraint. He leans up on his elbows as I start to glide up and down. His movements mimic mine. I can't find the words to describe what's happening between us. His forest-green eyes strip me bare of any worries or insecurities.

"You take my breath away. I could watch you all day when you look high on me," he says in between teasing movements. "Take control of me. Let me watch you as you let go."

He doesn't have to say any more. My body takes control of his before my mind can catch up. I do things to myself I never thought I would be brave enough to do in front of a man. *Where is the old me?*

*I hope she never comes back.* With his glistening eyes, he watches every movement I make. It empowers me, knowing it's me he wants to devour. I stay at a slow pace so I can beautifully torture him.

I'm stark naked in front of him, and I don't mean without clothes. Every one of my walls have been burnt down since we met. He has helped me become the woman I have always wanted to be but never thought was possible.

His hands move to my hips, moving me faster. "Lisa, I can't get enough of you. I want to stay like this, but I can't hold off much longer. It's my turn to control you."

He grabs me with his strong hands and flips me onto my back without separating us. He has me in a position that touches all of my sensitive spots. The buildup is so bittersweet. Hot honey flows through my blood, igniting sparks as it travels through my body, down to my toes. The sparks become explosions as we finally fall off the cliff together.

Holding on to each other like parachutes.

Afraid to let go.

# Chapter 45

## Lisa

"I love you. I'm sorry, Jessica! I will always love you. Please don't walk away from me."

I lift my head off the pillow. Did I hear him correctly? Did he just say Jessica? I sit up in bed to hear if he says it again.

"Don't leave, Jessica. Please don't walk away!"

I gasp and put my hand over my mouth. I can't seem to move as my stomach swirls. I feel my heart dissolve into sand. We have spent the past months and hours together as much as possible. I have been floating on air since we met. I know what being in love with someone truly feels like now. We melt into each other when we make love, especially tonight.

What kind of game is he playing? My heart aches hearing her name, not mine, come out of his mouth. It's poison to my ears. He'll never let her go or be able to love me the way I want or deserve.

I have had enough of this shit and can't stay here another minute—even if it is three a.m. I pack my bag as quietly and quickly as possible. I sneak out of the bedroom and close the door. I search the apartment for a piece of paper and pen. We just had the most perfect night. So romantic, so playful, and what I thought was full of love.

Of course, he never said those three words to me. He never says those three words. I am so fucking stupid to think he is in love with me. It's all a fucking act. And here I thought he was trying to tell me he loved me by playing the "Jersey Girl" song. A song about loving a Jersey girl. *I'm such a fucking fool*. Again! I want to scream.

I know he cares about me, but I want and deserve more. I love him more than anything, but I can't compete anymore. I shouldn't have to. All this time I thought he was making progress. Am I expecting too much? I never ask him how he's feeling because I am afraid of what he'll say. Hearing him talk in his sleep just confirmed my fears.

I sit on the couch and write him a letter. I leave it on the coffee table for him to find whenever. This is the last time he will hear from me for a while, maybe forever. He needs to choose to live with her in the past or with me in the future. His fate is in his own hands.

I need to use the bathroom before I leave. As I am finishing up, I glance down at my underwear. What the hell is with my period? It's so damn abnormal. I have minor cramps, but it doesn't feel like my period. We were out of control tonight. I experienced slight pain afterward. I shake my head out of frustration. It's not the time to deal with this. I need to get out of here.

I walk out of the bathroom and look at the kitchen table, still set up from tonight. The candles, the half-eaten grilled cheese sandwiches, champagne glasses... It's not possible I'm the only one who is in love. *Should I really leave the letter?* Yes, I need to be bold and stand my ground. He needs to make up his mind. The old Lisa would cling to him out of desperation and settle for less than she deserves. That is not me anymore. She is gone.

I put on my jacket and bend over to grab my bags off the floor. Severe dizziness overwhelms me as I stand up too fast. I lose my balance and hit the floor hard on my left side. Right where I feel my cramps. The dizziness fades, but the pain on my side spikes. I grab my side and try to refrain from making any noise. I push up on my hands, but the pain becomes sharp enough I fall back down. As it continues to increase I feel a surge of wetness between my legs. It has to be my period. How will I get out of here before he wakes up? I don't want him to see me, but I'm frightened.

A few minutes pass, and the pain progresses. My forehead is sweaty, and the dizziness has returned. This is definitely not my period.

"James!" I try to yell out, but it comes out muffled. I yell again with every ounce of energy I have.

"*James!*"

# Chapter 46

## James

I feel the bed next to me and notice it's cold and empty. Lisa must have gone to the bathroom. I look at the clock as I turn over onto my back. Three twenty. I take a deep breath in pure delight. Tonight was amazing. I loved surprising her and seeing how her face lit up. We made love all night, spicing it up with things we have never done before.

I have never felt so relaxed about life. I'm not the inflexible, planning James anymore. My future is wide open, and I like it that way. Every day is new with great possibilities, especially when I'm with Lisa. She supports me with my new job, even though she isn't happy about it.

My fears have decreased, but I'm still not able to go back to medicine. I want to in the worst way, but the devil puts those ugly thoughts and images back into my head. How will I ever be able to go back if all I see is Jessica lying on the operating table and my stillborn child in my hands?

I almost told Lisa I am in love with her. I froze up and didn't go through with it. Instead, I tried to show my love through worshipping her body. It was the perfect time, and I turned into a coward. I never thought I could love someone again as much as I love her.

"James!" I hear her piercing cry from the living room. I jump in fear as goose bumps crawl up my entire body like spiders. I bolt out of my room and find her on the floor in the fetal position. Air is sucked out of my lungs, and my body freezes. For an instant, I have tunnel vision, like I'm being yanked back in time to when I found Jessica on the floor. *This can't be happening! This can't be happening! Not again!*

"James!" she bellows.

Her petrified voice pulls me back to the present. *No, this will not happen again! I am a doctor. I can take care of her.*

Energy pumps through me like an electric shock to my heart, and my lungs fill with air again. The doctor in me takes over.

I get down on my knees. "What's the matter? What happened?"

She cries in pain. "I went to the bathroom, and I noticed I was bleeding. Maybe it's my period, but I have never suffered like this." She murmurs in between breaths. "I fell on my side, and now there's stabbing pain in my abdomen. It has to be something else. Get me to the hospital!"

In less than thirty seconds, I have my clothes and jacket on and grab my phone and keys. I have her in my arms and run out of the apartment.

"I'll take you to the hospital instead of calling for an ambulance. It's quicker this way. Try to breathe through the pain. I need to drive fast, but I will be careful." I place her in my car and strap her in her seat belt.

"God, it hurts. What's wrong with me?" Her shrill voice gets louder.

I get into the car and look at her. Déjà vu. We were in this situation before. My worlds are colliding.

"Drive, James!" she screams out as I try to regain my focus.

I punch the gas, and for the first time I don't care how fast I'm going. I know in my gut this is bad.

"How much longer? I can't take it anymore," she moans. Her energy quickly depleting.

"Two minutes, tops. Trust me. I'll get you there." Cars honk as I swerve between them. I want to yell, but it won't help Lisa. I slam on the brakes and jump out of the car. I whip her car door open and lift her into my arms. The ER entrance is straight ahead.

I plow through the doors and yell to a nurse, "Help! She needs help. She has piercing stomach pain, and she thinks she's bleeding."

I see Dr. Kaplan in the distance. "Dr. Kaplan," I yell, "It's me. James Kramer. Please help her." He runs over to me. I explain to him what I know so far. Nurses rush over with a stretcher. I lay Lisa on it gently. My mouth drops open. I look at her pale face.

"James, what's wrong?" she asks in hysterics.

"You're bleeding. I see it on your pants."

They push the stretcher through the doors. I watch her move farther and farther away from me.

"James!" she cries out, reaching for me, but I don't move. I let the doors close, and she is gone.

My body shakes uncontrollably as it hits me I'm in the ER, and with Lisa, no less. How can this happen again? I feel like I'm watching a rerun with Jessica. But no, it's Lisa who's disappeared behind those doors, and I have no idea what is going on. I should be on the other side, helping her. Taking care of her. I slam the wall with my fists.

Maybe her problem has to do with her uterus. She has been experiencing light cramps and spotting the past weeks but said it was normal for her. Were we too rough tonight?

"What should I do?" I ask myself as I pace. It's the middle of the night, but I don't care. I pull out my phone and dial Alexa's number. It rings twice. *Come on, Alexa! Answer the damn phone.*

"Hello, James. It's after three in the morning. What's the matter?" She yawns.

"Alexa, I'm in the ER with Lisa. She fell and injured her side or her stomach. I think it's something serious. I found her lying on the floor in our apartment. Can you please go there and get her handbag? I forgot to grab it. I need her phone or a phone book so I can call her dad and sister." I can hardly hold the phone because my hands are shaking so bad.

"Holy shit." I hear her getting out of bed. "I can't believe you're in the ER. Can you handle being there alone?"

"It doesn't matter if I can or not. I need to be here for Lisa. Will you please pick up her stuff and bring it to me?" I ask with impatience.

"Yes. I'll leave right now. Hopefully, I can be there in less than half an hour. She *will* be fine. Have some faith."

I hang up on her and want to throw the phone across the room. I should be in there comforting her, but I am stuck out here. *Why? Why? Why?* Haven't we been through enough already?

I hear the doors open, and I spin around. Dr. Kaplan.

"Dr. Kaplan, what's going on? Is she going to be all right?"

He points to a chair for me to sit down in.

"I can't sit. I'm too nervous. Please tell me what's happening."

"You know we aren't allowed to disclose any information to nonfamily members. Since I know you and you are a doctor, I'll let it slip."

"Thank you." I sigh.

"We don't know what's wrong yet. The doctor taking care of her had to put her under anesthesia. She's bleeding internally in the lower abdomen."

"She was in a car accident when she was in high school. It caused severe injuries to her uterus. She has a scar in the area where it happened. Maybe it has something to do with that, even though it was years ago. She told me she fell and that was when the pain started."

"I see. I need to tell the doctor this. Please stay calm. She's in good hands. Someone will be out as soon as possible to give you an update. Did you inform her family members she's here?"

"I'm waiting for my sister. She's bringing me Lisa's bag so I can try to contact her family. Right now, I'm the only one who will be here. Even if I get ahold of her family right away, it'll take at least an hour before someone arrives."

His beeper goes off. His face becomes tense. "I need to go back in now." He pats me on the back as he walks away. "It's good to see you, James. I'm sorry it's under bad circumstances again. We have missed you here in the ER."

All I can do is nod. My thoughts are on Lisa, but I felt some pride when I heard that. I was a good doctor. I loved my job and working here. Why is everything so damn complicated in my life? I just want to go back to the way it was before Jessica died. It was so simple then. But I wouldn't have met Lisa if my life had never changed. I grab my hair because my head is about to burst. I can't handle this anymore.

I fall on a waiting room chair and cry. Yes, I'm a man, and I cry a lot. I don't care who sees me. I don't know how long I sit here, but I hear Alexa in the distance. I stand up and run to her.

She instantly wraps her arms around me. "James. You're crying. Is it that bad?" she asks with tears in her eyes.

I shake my head. "I don't know anything. I'm so frustrated, pissed, defeated. This is all too much for me. I can't do this again."

She takes my hand into hers and guides me to a chair. "Try to relax. You're not alone. I told Mom and Dad, and they said they'll be here as soon as possible. Tell me what happened." She digs through her bag and pulls out a package of tissues.

I take one and rub the tears from my face.

"I surprised her tonight with a candlelight dinner at our place. We had an amazing night. As I said, I found her on the floor in front of the door. I don't know why she was even there. She was dressed as if she was leaving the apartment. In the middle of the night, no less."

"Yes, I saw her things at the door, as well as the mess you left." She pauses. "Here's her handbag. Her other things are in my car. Hopefully, she has a phone in there."

"Thanks for picking her stuff up for me."

"I'm sorry to hear about all of this. I can't even imagine what's shooting through your head. You need to be strong for her and for yourself. This isn't the same as with Jessica. Please remember Lisa is not Jessica."

I don't respond because I know she is right, but it's easier said than done. That fear is a part of me. I'm not sure it will ever go away.

"Go through her bag and see if you can find her phone."

I pull the phone from her bag. My hands are shaking, so Alexa takes it from me. She clicks on it, but it requires a password. I don't have it. *Shit!* Most of her numbers are probably in her phone. *Please let there be a phone book in her bag.* I rummage through it and find a little sapphire-blue book. Alexa takes that too.

"Her last name is Schmitt. Her father's name is Mike."

"Here it is." She dials the number for me. I press the button and hope to God someone answers. I walk away from Alexa to have some privacy.

I hear a man's groggy voice on the phone. "Hello?"

"Mike? It's James."

"*James.* Why are you calling and not Lisa? What's wrong?" he says with fear in his voice.

"Mike, Lisa's in the ER. Something is wrong with her lower abdomen. The doctors are with her now. Please come as soon as you can."

"My God, James. We'll be there as soon as possible. I'll call Tina. I'm glad you're there with her! See you soon. Do you have my cell phone number?" I search through the book and see it.

"Yes, I have it. I'll call if I hear anything. Drive safely."

# Chapter 47

## Lisa

Why do my eyes feel glued shut? I try to open them, but it's too exhausting. The smell of disinfectant is dominant in my nose. Am I in a hospital? Maybe I fell asleep. What is making all that racket? I try to move, but the sting of pain stops me. Something squeezes my hand.

"James?"

Another squeeze. "Lisa, are you awake? It's me, Tina. Dad and Beth are here too."

With the sound of her soft voice, I force my eyes open. I blink excessively to focus and look around. There are typical machines you would see in a hospital room. Why are they attached to me? I'm very confused. I look at Dad, Beth, and Tina, and I try to read their facial expressions. I try to speak, but my mouth is too dry. Did someone put cotton in my mouth?

All three sets of eyes study me. Dad's are filled with tears. Beth has her arm around him as she rests her head on his shoulder. Tina sits quietly on the edge of the bed as she strokes my hand with hers. Something's obviously wrong. When I go to speak, a nurse walks into the room.

She smiles at me and checks the machines. "You're finally awake. That's great to see."

"Can I please have some water?" I ask with a scratchy voice. The nurse takes a little cup of water with a straw from the side table and carefully hands it to me. My hands shake. Tina takes the cup from me and holds it in place so I can drink from the straw. I start coughing. It hurts to swallow. "What's going on? Why am I in the hospital?" I mumble.

The nurse touches my arm lightly and wipes the water drops off my chin. "I'll page your doctor to come to your room. Your family can tell you why you're here." The nurse walks out and closes the door.

"Would someone please tell me what the hell is going on? Why am I here?" I struggle to sit up.

Tina moves closer to me. "Please stay still and remain calm. You might hurt yourself."

"Hurt myself? I'm not going to ask again. What's going on?" My voice is cold as ice.

Her eyebrows squeeze together. "You don't remember anything?"

I rub my eyes to recall something. Anything. My eyes sting with tears because of fear, sadness, and pain.

I grab Tina's hand, short of breath. I feel like this is a repeat of the time I was in the hospital, after my accident.

"Where's James? He brought me here."

"He's in the waiting room and has been here the entire time. It hasn't been easy for him."

"What's wrong with me? Did the doctor tell you anything? Is it my appendix or something?" I look from one face to the other. I can't read their faces.

"No, it's not your appendix. The doctor told us what the diagnosis is, but we want him to tell you first." She has a little smile on her face. Why would she smile at a time like this?

We all turn our heads when the door opens. A bulky older man with a white coat comes in. I guess he's the doctor. Tina moves to the other side of the bed to give the doctor space.

"Hi, Lisa. My name is Dr. Kaplan. I'm the chief of staff here in the ER. I worked with James in the past. I told the doctor who is responsible for you I would explain everything."

He looks at me for a reaction. I don't know how to react.

"Is that okay, Lisa?"

I nod. "Yes. I'm sorry. Please go ahead."

"You were bleeding when you arrived. We didn't know where the blood was coming from. I spoke to James, and he explained to me that you'd had an accident in the past and some of the symptoms you were experiencing when you arrived here today."

"Is there something wrong with my uterus? All I did was fall on my left side. I don't understand why I would have so much pain from that."

"Let me explain further. We immediately performed some tests and scans to find where the bleeding was coming from. During that time, we had to put you under anesthesia."

"Can we cut this story short and get to the point? What did you find?" I ask, thick with impatience. Tina's mouth drops open in response to my sharp tone.

He hesitates for an instant. "The tests revealed you are pregnant. Our estimation is that you are about sixteen weeks now. If we are correct, your due date will be around July fifteenth. We can confirm this later."

The room starts to spin. I cover my eyes with my hands and try to gain control of myself. "Wait a minute. Wait? What?" I stammer. "*I'm pregnant*? This must be a mistake. I was told I could *never* get pregnant. Do you know my medical history?" I challenge him. Now I know why my pants are tight and my boobs are so sensitive. I thought I was eating too much fast food.

"Yes. James and your dad explained to me what happened and what the prognosis was. For some reason, you have been blessed. Your body wants this baby."

I look at Tina in panic. "Does James know I'm pregnant?"

She shakes her head. "Absolutely not. We have no right to tell him something like this. He needs to hear it from you."

This will not go over well when James finds out.

"I have a feeling there's something more to this than my pregnancy. I feel a *but* coming along."

"Unfortunately, you're correct. The placenta did not attach properly to the uterus. When you fell, it separated a little bit from the uterus, hence the bleeding and pain."

I place my hand on my stomach. "Will my baby survive?" I ask with sudden panic. "Can I be happy about this pregnancy?" I try to sit up.

He puts his hand on my arm. "Please relax. Your baby is healthy and has developed just as any other baby at sixteen weeks. However, you have a very rare, serious, and complicated condition. You must be on strict bedrest. I repeat *must*. Any major movement can cause it to happen again. This is not only dangerous for the baby but also for you. If it happens again, you have the potential to lose an excessive amount of blood. The baby's life will be in danger, as well as your own."

I try to swallow, but my mouth is a desert. I'm terrified.

"In a couple of days, you will be transferred to the obstetrics department, which will monitor your progress. If you do well for the next week, you will be allowed to go home. You will need to be home for the rest of the pregnancy. You cannot work or do any excessive activities until after the baby is born. You can go to the bathroom and take a shower. That's all. Do you understand how serious this is?"

I nod as a tear traces my cheek. One part of me is deliriously happy I'm pregnant. The second part is in denial I'm pregnant, and the last part is frightened I could lose the baby or die myself. I was with Bryant for years, and I never got pregnant. If I am four months pregnant already, it means I became pregnant one of the first times I slept with James. How is that possible? That seems to be the main question ever since I met James. What is the reason for all of this?

I take a deep breath. "I would like a moment to myself, please. Can someone please ask James to come in here? I need to tell him."

"I'll go and get him. Dad and Beth, let's give them some privacy." Tina motions toward the door.

Dr. Kaplan gives me a gentle smile. "No problem. Please have the nurse page me if you have any other questions."

"Thanks, Dr. Kaplan. I need some time to let this sink in. I'm quite overwhelmed with everything. I'm happy but terrified."

"It's understandable with your rare condition. You can do this. I'll talk to you soon." He walks away from my bed and is out the door.

Seconds later, James runs to me and kneels at my side. He presses my hand against his cheek. "Lisa, what's going on? No one will tell me anything. I'm jumping out of my skin." He looks like he has been crying. Is it because of me or being in the hospital?

James squeezes my hand tightly. "I'm so worried. Please tell me what's going on."

I need to come right out with it, like ripping off a Band-Aid. "I'm pregnant. About sixteen weeks. Our baby is due around July fifteenth, but it hasn't been confirmed yet," I say without emotion.

His face loses all color. He lets go of my hand and stumbles to his feet. He backs away from the bed. His face transforms into a scowl. *Well, that's not the reaction I was hoping for.*

"I thought I could never get pregnant. We have created a true miracle, and I'm ecstatic and thankful. It's a blessing for both of us. But this pregnancy is extremely dangerous. I need to be on strict bedrest for the rest of the pregnancy. There is a chance the placenta can separate from the uterine wall, which could be life threatening to me and the baby." *Please come to me. Hug me and tell me everything is going to be all right.*

"When we first met, you made it very clear to me you weren't sure you could ever get married or have a child again. You are being blessed with a second chance to have a child of your own. Please be happy about this," I plead. "I need you more than ever. Please be happy for us." I shouldn't have to beg.

His face becomes stone, and his hands clench. I take a deep breath and know what I need to do. "Your face and body language reflect all I need to know and confirms my instincts. I don't know if I should be angry or sympathetic to your feelings." *Do not cry. You need to be strong.*

"Ever since we met, I've faced my fears with you by my side. I have become the woman I always wished I could be. Finally, I feel free from my insecurities and have found peace within myself. My life has forever changed in a positive way. Even more so, now that I'm pregnant.

"You're stuck in your own little world. This is reality, James. You are going to be the father of *our* child. I don't know why this is happening, but it is. If you don't want this, that's fine. It will crush me, but I and our baby will survive, literally. I'll make sure of it. I'll do this with or without you. Our baby needs love, and I'm prepared to give all the love I can give."

The silence is so loud.

"Since you are not going to speak, I will continue." I close my eyes and take a moment to gather my thoughts. I open my eyes and look directly into his glowering dark-green ones. "I'm going to give you some advice." *Stay calm. Say what you have always wanted to say.*

I squeeze the bed sheets. "Go find yourself. I tried to help you, but it didn't work. You made me face my fears, but you wouldn't confront your own. Any time I wanted you to open up to me, you would get annoyed and change the subject. A clear sign of avoidance. You will never be able to move on if you don't come to terms with your past." My throat hurts, and I realize I'm practically yelling. But I'm not done yet. "Jessica and Jacob are never coming back!"

He winces in response.

"I will not be a substitute for her anymore. I love you so much, James. Parts of my heart have belonged to yours since I was fifteen. Over the past couple of months, one piece at a time, my heart fully became yours." *This is not how I wanted to confess my love for him.*

"I promised myself I would never give my heart to any man again. You changed that for me. Every piece of my body and soul loves you more than I ever thought was possible. But I can't do this if you don't feel the same. I will not settle for anything less than true love.

"You need to get over your fear about being a doctor, about being in love again, about having another child. What happened to Jessica and Jacob was not your fault. How many times do people have to tell you before you believe it? Your goal was always to become a doctor. You are one, and that will never change. You're in the hospital right now, and you survived. A career in real estate is not your calling, and it never will be." I inhale deeply.

His fists open and close several times at his sides, but he remains catatonic. He teeters from side to side, which gives me a glimmer of hope. That vanishes when he turns around and walks out the door without looking back.

My face burns like fire. "Yes, leave. That'll make it all go away. Run away from your problems. You are such a fucking coward."

I deflate and sob more than I ever have since Mom died. My rage bleeds out of me through my tears. I have lost him. Well, isn't this fucking ironic? I can't keep a man because I can't get pregnant. By a miracle, I get pregnant, and the one man I truly love walks away.

I shake my head and wipe the tears from my eyes. It doesn't matter. My main focus now is the miracle growing inside me. I'll do anything I need to, to keep my baby healthy and in my belly for as long as possible. I'm in charge now.

# Chapter 48

## James

She's right. I am a fucking coward. I storm out the door that leads to the waiting room. Everyone stands up and smiles. I ignore them and continue to walk right past them. I can't look at them, because if I do, I will fall apart. I need to get away from here as fast as possible.

"James, where are you going? You can't leave now. What is going on?" Alexa yells.

But I do just that. I leave.

I slam my fist on the kitchen table. I'm back to this. Getting drunk on whiskey. I'm sitting in the kitchen in the dark. The only glimmer of light comes from the living room window. Lisa is pregnant. Pregnant! She tells me this, and what do I do? I walk away like a selfish asshole. She is pregnant with our child—a dangerous pregnancy, no less—and I walked away. It was the only response I could give. What she said to me was completely true.

I am in limbo. I haven't fully dealt with Jessica's and Jacob's deaths. Working in the ER was my dream, and I can't even do that. I obtained a stupid real estate license instead. Lisa has been a distraction from all of this. Being with her has helped me avoid all of my problems. She doesn't deserve that. *I don't deserve Lisa.*

I down the last drop of whiskey in my glass and reach for the almost empty bottle.

"James!" Alexa yells as she slams the door. "Where the hell are you?" She turns the light on and groans. She stands there with steam coming out of her ears. "Boy am I not surprised. Turning to whiskey again. Every time you are faced with something difficult, whiskey becomes your new best friend." She shakes her head in disgust.

"James, what the fuck is your problem? How could you leave Lisa alone? That was beyond unforgivable!" Having Lisa in your life was a blessing. Now she's carrying your child."

"Who told you?" I snap.

"Lisa told the entire family. She's a mess, James. Why the hell did you walk away from her? Don't you see this as a miracle? You are going to be a father!"

"You have no idea what I'm going through! Not a fucking clue. You think you have all of the answers!" I yell as I stand up quickly from the kitchen table, and my chair shoots backward.

She stumbles back. "Then tell me. Talk to me! Make me understand."

"I can't go through this again. I can't sit here and watch the woman I love die along with my unborn child. Not again! *The woman I love*. Do you know how dangerous this pregnancy is? I'm a doctor, so I know exactly how dangerous it is."

"So walking away from her is going to help her? If anything, it's the worst thing you could have done. You can't even imagine what's going through her head. I spoke to her."

She gets in my face. "She was told by several doctors she could never get pregnant. She felt broken for most of her life. She felt no man would love her because she couldn't get pregnant. In the end, she loses the man she loves because she unexpectedly *gets* pregnant. Tell me how you would feel."

"I'm a fucking mess and a coward. I'll never survive if I lose her and the baby." I want to throw my glass against the wall again, but I refrain.

As Alexa's voice rises, she points her finger at me. Her head moves back and forth with attitude. "You know what you are going to do? You are going to pull your head out of your ass. You are going to stop hiding. I know you loved Jessica and Jacob, but they are gone,

James. Gone! Stop feeling guilty. You have a right to be happy again. You are a wonderful man with so much love to give. What happened with Jessica and Jacob was a tragedy, but it wasn't your fault." She grabs me by the arms. "It wasn't your fault!"

I yank my arms away and pull on my T-shirt. I lean against the counter and wait for the next lecture.

"I think I need a whiskey now. Even though I hate the stuff." She walks to the cabinet and retrieves a glass.

"How did you feel at the hospital today? Did you panic?"

"I couldn't think about it. I was there for Lisa. She means more to me than my mental issues."

"I know you miss it. It was a part of you. You worked so hard for your career, and you are a damn good doctor. It's time you fight to get it back. Go to Dr. Kaplan. Suck it up and be a man," she says after she swigs her whiskey. Her face contorts as she shivers from the taste.

"You have a second chance for real love, to have a family. Don't throw it away because you're afraid. Since when did that ever stop you from doing something? That's not the James I know."

She takes a deep breath. "You have fallen in love with Lisa. I know you are scared to admit it, but you have. Just accept it! You don't have to convince yourself anymore, but you will need to convince Lisa."

"I need to sit down." She walks over to the couch and places her whiskey on the coffee table. "James, what's this?" She waves a piece of white paper in the air.

I squint my eyes. "I don't know. What does it say?"

"It has your name on it." She hands it to me.

I run my hands through my hair. I recognize the handwriting. "It's a letter from Lisa. She must have written it before she tried to leave." I sit on the couch but don't read it right away. Out of fear again. I take a deep breath.

*Dear James,*

*By the time you find this letter you will see I have left. I can't describe in words how this night was a life-altering experience* for me. I have never felt something so binding and emotional between me and another person. I truly felt my soul connect with yours. It's another moment to put at the top of my favorites list. I thank you for that.

After all we have been through and spending so much time together, I thought it was finally going to be the time we say those three special words to each other. As usual, the time came and went. I always hesitate because I'm not sure you are ready or even want to hear it from me.

You talked in your sleep tonight. You were saying "I love you." Unfortunately, not to me though. You were saying, "I love you, Jessica. I will always love you." It hurt me more than any physical pain could. It was a wake-up call. You might love me, but you are not in love with me. Jessica will always be the love of your life, even though she is not here anymore. I can't compete, and I won't compete.

Ever since I've met you, I've become so much more confident and mentally stronger. Because of that, I'll never let myself be second best again. You are living in the past and holding yourself back.

I can't do this anymore. Leaving this apartment will be the hardest thing I ever do. I love you more than I ever thought I could love someone. See, I finally said it. I never knew the kind of love I have for you really existed. It frightens me, but I know I could never live my life without you in it. I tried to be patient with you. You refuse to move on, and don't know what you want. I need to leave you so you can find your way. Look for and find what will make you truly happy again.

My heart will always beat for yours.

What have I done? What did I dream last night? *Think, think, think!* The letter drops from my hand and floats to the floor like a feather. I lay my head on the back of the couch as the dream replays in my head.

"What does it say? Or is it too private to tell me?"

I motion for her to pick up the letter and read it.

"Are you sure?" She hesitates.

I shrug. Her eyes rapidly go back and forth as she reads it. "Do you remember the dream?"

I nod. "I told Jessica about Lisa and that I'm in love with her. I explained to Jessica I'll always love her, but I needed to let her go if I want to be with Lisa. She tried to walk away from me, but I told her not to. I kept saying I was sorry." I stand up and kick the table. The whiskey glass rattles in response.

"Watch what you're doing. Don't damage my furniture!"

"Now I know why she was dressed when I found her. I have hurt her in ways I was afraid I would. She thinks she's second best. On top of that, now she thinks I walked away from her because she's pregnant. It's true to an extent, but not for the reason she thinks."

Alexa sits on the edge of the couch. "How do you feel after remembering the dream?" She empties her whiskey glass.

I'm numb at this point. "I don't want to talk about this anymore. I'm completely exhausted and need to be alone. This is for me to figure out by myself." I reach over and give her a hug. "Thank you for always being here for me. I sound like a broken record these days."

"Just listen to me. I would do anything to find love like you have experienced. Don't fuck it up more than you already have. You are going to be a father. Be brave." She turns around and disappears into her room.

# Chapter 49

## Lisa

"Are you sure this is what you want to do? It's a lot of change all at once," Tina expresses with concern.

"Yes, Tina," I confirm as I sit up in the hospital bed. "Dad and Beth asked me to stay with them until the baby is born. It's the most logical option. They have the office and a bathroom with a walk-in shower on the first floor. Beth will move her office upstairs into one of the bedrooms.

"Beth works from home, so she'll be there to help me. Dad or Beth can drive me to my doctor appointments at St. Vincent's hospital nearby. It'll save me money, because I won't be able to afford rent."

"What about your apartment and all of your personal things?" She leans against the bed.

"I broke the lease. I called the landlord and explained the situation. He has a waiting list for people to rent the apartments. He didn't seem to care if I break the lease and move out."

"At least something was easy for you." Tina walks over to a pile of my dirty clothes and puts them in a bag. I can't stand wearing hospital gowns.

"I requested sick leave from my residency. Thankfully I will still have insurance for the next couple of months. I have no idea what I'll do once the baby is born. The worst part is I won't have an income. Dad keeps reassuring me they will help me. My health and the baby's are top priority right now. Nothing else." I stare outside, watching the pouring rain splash against the window, wishing I could say James is still one of my priorities.

I haven't heard from him since I was admitted to the hospital two weeks ago. I was told I would only be in here for one week, but the doctor wanted to perform a few more tests to ensure it's safe for me to have bedrest at home. If all goes well, once I hit six months, I'll be admitted to St. Vincent's for twenty-four-hour monitoring. I'll be at a higher risk the further I'm along in the pregnancy.

Bedrest is horrible. I can only get up to go to the bathroom or take a shower. My back hurts from constantly sitting or lying. Even though I hate being stuck in bed, I would do anything to protect my baby. I need to focus on the baby because if I don't, I'll start analyzing every moment I spent with James. I miss him more than I can breathe. I refuse to talk about him. I asked Tina once if she has heard from him or even his family, and she said no. It made the boulder on my chest even heavier. I can't believe even his family hasn't visited or called. I feel abandoned by them.

Tina drops the bag of dirty laundry on the floor by the door. "I'll take care of your apartment since I had a feeling it would come to this. I spoke to Emily the other day. She will help me pack your things. Her boyfriend will help us move out the furniture. You need to figure out what you want us to do with all of your stuff. Dad's house doesn't have room to store all your furniture."

"Let me think about it and call some people I know at the hospital. Maybe they need some furniture." I groan. "I'm sorry any of you have to deal with this. You know how independent I always am. It's hard to rely on you, Emily, Dad, Beth, and whoever else! If I'm this frustrated already, I can't imagine what I'll be like after being bedridden for the next months."

The bed squeaks as Tina sits at my side. "Well, get used to it. This is the one time you will need us more than ever. I'm excited you're moving closer to me. We can see each other more often. I can watch you grow nice and fat. I guess I'll also get fat because I'll be eating a lot of ice cream with you. That's what pregnant women eat, right? Or is it pickles?" She laughs at her own joke.

"This is when I miss Mom the most, Tina. She should be here

with me. Holding my hand, telling me everything will be fine and dandy. She would be a grandmother soon."

Tina leans over and squeezes me against her. "I know. I miss her too. Beth and I will hold your hand instead. We'll get you through this. I know it's hard for you, especially since you haven't heard from James. He'll be back. I have a feeling this is what he needed to get his shit together. Focus on your health and that baby of yours. God didn't put you and James together so many times to let this rip you apart. It will work out in the end."

She puts on her coat and picks up her handbag from the chair.

"When you go to my apartment to get some of my clothes, can you please bring me James's leather jacket?"

"Are you sure? You don't want me to burn it or shred it with a knife?"

"Believe me—I've already thought about doing that once I get my hands on it again." I smirk.

She stands there with her hands in her pockets, jiggling her car keys. "It won't upset you to wear it?"

"No." I recline my bed so I can lie flat. "It has comforted me for years. I need it now more than ever."

She shrugs. "If you say so." She walks to the door and leans on the frame. "Dad and Beth should be here in an hour to pick you up. I'll go over to your place now and get your things. Don't forget the bag of laundry here on the floor. See you tonight."

"Thanks, Tina. I hope I can help you one day the way you always help me. I love you." She blows me a kiss and walks out the door.

Only one hour left in this stuffy hospital room. I'm alone, and the quiet makes me think too much. If I could take a run right now, I would. I need that feeling of being completely breathless. The desperate need to see James won't fade away though. I miss his face, his dazzling eyes, and his soft lips. I want to feel his hand on my swollen belly, hear him tell me how happy he is. I'm so furious with him, but I would take him back in a heartbeat.

However, I don't miss competing with Jessica for his attention.

I need to keep telling myself I made the right decision to tell him to leave. And even if he did come back, what would I expect from him? How would I know if he is speaking the truth?

I sigh. I need to get these fantasies out of my head. If he ever comes back, it will likely only be out of obligation. Not because he loves me.

# Chapter 50

## Lisa

"Lisa, everything appears great for twenty weeks. The baby is developing perfectly, and the placenta hasn't changed," Dr. Stuart says as she prints out pictures of the baby. "Have you changed your mind about finding out the gender?"

"No. I still want it to be a surprise. I have a feeling I know, but I'm not telling anyone." I smile as I look at the pictures.

"You look great. I know it's hard lying in a bed for so long. It would drive me nuts."

I support myself on the bed to pull my leggings up. It's not easy. "I feel like I walk like a penguin. I'm sure my thighs are spreading from sitting all the time. I have never been this heavy. Is there anything I can do to relieve the stiffness of my back?"

"Try lying in a warm bath. Not too warm and not too long. It'll relax your muscles. I can also give you contact information for a good physical therapist who focuses on pregnant women and makes house visits."

"A massage, now that sounds good to me." I smile as I rub my back.

"Promise me you'll alert me at any time if you are spotting or cramping. It's very crucial you come to the hospital immediately when that happens. Understand?"

"Yes, Dr. Stuart." I stand like a soldier and salute her.

She chuckles. "It's nice to see you still have a sense of humor. Keep it. You'll need it when the baby is crying all night."

"The baby can cry all night as long as she or he is healthy."

She sits down on her roll chair. "We want to make sure the baby stays in your belly for at least another four weeks. Any time after that, the baby has a better chance of survival if you have an emergency. Please take care of yourself at home. It's a lot nicer to stay at home than to be here in the hospital. Be thankful. You only have one month left at home. Then you will be stuck here until the baby wants to make an appearance."

She tries to be funny, but it's not helping. It will suck to live in a smelly hospital for several weeks again. I didn't enjoy it so much when I worked in one every day. I should be used to the smell.

I'm definitely thankful for plenty of things, except one. I still haven't heard from James. I want to call Alexa, but I don't have enough nerve. I'm floored and hurt neither she nor her parents have contacted me. I miss all of them. We became so close so quickly. I have never experienced that kind of love before. I clench my jaw. I need to stop thinking about them. It only makes me want to eat more ice cream and peanut butter.

"See you next week, Dr. Stuart." I waddle out the door and spot Beth waiting patiently.

"I'm here." She walks over with a wheelchair.

"Everything is on schedule and looking good," I say brightly.

"That's terrific, honey. Want to go get some ice cream? It's a bit cold, but who cares! I can get it to go so we can enjoy it at home."

"Sounds like a good plan to me! I'm lucky to have you, Beth."

She rubs my arm. "Thank you for letting me in, Lisa. I have said this so many times, but...I know I'm not your mother, but I can be something close to it. I have no children of my own. To me, you and Tina will always be my daughters."

Oh no, the floodgates might open for both of us. "Let's get out of here before we start crying in front of all the other pregnant women. It will cause a chain reaction of crying women."

I stare down at the wheelchair. "Do I really need to be pushed in that thing again? I'm not an invalid."

"You know what the doctor ordered. Now sit down." I ease into the chair and cover my face. This is so embarrassing.

# Chapter 51

## Lisa

I can't hold off anymore. "You haven't spoken to him at all, Tina? He hasn't contacted you?" I ask, trying hard not to throw my book across the room.

She frowns. "I'm sorry. He hasn't. I don't know what to tell you. You need to calm down. Dr. Stuart says stress isn't good for either of you."

I know she feels bad and is frustrated. I can tell by the way she is aggressively sterilizing and straightening the room while I sit like a tub of lard on the bed.

"Why don't you take a shower? You have been in those pajamas for three days now. It smells in this room. Your hair looks like a bird is building a mansion in it."

"Thanks for the compliments, sis." I lift one arm up to smell myself as my other hand tries to mat down my hair. I crinkle my nose. "I don't smell that bad." *Yes, you do.*

She laughs and buzzes around the room. "The sun is finally shining today and it's above average temperatures for March." She neatly stacks my magazines on the nightstand.

"When you're done, I'll make you breakfast in bed. And when you're finished eating, I can French braid your hair like Mom always did. Would you like that? A nice warm shower will cheer you up." She definitely has something up her sleeve. She's way too happy.

"Do you have a hot new boyfriend or something? You're acting weird today. Like you have a secret."

She waves her hand but doesn't look me in the eye. "I wish. Sadly, no hot new boyfriend begging me for attention. I just want to cheer you up. I can't imagine being stuck here day in and day out. Someone has to be cheerful."

"Please make something really fattening and sweet for breakfast." My cravings have been out of control. As long as it is sweet, I'm happy.

"No problem. You know how I love to make any kind of fattening food."

"It must be nice to eat whatever you want and not gain weight. You don't even exercise."

"Yell when you get out of the shower so I know when to bring your food." She walks off, humming away.

I carefully rise from the bed and waddle to the bathroom. My butt following me from behind. Can my thighs get any bigger?

I let the warm water run down my body. I look at my belly and put my hands on it. It isn't too big yet. I'm only five and a half months along. "Please stay in there as long as you can, little peanut. You need to stay healthy. I'm going a little batty right now since I'm stuck in this house. You are worth it though.

"I haven't heard from your daddy yet. I guess it's time to give up. He's made up his mind and has left us. We'll be fine, I promise. You're a dream come true." I feel a tap on my hand. I start to laugh for the first time in days, which turns into tears. "Are you listening to me in there? Are you agreeing with me we'll be okay?" I feel another tap. Right then I know in my heart, everything will work out just fine. I wash my belly with soap and rinse off.

Some days I only talk to my baby bump. I lie in this room and avoid human contact. I don't want to talk to anyone or to see their sympathetic faces anymore. Moving to the hospital will be easier for everyone. No one deserves my bad attitude. I'll be different once the baby is born. I hope postpartum won't make an appearance.

I turn off the shower and grab the extra-large, luxurious powder-blue Egyptian cotton towel Beth bought me. I'm spoiled in this house. I look at myself in the mirror and see a chubby, depressed woman.

I'm pale, like I haven't seen the sun in a year. My cheeks bulge like a chipmunk's. When I gain weight, it always goes to my cheeks first. My eyes look tired and puffy. Probably from all the crying. I should ask Tina for some cucumber slices to put on my eyes.

My boobs have never been this big. I guess that's an advantage. However, I refuse to weigh myself. When Dr. Stuart weighs me, I don't look at the number. I don't want to know how much I've gained.

A little makeup wouldn't hurt today, and some fresh clothes. I wrap the large towel around me and open the bathroom door. The smell of pancakes is overpowering. Tina's the best for making me pancakes. It makes my stomach growl, but it also makes me sad, since it was James's and my favorite breakfast. I walk across the hall to my room and close the door behind me.

Bright sunshine beams through the window. I stand in front of it to enjoy the warm sun on my face. I'm in desperate need of vitamin D. It has rained for a week straight. The amount of tears I've shed reflects the pouring rain.

Tina is right. This room is stuffy and needs fresh air. I open the window and enjoy the breeze that sweeps in. I close it after a few seconds though because it's still too cold for me. But it felt good. Taking a shower, putting on clean clothes, and a dose of fresh air works wonders. I might crack a smile today. If it doesn't hurt my face.

I apply some makeup and brush my hair. James's jacket hangs over the desk chair next to me. I pick it up. One time when I was at his apartment, I sprayed it with his cologne. It still faintly smells like him as I lift it to my nose. How can something like this bring me so much comfort even though I want to strangle him? I toss it back over the chair.

I peek my head out of the door and yell, "Tina, I'm ready for breakfast and for you to braid my hair."

"Breakfast is almost finished. Give me five more minutes." I hear dishes clatter and hushed voices in the kitchen, probably Tina and Beth fighting over the stove again.

I close the door again. If they want to fight over who's making breakfast, I don't care. I need to lie down, since I shouldn't be on my feet this long. I wish Tina would hurry up though, because I'm dying of hunger.

Tina opens the door but comes in without breakfast.

"What was all the ruckus out there? Did you burn the pancakes? If you did, I don't care. I'll eat them anyway. I'm a ravenous pregnant woman." I sit up straight.

"No, I didn't burn the pancakes. I wanted to surprise you with something else in addition to pancakes."

I lift one eyebrow. "What's up with you? I smell the pancakes, so where are they?" She steps to the side.

"I have your pancakes." Standing in the doorway is handsome James with a tray full of food. My heart rate shoots through the roof. My makeup is useless because I'm sure I'm the shade of scarlet right now. I look at Tina, but she's already sneaking out of the room. She turns around, and as she closes the door, she gives me a thumbs-up.

"Hi, Lisa."

Just the sound of his voice makes me warm. He's finally here, but I have no idea what to say or do. I stare at him because it's all I can do. Tears are already surfacing. *Damn him and my hormones.*

"Are you hungry?" He walks toward me with the tray.

I raise my chin without breaking eye contact. He's more beautiful than the last time I saw him. *Jerk.* Almost more mature or confident in a sexy way. I have missed every detail about him. I want to jump into his arms and kiss him until we can't breathe anymore. But I can't, and I won't. It won't be easy for him. He has a lot of explaining to do. He might be here just to see how the pregnancy is progressing and nothing else. I start to quiver and am suddenly not hungry anymore.

"I've lost my appetite." I point to the dresser. "You can leave the tray there."

He doesn't listen. "You should try to eat. You love pancakes."

"Your visit is quite unexpected." My stomach is in knots now. I place my hands on my belly. I watch his eyes travel to where my hands are.

307

"James, I don't care about the pancakes. What do you want? I haven't seen or heard from you, or your family, in almost two months." Shit, the tears are ready to break loose. I want to be strong, but I can't when he's in the same room. I don't have the strength.

He finally puts the tray on my dresser.

"I am extremely disappointed your parents haven't even contacted me. I'm carrying their grandchild. Don't they care? What about Alexa? She was like a sister to me. I feel abandoned by you and your family."

"Can I sit down?" He turns around and takes hold of the desk chair, noticing his jacket is hanging on it. I see a hint of a smile as well as his dimples. *Damn him!*

"I guess so, since you seem to be making yourself comfortable already."

# Chapter 52

## James

I sit down and suck in every inch of her. I have missed her beauty, her smile, her big blue eyes, her kissable neck. That should be my hand rubbing her belly.

I have come to beg her for forgiveness and to take me back. Where do I start to explain my disappearance these past several weeks? I may have been gone, but I haven't been sitting around dwelling in my own misery.

I want to kiss her tears away. I hate myself for making her cry. However, she has every right to be mad at me. She still has my jacket, which is good sign. Maybe I do have a chance.

"I asked my family not to contact you. They weren't happy about it, but they did it for me."

"Why would you do that? You know I love your family. Why would you hurt me like this?" She turns her head away and wipes tears from her face.

"Lisa, please look at me. This is very hard for me too. The past months have been total hell."

"Oh, it's been hell for you! I have been stuck in this bed for weeks. Replaying every single moment we spent together, wondering why I gave you my heart. That's what I did, James. Every little piece of it was yours. The second you walked out of that hospital room, my heart jumped out of my chest and ran after you, screaming *don't leave me!* It's still lying in the hospital, waiting for your return. It's probably shriveled like a raisin by now." Her hands grip the blanket like she's going to hurt someone.

"You did the one thing to me I never thought was possible. You left me in the hospital because I was pregnant. You knew I believed no man would ever love me. Remember? Or did you forget about that while you wallowed in your own misery, thinking about Jessica?" she hisses.

*Wow, that was harsh.* But I deserve it.

"I get pregnant, and you walk away." Her eyes turn to deep sapphire-blue slits.

This might be harder than I thought. She has every right to yell at me. I have never seen her so pissed.

"Lisa, please calm down. It's obvious the very sight of me makes your emotions boil over. I only ask for a few minutes of your time to explain the last two months. If you don't like what I have to say, then I'll leave."

"Fine." She closes her eyes and takes a deep breath, as if meditating. She places a tissue box from her table next to her on the bed.

I want to take her hand in mine, but I'm not going to push my luck. "I have spent the past two months trying to get my life back in order. When I walked out of the hospital, I nearly broke down right in front of the ER entrance. I didn't want to talk to anyone. I needed to escape." I push off the chair and walk back and forth in front of her. I'm too nervous to sit.

"Of course, I drove straight home and aimed to get drunk. I was petrified and shocked. I've lost two people I loved already in my life. I looked at you and thought it could happen again. Your pregnancy is life threatening. I panicked." I stop and face her.

"I sat in my apartment in the dark. Pissed at myself, overcome with angst I could lose you both, not having a clue what to do. Every horrible scenario was going through my head." I scratch my chin.

"Alexa came home and let me have it. She had every right to scream at me. You and my family have been nothing but patient with me. Especially you. You didn't push me. You didn't ask me questions about how I was feeling, how I was dealing with Jessica's and Jacob's deaths. You just loved me for me. You were completely selfless, and I was incredibly selfish. I pretended my past didn't happen.

"What I didn't pretend is how I felt about you. The one thing I was clear about—but was too afraid to admit—was that I was and still am completely in love with you."

Her shimmering blue eyes grow wide open now.

"Valentine's Day was a night I'll never forget. I wanted to make that day special for you. How our bodies and souls intertwined that night showed me the passion and love we have for one another. I wanted to confess my love for you, but of course, I chickened out.

"You mentioned you heard me talk in my sleep. I did have a dream that night, but it wasn't what you think it was. In the dream, I told Jessica about you. That I'm in love with you and you make me happy and excited about life again. You have filled my heart with yours. It beats in sync with yours."

I can't stand it anymore. I need to touch her. I push the chair away so I can kneel next to her bed. I slowly reach to take her hand, and she meets me halfway. My eyes close to enjoy the sense of relief flooding through me.

"I went to see Jessica's parents."

Her hand squeezes mine.

"I told them about you. They remembered you from the night we saw them at the theater. They could tell then something was going on. Even though nothing happened between us at the time. I apologized I didn't contact them or try to reach out for so long. It felt good to tell them what was happening. I thought I would feel guilty. But I didn't. I was proud to tell them about you. They were thrilled and relieved I'm living my life again. A huge weight was lifted off my chest."

"I know how hard that must have been for you."

I put my fingers to her lips. "Please let me finish."

She tries not to smile, but it finally breaks through. "Sorry, I'll be quiet." She presses her lips together with her fingers.

"The hardest thing I did was visit Jessica and Jacob's grave. I hadn't been there in several months. I sat there and told them about the past months and how I met you. I told them how scared I am about possibly losing you and the baby. I reassured them I will always love them and never forget them. But you and our baby are my life now. My future.

"It felt good to tell them about you and to accept how I feel about you. Loving you isn't wrong. It's absolutely right."

She closes her eyes as I kiss her shaky hand softly.

"When I was finished talking to them, I stood in front of their gravestone in silence for a little while. Out of nowhere, a strong smell of roses overwhelmed me, as if Jessica were there giving me her blessing. It was the dead of winter. After that, I finally let them go."

"I hope you feel at peace with yourself."

"There's still more to say. All right? Be patient, petite one." I tap her nose.

"When I found you on the floor like I did Jessica, the doctor side of me took over. I didn't think of my fears. I only thought about you and your safety. The entire situation was unbelievably similar to your car accident. You were sitting in my car like you did years ago. Your big blue eyes pleading for me to help you. The difference this time was I knew what to do. I didn't hesitate to run into the hospital. A part hidden deep within me was ecstatic to be in the environment I used to love and still do. I had the knowledge to explain to the doctors and nurses what happened.

"Lisa, you were right all along. Medicine is my life. My calling. I called my old boss, Dr. Kaplan. You met him that day when you were admitted to the hospital. It killed me I couldn't do more for you. I wasn't allowed to be behind those doors in the examination room with you. I couldn't help you."

She puts her hand on my cheek. "James, you saved me that day, just like you saved me when I was a teenager. If you weren't there to help me, my life would have been at risk. Maybe I wouldn't even be sitting here right now with our baby growing inside of me."

She takes my hands and puts them on her belly.

"Our baby," I repeat.

I hold my breath as tears pool in my eyes.

# Chapter 53

### Lisa

I look down at his hands and know they are right where they are supposed to be. I have prayed for this moment for so long.

He continues. "I called Dr. Kaplan and spoke to him about my future. I want to work in the ER again. Since I took off so much time, I asked how that will affect my career options."

I never thought I would hear him say these things. Hope floats through the air.

"I spoke to him about our situation, how you moved back home to New Jersey and had to stop your residency. I knew your new doctor works at St. Vincent's hospital. I asked him if he could call in some favors to have me transferred to the ER there, so I can perform a fellowship to get me back on my feet."

"What? Why would you do that? I don't understand." I don't know if I should be happy or mad.

"You are here and having our baby. We'll need as much help as possible. Both of our families live in this area."

"How did you know who my new doctor is?" I yank my hand away. "When did you speak to my family?"

"I have spoken to them all and asked them for their help, since you still need to finish your residency."

My head extends off my neck. I feel like E.T. "You have been in contact with my family this entire time?" I ask through gritted teeth. "Tina knew you were coming today, didn't she? I am going to kill her."

His shoulders slump. "Again, I asked everyone not to tell you. Be mad at me, not at them. Please let me finish before you get upset with them." He sighs.

"I did a little research about the hospital to see if there's a residency program for your field. There is one available. Dr. Kaplan offered to put in a good word for you if you want to live near our families. The hospital also has daycare services for employees."

"You did this without asking my permission." I sound pissed, but I'm really not. He deserves to be given a hard time though.

He raises his hands. "I didn't do anything. I only asked questions to see if these are possible options."

I squint my eyes. "Why are you doing this? What do you want from me?" Who does he think he is, making these decisions without asking me?

"Lisa, deep in your heart, you know why." He places his hand on my heart. "As I said before, I'm in love with you. I have been for a long time, but I was too afraid to admit it. I'm so sorry I hurt you and you have been dealing with this alone. You are the best thing that has ever happened to me. We belong together. We both know that, after all we have been through.

"I never thought it was possible to have more than one soul mate. My connection to you is proof I was wrong. Jessica was the old James's soul mate. The new version of me is bonded to you permanently and may have been since we were teenagers. The last months have been so difficult because my soul ached for yours every second we were apart.

"No matter how much I longed to see you, to touch you, I had to stay away. I needed to do this to prove to you I'm ready. It was best to do this by myself."

He grabs my hands and brings them to his cheek. "Please tell me I'm not too late. Please tell me I still have a chance."

I might be a bitch for this, but I like it that he's pleading.

I remain silent for a few seconds, trying to absorb all he has said. This is what I have waited to hear for so long. My heart flutters like butterfly wings, and my lower lip trembles.

My eyes find his, and my smile becomes bright. I grab his face and kiss him passionately. *I'm so glad I brushed my teeth.* "I have missed you so much. I wanted and tried to hate you, but I can't. I love you too much."

"I'm so sorry. Please let me make it up to you. Yes, I'm scared you are pregnant. You know why though. Please believe me when I say this. I'm beyond happy you are going to be the mother of my child. I promise I will never leave you again."

"I believe you. I know I should be mad at you for a lot of things. Such as assuming I would want to move back here and continue my residency at another hospital. But I can't believe you would change hospitals for us. Does this really mean we are going to be together? Forever?"

"Yes, we are going to do this together. Forever."

He pulls away from me and puts his hand in his pocket. What's he doing? He takes a ring box out of it. My breath catches.

"Being away from you has made me realize how much I can't live without you. I threw away the key to my heart after Jessica died. Vowed to never open it again. Somehow, you found it and unlocked it again. You have shown me life is worth living and how beautiful it can be. I look forward to all of the wonderful memories we will create together as a family."

He opens the box. "Lisa, will you marry me?"

My hand goes over my heart. *Oh my gosh, it's stunning.* A sparkling solitaire with smaller round diamonds on each side. He knows me so well—I don't wear flashy jewelry. This ring is simple and petite just like me. It's absolutely perfect.

"I want to spend the rest of my life with you and our baby. I will promise to be the best husband and father I can. You complete me like no one else. The next months will be difficult, but I promise we'll get through them together. I will take care of you and never leave your side. Please say you will become my wife."

Tears run down my face. "I would jump on you if I could, but you'll just have to come to me." He takes his shoes off and crawls onto the bed.

316

I grab him by the collar and pull him close to my face. "Of course I'll marry you. It has always been you and only you who I love. The ring is beautiful. Please put it on my finger and then show me how much you missed me with those delicious lips of yours."

He slips the ring onto my finger, and it fits perfectly. As if it were made specifically for me.

"Before I kiss you, I have one request."

"What is it?" I stare at his lips like they are a piece of steak. I'm pregnant. What can I say?

"Please marry me soon. Before you move to the hospital for the next months. I don't want to wait until our baby is born or until you finish your residency. I want you to be my wife as soon as possible and to start our new life together. I would do it right this minute if I could. We can have a big wedding after the baby is born if you want." He teases me with kisses along my jawline. "What do you say? Will you marry me tomorrow or the next day?"

"You're driving me nuts. If I say yes, will you finally kiss me? We need to make up for lost time." I feel another kick from the baby.

He comes even closer. Our lips are almost touching. "Say it then."

"Before I say anything, put your hand on my belly."

He lays his hand there, and I put mine on his.

"Today is the first day I feel the baby. He or she just moved. Let's see if it'll happen again."

We wait in silence. He moves closer to my belly. "Come on, little one. Daddy is finally here. I want to feel you move. Can you please convince your mommy to marry me?" As if on cue, we both feel a tap. He stares at my bump with such amazement and love. I wish I had a camera to capture this moment forever. Now I can answer his question.

"Yes, I will marry you right this second if it means you will finally kiss me. I'm a pregnant woman with raging hormones. Kiss me now and show me you love me."

"So bossy and damn sexy." Our lips finally touch, and the pulse of electricity I have missed so much shoots through every cell in my body. It lights me up like a Christmas tree. I have missed us so much.

He leans away from me. "Seriously. Will you marry me as soon as possible?" He looks at me with eager bright-green eyes. Oh, how I have missed his eyes.

"I wouldn't have it any other way. You'll need to plan everything. I can't do much from this bed. Nothing fancy. I just want us to be together from now on."

"That's my intention," he says as his hands start to roam over my body. "You are so voluptuous with your new curves. I love it."

"I want to make love to you so badly, but I can't until after the baby is born. Doctor's orders." I pout. "It's not fair. I need the touch of your skin against mine."

He looks at me with hooded eyes. "It doesn't mean we can't kiss." I can't talk anymore, because his lips are on mine again. Exactly where they belong.

# Chapter 54

## Lisa

I rub my lower back. "Debbie, I'll miss your back massages once I leave this hospital."

"That's my job. To make your life manageable while lying in bed for so long."

I'm officially seven months and two weeks pregnant, as well as a married woman. A justice of the peace married us the day after he proposed. Since it was a Saturday, we had all our family and friends around us. I never thought I would have a family like this. I couldn't be happier.

So much has happened since September. It's weird how someone's life can change by one random decision. If I hadn't gone for a drink at that bar in September, I would have never met James officially. But would we have met anyway? I don't care anymore, because I am exactly where I want to be at this moment.

The pregnancy continues to go well. The baby is developing right on schedule. The doctors are amazed how smooth it is going. I think they assumed there would be more complications and the baby would be born sooner. The doctors and nurses have explained the kind of complications the baby might have if delivered early. Steroids are being given to strengthen the baby's lungs.

Now that James and I are married, my patience, strength, and determination are better than ever. I'm truly blessed I have been given this chance to have a baby. It's a true miracle, actually. Never in a million years would I have thought I would be sitting here pregnant. Don't get me wrong. I hate being stuck in this hospital day in and day out. It makes me nuts, but I do see the light at the end of the tunnel. I don't know if I'll ever get the smell of disinfectant out of my hair and skin though.

"Lisa, I need to get a hot compress for you to lay on. I'll be back in a few minutes."

"No problem. I need to use the bathroom anyway before Dr. Stuart arrives in a few minutes. Take your time."

She walks to me and takes my arm. "Should I assist you?"

I wave her away. "This is the one thing I'm still allowed to do by myself." We both laugh. She trots out of the room and closes the door.

James has officially transferred to this hospital. He applied for a fellowship here in the ER, and he was granted it. We had a bed moved into this cramped hospital room so he can stay with me every night. He hovers over me, but I wouldn't have it any other way. I know why he does it. He's nervous and hates he has no control over what happens. Now that we're married and he's working in the ER again, I've never seen him happier. No offense to him, but he wouldn't have been a very good real estate agent.

We'll officially move into James's parents' house after we're released from the hospital. Since James isn't making a lot of money, this gives us a chance to save for the future. Their house is big enough that we'll have our own space.

Getting pregnant has made me reevaluate my life. I stopped my residency to become a psychiatrist. I can't imagine working nonstop for the next four years while I have a little baby at home. I want to enjoy every second being a mom.

There are different career paths I can follow. After a lot of thought and discussions with James, I have chosen to go back to get my PhD in psychology instead. It'll still be a lot of work, but I'll finish my studies and training faster. This route will allow me to do the same work, without prescribing medication. My main goal has always been to have my own practice. I don't need to be a psychiatrist to do that. If some patients need further therapy, such as medicine, then I'll recommend them to someone else.

Kathleen and Beth have offered to watch the baby when James is working and I'm studying. They will switch days, or we can utilize the daycare services at the hospital. I would rather the baby be with them though. I don't know what we would do without their help these past months, and after the baby is born.

James will be back later tonight. His dad wants to finish the baby's room. I wish I could help them. He's so excited to become a grandpa. Getting married and having this baby has brought our families close together. We're happy to be living near everyone again.

It's amazing how everything falls into place.

I ease myself off the bed, holding on to the sheets for balance. I move along the side, but my shirt gets caught on the rail and I'm yanked backward. I try to grab the footboard, but my fingers slip off. I lose my balance and fall onto James's bed. The pain stabs my side like a knife. I tumble to the floor because my legs can't hold me up anymore. *Please! Not like this.* The emergency cord hangs not too far from me. With every ounce of energy I have, between moans, I push myself across the small area between our beds and yank it down. I scream out in pain when the door swings open. "Help me!"

"Get her to the OR. Now!" Dr. Stuart yells.

# Chapter 55

## James

I yawn as I enter the elevator going up to Lisa's floor. One more box ticked off the list. Dad and I finished the nursery a little while ago. I rub my eyes, hoping for a good night sleep. Lisa and I are tired of living in this hospital.

I step closer to the doors as it approaches her floor. As they slide open, I hear the emergency alert signal radiating through the floor. *Lisa!* I run down the hallway and see nurses pushing a gurney and Dr. Stuart running briskly down the hall toward the OR. *Please don't be Lisa!*

"Prep her for surgery!" Dr. Stuart demands in the distance.

*Oh my God!*

I run into Lisa's room. I look around and see the blood on the floor. "No! Lisa! No!" I scream in hysterics. I bolt out of our room toward the OR. The hallway feels miles long. I dive through the doors.

"Where's Lisa? What's happening? Where's Dr. Stuart?" I'm acting like a crazed lunatic.

A nurse rushes up to me. "Dr. Kramer, Lisa fell in her room and started to hemorrhage. She needs an emergency C-section. Dr. Stuart is washing up now."

"I want to be in the room with Lisa. She needs me there." I push my way past her. I look around frantically, banging into other nurses. "Where is she?" I scream.

I see Dr. Stuart run into an OR. I dash in her direction, but the doors close before I can go in. "Lisa!" My fists bang on the hard, thick doors, almost leaving dents.

"Get him out of here. He can't be here when he's like this," another doctor yells.

A male nurse grabs me by the arms and pulls me away from the door. I struggle against him. "No, I need to be with her!" I cry out. He pushes me against the wall and holds me there.

"Dr. Kramer, they will do everything they can. You need to trust them. Please calm down."

"I can't calm down. They could die, and I'm out here. How would you react?" *Take a breath, James! They will throw you out of the ward if you are disruptive.*

I rip my arms away and push him back. I fall against the wall and slide to the floor. How can this be happening again? They were doing so well. I tap my head on the wall repeatedly. "Jessica, I know you're watching over us. Please don't take them away from me. Help them. I can't do this again." I keep repeating this.

I'm so focused I barely hear a baby cry behind the door. My head shoots up, and then adrenaline yanks me up off the floor like two arms. I cry and smile at the same time. The smile is ripped off my face when I hear the monitor alarms pulsing through the door. "What's happening? Will someone please tell me what the fuck is going on? Lisa!" I pound on the steel door. "Don't leave me. Please don't leave me."

Minutes pass by. My energy is at zero. I still hear the baby cry. I lean my forehead against the door. I say quietly, "I love you so much. Both of you are my life. My life is nothing without you by my side. We have a baby to take care of together. You are a mother now. I can't do this without you." I sob but jump back when the door slowly opens.

Dr. Stuart walks into the hallway.

I pounce at her. "What the hell is going on? Where is my baby? Is Lisa okay? No one is telling me anything!"

She puts her arm up to add space between us. "I need you to calm down, or I will have you physically removed from this department. I don't care that you work here or you are her husband. You are chaotic right now and disturbing the other patients."

I take a step back and try to compose myself. "Please tell me. I'm losing my mind." My chest heaves as my head pounds.

Her angry face transforms into a smile. "I would like to say congratulations first. You have a baby daughter. She's as healthy as can be and can breathe on her own. She is a true miracle. I will bring you to her in a minute."

New tears are pushing behind my eyes, but I won't let them come yet. Not until I know how Lisa is.

"What about Lisa? I heard the machines through the door. What happened?"

"She lost an excessive amount of blood due to the separation of the placenta and the uterus. She needed a blood transfusion. I had to remove her uterus. In that short amount of time, she took a turn for the worse. We lost her for a few seconds. Thankfully, we were able to revive her. She's still asleep, but she is stable right now. We will monitor her closely for the next few hours."

I shake her hand repeatedly. "Thank you for taking care of them. Thank you so much. They are my life."

"Lisa's a fighter. She has been this entire pregnancy. She'll be fine, but we still need to be careful."

"Please let me see them."

"How about I introduce you to your new daughter?" She rubs my arm and gives me a reassuring smile.

*I have a daughter, and she is healthy.* It can finally sink in. I take a deep breath as my heart grows even bigger. "Please. I can't wait any longer."

She pushes the button to the sliding door.

"Please wash your hands first. You know the drill, Dr. Kramer."

I laugh and do as she says. I follow her and watch her pick up my daughter. I'm shaking because I'm excited, nervous, delirious...

She lays her in my arms. "Go sit in that chair in the corner with her for a little while. I'll let you know when you can see Lisa."

I nod. My eyes can't leave her face, even though they are flowing with tears. She is so beautiful. I kiss her lightly as she sleeps peacefully. She is so tiny but so perfect.

"You are beautiful like your mom. I can't wait until you meet her. You are a true blessing for both of us. I promise to be the best dad."

A lone tear drips from my eye onto her cheek. I sit with her for what feels like an hour in silence. She stirs in my arms. Her eyes flutter open, and all I see is Lisa. She has her heart-shaped face. She stares at me for a few seconds, then starts to scream. I never thought I would love to hear a baby scream.

The nurse comes over. "Your daughter needs to have more routine tests performed. I will take her for a few minutes. Please go to Dr. Stuart through that door. She'll take you to see your wife."

I'm so scared to see her. I know what people look like after critical situations. That's my job, but it's never a nice picture. I remember how terrifying it was to see Jessica lying on the operating table. Please don't let her look like that.

I follow Dr. Stuart through a set of doors. She walks around the corner to a row of beds. She motions me to the first bed. I run to Lisa's and grab her hand. I let more tears flow all over again.

"Lisa, Lisa, Lisa. Please wake up. I can't do this without you. Please, please, please wake up."

I press her hand against my cheek. A nurse brings me a chair. "You can do this, Lisa. You are so strong and have been through so much. Your body can handle this. Your daughter and husband are waiting for you. We need you!"

# Chapter 56

## Lisa

Everything looks blurred. I don't know where I am. Wasn't I just in the hospital room getting a massage? Out in the distance, two foggy figures glide toward me. I can't tell if they are people or just shadows. Slowly, the figures become clearer. *This can't be real. It's only a dream.* I see Mom and Jessica. Jacob is cradled in her arms.

I reach out crying, "Mom, I can't believe it's you. I've missed you so much. You look just like I remember you. So beautiful, like an angel. I wish you were still with us. Am I in heaven? I don't understand what's happening."

She smiles at me. "I've missed you too. I've always been with you, but not the way you think. I'm so proud of you and what you have become. James and your baby are waiting for you. You need to go back to them. Go back, be happy, and live your life to the fullest."

I turn to Jessica. She's wearing a beautiful lilac-purple dress. It has short flowing sleeves with a low-cut neckline. Long layers of sheer material and satin cascade from the waistline. "Don't worry, Lisa. You were meant to be together. Take care of James. He told me about you in his dreams. He loves you more than you'll ever know. This is the way it's meant to be. Your mom and I will always be watching over you and your family. Go ahead. Wake up now. They need you."

Are they angels? Am I hallucinating? "Don't go. I have so much to ask. Please don't go." I plead. I reach for them out of desperation, but they fade away in the distance. Disappearing into the fog. I hear my name echoing in the far distance. It's James, calling me. Where is he? My eyes dart back and forth, searching for him. I don't see him, but I hear him. I jerk my arm in response to something squeezing my hand. I close my eyes and try to hear where the sound is coming from.

James sits near me. His fingers are entwined with mine. His head rests on our hands. I squeeze his fingers. He jerks up. "Lisa? Lisa!" He stares at me with sadness but also relief. He leans down and showers me with kisses all over my face. "Thank God you are awake. I thought I was going to lose you." He presses my hand against his face as tears run down his cheeks.

He wipes them away. "I can't stop crying."

I'm so confused and lethargic. Out of instinct, my hand aims for my stomach. It's flat. "Our baby! Where's our baby? Is the baby okay? Am I okay?" I mumble, shaking my head back and forth in panic. My body throbs in pain.

"Lisa, stay calm and still." He rubs my forehead. "We have a beautiful baby girl. She's small but very healthy. I'm so proud of you. You are both going to be just fine."

"What happened? I remember getting a massage, but everything after that is fuzzy."

"I came back to the hospital just as they were rushing you to surgery. During surgery, you lost a lot of blood after they performed an emergency C-section."

He continues to brush his fingers through my hair. He takes a deep breath. "I'm sorry to say they had to remove your uterus. They lost you for a couple of seconds, but you came back to us. Thank God you came back to us." He kisses my forehead.

"I don't care as long as she is healthy and I'll have a quick recovery."

"You are going to be on your feet in no time. Let me go tell the nurse that you are awake. I want you to meet our daughter." He rushes off in excitement.

He's a proud daddy. I can hear it in his high-pitched voice and see it in the grin on his face when he said *our daughter*. I'm surprised there are no cigars sticking out of his shirt pocket.

I sigh in relief. As soon as I found out I was pregnant, I knew the baby was a girl. I don't know how, but I did. Mother's instinct maybe.

"I'm here again. The nurse is going to bring her to us." His grin larger than before.

We're interrupted by the nurse, holding our daughter who is swaddled in white. "Mrs. Kramer, would you like to meet your daughter?"

I'm suddenly nervous. The tears form as I nod. I try to lift my arms, but don't have the energy.

"Don't worry, dear. Let me lay her on your chest." She's light as a feather. "Now I will put your arm around her like this but you don't need to carry her." There you go. She's a real cutie." She rubs my hand. "Congratulations."

"Thank you." I beam, of course, with tears in my eyes. We cry way too much.

"I'll come back in a little while to check on you both. Your daughter needs to nurse soon." She slips away to give us privacy.

My eyes memorize every line of my daughter's face. "She's so beautiful. I can't believe she is finally here. Against all odds, we made it through. She's absolutely perfect."

She is real, and she is my daughter. I trace her sweet cheeks, her little nose, her pointy chin. Every little facial feature as she sleeps. I look to James. "We are a family now. I love you both so much."

"I know. But you did all the hard work keeping her safe," he says. He lays his cheek against mine, and we cradle her together. We stare at her in amazement and block out our surroundings.

"I have an idea for her name," I whisper.

His head perks up. "You do? I thought we agreed on Katie."

"We did but how about Felicia Rosa? Felicia for my mom, and Rosa in remembrance of Jessica."

His eyebrows furrow together. "Why did you change your mind?"

"Before I woke up just now, I had a weird dream. My mom and Jessica were in it, as if they were angels. They gave us their blessing and promise to watch over us. It felt so real, James. Felicia Rosa just feels right to me."

James remains quiet. "I'm speechless. I don't know what to say, other than yes. You always amaze me. I'm so lucky to have you as my wife." He kisses my lips lightly.

Now I feel completely at peace.

I put my hand on his cheek. "I know what the reason is."

"What do you mean? The reason for what?"

"We always questioned why our lives were so connected and why they collided when they did. I know the reason why."

He looks at me with one eyebrow raised.

"It was for this moment. For us to become a family with Felicia. We are right where we're supposed to be." I can't hold back the tears. "You both are my dream come true."

"And you are mine." He leans down and kisses my forehead and then Felicia's. No more words are needed. We finally know why.

# Epilogue

## One Year Later

"Tina, can you please tie the balloons to the back of the chairs? I don't want them to blow away. I need to arrange Felicia's birthday presents on the table here. I think the cake should be placed next to them."

I'm glad we have his parents' house for her birthday party. Even though it is quite windy, it's a perfectly sunny spring day for a party in the large well-manicured garden. Petals from the flowering trees are blowing in the wind. Bundles of vibrant-colored tulips and daffodils are basking in the sun through the garden borders.

"I can't believe Felicia is one today. Time flies. Look at all these presents. She's spoiled rotten." Tina ties another balloon to one of the chairs.

"As she should be. She's such a blessing to our families." She truly is. I have never been this happy in my entire life. She is a good girl, but she has her moments. She can be quite feisty when she wants something. James is wrapped around her little finger. She has a spunky personality, just like Tina and Alexa. She has big aquamarine eyes. Her hair is pure peach fuzz still. I don't even want to think about how many boys will show up at our front door when she is older. James will need a lot of patience and control not to throw them off the property.

James finished his fellowship and officially works in the ER and receives a good salary. He loves the hospital. It's written all over his face when he comes home every day. I still have another year until I'm finished with school and training. I'm already researching how to open my own practice.

We still live with his parents, but we'll close on a house in two months. His father found a sweet house for us, two towns over. It's the perfect size for our family—three bedrooms with a separate apartment attached, which I can use for my own practice one day.

Our families and friends will be here soon. I hear Felicia crying in the house. She has awakened from her nap. I'd better feed her because the guests will be arriving soon. James went to pick up the last gift for Felicia. It's the biggest surprise of all. His parents went to pick up her big birthday cake.

"I'll take care of her. You finish up what you need to do. I know how to change her diaper and what she likes to eat," Tina says over her shoulder, already running into the house.

I giggle. "Thanks! It gives me a few minutes to set up particular pieces that go along with our present for her."

Slowly, everyone starts to arrive, adding more gifts to the table. I shake my head in disbelief—we will be here all afternoon opening all of them. Tina comes out with Felicia and greets the guests. Hopefully that will distract Felicia from seeing her mound of presents.

I hear James's car in the driveway. I walk up to Tina and say, "James is home. Can you please get everyone in place for the big surprise and sit Felicia in the grass in front of the table with her presents? Yell when everyone is ready."

"No problem. I'm so excited!" She picks up Felicia and tickles her.

We don't want to bring her gifts out until everyone is in place and she's sitting in the grass. It isn't easy to hold off bringing them out.

I run to the driveway, where no one can see me. I laugh out loud when I find James trying to control the gifts.

"Need some help, handsome?"

"Please!" He struggles. "What made us think I could pick them up by myself? That was a disaster." He half laughs. "The car is a mess inside."

Tina calls from the garden. "Lisa and James, we're ready when you are. You can bring them out."

I put one in my arm as it squirms. "Everyone is waiting. Let's go."

I can't help but giggle. We walk around the corner straight toward Felicia. I hear our guests laughing and saying how cute they are. We approach Felicia carefully so we don't scare her or them. She instantly starts waving her arms and squealing. Two blond Labrador puppies with pink bows around their necks tumble around her. Sniffing, licking, but hopefully not peeing on her. One pushes Felicia over in its excitement.

James has said the moment his heart opened up to me was when he saw me playing with those puppies in the park. We both thought these would be a perfect gift for her. She won't have brothers and sisters to play with, but she will at least have her dogs by her side.

# *Acknowledgments*

First, I would like to thank my husband, Christoph, for encouraging me to write my first novel. I've always had the idea for this book, but his persistence is what's driven me to where I am today. To my children, Sarah, Anna, and Lucas—you have been great cheerleaders throughout this entire experience. I couldn't have done this without your support. I love you.

To my editor, Dori Harrell, at Breakout Editing. You were supportive and easy to work with from the start. Your guidance and eye for detail were invaluable and consistent. Thank you for your patience with my nonstop questions. Your praise was provided at the perfect times. To my proofreader, Rachel Overton, at Wordscapes. Your last-minute recommendations and changes helped push my book to a better level. Thank you so much.

Thank you to Sarah Hansen at Okay Creations LLC for my book cover. I gave you a description of what I envisioned, and you made it come true. You were easy to work with and responded to all my little detail changes. You are brilliant at what you do. It was a great learning experience for my first book.

To my sisters, Deanna and Betsy, my friends, Silke, Liz, Susanne, Ingrid, Annette and Katharine in the Network of English-Speaking Women, my friends in New Jersey, and Miriam—when I finally told you I had written a book, your enthusiasm, support, and encouragement were unlimited. When I had doubts, you were always there to pump me with confidence. Thank you!

Thank you to those who have taken the time to read this book. I hope you enjoyed reading it as much as I did writing it. My goal is to make at least one person smile or even drop a tear or two while reading this. Today, there is so much tragedy, hate, and negativity surrounding us. I hope this book helps my readers block out that negativity even for just a few minutes a day. There's nothing like getting lost in a good book.

If you are curious about what whets Tina's appetite, find out in book two, *Dreams Collide*. Please follow me on my website or social media for any updates on future books.

*www.kristinabeck.com*
*www.facebook.com/krissybeck73*
*www.twitter.com/krissybeck96*
*www.instagram.com/krissybeck96*
*www.goodreads.com/kristina_beck*
*www.amazon.com/author/kristinabeck*
*www.bookbub.com/authors/kristina-beck*

## Other books by Kristina Beck

### Collide Series
*Dreams Collide*
*Souls Collide*

# About the Author

A Jersey Girl herself, Kristina was born and raised in New Jersey, USA, for thirty years. She later moved to Germany and has lived there for over fourteen years with her German husband and three children. She is an avid reader of different genres, but romance always takes precedence. She loves coffee, dark chocolate, power naps, and '80s movies. Her hobbies include writing, reading, fitness, and forever trying to improve her German-language skills.

37256513R00203

Made in the USA
Middletown, DE
24 February 2019